I0583425

THE LAST ASTRONOMER

Axis Gate: Book I

Daniel Athas Holly

AXIS
PRESS

This is a work of alternate-history science fiction/fantasy. Many elements contained herein relate to real history, quasi-real history, or at least to events, myths, legends, and individuals (or relatives thereof) *of* real history, except for the things which are entirely made up. All such references in this book are reasonably accurate to their original sources, except for the ones that aren't. Only minor changes were made for the sake of historical timing and not excessively offending the dead beyond absolute necessity. Nevertheless, this book is a product of the author's mediocre imagination at best, and should be regarded as such. No constellations were injured or killed in the process of penning this novel, though a few were malnourished.

Copyright © 2025 by Daniel Athas Holly

First U.S. paperback edition 2021
Second U.S. edition 2025

All rights reserved solely by the author. The author agrees all contents are original and do not infringe upon the legal rights of any other person or work. No part of this book may be reproduced, transmitted, or stored in an information retrieval system in any form or by any means, graphic, electronic, mechanical, or psychic, including photographing, photocopying, taping, and recording, without prior written permission from the author.

This book was typeset in Minion Pro.

Hardcover ISBN: 978-0-578-91804-4
Paperback ISBN: 979-8-9926158-0-7
E-Book ISBN: 979-8-9926158-1-4
Audiobook ISBN: 979-8-9926158-2-1

TABLE OF CONTENTS

FORWARD

in which the author says much, some of which could possibly be considered interesting, especially if the reader possesses low standards for intrigue.

It will likely either comfort or trouble the reader to know that this forward does not conclude with the author becoming a flat-earther. I'll understand if you stop reading, now.

This edition of *The Last Astronomer* is a drastic update, in the same way that the Second World War was an update of the First. This day in age, call it a patch—bug fixes, revamped combat system, new maps, DLC integration, and FMV cutscenes. Maybe not that one.

Stories grow, sometimes in surprising directions. There was always an idea of what the next "areas" of the narrative would be, but most of it has been developed, mapped, and planned in the months following publication.

In its infancy, childhood, and even adolescence, *The Last Astronomer* began as an undergraduate short story assignment in a fiction writing class, though its true origin was a cold January night in our cottage in Wisconsin. One of our bedroom windows was cracked and it made the room quite cold. Elizabeth rolled over and took a large percentage of the blanket with her (as wives do), and my knee was left in the cold air. It put my sleepy mind to pondering existence in a safe and sealed shelter in a remote and bitter wasteland, and a great bay door open, with only a young boy standing at its maw. I went to sleep wondering: *what would make someone leave that?* The following morning, I drafted the short story.

Move a few years ahead to graduate school at Hamline University. I drafted my first run of the story as a full novel. At the time, I was working on two *other* short stories, and something about them felt inextricably linked to the same world, even though this wasn't the case. During my time at Hamline, *this* book went through several full drafts (out of an eventual fourteen), as did one of its "companion" parallel books.

The industry's narrative push at the time—it was an *intense* push—was for young adult or similar work to become as gut-wrenching, emotional, dark, and we were consistently reminded to avoid intellectual depth. Three drafts of the book came and went during my time at Hamline, and by the end of it, I came to an unpleasant and reluctant conclusion: the novel had become so dark, so depressing, that I couldn't stand to read it. I'd come to hate my own work.

Almost three years would pass before I would touch it again, but one day (a Thursday, probably), I was watching a favourite documentary on whaling, and within it, unsurprisingly, excerpts from *Moby Dick* were quoted. *Moby Dick* was the first true novel I ever read, and it has maintained a special place in my life. Having been at least a decade since I'd read it, I was moved by Melville's eloquence, and it put me in mind of how few of "today's" books will ever be quoted like that, if we continue down the literary path of trend. So I decided, well, I love a lighthearted adventure novel to this day, as well as prosaic language, so hang the industry—I'll write what I like, and then knock off for lunch.

As the story involved the myths of paradisean land, I set out to read and analyze every utopian novel ever written, including ancient religious texts of paradise, esoteric or otherwise. It took seven years, during this, this book underwent many redrafts. The process gifted me with a treasure trove of obscure mythologies, however, especially regarding the axis.

So what happened after the original publishing in 2021?

Like any creator, authors and their work are influenced by many things, and I came to see too many voices affecting the story, in reflection. My Master's Thesis at Hamline focused on narrative arcs across multiple volumes, so, book series, and I was no stranger to the challenges of prediction. Even Tolkien himself changed *The Hobbit* post-publication in order to better align it with *The Lord of the Rings*. Far be it from me to compare myself, but I suppose I just did. Anyway, some minor alterations regarding series staging and better integration kept going, and going.

What then began as a brief edit for new cover art and some continuity details became … well, it's in your hand.

I likewise found myself, as drafts of future installments rolled on under finger-press, lightening the tone further and further, especially regarding the culture of Orphan Towne as time went on, and wanted to bring more of that more jovial mood into this test, to better smooth the transition(s).

But there's one more thing. Tolkien again: erring on his side vs. C.S. Lewis's (yes, it's s's, when a proper noun—deal!) regarding allegory and narratives having messages. While I never set out to pen a message, I felt strongly that this edition must be the purest story for story's sake. Those are the ones that stand the test of time. Yes, I love *Narnia* too, settle down. But as I said before, there were a few too many cooks in the kitchen.

This edition is *purest*, if I could venture to call it that. It's also the *cleanest*. Like any worldbuilder, the biggest hurdle to overcome is keeping the world on the back-end of the story, as even the most elaborate Herbert-worthy setting (see? A non-Tolkien reference!) is a nimbly-pimbly nothing without the beating heart of the characters' story and struggles. This edition better simplifies the details, clarifies the science fiction elements, and reduces the active players. Always a good writer's goal is fewer active characters and elements with more involvement and agency. For example, in the old drafts, Hana was *two* girls, sisters, an elder (Sara, who became Agnes) and a younger (Helen, who became Hana). Here, the cast is tighter, more involved, and (I hope) still a little lighter in tone. A little levity never hurt.

Here's hoping you enjoy it, or at least don't hate it.

*For my little astronomer, Nevæa Raen
whose skyward eyes draw me away
from life's common pathways
onto roads that lie bricked
with the extraordinary*

— PART I —

Discovery

CHAPTER 1

in which a bedraggled discovery is made

THE STAR CAPELLA ASCENDED INTO THE OCTOBER SKY at 36° azimuth, 79° ecliptic, twelve minutes before Junior Engineer (Third Class) Alvin Esker would make the greatest discovery in the long and storied history of Orphan Towne, which wouldn't be the end of the world, except that because of it, Alvin would inadvertently obliterate a continent. So maybe it would.

Now that discovery perched outside the Agromatic Gardens, on the other side of glass—*a girl*.

A girl made of bone and hair and flesh and everything that Orphan's utterly ordinary girls were made of (so far as Alvin knew), a girl who looked back at him like a startled animal. He was afraid she might bolt like one into thickets of shadow and rock. Her alarmed eyes shone from behind old wind goggles.

His satchel slumped, and she watched him drop it. She *watched* him— like a human might do, one with hair and fingers and a respiratory system.

Alvin's heart raced because this girl-beyond-the-glass could not possibly exist. This was Orphan! Orphan Heights was the 'finest towne at the end of the world' (which was conveniently written on all the signs). Clad in glass and limeiron, it quickly turned to industry and invention so it might survive in the crippling rock land of the continent, because nothing else could.

Yet there she was, the girl who couldn't exist, because nothing lived in

1

the Expanse, nothing beyond the scattered fowl or shrub.

She reached into the thick of her hair under her hood, and fiddled with something. She pulled loose her goggles and nested them in the piles of bright, golden hair on her head as the hood drew back. Alvin's mouth fell open. He'd never seen golden hair before. Nobody in Orphan had hair like that—nobody.

She had a face. A *real* face.

Alvin waggled his fingers at her. To say hello. She said something back at him, but of course no discernible sound passes through glass that thick.

"What?" he answered, as if it was a good idea.

Then she started talking, fast and loudly, not that he could hear her, and she soon figured that out. Her mouth pressed in a thin surrender. Alvin stepped up to the cold barrier and rested a hand against it, inside a circle in the iron filigree. She put her own small hand opposite it.

"I'm Alvin," he said, as if it mattered. He might as well have been nestled aside a cozy fireplace while she was on the surface of the moon. The hair on his neck stood up.

The gates of Orphan would have to open.

He made his fingers walk on his palm, and gestured them through an open door. He pointed downward toward the great doors that hadn't opened ... well, they were *meant* to never open again. The girl looked apprehensive about this plan, but the thunder convinced her. As it does.

The great discovery of the existence of the *girl-who-couldn't-exist* began only twelve minutes prior. He'd glanced through a broad lens at the vast Expanse beyond the dome at the end of a long moment of daydreaming of places far beyond Orphan. As one does. He penciled a few thoughts in his notebook about people who went to such places and the wonderous discoveries they made there. He took another look through the glass eye, and was about to slip the lens back into his satchel when something out there *moved*.

Had it moved? Alvin Esker let his mind roam, and it took a perilous long time to find it again.

"Ow!" he yelled, yanked his palm away and swore at it under his breath.

His hand had previously been busy mounting a little star of his own into a lectral socket. One by one, he'd installed them on a pergola rooftop in Orphan Towne's Agromatic Gardens for the sake of all who strolled with their sweethearts of an evening, and forgot to let go once the power came on.

Incandescents are hot, he noted.

And then, Alvin did something wrong: the 'something moved' notion tugged at the collar of his mind, and while it meandered, he attached the positive lead and the ground to the same terminal on one of the sockets.

The entire system shorted out. His bare forearms burned from the sparks below his rolled sleeves.

"Esker you idiot!" shouted Ellery Hartchild from atop the nearby tram car. He was about Alvin's age, with more experience but less sanity.

"You gentlemen mind telling me why I'm unable to properly see my vacuum tubes in here?" That was Baron Lorecroft, the head of the project.

"Esker mucked it up again!" Ellery echoed. "Leave Esker to the Tramrunners, for all the good he is here."

"You didn't have to rat me out, you piker!" Alvin swiftly searched for his mistake, frantically feeling his way across the lines. From his belt, he pulled his lectral lantern and flared it into life.

Alvin seized when Lorecroft's sturdy hand gripped his shoulder, mounted firmly on the stepladder. "Hurt yourself, son?"

"It—it's nothing, Professor," Alvin insisted.

Lorecroft plucked up Alvin's notebook and scanned the page briefly before putting it back. "Woolgathering, were you, Master Esker?"

"Sir?"

"To um … meander in your thoughts. To go elsewhere in your mind and lose your sense of time. Woolgathering."

"Oh. Never heard that one, sir! And I've heard a lot of 'em! I weren't doing that, though. Woolgathering, I mean. There's only me and the pergola beams up here, Sir, and all them incandescents."

Baron Lorecroft eyed his work like a bird of prey scanning its meal, and with his blue cravat tucked roundly at his neck, he indeed carried the look of a proud avian with feathered chest. A pigeon waddled along the walkway below, head flicking like Lorecroft's sometimes did—an observation which made Alvin snicker, and pretend it was a cough.

"Master Hartchild?" the Baron called. "I'm off to fetch a fuse. Kindly carry my tools, will you? You seem like you need some respite from your own temper."

"Temper's fine when Esker's not around, isn't it?"

"Yes, well we'll give Master Esker a moment to marshal his focus."

They left Alvin alone at what may as well *have* been the top of the world, since the Agromatic Gardens perched high on the West/Northwest Eighth of Orphan's fourth and uppermost perimeter story. For the first time that evening, Alvin had little to do but wait for his hand to stop throbbing. He slid the old heavy lens out one more time. Through its eye, Capella glowed, grown from cosmic boughs. His gaze fell to the stony slope outside Orphan.

"Esker?" called Ellery Hartchild.

And that was when it happened. This time, there was no denying it.

He scrambled, dropped half his tools from the pergola and found Ellery Hartchild in his way. "I said, 'your brother is here and looking for you.' Git can't even follow a sentence…"

Alvin's brother?

Oh no.

"Forget something this evening, Al?" Alphonse was waiting. Alvin couldn't afford to stop. He'd seen the *thing-with-nimble-feet* move down below. He tried to push his way past, but Alphonse was bigger. "Father's angry, and mum was crying, when I left Chapel Hill. You know, the one just down the lane?"

"I'm heading out now!" Alvin insisted. "I'll meet you all at the grave."

"Meet them—it's already over with!"

Alvin kept scooping up his falling tools that overflowed his bag like a rising muffin.

"I've made you angry."

"Obviously."

"I'm a poor son."

"Increasingly."

"I'm a poor brother."

"Frequently."

"I'm a poor engineer, probably, too."

"One day a year is not too much to ask you to show up."

"I know I just…" Something stopped in Alvin's throat, when he thought about the chapel, the grave, and the flood of other thoughts that came with them in hideous parade. "Guess I don't see much point to standing over a stone like she can hear us still, is all."

Alvin's mind was still fixed on the *thing-that-moved-out-there*.

"Al, it really hurt mum. That ain't something you can undo, you know. You didn't used to think so little of things like this."

"I didn't used to think that the earth were round, also. Or that touching your tongue to a lectral tank makes you taste metal for hours."

"You did that?"

"Ain't ready to talk about it. Anyway, I have to go! Father always says to be responsible! I'll drop my tools and head—"

"Father would raze Orphan to the ground with his bare hands before he would miss Agnes's memorial."

Alvin managed to snake his way past his brother and deposit his tools in the old tram car he delivered to the LIT Corps. as a workstation. He was free and clear until—"Alvinheim Esker! Where were you?!" Author help him, Ellery's sister Tabitha had arrived.

He might as well have had his mother walk in on him after turning her newly 'dismantled' perfume bottles into lenses for his engineer goggles … not that he ever did such a thing.

"I've half a mind to give you what-for, Esker," she lectured.

"I know," Alvin agreed, and sidled his way around her on the stairs. "And—and you don't got to because Alphonse has done it plenty and I done it enough to myself for the both of you, so you can be assured I'm—I'm frightful angry with myself! So angry I'm—I'm going to go and not eat my supper tonight."

"Your mother started bawling, right there at the memorial. In front of everyone! Saying how much she wished *both* her sons were there in her company—Alvinheim Esker you stop and listen to me! I'm not finished with you! Alphonse, stop him!"

"If *you* can't, I can't," Alphonse added.

He stumbled his way backwards down the stairs. "I—I think I left my notebook on the parkway earlier when—when we were working on the thing!"

"Alvin!" they both yelled.

But Alvin was not about to stop running.

Eight minutes later he was running again, this time to meet the strange and alien girl at Orphan's ancient West Gate. Now, those gates had not been opened—save one instance—for several hundred years, and even in that one instance, the Founding Order was not broken: *Permit nothing external to infect the system.*

Layman's terms: *don't ever let anything into towne, you imbecile.*

Alvin ran anyway, fled down the flights, over garden bridgeways past circulation labs and down to Orphan's lowest level. Then he took the nearest tunneling stairs down into the Recess, where all of Orphan's operational machines churned endlessly.

And where old Westgate was.

There beside the gate hung a dial lock, small ceramic cylinders marked with numerics. Alvin paused in front of it and (as he phrased it), "spun the old lens around."

In his mind there was what Alvin pictured as a great observatory, a circular, glass-clad dome that he imagined occupying the space within the top of his skull, and at its center hung a spyglass enthroned atop great gears and mainsprings, able to peer into the furthest reaches of his personal cosmos, where all his memories resided.

All he ever needed do was angle the lens to the memory, and bring it into focus in order to recall it with astounding clarity for a boy his age.

So he spun the lens around to the last time he'd stood in that very spot, to the hand that had once turned the dial locks. Each one clicked past number after number until he set it how he wanted, every click breaking a little more of the law of Orphan Towne.

Billowed undertow of dust and earth rolled in around Alvin's ankles and blew into the entry when the door lifted. Alvin had only once *truly* seen the vast, dark plates of stone that rose into crests across the middle distance, and it all reached out from Orphan Towne until it could reach no more.

And there she stood, a paradox with skinny legs and goggles.

But when the thunder peeled, she lunged through the door and sat herself next to it. She asked something in some butchered form of Anglish he had trouble following at first. Her voice was raspy for a girl her age, as if the dust and crystalline sand in the Expanse had long infected her lungs.

"What did you say?" he asked, as if that would help. He was surprised to learn that it did.

She searched his face. "Door. Door is cold. Please shut?"

Alvin complied, and the old door severed them from the wild Expanse.

"Thank—um—thank you," she panted.

Then the girl drew off her scarf and hood, and Alvin's astonished eyes gazed at a sight he'd never seen. A great mane of sunlit-golden hair spilled against her shouldertops. She swept it all back with one motion, and shook it free from her face. Everyone in Orphan had dark hair, mostly brown like Alvin's, and brown eyes.

There were no blondes.

He'd read legends of blondes in his mythology classes, but this girl, for all the filth and grime layered in her hair, was a walking torch of silvery-golden fire.

"You let me *in*," she said.

"Course I did. You were in a bad way, and I could tell. What sort of person would I have been if I hadn't? Rotten one, that's what sort."

"Thank Jalós you did."

He knelt, inspecting her, tilting his head this way and that, tapping the same spot on his temple he always tapped when thinking. Maybe she wasn't even there. Maybe he breathed something rotten during his time in the

Gardens. He did used to have allergies to pollen. Gingerly, he reached out a hand, and one finger. The girl looked at his hand, at him, and back again.

Then she poked him hard in the arm. His yelp amused her. "Why'd you do that?" he demanded.

She laughed. "Why? Not want me to?"

Her eye-teeth were a little shorter than the rest, her crooked smile drawing back like a curtain to one side when she grinned.

"I were only trying to determine if you were a figment or not. Didn't have to jab me."

"Fig … ment?"

"You know, an apparition, 'cause if you're human and you're actually sitting there, then I've a great deal of explaining to do because this is not what's supposed to happen on Thursdays. Just wait until the *High Times* gets a hold of this tomorrow. 'Local Git Rediscovers Humanity,' or the like, that's what the headline will say, and no mistake."

"You talk a lot."

"I don't," he defended. "Especially to an aberration."

She scowled. "Touch." Her thin hand reached out and spread. It trembled a little from exhaustion, probably. All of her did. Their fingers laced. "See?"

Yes, Alvin saw. He saw the impossible, sitting in the loading bay with silver sand spilling from her blinding hair and irritating him.

"So. Inside Iron Hollow…"

Was that really the name of Orphan, outside of Orphan? But how could it be? There was nobody outside of Orphan to name it! She reached into the back of her hair and fiddled with something like she had before, apparently a fussy clasp to the strap of her goggles. "Help? It gets stuck."

Cautiously he reached behind her ear (she had ears!) and found her fingers pulling on a little metal clasp, rather bent and poorly made. No wonder it locked. It hurt his fingers to pry that hard, but he snapped it free, and the girl shook out her long mess of radiant mane and swept it back with her hand. Her nose looked like someone had dusted it with cinnamon—freckles.

She had *freckles.*

Alvin pulled her to her feet. Her tired face finally came into full view, close to him, and she looked with colors that bulleted through the lens of Alvin's mind. A thin ring of dirt lay across her cheeks where the goggles sat.

"Your eyes … are different colors," he said.

The girl drew back, looking at the floor so he couldn't see them. "Yah. Listen, will you trade?"

"Trade?"

"For water? Maybe for food?"

"You want to trade for water?"

Thunder bore across the outer sky. The girl jolted.

"Trade?" she implored, swinging her rucksack around to where she could reach it. "Have not eaten for two days. Out of water. Can trade. And mending! Good at mending. Trousers need stitching, maybe?"

"Look—off my trousers! I'll see that you eat, okay? You can keep your … things." Though he was utterly fascinated to know what she had in that rucksack.

She finally glanced around at the great old entrance to Orphan Towne, and her mouth fell wide. "So … big."

At first, her speech seemed almost childlike, and he even entertained the thought that she might have some kind of retardation, but quickly decided no. The Eskers hardly spoke with perfect diction, though their frankness was stuff of folklore.

"Who are you? Seem young to open doors like this."

"I'm Esker. I mean Alvin! My name's Alvin. Alvin Esker. That's the name I were given. By my parents. Alvin, so you can call me that. Well, don't call me 'that.' That'd be stupid. Alvin's fine. Actually, my name's Alvinheim—old family name—but no one calls me that. Almost no one. Well, Mum does."

She looked at him strangely, curious wide eyes on his rambling gestures. But her existence still confounded him.

"How could you even survive out there? The air ain't even breathable, but you've got nostrils!"

"Got what?!" She looked herself over frantically.

"Relax! A nose. You've got a nose. And freckles?"

She was such a curious thing, cocking her head when she didn't understand. Her eyes never seemed to relax or soften, always searching, always finding. Then they stopped searching and focused on something; Alvin thought it might be his shoulder. She cocked her head again, and the full colour of those eyes of hers mesmerized him, framed in a mane of wild sunlit yellow. Why was she looking at him like—

"Who is your friend?" She nodded towards whatever was behind him.

"Who's my..."

Alvin's blood stopped. He didn't know it could do that. He turned, his shoulder tight and ready for something to hit him.

But not ready enough.

in which both bickering and planning come about

NO VOLUME OF HELD BREATH COULD EQUIP ALVIN ESKER to face Tabitha Hartchild's astounded eyes or hanging mouth. He was caught, and caught by the worst catcher he could fathom. She braced herself against a pillar behind them, stark white and silent. She clutched the collar of her blouse like a rope.

"When you when you ran off I thought … I thought something was amiss, so I … my word, Esker, you let somebody *in!*"

"I … I might've. Yes. Seemed a good idea, at the time, but I still happen to think it was—"

"Who is she?"

"She's … I didn't think to ask."

"You didn't think?!"

"Right. I ought've asked, by now."

The strange girl's eyes flared wide when she looked closer at Tabitha. "Whoa! Black hair?!" She reached for it like Alvin would reach for the first incandescent he'd ever seen as a boy, and the result was the same. "Ow!"

"Kindly leave my hair alone," Tabitha demanded.

"Just—just calm down," Alvin fussed. "Miss Expanse Girl? So, I'm Alvin. I told you already but just a reminder. Oh, and that's Tabitha, who smacked your hand and all."

"Esker!" Tabitha snapped.

"Right. Would you be kind enough to tell me who exactly you happen … to actually be?"

The girl eyed them both, glanced between the two of them for a confused moment. "Lofthana Engindaut cín Jalóheim fra Sóholdt."

"Right," he said. "Miss Hartchild, this is—um, this…" He bit his lip. "This is Hana."

Tabitha visibly waited for the rest. He turned back to Hana, who only seemed confused.

"Could you repeat it because I could use some help with—"

"Lofthana Engindaut cín Jalóheim fra Sóholdt."

"Right. That's it." Tabitha didn't move, and only raised her eyebrows higher. "I'd like to introduce—introduce Miss Sóholdt. From. From the Expanse. If that's alright."

"And what is Miss … *Sóholdt* doing *inside* of Orphan?"

"I…"

"Did not think to ask," Tabitha finished. "Miss Sóholdt, what are you doing here?"

"Huh?" said Hana. "Oh. Long way to go across Svaraheim. Got lost. Needed shelter."

"See, Hartchild?"

But Tabitha still pointed to the almost otherworldly girl. "Esker, she's from *outside*…"

"Rubbish," Alvin insisted with an awkward laugh. "You know that … please don't tell Ellery. It's all he needs to make my life miserable more than he already does."

"Where did she come from?"

"Sóholdt," repeated Hana. "In Jalóheim, in the Rift. North side."

"I couldn't very well leave her to rot out there in the cold, could I?" Alvin defended. "You should have seen her shiver. I can't watch someone shiver like that and do nothing about it, can I?" He kept himself from saying 'a girl' because Tabitha would've rolled her eyes at him, and Alvin didn't like it when people did that.

"Esker … if any of the Scholars—if anyone at all sees her? Land's sake, if the *Times* hears about this?! Or the Broadcast!"

Alvin didn't know what she was driving at. Hana apparently grew bored and started feeling her way around the entry, running cautious hands over the rungwork and arches, picking off anything that would come loose and looking at it as if she might eat it.

"I don't think I understand."

"Parading this wretched girl around like the belle of the ball will destroy lives' worth of work, and that's only the beginning of the damage. We can hardly hide *hair* like that! There's contamination to think of and biologic effects and … and you can't just open Orphan's gates like this! It's a closed system for a reason."

"I think you're overreacting," Alvin defended. "They'll want to know the truth about her. I'm sure they will."

"That is not how Scholars operate, Esker. I'm telling you for your own good and for hers, Miss Sóholdt must go back to wherever she came from"

"Go back?"

"And we must never speak of today again. Alright? We will bandage over this wound and let it quietly—Esker, she's climbing on the arch."

Hana had found her way up aside the bay door and was glimpsing the Expanse from that vantage.

Alvin fretted. "Hey! Hey get down! You could break your neck!"

"See better up here," she returned.

Alvin was caught between these girls, and turned back to Tabitha. "I won't send her into that cold again, Hartchild, and that's all there is to it."

"You are such a male."

"I don't think I know what that means. Come on, Hana," Alvin called without taking his glaring eyes off Tabitha's glaring eyes. "I'll take you home, okay? You'll be safe there. You can eat with us, too."

"Really? To water!" Hana exclaimed.

"She's not a puppy, Esker!" Hana hopped down from her perch and joined him. "I—I could speak to father about this?"

A cold horror curled around Alvin's neck. The Inspector General? Knowing about the existence of this wilderness girl? She wouldn't. But what if she did? What would they even do with … her?

Tabitha hesitated for a long, breathy moment, pinching her eyes, and suddenly found the ceiling fascinating. "We'll acquire some supplies for her, alright? We'll get food and water and send her on her way."

"Hartchild—"

"Or I can talk to Father about this."

"No!" Alvin repeated, and not nicely. "No you won't do that. You're not your brother. You wouldn't act like some clout from Wesbeldt!"

"I will!" Tabitha stolidly crossed her arms. "And so help me!"

He pressed his mouth into an impassible line, and waited for a response from Tabitha. This was a smug-off. It lasted until a deep growl sounded through the echoing hall, and drew both of their notice to the strange blonde newcomer, holding her stomach. "Is there food anywhere?"

Tabitha didn't have anything to say to this, and visibly relented. Alvin turned his attention back to his discovery. "Follow me, Hana Sóholdt. I'll introduce you to the cooking of the famous Mrs. Elise Esker! Esker mothers are known across Orphan for their culinary—"

Tabitha's arm stopped them both. "Wait," she said, and sighed long and loud. "I'm coming."

The walk to Irra's Landing was quiet, or rather spent trying to keep Hana quiet. They couldn't let her and her impossibly-blonde hair in sight of the locals. It didn't help that she tried to keep touching Tabitha's own black curls. It had been quickly decided (by Tabitha, with no vote) that they would take her by way of the tram, but when they arrived at the station, they found its lights dark, and the platform silent.

"Right," said Alvin. "It's half five. Trams are done for the day."

"He's right," said Tabitha. "Guess there's nothing for it but to send her on her way to wherever—"

"No need for that," said Alvin. "Got a better way, I do."

Alvin quietly led them to the higher ring of the perimeter, and to the Agromatic Gardens where he'd first spotted her. Alvin poked his head out from behind the occasional hickory to make certain the LIT Corps. had already gone. They had, and there sat their salvation.

"You're going to take us on the *work* tram?" Tabitha complained.

"Water?" was Hana's only complaint, and not even that.

Alvin and Tabitha argued their way over to the drinking fountain. Alvin pumped the lever a few times, and Hana yelped when it spilled.

"What's wrong?" asked Tabitha.

"Water's going everywhere!" Hana shouted, trying to catch it before it hit the ground where the drain was.

"It—it's alright," Alvin assured. "Orphan's wells are deep and we've plenty. Drink."

Hana looked at him like he'd asked her to commit a crime. He and Tabitha both had to urge her again. It splashed on her trembling fingers, and she cupped it in her dirty hands. Her face lit.

"Go ahead, Miss Sóholdt," Tabitha prodded.

Hana held it to her mouth, and drank, eyes falling shut in the apparent pleasure of how clean it was. She took more and splashed it on her face, then drank again, and snapped her head to fling her mane dry.

"Alright!" said Tabitha, and even she almost laughed. "Let's keep moving. It's the labour tram, I suppose."

"What is it? Little shelter?" asked Hana, batting her hands dry.

"No, Miss Sóholdt," Tabitha explained. "It's a tram. It moves. You'll see. Apparently."

Most like a trolley, the trams all featured comfortable seats and lighting, and windows that could close, even curtains, but this one had long since been converted into a mobile work station for the engineers.

There were a few seats left, though.

Alvin eagerly went to the controls and started flicking switches.

Hana Sóholdt (as Alvin would forever call her) ran quick fingers across the arch of woven bronze over the trolley door, then over the tarnished brass handrails before taking a cautious seat in the back. She rubbed the velvet cushion. "So soft," Hana said, and examined the stitchwork and the underside of the corners. "Why does it have a roof?"

"Pardon?" Tabitha answered.

"Why a roof? This whole *village* has a roof. Why does it need one? Or the buildings over there?"

"Privacy, I suppose," said Tabitha. "Never considered it before."

Alvin, quite pleased with himself, gripped the throttle, and the lectral lights in the car glowed softly. "Ready to go?"

Hana's mouth fell open and she gazed with the widest eyes Alvin had ever seen. She slowly rose in her seat, and reached an open hand towards one of the suspended bulbs overhead. "You trap stars..." she awed.

"Not stars," Tabitha corrected. "Simple lectral power, Miss Sóholdt, run by Orphan's steam engines in the south part of towne."

The jolt of the train moving out of the stop spilled her clear onto the floor. Tabitha helped her up.

"Jalós, it moves! Where are you taking me?"

"Harchester," Alvin told her. "That's in Algary, the southeast quarter."

Alvin gave the tram a little more speed, and some of the open windows made Tabitha hold her hat on tighter. It was the closest thing an Orphanite ever came to feeling wind.

"No need for rushing, Esker!" Tabitha reminded him.

"This is fast!" Hana yelled, which caused Alvin to open the throttle lever all the more. The tram sped and swung around the northwestern quarter like a bird on the wing. The tracks were often suspended over nothing, or descended onto the main walkways and divided the roads on either side, cutting through small platforms and landings as it sped across Orphan.

"Should see it during the day," Alvin called over his shoulder. "Normally there's near a hundred of these running everywhere. Father's a Tramrunner, too," he bragged. "Fores the crew for all of Harchester, he does!"

Meanwhile, Tabitha fought to shut the window by her head, but Hana only opened the one in front of it so she could lean out.

While Orphan's skeleton and primary arches were of folded limeiron alloy, much of the interior was of intricate white birch, from the days when the Expanse still had forests, or of plaster, when the birch wore out. The houses were all of high peaks and lattice bracework. Orphan was noisy, a cacophony of building-sized steam engines, rail traffic, and populace, all trying to out-drone each other so nobody had to deal with any of that obnoxious quiet.

Orphan was a snow globe of a towne that Alvin sometimes pictured himself picking up, tipping upside down, and giving a good hard shake until all the specks of tiny people would whirl around all over the place, though he rarely mentioned that to anybody.

Most of all, Hana was busy staring intently at the apex of the vast enclosure that was the *finest towne at the end of the world*, where the Heuridium tower hung suspended, and she cocked her shaggy head at the inscription high around its beams.

"'There shall come a day,'" said Tabitha.

"Huh?" said Hana.

"It is the motto of Orphan, Miss Sóholdt. 'There shall come a day'."

Hana gazed up at it again. "Yah…"

Around its white frame stood the Colonial Academy of Science, scattered across building after building on vaulted campus platforms above the lower street rows.

She seemed transfixed by it.

"It was designed by our Scholar Patriarch, Cornelius Hickter, Miss Sóholdt," Tabitha explained.

Hana gawped at everything. She kept saying things like "do you see that?" or "what is that for?"

"Hey, um … Miss Sóholdt?" Alvin asked. "Hana? What's … out there? In the Expanse," he continued. "Nobody's supposed to be alive still."

"Esker," Tabitha cautioned. "Best not to ask."

"Endless stone," Hana mused while her eyes soaked in every inch of Orphan Towne. "The Clans are far apart."

"Cla—Clans? How many people are still—"

"Esker!" Tabitha barked. "She's an anomaly. Leave it at that."

Hana's flushed face spun into questioning glare.

"It's not an insult!" Alvin insisted. "She—she wasn't insulting you."

For the moment, Alvin swallowed his curiosity; after all, his universe had already been uprooted enough for one evening. He pointed out the Merchant Circle on lofted disks below and around the Academy. He pointed to Rosewater Way and the Merchant Circles, the curving promenade where all the everyday restaurants stood, including the Songbird, a favorite of the Eskers, and of most of the working men. The *Lager Than Life* wasn't far behind it, the favourite pub of Harchester.

"She hardly needs a tour," Tabitha lectured. "Since she's not staying."

When finally they came to Tanno's Landing, Alvin drew back the throttle and cranked the brakes into place, and with a cry that caused Hana to cover her ears momentarily, the tram stopped, two streets down from London Row. Hana stepped off the trolley like one stepping into a cold river. Alvin helped her but she would not stop gawping at everything.

"She'll give us away if she keeps doing that," Tabitha remarked.

"No one notices a couple of adolescents in the side rows," Alvin said. "They usually don't bother to look because they'd expect them to be giving each other one on the mouth, or the like."

"Must you always be so crass?" said Tabitha. "It's embarrassing to even be seen with you."

"'Giving one'?" asked Hana.

"It means a scandal in the making, and nothing suitable for polite company," returned Tabitha, while Alvin snickered. "Though it's to be expected in a place like Harchester."

"Eskers are never crass," Alvin answered. "We're just pleasantly forthright, we are."

Orphan's outer streets were tiered, one atop the other in ever-widening circles around the perimeter of towne. Dim light was common at that time of year. One either developed good eyes or rugged shins.

They had to stop Hana from climbing the lampposts now and then.

Alvin's home was a noble little two-decker brownstone in the middle of London Row with an antique turret on the north corner, where his bedroom was mostly housed, and on the front, an old family plaque.

"Any thought as to how to sneak Miss Sóholdt in?" asked Tabitha, clearly still preferring her *exile-the-girl* idea.

"Give me a moment," said Alvin. "Easy enough, if we think about it. Though, keep out of sight of Mrs. Dutch, in the next house. Woman's a nosy-parker if ever there was one, and a gossip, also."

Alvin tapped his temple as he often did, swirled his hand about in the air as one thought after another paraded behind his eyes and he mumbled to himself. "No, not if that happens. Could do it this way—but not if Mum's done the wash already—and if the sill's still warped..."

Tabitha rolled her eyes.

Hana just watched.

"Got it!" he started. "It'll be easy! I'll just—"

The rest of whatever Alvin's plan had been was heard no more. Tabitha shoved Hana out of sight with her as the front door burst open, and Hugo Esker loomed through the opening.

"Hello, son!" he said, his left eye angrily twitching at his boy in a way that made Alvin recoil. "Why don't you come on inside and we can have a little chat?"

in which Alvin poorly circumnavigates a disaster

THE GREASY SMELL OF THE ESKER BROWNSTONE welcomed Alvin, as always—not greasy like sweat or fat runoff but like petroleum from one of his father's recent engineering projects that usually found its home on the dining table for weeks on end. It had spread to the coffee table since that morning, the water pump and the distributor apparently having been fruitful and multiplied.

Alvin debated exposing Hana to the sight of his entire family. Why not? A walking marvel, that's what she was! And blonde, to boot! Maybe it was Tabitha's doomful attitude getting the better of him, but he did wonder how everyone would react.

His father tapped the spanner in his hand as he prepared to lecture. This was his way of still being intimidating, the family assumed.

"Mind explaining?" he asked.

Alphonse sat on the divan, trying visibly to mind his own business.

"I'm going venture you noticed that I weren't at the—"

"I don't take kindly to having to make excuses for my son. You embarrassed this family today. Even Inspector Hartchild came with his daughter, and he already thought less of us than the mire on his boots."

"Father—"

"I'll not tolerate your mother's tears on account of you, boy."

This was only partly true. She wept because of the memorial, surely. Alvin's absence likely just made it worse, but he wasn't stupid enough to say that aloud. He *was* stupid enough to say something else, though.

"I was—was caught up with work, is all. It were my duty to finish—"

"Your duty is to your family long before it's to any of your bulbs, Alvin. You're an Esker."

"Mr. Esker, maybe today isn't the best day for this?"

"Albany's here too?!" Alvin hadn't noticed Albany Finch in the corner, fingering his way through the bookcase, kicking himself for not recalling that Albany *always* took his dinner with the Eskers after the memorial service.

"Albany's good as family. They might've never tied the knot proper but he'll always be family here—and *he* had the good sense to come to the memorial!"

"Please, Mr. Esker, do leave me out of this. It's the last thing Aggie would want. Can we not just go back to how things were?"

"Can't go back, Albany. Alvin made his choice and has to live with it."

His mother came into the sitting room with a pile of trousers she was likely settling in to stitch. "Hugo," she told his father with a hand on his shoulder. "He's a growing boy."

"Eh?"

"He's at that age where he's wrestling with things. And you know how Agnesine's loss affected him. He'll come around in his own time. Have you seen my needles?"

"How can you be on about needles when you was crying not an hour ago?" Hugo ranted.

"Life goes on, as you've always said. Then was a time for mourning. Now is time for trousers. Don't be so hard on Alvinheim. He's been different since Agnesine died."

"Different?" Alvin defended.

Alphonse and Albany over at the bookcase both said at the same time, "Here we go."

Elise Esker paused with the trousers, and took a long breath in through her nose. "I remember a little boy with wonder in his face, would dream about flying and adventures and make castles out of my sofa. And then one day, he grew up. Maybe a day too soon, and a little too much. Alvin," his mother added. "Eat your dinner before it gets even colder. Where are the blasted things?"

"Put your rubbish away, first," his father added.

Albany assured him, "Dinner was wonderful, Al. Delicious as always, Mrs. Esker. I miss our Sunday evening dinners like we used to have."

"You can have dinner any time you want, Albany."

Alvin went to his bedroom, the third door on the elevated landing, and slumped the satchel just inside.

Of all the many ways he'd considered his little bedroom, it never crossed his mind whether or not it could securely harbor a girl, and this was a lousy introduction to that train of thought.

His father was busy summarizing what was wrong with "this generation," which Alvin and Alphonse could recite verbatim: "No consideration for anything," he ranted, "except the newest this-or-that buggery. And why? They think times change. 'Times have changed, Mr. Esker, Sir.' 'Times have changed, you know,' or 'you've got to change with the times, Sir!' Rot and rubbish, is what it is, and it's bleeding over onto our boys, is what!"

Through the hazy little round window on the front door, Hana's curious face suddenly bounced into view, apparently too short to see through it on her toes. She popped up again, and again, which told Alvin she was hopping.

When his mother vanished into the back room to find her needles, his father followed. The ear for his lecture had to stay in range, after all.

"What is the matter with you?" Alphonse asked, perched on the divan with his back to the door. "You know what today means to them."

"I know," said Alvin.

"I don't understand how you can *forget*. You of *all* people!"

"Oh be nice, Alphonse. Today's hard on all of us."

Forget…

There was so much Alvin would've said, *should've* said. "I'll check the post," is all that came out.

"Wha—are you even listening? And I already checked the post…"

Alvin used the moment to usher the girls in, gesturing for them to keep low and follow his direction, not that Hana understood this. She seemed to think it was a game. They crept behind Alphonse on the divan while Albany flipped open some book on heraldry while Tabitha yanked Hana down behind the divan by Alvin's legs.

"No post," said Alvin, which made his brother roll his eyes.

Hugo Esker came back, still following Elise. "…never solves anything, and he ought to know that," he lectured.

"He just needs more time," his mother added. "Alvinheim's growing up, isn't he? That's all. You know what schooling does to a lot of children."

"Well problems don't go away by giving 'em time, is what. Know what happens? They grow fat. You want fat problems on your hands? Do you?"

"Already have one," she chuckled, patting Hugo on the stomach.

Something fiddled with Alvin's boots, likely Hana trying to figure out how they worked. He flicked his foot but she kept doing it until he heard a tiny slap, which ended the fiddling. His mother invited Alvin to his cold dinner—over at the table on the opposite side of his parents.

"Not hungry, son?"

"No, Mother, I am. Just comfortable here, is all. This is a great divan. Always liked it. Haven't you?"

Alphonse made a face up at his little brother, his usual *are-you-an-idiot* look he so often gave him, while his mother could only blink a few times. If only he knew his back was inches from two stowaways…

"I … suppose so?"

"Your mother's right, you know," Hugo Esker continued. "You *have* changed, Alvin. It's all books and scholars, now."

Alvin would have to keep his parents' (and Alphonse and Albany's) attention on himself, so their backs would be to the girls. There was only one certain way to do that, so Alvin drew in a deep breath: "If … if Agnes's pseudo-science and daydreams hadn't been so encouraged, we wouldn't be one family member low."

His mother gasped, actually gasped aloud; Albany dropped his book.

It made Alvin's whole body cinch up, and the rasp of crumpling paper told him Alphonse' did too. And as the girls crawled right out from the dividing wall behind the divan, behind his father and mother Alphonse, Alvin steeled himself.

"Oh Alvinheim…" his mother sighed. "You don't mean that. Really, you can't! You know that's not true."

"She wouldn't have done what she did if she weren't prodded—"

"Alvinheim Lockwilde Esker," his father said calmly. "Your sister was a gift to this family. A blessed angel, she was, and when you speak like that…"

Alvin's mother tensed, her mouth thin and back straight. She always tensed when her little girl was spoken of, but she put her hand on her husband's shoulder, which seemed to calm him somewhat, but it gave Tabitha and Hana enough time to sneak into the kitchen and creep around behind the serving counter.

"Don't get too comfortable with them Scholars, Alvin," said his father. "There's more going on there, and I don't like it."

Albany reminded Hugo that he was there. "Would you like me to step out, Mr. Esker? I'm frightfully close to the Scholary, in my job, remember."

"And you've got more sense than most of 'em. No, you stay there."

"Yes, Sir."

Hugo, with a heavy brow, turned back to Alvin. "You're starting to sound like that fool Hartchild when you talk like that."

"I…" (*Alvin did not like Ellery, and remembered that Ellery's sister was in the room*) "Ellery's a smart fellow."

"He's an idiot. Always was. Boy can't handle his own shoelaces in the morning. Probably drools when he sleeps. He's a 'times-have-changed' blighter, too. Only reason he even made the Corps. is he's Hartchild's boy, and that man's a roaring imbecile already so the fruit ain't fallen far from that bug-eaten tree."

Alvin shut his eyes and couldn't bring himself to look at the face Tabitha must've made. A knock sounded at the Esker door, and Alvin near bolted out of his own skin. *Now what?* The girls were only a few feet from him in the kitchen!

Alphonse answered it.

"Professor Lorecroft!" called Alvin's mother. "And young Master Hartchild! Won't you come in?"

"Evening, Mrs. Esker. Mr. Esker," said the good Professor, removing his ivory coachman. "I don't mean to intrude at such an hour. Ah! Young Master Finch! I forgot you'd be here."

"Baron," Albany bowed.

Ellery Hartchild followed in after him.

"It's no intrusion," Alvin's mother insisted. Elise Esker was the sociable one. Even old Mrs. Dutch next door would converse with her, and she didn't talk to anyone but cats.

She headed for the kitchen. "Come in, please. I'll make some tea."

"No!" Alvin shouted.

"Excuse me?" said his mother, pausing by the serving counter.

"It's—Professor Lorecroft hates tea, is all," said Alvin.

"Really?" his mother asked, for such a thing was unheard of in the annals of Orphan Towne.

Sure enough, the Professor cocked an eyebrow. "As it happens, I've quite a weakness for earl grey, but I'm afraid I cannot stay."

Thank the Author, Alvin muttered to himself.

"*I'd* love some," Albany noted.

"No you wouldn't," Alvin growled, and he let out the breath he didn't know he was holding.

Ellery Hartchild was eyeing him coldly, as he often did. "Where's Tabby?" he asked.

"Excuse me?"

"She ran off after you, just a few moments after—what were you doing again? Oh, right. Looking for your notebook."

"Didn't see her, much. I mean, I saw her, but she didn't stay. Said she had to—to go."

Alvin was a horrid liar.

"Go where?"

"After you."

Meanwhile, Alvin's father slipped his hands into his pockets, probably as excuse to not have to shake Lorecroft's hand.

"What brought you this evening, fanc—er—Lorecroft?"

"I'm actually on my way home for the evening and thought I'd stop by to drop this off. Young Alvinheim left it at the work site."

From his coat, the Professor drew Alvin's notebook.

Every Esker knew that London Row was nowhere near "on the way" for Lorecroft; he lived back in Edgemeadow near the Gardens with most of the nobility. As Alvin gingerly took it from his hand, he cautiously traced his gaze up the Professor's arm, but the Professor's face seemed all but cordial in his way.

Ellery Hartchild's on the other hand…

"I also wanted to thank you both personally for um … *loaning* us your son for the Lectral Incandescent Transition Corps. While I'm certain your crew felt his absence, we wouldn't be so ahead of schedule were not for Master Esker's admirable work ethic."

"Thank you, Baron," said his mother.

"Oh, my name is fine, if you please, Mrs. Esker," said the Professor. "I've never been one to stand on titles."

If Ellery Hartchild caught his big sister here in the Esker home, crawling around on the floor in hiding? Alvin couldn't even fathom such doom.

"I um … I also believe I owe you all an apology," said Lorecroft, which pulled Alvin's attention back. "It would've been proper of me to attend the memorial for Miss Esker today," he said.

"You?" said Alvin's mother, then caught herself.

Lorecroft shrugged. "Is there any reason I cannot attend a time of remembrance for a remarkable young woman? She was a student, after all. While I might not be so *traditional* as yourselves, I held Miss Esker is extremely high regard. I certainly hope you all know that."

Albany politely answered, "We do, Baron, but it's good of you to say."

Alvin positioned himself in the kitchen, again standing right between the crouching girls, who sat with their backs to the cupboards, just under the counter, while Alvin saw to the kettle.

When he turned the spoked handwheel over the sink and water poured, Hana nearly leapt up from the floor like a pup for a biscuit.

Tabitha's jab to his knee suggested to Alvin that she needed him down there, so he "dropped" the dishrag onto the floor and ducked to get it.

"Do you have *any* idea what'll happen if Uncle Hiram finds her here? Or Ellery?" Tabitha whispered. "Get. Them. Out! This oughtn't be hard for you. Not corking your mouth is what you're best at, so why don't you put that to use?"

"You can *send* for *water?*" Hana awed, and tried to reach for it.

Alvin pushed her back and told Tabitha to, "get Hana to my bedroom. It's the corner door on the far landing—"

"And how am I supposed to get us there? This whole thing's a scandal in the making!"

"I'll figure something out. Look, you can climb out the casement into the alley—"

"Through a casement?! You're daft!"

"It's nice to hear, Baron," said Alvin's mother, then corrected herself: "*Mr. Lorecroft.* You sure I can't make you that tea?"

"Professor," Alvin interrupted. "Don't you have to be back at the site early in the morning?"

"Indeed. I ought be going. Come, Ellery. We've pestered the Eskers enough for one evening."

He donned his ivory coachman again, and opened the old latch door into the cool, gas-lit evening, but he paused in the doorway. "I look forward to trying the tea, next time. Be sure to save some earl grey, won't you?"

He gave a curious nod, and the kettle whistled. He was gone before Alvin looked back again, after pouring the tea for his mum, and once he was, a deep quiet settled over the Esker home. His father slumped onto the divan. He was a tired man, always a tired man. Hugo Esker was the man to go to, the one everyone trusted. Everyone.

"Hugo?" said his mother. "You alright, Dear?"

Alvin motioned when Tabitha's eyes peeked out from around the cupboard, hoping she would move to his bedroom. Tabitha and Hana crept out toward the landing steps again.

His father turned on the divan, toward a full view of the girls.

"Father!"

"Eh?"

"Um … what—what if we had a plaque dedicated to her. That old gazebo she loved! We'll do it tomorrow! I'm sure Albany could arrange it with with municipality." The girls crept silently, not ten feet behind his father. "Alphonse can make up the plaque, and I can come tomorrow, if that'll make it right. Just us and—and Albany, and I'll bet I can get Tabitha to come. We'll go to Chapel Hill and…"

"Really, Alvinheim?" said his mother. "Would you?"

His father cocked an eyebrow, and turned to go.

"Remember—remember when the Chancellor said he'd wished she would marry one of his boys?" Alvin forced a laugh, and everyone looked at him funny. "And he—he didn't even care which one? But Jack and Morgan married them girls from the Erskine family, instead? Remember? Twins, I think. They were Sam Erskine's girls, they were. And their mother's too. They were hers, I suppose. A Branton, she was. But Albany sure caught her eye! Almost a Viscountess, Agnes was. Ever think about that, Mother? Seems so strange for an Esker."

His father blinked. "Alvin?"

Tabitha ushered Hana into Alvin's bedroom. They didn't shut the door tight, but hopefully hid behind it.

"Yes, Sir?" said Alvin.

"You said you'd be there *today*. Man's only as good as his word."

"I'll come. I swear I will."

"I'm sure we can arrange it, Mr. Esker, if it helps the family," said Albany, a good fellow, for a politician, as Hugo always said.

Hugo Esker drew off his tramrunner's coat and draped it on the rack in the corner, plucked the bronze Engineer badge from his belt, and hung it where it belonged. "If you miss it again … anyway. I'll say goodnight, Albany. Let yourself out?"

"Of course, Sir," said Albany fetching his coat from the rack.

"I'm off too, boys," his mother said, taking her tea with her, as she often did of an evening so she could read in bed.

She kissed Alvin on the head.

"I'm sorry, mother."

"He loves you," she whispered.

"I know."

"I do, too."

With the click of the door, Alvin's heart sank, as if it had held a tremendous breath for so long. He picked up his cold dinner and tried to get past his brother.

"So. How was the *hour* it took you to grab your notebook? You know, the one Lorecroft brought by just now? And don't think I didn't notice Hartchild, by the bye." *Ellery? Or Tabitha?* "What exactly happened?"

Alvin's shoulders fell. "Nothing happened."

"Bollocks if I believe that."

"I'm going to bed."

"What—with your dinner?"

"Yes, with my dinner. I'm feeling eccentric tonight! Maybe next, I'll wear an oil pan for a hat and sleep on the counters. Goodnight, Alphonse."

"Alvin?"

Alvin stopped. "Oh. Sorry, Albany. Didn't mean to not say goodnight."

Albany Finch stood in the Esker door, donning his wool cap. "Are you alright?"

"What do you mean?"

"Your mother's right, you know. You *have* changed. They miss the way you used to be. Agnes would, too."

Albany quietly shut the door, and left him with his thoughts. And Alphonse, though he seemed to have nothing else to say. Alvin trudged off with dinner in hand, and went into his room as exhausted as he was eager to find himself alone with the greatest discovery in Orphan's history, who just happened to also be a grimy, pretty girl.

Who drew a knife on him the moment he entered.

ENTRY 8: "A MAN FOR ALL HOURS"

"Were it not for the zeal and fortitude of great Hickter, would not this indomitable beacon of the Expanse, with all rightful splendour of illumined minds, remain in lowly squalor and vain ignorance of its fallen and forgotten predecessors? Doubt it not!"

—Solomon Day, 11ᵗʰ Marquess of Highshire, Orphan Colony

Orphan Heights holds surprisingly scant records of Hickter, outside genealogical, and those bear little resemblance to one another and are largely believed apocryphal. The following is from the Archive's entries, unavoidably the sole available source:

Inventor and scholar of Newtonian Physics, Hermetic Philosophy, culinary art, gravitics, Byzantine architecture, algebra, psychology, chemistry, statecraft, non-Euclidean geometry, the works of Plato, Agrippa, 14th Century French literature (and of course Shakespeare), Cornelius Erasmus Hickter would perch along a low wall outside the newly-erected Academy of Science at age eight and question the Scholars on Unified Field Theory. Admitted to the Academy at eleven, his theories on gravitic constants allowed for development of Orphan's air cycling systems, as well as the phonometric orchestra. By twenty, he'd patented Orphan's first combustion engine, rocking chair, and a popular garlic tomato sauce. One colleague, Stanis Morley, was so affronted by Hickter's criticism of his work on gravitic echos that he challenged Hickter to a duel. Hickter, being a master of both the fencing blade and the powdergun, handily defeated his counterpart when the latter stumbled over a railing and fractured his leg. Hicker set the bone, made peace, then co-wrote a seminal work on magnetic fields that elevated Morley into notoriety, as well as reconciling his marriage.

CHAPTER 4

in which a careless girl climbs on all of Alvin's things

MOTTLED GLINT OFF HANA'S BLADE made Alvin's heart race as he backed up against the door. Her eyes blared wide, alarmed, her body heaving sharp breaths in his face. He dropped the plate of eggs.

"Hey!" Alvin barked. "Blazes are you doing?!"

"Too young for *those* kind of things!"

"Too—*what* kind? What're you suggesting? I'm an Esker, I'll have you know! Eskers don't take advantage of a girl like some motherless cad from Wesbeldt! Honestly…"

She cocked an eyebrow. "But … the bed…"

"You don't sleep where you're from? I had to hide you *somewhere!* This is my room!"

"Oh." She eyed him carefully, cautiously. "All of this is *yours?* Sorry. Five days with no food and…"

Her eyes hazed and couldn't track him. The knife wobbled in her hand. Breaths came in sharp draws, and before he understood what was happening to her (or to him), Hana slumped.

"Hey!" He caught her, sort of, and lay her down along the floor. "Hana? Hey!" He shook her and tapped her face. Her eyes fluttered a little and she would only moan.

Oh, how he wanted to summon his mother!

"For Author's sake! It's okay. It's alright, Hana. Understand? Course you don't. Can't hear me. Blazing fool, that's what you are, Alvin Esker, and no mistake."

He cradled her head and spun himself over her to reach for the pillow on his bed. He caught it with his fingertips and pulled it under her.

Now, Alvinheim Lockwilde Esker was all Esker, but every now and again, the Heinrich side of Alvin (being of his mother's good-natured family) would show itself in an impulse to bring somebody food or put a pillow under their head. He bounded up and peered through the door. Alphonse was still on the divan, but what choice did he have?

"I thought you were off to bed," his brother mused.

"Thirsty after all that supper!" he countered, and filled the largest glass of water he could without spilling.

"The supper that you ate in two minutes? What was that noise in there?"

"I dropped my plate."

"You dropped it? Maybe that's why we've these amazing modern machines called 'tables.'"

"I'm a natural innovator. Can't advance society without dropping a plate or two, can we?" He rushed back to his room. Hana lay there and breathed in staggered, ragged draws. "Water. Drink. Come on. Drink."

Some trickled down her chin but it startled her enough that her eyes fluttered as a little went down her throat. For a moment, the fierceness came back to her eyes when she saw him over her. Her fingers drew forward as if expecting it to burn, and handled the glass like it was a newborn, looking to Alvin as if for permission, and he nodded. She drank, and she drank, and she drank until it was gone, and when it was, she held it upside down over her mouth and tapped on the bottom before tonguing the rim like Alvin had often seen his father and his mates do with widowmakers down at the *Lager Than Life*.

When she was done, her mouth fell open and she gasped from the pleasure of water on parched dry throat. Alvin noticed her knife still on the floor. He took the chance to quietly slip it into his hand and back onto a shelf behind him. "You need food."

He lay her head back down and scooped the partly-spilled dinner back on the plate, and doubted she would care overmuch.

"Oh." She said, eyeing the plate in his hands, looking between it and his face as though looking at it was dirty somehow.

"I brought it for *you*," Alvin assured her, the Heinrich side of him quite pleased with itself.

"For what trade?" she asked.

"No trade necessary, is what any good Esker would say!"

"But your ration … you cannot give it."

"Ration? We've plenty of food."

Hunger overcame her curiosity, apparently. Once the plate was in her hands, she bore in. The eggs, she devoured without wiping off her hands, and went from there to the sandwich and lettuce, piling them in her mouth like they might scurry away.

Then Hana belched loud enough for half the brownstone to hear.

"Blazes, Al!" Alphonse yelled from the other room. "Don't let mum hear like that!"

Hana sighed pleasantly. "That is best food. Ever."

"Someday I'll tell mum you said so," Alvin assured. "Oh. What happened to Tabitha?"

"Left through that," said Hana, pointing to Alvin's casement window. "She said really bad things, most about you. Pushing her helped, but it made the bad words worse. Knife?"

"Huh? Oh! I don't know where it could've…"

"Give," she insisted. Against his better judgment, he took the knife from its hiding spot. Hana sheathed it. "You, your towne, you can do so *much*."

"Think so?" he said, drawing from his belt his great innovation, the Apparatic Micro-Induction Incandescent Lantern—*patent-pending*. He clicked the little dial on the base and it flared into glorious life. Hana's blue and green eyes shone with gold from the lamp.

"We call it 'lectral energy,'" he bragged. "Like it?"

She nodded seriously.

He put out the light and set it back by his bag. Hana eyed it for another

few moments before turning her curious gaze on his bedroom. "This is …
this whole building is yours? Only you four? Does that other man live here?
Or is he a different clan?"

"Albany? No!" he chuckled. "He lives way over in Edgemeadow, near
the Gardens where I saw you. Most of the Nobility live there."

"Nobility?" she asked.

"The Aristocracy," he explained.

She scowled, apparently not understanding and annoyed by it.

"Don't you have any leaders where you're from?"

"Chieftain," she said. "And the Priestess. Like that?"

"Uh … sort of?" he mused. "I mean we've a parliamentary system but if
you want to think of it—"

Hana rushed to the door and peeked back through the crack, which
Alvin quickly shut. "Can you all open the doors of Iron Hollow like the one
you opened for me?" she asked.

Alvin laughed. "Alright, first priority: it's called 'Orphan *Heights*,' or
'Orphan Towne' if you're a reasonably normal person. Only the Aristocracy
or Scholars or uppity types call it 'Orphan Heights.' Or you can just call it
plain old 'Orphan' like most of us do. Try it."

"Orphan," she repeated flatly, apparently unclear why he asked her to.

"As for the doors, it's pretty much just me who can open them, least of
anyone you're going to meet on the street. I mean, I'm sure Chancellor
Finch or Inspector Hartchild knows the codes and all but I happened to see
it once and remembered it. I'm good at remembering things, I am."

She turned her attention to the rest of Alvin's remarkable little home.

It all formed a ring around the room, Alvin's bed and surrounding
pillow horde, shelves lining its headboard and the bookcase next to that. His
desk sat beside the door. No inch of Alvin's was empty, save for the one spot
of wall beneath the window at the foot of his bed. The lamplight made it
warm, and his books and projects and papers and charts and models spilled
or hung tacked everywhere. Tools and parts littered everything. His 'nest,'
his mother called it.

Hana first scanned the high shelves, and a cocked brow phrased her question for him.

"Oh. Those are nothing, just some … ornilofter designs."

"Orni—what?"

"They're just…" His voice fell.

"You people can fly, too?!"

"No, just—just things I made as a boy. Lofters. Flying machine models. I've loads of books on it—heavier-than-air flight ideas, I mean. Toys and wishes, you know? They ain't real, not yet, anyway. Should take them down, really, just haven't done it yet."

"What is all this?" she asked, gesturing at the modest spyglass in the corner, the old drawings of constellations, planets, temples, monster, etc.

"The telescope was my sister's. She was an Astronomer, Orphan's only one, actually." He breathed on its surface and wiped a smear with his sleeve. "Worked for six months to afford the materials for this, and the labor, though Alphonse did most of the work. A master brazesmith, Alphonse is."

"What is her name?"

"Name? Oh. Agnes—Agnesine, actually."

"Agnes," Hana repeated. "'Aggie,' that man called her. Like you call me Hana. And she was what?"

"An Astronomer. Star-watcher. You look through the telescope and you can see stars close-up."

"Huh."

Hana got up, and went to the desk, where many of the papers hung. She climbed onto it for a better look at the higher ones. Hana mountain-goated her way across his furniture, since he'd hung most of his crude charts up over the moldings. Alvin chose to let it go.

"You think about far-away a lot, yah?"

"Wha—what?"

"Far away. Places. You watch stars. You play flying machines. You think about far away." Alvin puzzled over this. Nobody had ever pointed out such an obvious thing to him, so obvious he hadn't ever once considered it. "What do they look like? Stars?"

"Ha, um … Hana, stars are spheres of burning gas, thousands of miles wide. That's all, so they look like that up close, I suppose."

A wide grin drew across her face, swelling to overfull before coming out in a burst. "Nah!"

"No, really!" he said. "We're not that different."

"What do you mean?"

"You and me. Humans. Our bodies are just carbon and the like. 'Dust and windsong,' Professor Lorecroft calls it. Here, look at the star…"

He would prove it. He kept enough of his old textbooks, and promptly displayed a page for her. She *ooed* a little at the penned illustration of the pockmarked orb.

"Never seen one big like this."

"That's why we have telescopes. Haven't you ever looked in one?"

She shook her shaggy head, and pointed to his. "Show me."

With the tiniest nod he'd ever given, Alvin reached to his satchel, and pulled the brass-edged lens from its cotton sleeve and put it back where it belonged, on the end of the mounted scope. He threaded it into place and set it on the casement sill until he spotted a star, fuzzy through Orphan's glass up overhead, one of the stars of Leo, he thought.

Hana took it eagerly, and likewise aimed her face with Alvin's help. He held her arms and lifted her chin. "Somewhere around—"

"There!" she said, and Alvin had to shush her; her mouth fell open as she gazed.

"What do you think?" he laughed.

"Amazing!" she said. "It looks like it does *without* a spyglass!"

Alvin promptly took it back. "Telescope. We can't see much from here, but I'll take you to the Gardens tomorrow! The Agromatic Gardens? Where we met? There's a stellar view from there. Ha! See … 'stellar'? Because … nevermind."

He collapsed the scope, thanks to Alphonse's forethought to make it portable for Agnes, capped the lens, and slid the whole affair into his satchel, where they barely fit.

Hana could no longer hold back a deep yawn. "Atí lagi," she said, and planted herself back on the floor.

At one point, she fixated on his bed. She first propped an elbow on its edge, and slowly advanced to fondling of the mattress. Alvin, being raised mannerly toward the fairer sex, insisted she have it.

"Nah," she said. "Not for me."

"No," said Alvin. "Really. I insist you take the bed, and I'll have no quarrel over it. You're safe here." He was stalwart on the issue, and she seemed to realize it.

She pulled off her outer wrappings and tossed them to the floor. She ran her palms up the bed, under the covers, let the wrinkles go between her fingers. Slowly she burrowed in from the foot, as if she'd no idea how you were supposed to get into a bed properly. By the time she was fully under, Hana was squeezing the quilt and letting out heavy sighs.

It was not so much a question of *who* she could be, but *how*. If only he could puzzle it out! He looked again and again, each time with a thought's beginning: "Maybe..." but there never came an answer.

He would muse over this blonde wonder in and out of shallow sleep until morning, when, after sleeping far too late, he would rouse to find his bed empty, and the girl gone.

C H A P T E R   5

in which valuable lost things are wished to be found

ALVIN'S FIRST THOUGHT OF THE MORNING on the 2nd of October was whether or not he'd fallen onto the floor during the night. It often took a while for the cobwebs to dust off the windows of his little inner-observatory of a morning, but not that morning. No note. Just an empty bed. He bolted from his room and made Alphonse's brow rise as he sat with his breakfast.

"Author above!" Alphonse exclaimed. "You look like you greased and guzzled proper. Sleep in your clothes last night?"

"What? Clothes? Oh. Yes. I was comfortable."

On the kitchen counter behind Alphonse stood eight empty glasses that looked to once have held water. Over them hovered their mother, scratching her head at their existence. "Alvinheim? Was it you who left these here?"

"Um … yes. Last night. I was thirsty."

"And kept getting down more glasses?" asked Alphonse.

"I … thought of mastering waterglass music for a moment. Had a dream about it and it couldn't wait. I gave it up after while. Father at work?"

"Of course he is!" his mother reminded him. "Orphan doesn't run on sloppy clocks! The Academy has his crew overseeing those new underfittings he complains so much about. Don't sleep so late, next time."

"Got the Tramrunners working overtime for the election, don't they?"

38

said Alphonse, tearing off another piece of his rye.

Alvin tried to interject before his mother and brother lost themselves in the inevitable politics of Orphan's coming elections.

"Did anyone—"

"You know how this sort of showmanship works," his mother continued. "They want to play up the tension between the Bankers and the House of Commons and every Baron and Viscount is playing like they aren't all selling the same nonsense to the Chancellery—silliness, you ask me."

"Hey," said Alvin. "Did anyone—"

"Well I don't see why *we've* got to pay for their posturing with all this overtime," Alphonse barked. "And have you seen this equipment they've got us installing? Bonkers, is what."

This was going to escalate. "Excuse me!" Alvin shouted. "Did anyone stop by this morning?"

"Someone's testy," his brother mused. "Nobody but Constable Pines."

"What?"

"Mmm hmm. Something about a thief. Apparently Mrs. Dutch's linens were stolen off the clothesline. She's in a frightful state." Alvin weighed the likelihood of it *not* being Hana, and came up with nothing. "Pines is thrilled, meanwhile, finally has a crime. You'd have thought it was Christmas..."

His mother took a long drought of her tea. "Don't be late for this dedication idea of yours, please, or your father's liable to rupture a seam. He's already in a mood because he had to stop off at Pike's Bank this morning. You know how he feels about bankers."

"I know how father feels about most things. Everyone does."

Elise Esker let out a long and tired sigh. "You know, when you say things like that, you're talking about the man I married."

"I'm sorry, Mum. Didn't mean it poorly."

"You'll be a father someday, too, you know. You might see things differently, then. Now, I left you some rolls."

Alvin shoved them into his satchel, which made both his brother and mother look at him funny.

"Maybe later," he said.

But there was no sign of Hana except some odds and ends moved around across the living room, and the glasses on the kitchen counter that so perplexed his mother, who went straight to washing them with little comments like "what would possess that boy" falling like crumbs.

Once she was done, she left Alvin and his brother momentarily alone.

"You're leaving without combing that pilfer's nest you call hair?" said Alphonse.

"Alvinheim, comb your hair!" his mother scolded from down the hall.

"Have to keep the girls off me somehow," he answered as he pulled on his shoes and old copper Tramrunner jacket. Orphan's mornings were chilly, as his mother reminded him hourly.

He made it to the door before Alphonse called after, "Speaking of … your nerves have anything to do with harboring a girl in your bedroom overnight?"

Alvin white-knuckled the handle.

"It had to be a sight," his brother said. "There was I, emerging early this morning—in my night trousers, mind you, the ones with the big hole in the thigh—to find a girl I very much didn't know standing in the kitchen, having polished off a seventh glass of water, draining the eighth into this ruddy little flask she had on her."

"You … you didn't you tell Mum?"

"Ain't in the habit of snitching, least not without a story. I thought she was a burglar, at first."

"A burglar!"

"It was dark! And anyway I know it was her what stole Mrs. Dutch's linens. Can't blame the girl, seeing the rubbish she wore. We had a brief talk … extremely brief. Don't seem the talkative type. My second thought was that you've been hiding a girlfriend, but then I saw that *hair* of hers. 'Not from around here,' I tell myself."

"Alphonse—"

"And then I tell myself, 'well then, where can she be from? ain't like there's any *other* place. But. There she was! She seemed anxious, and left."

"Where did she go?"

"She's dreadful cute, is what I think, and I don't mind telling you. I mean, Father would skin you if he knew about this, and no mistake, but I'll have the rest of my life to hold this over your head."

"I weren't indecent," Alvin insisted.

"Oh, I know my little brother enough to know that much. Mind you, whatever comes of this, I'll make sure we green-gauge it with Newkirk's column in the *Hilldiver*—hey, where are you going?"

"Well I have to find her!" Alvin called back, and was out the door and onto the cobbled avenue before Alphonse could holler back.

London Row stood quiet. The working men of Orphan Towne would already be at their stations since 6:56, running the substations, the plants, and the tram freight lines. Even the milkmen would be out, though wouldn't come to Alvin's third block of London Row until 9:48.

"Hana!" he called. He was answered by old Margaret Dutch's rooster, Nuggets, next door down.

So he ran.

Up and down every residential row, Alvin looked, starting at Baker and working from there. By 9:40, he'd left the Residential 16th and made his way to Tanno's Landing.

"What are you doing, kid?" someone shouted when he leapt the fence and pulled himself into the open tram car.

He thought he saw her around the north end of the Municipal District, and promptly jumped from the moving car while the workmen condemned his stupidity for jumping on a moving tram. Hana wasn't there.

He found himself by the Songbird Café at 11:14, and planted his tired self into a bench. He would've eaten the sweet rolls, but feared it would be rude to the owner, who leaned over the counter across the patio and bid him good morning.

"Knocking off for lunch early there, Al? Good timing. The rush won't hit for another nine minutes-thirty."

"No. Thank you, Mr. Dewitt. Not very hungry."

"What brings you here, then?" The little birdcage next to him sang with chirpy birdsong, as usual, the Dewitts being Orphan's only bird-breeding family of note.

Alvin watched the clattering trams, shipping the workmen off to the perimeter rail projects, the smoke rising from the Songbird, the timely bustle of foot traffic around the lofted Academy campus.

"Lost something, is all."

"Oh? Sorry to hear that, Al, but I'm sure you'll find it if you look hard enough. Always in the last place, I say. Here. Have a half mutton sandwich. Fella left it. No charge."

Alvin took the sandwich morosely and ate it. How could she have just *vanished?* No word of her came from anyone, and if they knew ... well, word traveled fast in the 'finest towne at the end of the world,' and the Constables were still circling the residential areas. Orphan was big, sure, near two miles across, but not *impossibly* big.

Alvin swallowed the last bite, stood, gave up, and then spotted her.

From his satchel, he pulled the small spyglass that he insisted was a telescope, spun off the cap, and put it to his eye, bringing into relative focus the *girl of elsewhere*, through the few smatterings of clustered people, adjusting that tattered old hood she wore. He'd only seen a fleeting glimpse, and seen it just in time to catch her talking with someone, her head craned to see a higher face.

Dread gripped him, and when someone moved out of the way, Hiram Lorecroft came into focus above her.

Baron Hiram Alberstein Lorecroft was a curious man, a matchless mind, called everything from 'The Bright Star of Orphan Heights' to 'Cornelius Hickter Reincarnated' by the time he was Alvin's age, the man who practically *invented* light. Descended from a long heritage of brilliance among even Orphan's storied inventors, the Lorecrofts had been the minds behind many of its wonders, from cycle-filtered ventilation to the rotary ceiling fan—and now, lectral luminescence. Every toe un-stubbed and every un-strained eye reading late of an evening was owed to a Lorecroft.

What in blazes was he going to do with Hana? And while Alvin's heart pounded like a bird trying to batter its way out of his ribs, he jammed the spyglass back into his bag.

Nobody in Orphan ran. It simply wasn't done.

The schedule was too tight for that. The cams and mainsprings of its culture were oiled too well for that. The certainty of life was too known for that. Such haste implied imperfection in Orphan's order, and only small children attempted it.

The trams ran on time, but nobody *ran*.

The very idea.

The straight elevated road of Wells Commons was thick with another political rally of some sort. Alvin couldn't get through clearly enough but shoved his way rudely through the huddled masses listening to some or another person mounted on a table to preach about the injustice of the Bankers or the Chancellery or whatever.

Alvin hated politics.

"Young Master Esker!" called Constable Pines. "Seen something, have you? You be sure to let me know, now!"

His son Martin Pines was with him, as usual. "Esker!" Martin called, echoing his father. "Where you running to?"

But Alvin didn't indulge either. He pressed his way through the side of the crowd and ran for clear streets.

Up and down the bridgeways, the masses of Orphan flowed around the singular boy. Scholars poured from the campus on their lunches. Alvin spun, lighthousing his gaze down every alleyway in sight until an ivory coachman hat stood out, heading away toward the library on the south end.

Where was he taking her?

"Excuse me," said Alvin. "Excuse me!" He pushed and slid, angled and wove through the ranks.

So up the outside steps of the Songbird's veranda he ran, bounding over the railing while everyone gasped and called out, astounded at this obnoxious boy's erratic behavior. He spotted Lorecroft and Hana below, as

Lorecroft ushered her swiftly on the lower bridgeways, to (of all places) the sprawling curves of Bellamy Park.

Lorecroft took her to the east fountain, where Alvin was relieved to find no one else at all. Under the nearby gaze of the three marble figures of the fountain, Hana stood before the Professor, clad in Mrs. Dutch's lousy linens over her own ragged clothes.

What a sight she was.

Alvin caught his breath along the upper bridgeway and watched them down below. Lorecroft gingerly lifted the crest of her hood enough to get a peek at the lustrous hair underneath, nodded to himself, and carried on as if she was only showing him a new bonnet from *Sophie's* down the lane.

"You just … shoot it in the air?" said Hana. "All that water?"

"What? The fountain? It's designed for aesthetic appeal. That means it's beautiful to look at. Don't you think it's beautiful?"

"Yah," she said. "Just … so much water. Goes nowhere."

"Indeed. I'm sure it's a different sort of decoration than what you're accustomed to," said the Professor. "Though the water is pumped back through the system. Orphan wastes little."

"Never seen so much water in one place," she repeated.

"No, not since the Yedack River dried up, I suppose, and that was long before your time. Now would you mind telling me how it is you come to be in our little towne?"

Hana looked apprehensive, holding her arms and seeming cold, or maybe just anxious.

"I can discern the basics for myself," he added, "though one detail is missing. I suppose that if *you* don't feel comfortable telling me, I might just ask young Master Esker myself, if he would be polite enough to step down here and join us."

The doomful feeling of the night before settled back over Alvin. He wound down a spiraling brick stairway a little further up. Lorecroft gave an unhappy glance to him as he descended, a good match for the stoic faces of Megillius, Clinias, and the Athenian, who all stood in gleaming marble, their backs together, staring to the sky from atop the fountain.

"I'll be asking you about a certain gate protocol shortly," said the

Professor, then turned back to Hana.

Before they could continue their conversation, Alvin interrupted. "Why did you come here, Professor?"

Lorecroft did not seem especially amused. "Barring an atypical variable, Bellamy Park's sculpture walk remains vacant from 11:06 to 11:24. That leaves us with eight minutes to…" He checked his timepiece. "Seven, with your interruption. Now, Miss … I'm sorry, young lady, but I'm afraid I didn't hear your … young lady?"

She was in the fountain.

"Lofthana Engindaut cín Jalóheim fra Sóholdt," she answered, drinking down the contents of a little flask and filling it in the fountain's falling stream. "See?" She showed them the flask. Her name was cut into its edge.

Alvin again interjected. "I don't understand why'd she run away— why'd you run away?"

She didn't answer.

"I think this young lady has come to Orphan Heights to propose a bargain, assuming she doesn't linger in our once-elegant fountain all day."

"Yah," she stated. "Brought things for trading. And mending!"

"Wondrous things, no doubt," said Lorecroft, circling the fountain and keeping a dry distance as she splashed. "But I'm curious what it is you hope to gain in exchange for your wares?"

She seemed transfixed by the water, fingering the downward stream until a little splashed off her hand and hit her cheek. She started back, beaming eyes like a toddler, and answered wistfully, "A <u>Dark Illumined Eye</u>."

"The—the what?" asked Alvin. "Wait—Professor, ain't you gonna ask her about the Expanse? And *what* Eye? Hana? What in blazes are you on about?"

"<u>Dark Illumined Eye</u>," the Professor mused, and squinted, thought a moment. "A book?"

"Yah."

"Its existence is a folk tale, if I remember? If only your dear uncle Otto were here, Master Esker. He would expound on it for hours, no doubt."

Hana nodded, and dried off her hand as she hopped out of the fountain,

45

boots sloshing water everywhere. "It is in that tower, yah?"

"Wait," said Alvin. "You came all this way, for a magic book you think is in the Heuridium?"

Hana slumped her rucksack to the now-soggy ground. "Look, brought things to trade." Her hair spilled down over her face. She swept it back and reset her hood as they talked. "Got tools and good weave and if anything needs need mending—"

"Really, Miss Sóholdt," said Lorecroft with a hand up, "I've a maid to see to my mending. You've come to see some sort of iconographic object, by the sound of it, but what precisely makes you believe you'll find it in the old Heuridium of our Academy? Four minutes left."

"And what even is it? What makes this book so important?" Alvin pressed.

"It is from Agarta," she said, as if he ought to know.

"From *what?*"

Lorecroft opened his mouth, and something made him stop. He thought inwardly for a moment, and a little smirk came across his face. Whatever the Professor summoned, it sounded old, and strange: "'Know none before us, self-begot, self-rais'd by our own quick'ning power, when fatal course had circled his full orb, the birth mature of this our native heaven, ethereal sons.'"

"Sir?"

"Thule, Master. Esker. That's what our ancestors called it. Your might better know it by that name." This sent a cold ripple through Alvin, but even he couldn't pinpoint why. He knew the word, but didn't stop to spin his lens around at the moment, because Lorecroft kept talking. "Of course, Miss Sóholdt, you know there is no such book as this … <u>Dark Illumined Eye</u>. And the myths of your … *Agarta* are only that."

"Nah!" Hana insisted. "Agarta *is* real! And the book *is* here! Put me to the Proving Tree and test it! You—you have to have—"

Lorecroft cut her off. "I am sorry, Miss Sóholdt, but the Heuridium, in spite of its grandeur, is only a relic. Today, it's little more than a monument, not unlike the North Operations complex. We use it to store old landscaping machinery and excess linens from the Weaver's Mill. It houses no books but old note papers. Now, we have only three minutes."

"But you have to have it! It has to be there!"

"I could've brought you to him, you know," snapped Alvin, his pride suffering quite the tendering. "Could've brought you to whatever Scholar you wanted, if you'd asked."

"You already did enough," she muttered. "And you would have talked about it for hours."

"I wouldn't!"

"Children!" Lorecroft snapped. "This is not a light matter. Miss Sóholdt's appearance obviously carries great weight with it. For now, I would recommend keeping this among ourselves while I ponder the best course. Now Master. Esker, I will escort you both back to Willowbough, my estate in Astorhill until—"

A sharp whistle sounded off from a constable down the lane, and it was only then they realized that not only was she boldly displaying Mrs. Dutch's scarf, but her hood was down.

"What is that?" said Hana.

"That is an atypical variable," Lorecroft returned. "Run."

"What?" she asked.

Alvin grabbed her hand. "They've seen you! Run!"

But the Professor caught Alvin by the arm, with more strength than he ever expected a thinking man could. "Get her to Willowbough, but be wary of her, Master Esker. You do not know what she is."

And then he let go.

Alvin tugged on her arm, bolted from the middle of Bellamy Park, and they bounded onto a half-empty freight car one row up, rode it one stop up and jumped off at Senna's Landing while the constable chased after. Alvin would've grabbed her hand for the running, if he possibly could've caught up. Hana soared like a rabbit in flight, landing foot-falls off banisters and bounding over corners and stairs.

"Hey!" he yelled, but she wouldn't stop for anything.

Somehow they'd circled back to the labor rally at Wells Commons and ducked their way between all the bodies that were too busy tilting up their eyes to the speakers to notice them.

Cries against the Bankers or the Chancellery shrouded them in constant, protective noise until they came to Edgemeadow, and realized they would not be making it to Baron Lorecroft's estate. Constables were gathering from the summoning whistle, finally having something interesting to do and making sure the Aristocracy was safe from the bother.

Hana spun into an adjoining alley, where Alvin finally caught up, but it did not go unseen. Someone among the crowd saw them, and rushed in their direction, shoving by others who were more interested in what the constables were doing. But the alleyway they chose was gated at the far end.

"Why'd you have to steal Mrs. Dutch's blazing linens?!" Alvin asked.

"Was three vials of allspice not good enough of a trade?"

"You left her allspice?"

She nodded. "Nothing to mend."

"Well—well I'd've given you clothes if you'd only—" Footfalls came rushing into the alley. "Bollocks!" They would see him, see *her*, see that firelit hair of hers and that would be that. This was fight or flight. Alvin pulled her hood down a little lower. And then, he did the only fool, stupid thing his panicked mind could conjure.

"Look, I'm really sorry about this."

Maybe whoever came for them would see two adolescents in a compromised position, and considerately turn away. Alvin pressed her to the wall, hands on her small waist, turned his back to the alley, and ignored the sudden gasp from her throat as he leaned in.

"Alvinheim Lockwilde Esker!"

He drew back just before making contact with Hana's mouth. Her alarmed face stayed like it was. Tabitha's did, too. Neither girl spoke, just glared disbelieving at Alvin.

"I—I thought you were…"

"What are you *doing* with her?!" Tabitha growled, with all the ire of a schoolmarm.

"She was—I only tried—"

"I see quite well what you tried!" said Tabitha. "You're no better than some block-headed bounder from Wesbeldt! Just because the girl's a foreigner doesn't mean you can take advantage!"

Hana panted. "You were going to…"

"I was trying to keep her hidden!" Alvin defended, vainly.

"I'm not even going to acknowledge your … *brutish* behavior," said Tabitha. "She cannot be out here like this! Have you both lost your minds?"

Hana quickly turned her flushed face to the ground, then yelled up at them, "*That's* what 'giving one' means!"

"Esker, you've got to get her out of here."

"Look, this has been really a bugger of a day. I was supposed to get her to Willowbough, but that ain't happening now, obviously."

"Willowbough? You mean—you don't mean Uncle Hiram knows!"

"He—he might. A little bit. Don't give me that look! We need somewhere to go, where they won't look for her, at least until we can get her to your uncle's."

Alvin was all set to explain, then decided it was best to not let her know more than he already had. He needed to think. He fingered through ideas in the air as if he'd written them on an invisible blackboard, and tapped his temple, muttering to himself about what wouldn't work.

"Idea!" he finally erupted. "Meet us over at Cavendish."

"Meet you?" she said, rather uppity. "*There?*"

"Right! But go to Eddington's first and buy her some ordinary clothes, will you? Something that'll cover that hair, too."

"Cover that much hair?! I'd need a barber, not a tailor!"

Hana drew herself over to a window and started peering in over the stone edge of the casement. "Why is my hair bad?"

"It's hardly bad, Miss Sóholdt," Tabitha explained. "Unwashed, uncombed, and uneven, maybe, but nothing a little care wouldn't fix. It's simply … unique, for Orphan Heights. And Esker, Cavendish is twelve rows over and locked up!"

"I may or may not have a key," Alvin confessed. "Stop looking at me like that, Hartchild!" He turned back to her more warmly, this time. "Oh and, while you're at it, would you kindly stop at the Songbird? I recently discovered these mutton sandwiches they have and—”

“How can you think about *food* right now?”

“Food is good any time,” Hana added.

“Well I can hardly think on an empty stomach, can I? I thought we could knock off for lunch, is all.”

Hana was busy watching people through the nearest window until Tabitha noticed and jerked her away from it.

“I am not your maid!” she reminded Alvin. “And who’s going to pay?”

Hana interjected, “Would they take linens?”

Tabitha seethed.

“I’ll pay you later, Hartchild. You know I’m good for it.”

“You owe me two-and-six from last time! Just, don’t let her be seen!”

Tabitha marched, in her proper custom, out of the alleyway, leaving the two of them alone and exposed, reminding Alvin of his behavior when Tabitha happened upon them.

“Listen,” he said. “About … I don’t normally do that sort of thing, and I know it weren't right of me. Forgiven?”

Hana searched his face for longer than he wanted. “Atí lagi,” she said.

“What’s that?”

“It is alright. Just … did not expect it.”

It would be a dodgy time getting her there. They would cross several bridgeways, each one over the crowded morning lanes of the market, Alvin keeping quiet footing over the limeiron grates that anyone could look and see through from below, and eventually cross one bridgeway by the Parkstone lookout, finally coming to Cavendish, № 138.

The last place Alvin ever saw his sister alive.

CHAPTER 6

in which old sins cast long shadows on young carpet

DESPITE THREE YEARS OF DISUSE of the lock on the alley door of № 138 Cavendish, Alvin's key still worked, the one he was supposed to give back to the Municipal General a year prior.

Oops.

The handle didn't turn without a jerk or two, and it took a few good shoves with his shoulder to make the door swing. Hana coughed at the musty air, the two leaving the clacking of tram cars and all the noise of Orphan Towne behind as they shut the door.

Beams of gold streamed in ribbons through dusty curtains.

"Where are we?" Hana asked.

Alvin stumbled on something, and felt around for the kerosene lamp he remembered being down by the side wall, but found the match well empty.

"Hold up," he said. "Matches are in the back."

He smashed his knee on something, then his elbow.

"Don't hit things," she told him. "It hurts."

"Really?" he barked, holding his knee.

Hana didn't seem to have any trouble, and it was her who reminded him of the obvious.

"What about your magic lantern?"

51

"Hmm? Oh!" He took the lectral lantern from his hip and flared it into life, casting streaks of shadow from a hundred shapes around the room. "Right. Can't believe I didn't think of it sooner."

"We use lanterns a lot in Svaraheim."

"In what?" Alvin asked.

"Outside. This land. You know. Svaraheim. You called it—"

"The Expanse," he said, setting the flame to the wick. "You obviously use goggles a lot, too."

"Dust storms. They itch."

Alvin lit another, and a third, illuminating the room to a soft glow. Agnes's old desk sat between the two front windows that now were covered with drapes. Crates stood in stacks, and furniture settled into disuse under ghostly sheets.

One even hung over the wall above her desk.

"So … what is this place?" Hana asked him again.

— — — — — — — — — — — — — — — — — —

Four years prior, Alvin pushed the door to № 138 open, as he usually did after his schooling, and had to step over unparalleled mess. Boxes sat open, blooming with straw and shredded papers, a garden of cargo.

Agnes didn't see him.

She was far too occupied sketching notes over her new, commissioned invention, a three-foot circular table, rimmed in hickory and bronze, a model of a flat globe surrounded by rings in alignment with the cosmos.

Her recent employment serving at the Songbird obviously circulated her earnings back to the Engineers.

Agnes? he called.

It was three nights since she'd come home.

He found her singing softly to herself, there in her 'laboratory.' *Ich denke was ich will und was mich beglücket.* It was some old folk song in a language he vaguely remembered hearing his grandparents singing. *Die Gedanken sind frei…* She loved that song, and sang it often. *Al!* she started.

Is it four o'clock already? It isn't four. Gracious, hadn't even realized! Well, doesn't matter.

Once she noticed him gazing at the new creation, she positively beamed, like a bride showing off her gown.

You like it? Isn't it amazing! Alphonse did a lot of the work on the engraving. You know how he is with reliefs, always carving something. He always did, didn't he? Anyway...

When he asked what precisely it was, she answered after blowing her mangled hair from her face, *It—it's the earth. An Orrery, actually but I focused on the extra-planetary elements. It's a flat depiction of the solar system but I've compensated for spherical numerics. I needed to visualize it all, you know? I had it all drawn up but I needed to see it as a linear plane, sort of the way a labe will bend a dome into a plane for charting.*

That tic of hers began, where she'd flick a pencil wildly in her fingers and blink fast. Alvin traced the arc of the widest ring. *Why the ecliptic?* he asked.

I've tried to map some things out, according to records of star positions. The patterns I was talking about? I think there's still another layer to in, in positions over time. Uncle Otto was here earlier. You ought've seen him beam at it! Went on for half an hour about Thule and how they knew about all this in that ancient land. You know Otto and his Atlantean lost civilizations.

Chalkboards hung mounted everywhere, some standing perched against chairs, all filled to the rim with equations, angular measurements, and constellations. She moved from one to another, tripping over the mess and brushing back her hair like a nervous tic.

I think ... I think I'm close to figuring out how to alter the patterns, Al.

Alter them?

Alvin only ever had a dubious understanding of physics.

She stuttered, eyes flashing like a girl possessed, her mind, even from Alvin's view, aflutter with boundless numerics.

I think I'm on to something with the cymatic wave idea. It's like tiny vibrations—sound waves, essentially—but if we can emit a frequency at a tight enough wavelength, it could realign the vibratory patterns of any particle! I'm sure that with the right Cymatic Induction Emitter, transmutation of matter is possible. The stars give us the pattern. Alter the pattern with the right vibratory wave, and you alter matter!

Uh … how would you do that?

Agnes went to answer, and sighed. *I'm not the engineer. I've no idea.*

She stepped back and awed at the illustrious orrery. She liked to focus on victories, not problems. Alvin showed his obvious admiration for the craftsmanship. He ran a careful finger across the Alps. *But … what's it for?*

Agnes grinned. *Confirmation.* She nodded with glee, joy bubbling out from her girlish, sparking eyes. *The Orrery? It's for confirmation, far better mapping of the planispheric patterns. They're like a fractal, repeating in intervals at any scale, from microscopic to planetary! The same patterns in seashells and the human strand are found in planetary positions and orbits! It's all one governing pattern of nature. Stars are just the easiest to see. It's almost like it was meant to be there. Microcosms and macrocosms...*

Coming toward him, she tripped over the splintered planks of the shipping crates. *Imagine the things we could do, Al, if we could alter the patterns of matter—potentially turn filthy water into clean, alter iron into soil, and that's just the beginning and no, do not call me 'Alchemist!'*

She took a few breaths, ran a hand around the rim of the orrery, then brushed a few strands away from her face, and some inward imagination shaped her face into subtle joys.

We could finally have a future without these walls, and without the dead world out there remaining a wasteland. 'Above my head, a boundless sky I see, and seem to scent the odorous west-wind's kiss. The soft rough grass seems pressing on my feet...'

Alvin swallowed the memory, as he had so many others like it, still trying to grapple with those days with no better luck than ever.

"It was my sister's laboratory, a few years back," Alvin explained to Hana. "Rather gloomy, these days."

"What is 'laboratory'? Does it mean 'gloomy'?"

"Place of *work*, like a home but for working on thinking or schooling or the like. 'Gloomy' means dark and sad and murky and sort of dull."

"What is *this* thing?"

"That is a duster."

"Hmm…" She turned it over in her hand and giggled at the feathers when they brushed against her nose. "Dusters are great! Where's her, um, 'gloomy work place' now?" she asked, tossing aside the duster.

"She's dead."

"Oh. That *is* dark and sad and murky and sort of dull. She was smart?"

"She was brilliant," he asserted, with more than a little puff to his chest. "If a touch daft, in that genius sort of way. She had the title of Orphan's last Astronomer, though … though we gave it to her so I don't know if it's much of a title. Huh. Forgot they put carpet in not long before she died…"

Hana promptly kicked off her boots and what passed for socks in her world, *ooh-ing* at the plush fabric between her toes. She picked up random objects and set them down with disinterest, usually harder than Alvin liked. She was busy scratching at the molding on the ceiling, standing on the back of an old armchair.

"Don't your family live together? Ain't they … worried about you?"

On the back wall hung thick curtains, floor to ceiling, cutting off another portion of the building, pins of light sticking through into the dusty room.

"No family," she said.

"What? You're an orphan, then?"

"Jalóheim *is* our family." She squinted like she could wring the thought from her soggy mind. "Our Clan. All are Galó, but Jalóheim is our Clan."

Alvin looked away when she peered into the back room, its high windows facing the outer southeast walls of towne (the reason she rented *this* space, for its astral view).

"Is your village the only one?"

"Nah," she said. "Or yah. Nobody knows, anymore. Used to be lots. There was Clan Ormison and Farason and Faldin … nobody looks, anymore. Only ever see the Istlunders, in the wild, from Clan Faldin." She was transfixed on the sheet that covered the wall over the desk, trying to puzzle out how it was hung. "They turned real violent. Food was little and trade stopped. They take travelers, sometimes. Especially very old. Sometimes very young."

"To build their numbers?"

"To sacrifice. Eat, we think."

Alvin's blood chilled.

Hana stretched cautious fingers, and pulled one of the pins. Alvin didn't notice in time to tell her not to.

The drape fell and revealed Agnes's old cork board, covered over every inch in drawings, sketches, notes, and a huge sheet of draft paper at its center. The drawings were quite good, art being his sister's least-remembered talent. But it was the draft paper in the middle that caught her eye, a single geometric shape intricately rendered. 'Metatron's Cube: Balance of the Fatherland' was scribed and underlined with it.

Hana eyed it for a good long minute, angling her head left and right like a pup. "Huh. Was she strange?" she asked.

This might've ruffled Alvin's feathers, but this was no insult for Agnes. Agnesine Elspeth Esker was the "Star Girl" of the finest towne at the end of the world. Among the more crass of the populous, she was quietly known as the "Heavenly Body," or among the loathsome and base, derided as "Virgo."

"Why was she like this?" asked Hana. "You said it made her farther from people. That she lived here alone. Why do that?"

"Agnes..." Alvin hadn't openly spoken about her in a long while. "Agnes felt trapped in Orphan. It was too predictable for her. She wanted her world to have purpose. She wanted a future, and couldn't see one here."

"And it made her *more* alone?"

Alvin nodded.

"So ... *why?*" Hana seemed almost angered, face hot with the question on her mind.

"Agnes ... chased fireflies," he said.

"Hah? Fire can fly?!"

"No it can't fly—look, forget I said it like that. She just felt like a—a gear in a clock. Oh nevermind."

"Don't sound real smart after all."

"Hey! Now you take that back!"

"Take…" She furrowed her brow. "Did not give anything."

"No I mean—forget it. When she was a girl? She'd paint places she imagined from reading old books. Uncle Otto would talk for hours with Agnes about mythic places he believed in, like Thule—your Agarta, I guess, how they knew all about stars and patterns and energy. Once he used his links with the Chancellor to get her access to Orphan's antique Archives. It started interesting her, before long, that maybe someone once had done what she was trying to do."

"What was she trying to do?"

Alvin never knew how to answer this. "She thought you could change the universe by altering patterns she saw in stars, or something. Like Orphan's Scholars, she wanted to remake the Expanse into a new—a 'vaterland,' she called it. Old family language for 'fatherland'."

"She believed in Agarta," Hana mused. "That is where we go, when the Last Journey Home calls us, far away in the north, beyond Niavellir."

"Niavellir?"

She only nodded.

"Agnes didn't really believe in Thule, but Uncle Otto did, said it was way up at the north pole on some lost continent there. He's actually Mum's uncle, but he and Agnes were close. Your people believe in stuff like that?"

Hana nodded. "It is where we come from. Giant trees, in Agarta, and things like your trains. Only bigger! And cross the whole land. And whole cities in the air. And books and rivers and food. And people can live forever…"

"You know none of that's true, right? It's impossible."

"But true."

"It's not."

"It is! We will go back there, when the Sign from Jalós comes. Our Last Journey Home."

"So your people have sailing ships ready? Oh! I'll bet they're like those longboats I've seen in that opera at the Orpheum! How do you keep them seaworthy?"

Hana glazed. She blinked, and cocked her head a little. "Sh—ships?"

"Um, yeah? Ships. Things needed to sail across northern seas? Enough to carry your whole Clan? Ships?"

"Ships…" Hana squinted. She had a way of shaking her head sharply as if she were clearing sleep from her eyes or shaking dust from her hair, and she did it then. "Look, the Sign of Jalós cannot be understood without the book, and neither can the way to Agarta beyond Niavellir. Cannot go home without it."

Hana turned her attention back to Agnes's curiosities. A cold feeling caught Alvin by his collar when he thought of what she was trying to do, the same that came over him whenever he let the broader light of what Hana was trying to into his mind.

"Why do you think this magic book is here in Orphan? Who told you?"

Hana didn't seem to notice, but kept looking at all the strange geometry, and a paper pinned beside it. "Is this a map?"

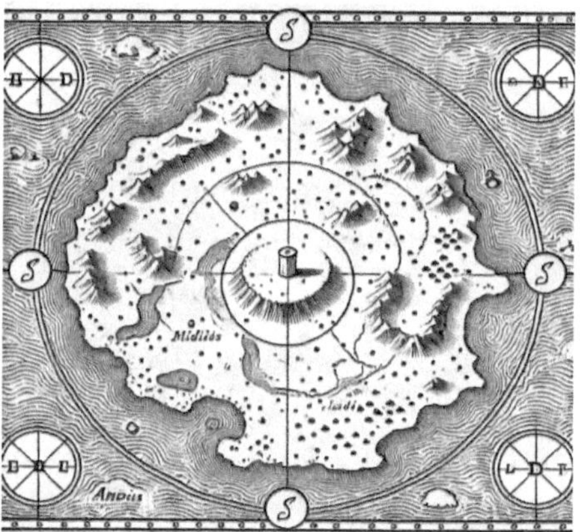

"Huh?" Alvin pulled himself out of his inquiry. "Oh. Uncle Otto gave her that. It's the Miocene Continent, the one at the north pole where he said Thule is. Took it from some old Mercator map he'd seen once in the Archives."

Hana touched the map's center. "Niavellir."

Hyperborea, Agnes had told him, the first time he inquired about her

58

new decoration. She stood back in awe of the imaginings that bordered her gifted mind. *Uncle Otto still assures me it's where the way to Thule lies, his 'Miocene Continent,' but you know your uncle.*

Why there? he asked her, and knew he'd opened quite the Pandora's jar (another phrase he'd learned from her) by the smirk on her face.

Uncle Otto says the ancient cultures imagined it like a pillar connecting heaven and earth.

Apparently he unconsciously expressed his confusion. *So … the pillar is an invisible axis?*

Ask your uncle … but yeah, I think that's right. He said the Orientals saw it more like a heavenly river flowing down, and the Nordics saw it like a great tree, the Greeks as a mountain, so on, but they're basically all the same thing.

Agnes pinned the corners of the map up as they started to come undone, knocking books off her desk as she climbed on top of it.

You know how he is. I told him I'm only interested in astral physics, not mystics, and he laughed, at least, said they're not so 'disconnected as I might think, young lady!' But … look, I know it's rather daft of me, but sometimes I like to think that somebody once knew how to … anyway.

She took one corner in her mouth, which made Alvin laugh a little, but she kept talking around the parchment. She got down off the desk and brushed her skirt.

Al? They're going to tell you a lot of things in school—especially about history. You're a bright lad, always were, and no mistake. You're an Esker, after all. They'll watch you. Smart ones are dangerous to them. Just…

She put her hand to the little necklace on her chest, the one Albany Finch gave gave her on her last birthday. Nine little wooden beads.

Don't let them steal away your awe. You hear me? That's what they want, even with physics, to reduce everything good in life to nothing more than swirling atoms and meaninglessness.

- -

Hana snooped her way deeper around Agnes's old workspace, pulling open drawers that Alvin would shut quickly. They were empty, anyway. She wouldn't stop until she happened to tilt her head around the side of the desk and ask, "What is that?"

"What?"

She found something peeking out from behind the back side, and pulled out a bound pile of pages.

"It's … it's her book," Alvin answered, having long forgotten that part of his sister's last months. He took it up carefully.

"She never managed to publish it. Thought mother had this…"

It sat in rough, bounded lambskin, stitched together by Agnes herself.

The Metarcanum:
A Theory of Linguistic Constitution
of Matter, Energy, & Form
by
Agnesine Elspeth Esker

"What is it about?" Hana asked. "Good story?"

Alvin never understood what it was, though he was certain it had to do with stars. Everything with Agnes had to do with stars. He almost put it back, and probably ought've. Sentiment alone urged him to slip it into the back pocket of his satchel.

"The Dark Illumined Eye is a book, too," she reminded him, with enthusiasm. Everything she did was with enthusiasm. "Teaches you how to open the Gate at Niavellir."

"Yes, I remember. Look, you came all this way to find this book, so you can open a gate to a magic Eden … and you think *I'm* strange?"

What was wrong with him? How could he keep listening to this drivel? A magic book about a lost civilization … the very idea certainly made every Scholar in Orphan cringe in that instant, and they hadn't even heard it. But this girl (ragged and withered as she was) had already done things he'd never dreamed, crossing the Expanse and piercing the border of Orphan, so maybe he ought've given her some leeway.

60

"Okay," he sighed. "How come you'd even know about something locked up in Orphan? Even if it did exist?"

"Was told about it," she said, rifling through the desk drawers while he'd been thinking. "A sage in Jalóheim said it was in your tower."

"A what? How could some old codger in your village know about the Heuridium?"

He turned and found her with a mouthful of very, very stale cracklebread in her teeth, and could only shrug. Alvin scowled, and chose not to calculate the age of it. After perching his backside on the edge of the desk and thought. What she was saying was ridiculous, of course, but he wondered what to say. "So … did they *send* you to find this book, then?"

"Yah." She hesitated, then unwound the wrappings that covered her right forearm. "That's what this means. See?" On the top of her forearm, her skin had been branded with a mark, several jagged lines in a row. "They made me take an oath to bring it back. This is my mission."

"It—this is a word?"

"Symbol. Means, 'remember your oath.'"

She blared her face at him in the exact way necessary to make him terrified to answer. The branded mark was covered again in a moment.

"Figured that … maybe you and me meeting was *meant*. You know? Led to you, maybe. You don't … believe in Jalós, do you?"

"In … what did you call it?"

"Jalós. The Many, the One."

"What, like gods or something?" to which she nodded. Hickter's Law was there on his lips, but he said nothing.

"You have things like that, yah? Your 'Author' talk?"

"No," Alvin corrected. "It's just an expression, like if there *were* someone pulling the strings, like fate or the like. Some folks believe more, I guess." *Like Father and Mum*, he reminded himself.

"Then you were meant to find me through that glass. Author *wanted* it."

"But … that's impossible."

"That is what you said about me." She held out her fingers to him again, open and spread, and took his hand and threaded them together with his.

"Feel skin? Nails? Scrapes? *Cannot* go home without the book."

She looked him in the eye for only an instant, the odd colors in her irises flashing at him like looking at a filament.

There was a day when he came into № 138, after supper at home. Agnes never showed up. He found the door at Cavendish open, and inside, Albany was fast asleep on the little divan by the door. A modest bouquet of flowers lay on the end table beside him. Agnes was working on waveforms at the blackboard, whispering to herself and tapping her temple to think.

Agnes? Alvin greeted her.

She startled, still wearing her sugar-dusted apron from her shift at the Songbird. *Al! Oh heavens. Is it—what time is it? Oh no. No it—it isn't half seven! Oh! Albany's...*

He was still snoring softly on the little sofa, his long legs dangling over its arm.

We had dinner plans. He'd come to pick me up.

Alvin pointed out the flowers and assured her of Albany's forgiveness, but that seemed to make it worse. Agnes slumped, and buried her face in her hands. She started crying.

Al, I—I'm so sorry. Three hours? How did I lose three hours? I only ... he's such a good man, Albany. He's too patient with me. I just wanted a better life with him, you know? I'd imagined watching him reclaim Orphan's future, giving it hope with alteration of matter, you know? Escape this everlasting loop we're in. 'There shall come a day.'

She fiddled with her beaded necklace.

Is it so wrong to want to give him that day? A Fatherland? A land to settle. Together?

Agnes breathed in slow heaves. A long time passed in silence.

If I ask you something, will you tell me the truth?

Of course he'd heard it around Orphan, the young woman who abandoned all her potential, all modern reason for idiotic hope of reshaping the universe with sound waves, wanting to find some purpose to the cosmos, who refused to acknowledge the obvious truth of Hickter's Law and fantasize about unobservable things.

Am I crazy?

Now, Alvin was not especially brave, not 'especially' anything, actually, even especially Esker. Brave young men did not fiddle with lectrics all day. He was fidgety, he scratched various parts of himself when nervous, and had a chatting problem, and none of those was much use now.

Or ever.

And when he thought about what he was considering doing, it made his bowels turn. He found himself sucking in a sharp, full breath and puffing out his chest for what was coming.

"I'll take you!" he blurted. "I'm going to help. No, I mean it." *He did?* "Absolutely! I'll get you into the Heuridium and we'll find whatever book is or ain't up there. I swear we will."

"You're going to *what?*" called Tabitha's loud voice from the open back door. "Tell me you did not say what I just heard leave your mouth, Alvin Esker," she said, flopping the Songbird's bag on the desk. "Tell me you would not actually do something that unfathomably stupid."

"This is entirely fathomable!" he defended. "It's not as though I'm going to blow off Orphan's windows as a diversion! I'll just get her in quietly."

"*You* are not even allowed in above the museum, quietly or otherwise!"

"Sure I am."

"Really..."

He put his hands on his hips and nodded, wishing he had a response. "Mmm hmm," he said. He had nothing, obviously, but held his ground until he did. "Of course," he said. "I *can* get us in."

"What?"

"The construction lifts," he said. "They use the same locking numeric as the outer gates—"

"Hang that Albany Finch," Tabitha hissed. "Hang his stupid codes and his foolish heart…"

She trailed off there. Hana just listened, keeping out from between the two of them. With a quick once-over of her, Tabitha hissed out the anxiety out of her lungs, took a long breath, and handed the Eddington's bag to her.

"Go put these on," she said. "Better than parading around in those vulgar dishrags."

Hana ran the fabrics over her palm where they protruded from the open end. "What can—"

"I don't mind," she told her. "Really. Please, change, and keep them. They're a gift."

Hana cradled them in her arms, took a step or two back, and turned to find somewhere to change.

"Esker," Tabitha said, calmly, almost in a whisper and not helping the situation. "You cannot do this." Here it came. She did not lecture. She came up to him, looked him square in the face, then down, and pleaded quietly. "Please."

"Um…"

"She's turning you back to how you used to be. Worse! And I'll not be party to it. I won't watch another Esker trail down this road."

"What do you mean, 'how I used to be'?"

"How you were when you would sit here, hour after hour, wanting to be just like big sister. Too much of her and too much of your uncle."

From the back room, Hana's raspy voice called: "How does somebody wear this?"

Tabitha's eyes fell shut, and she laughed a little. "I'll be right back."

Alvin found himself alone in Agatha's old office for a long moment. He ran a hand through his hair, moved from one spot to another, agitated and fiddling with his mouth, biting a cuticle and heaving a sigh now and then. He caught sight of the geometry on the wall again. *Symmetry to all things,* she once called it, *like the hand of a craftsman, or an author behind the paper.*

He was 'meant' to discover Hana.

At least, he wished he was. He wanted his room and some lunch.

Tabitha returned through the curtain, a little calmer and quieter. "Girl doesn't know how a proper dress operates, for land's sake. Esker, I'll say to you what I ought've said to Agnesine a long time ago: there is no grand pattern, no Thule, no meaning to the sky or to anything else. Esker, *all we have is us.* For everyone's sake, that girl needs to leave."

Neither of them noticed Hana, nor the red-faced ire that raised her hackles. "Should not have come!" she snapped.

"Wait!" said Alvin.

But Hana marched for the door.

"Esker, stop her!"

Alvin threw himself in front of her, and though Hana was faster and far more agile than himself, she wasn't a strong girl. "Don't," he asked. "Don't leave. It's going to be alright."

He'd forgotten the knife. "Whoa!"

"Move! Or be moved!" Hana gripped it ready to carve her way through him to reach that door.

"Miss Sóholdt!" Tabitha yelled. "Put that fool thing down!"

"Calm down," said Alvin. "Nobody's stopping you. Well—alright—I am, but just for a minute so you'll listen!"

"It was right to leave this morning!"

"Will you shut your gob and listen! You belong with me!" Alvin yelled, louder than he ought've, and it caused them all pause.

"Why?" she finally asked.

"Because I don't … think you're crazy."

"By finding a magic book to a fairyland!" Tabitha reminded them. "This is lunacy! If you think—if *either* of you think I'm having anything to do with this, forget it. I won't…"

"Hartchild, if you rat us out…"

"Agnesine is *gone*, Esker. She chose to do something stupid and she lost her life in the exchange. And you know what happened to her then? *Nothing.*"

It washed Alvin with cold dread, but Tabitha shoved him aside and was gone with a sharp slam of the door before he could muster up anything to say at all, and that was that.

Hana slipped her knife back into its belted sheath.

Alvin spun his lens around to a vision of Agnes sitting at her desk, reading something to his younger self that she thought would amuse him, and his stomach twisted up inside him for want of a reason for her absence. It was a perfect insane idea. Adventure, but without any of that nasty risk that would endanger somebody's life, something easy enough to reverse if it went sideways. Really, it would be little more than youthful tom-foolery, he told himself, and then told her, "I'll take you."

"Why?"

"Because…" He had no idea, but felt a sudden swell of *Uncle-Otto* that he wouldn't often admit to. "It sounds like fun," he told her. "Chasing after waterfowl—never mind. Look, Orphan could use a little non-orchestrated excitement, is what I think. You stay here and eat and—and I'll hurry home to get what we need. Deal?"

Hana cautiously took his waiting hand, and with one pump, the matter was settled. Alvin would hurry faster than he'd ever hurried before. He would give his mother a glancing hug, and fill his satchel with its usual necessities, most of which were not necessary at all, but such was Alvin's way. And as he ran for the door, his eye caught the copper gleam of his father's First Class Engineer badge, the one by his coat. He must've come home for lunch, as he sometimes did. Alvin would stare at it for a long moment. Ought he? He would weigh every variable, every contingency, every outcome.

Then he would snatch it off the hanger.

Alvin wasn't very good at weighing things wisely.

in which statuary becomes vertically advantageous

ALL HE WAS GOING TO DO was prove to Hana what wasn't possible, and probably show her the nature of terraforming machinery and bore her to madness. But it *did* sound fun, and was bound to get nobody killed. Still, amid all of Orphan's predictable comings and goings, something unexpected was a radical act.

Alvin and Hana stopped at the end of the bridgeway and craned their necks. In that day in age, there was no need for the lavish architecture of the past, the sort devoted to senseless myths and dogmas. But then, a little pomp never hurt anyone, and Orphan was not without its pomp. Overhead, the great motto: *There Shall Come a Day* loomed down at them, as if they were nothing more than impatient children.

Orphan was nothing if not patient.

The Great Initiative, they called it with due reverence and doffed hats, and among the elder generations, under-breath recitation of: *There Shall Come a Day*, often followed by a swiftly-swallowed beer.

"Is she your friend?"

"Huh?"

"With the black hair." Hana asked again.

"Tabitha? Remember that piker Ellery who was in my house last night? She's his older sister, Inspector Hartchild's girl."

"What is piker?"

"A piker? It's the sort of git 'would find a fellow passed out and nick his billfold."

Hana blinked. Several times, looking strained. "Many questions," she confessed. "He is a thief? Why is he free?"

"No he—it's just an insult, is all. Though he might've stolen a billfold! Who knows? Why? What how do they punish thieves where you're from?"

Hana craned up at the great heights of the Heuridium. "Harshly."

"What about someone worse than a thief?"

"It's the Proving Tree for them," she returned, and Alvin didn't ask further. "So … she is your friend? You quarrel a lot."

"Actually she was my sister's friend, but went to school with me."

"Oh. The dead sister?"

Alvin stumbled on his feet, and by her cocked eyebrow, he realized he not only stopped, but was apparently giving her quite the astonished face.

"Of course I mean Agnes! Who else would I be talking about! I'd only the one sister."

They walked on for moments in silence.

"Are you angry?"

"No. Just, you talk about things like that so … abruptly."

Hana didn't answer, at first. She pondered. "In Svaraheim, alive is alive and dead is dead. Why use more words?" Alvin had no answer to this, and turned the lens of his mind back to the task at hand.

Technically, anyone could come onto the Academy's lofty campus, its halls enshrined over the heart of the towne, but almost no one ever did. Why would they? Only the Heuridium's upper levels were off-limits, but anyone could visit the Museum of Science & Fabrication on the main level.

Hana flinched when the Broadcast came on, and the aged, chambered voice of the Academy's great patriarch came over the copper pipes placed around the vaulted grounds.

CITIZENS OF ORPHAN HEIGHTS: WE HAVE CROSSED INTO THE SUNLESS DAYS OF THE SEASON. THIS YEAR MARKS THE

FIRST IN WHICH MORE THAN FIFTY PERCENT OF OUR AVENUES WILL BE LIT WITH THE ADVANCEMENT OF LECTRAL INCANDESCENTS.

"What is that?" asked Hana.

"The Broadcast," Alvin explained. "Radio. Mostly it's in people's homes but there are a few public pipes out here. Any time the Chancellery wants to shout at the population, they use the Broadcast."

"Oh. Our leaders have ways of shouting at us, too."

The ancient voice of Solomon Day kept on talking about percentages and transition rates of oil lights to lectrics, but they didn't listen further.

"Don't gawp," Alvin scolded.

"What is gawp?"

He imitated her. "Like that! Gazing all open-mouthed at everything like a bloody tourist. Gawping."

"Oh. But is just so … *high*."

Tabitha had wisely gotten her something like a floppy charcoal beret with a narrow brim to hide her face and as much of her hair as possible. Only little tufts poked out like golden sprigs. Orphan girls preened their hair far neater than Hana bothered to, and she still kept her palms and wrists wrapped like a mountain climber. And while Tabitha had purchased her a fine overdress in Orphan's popular blues, greys, and coppers, she wore her old wide, leather belt over it anyway. She kept her boots, too.

Alvin failed to convince her to lose Mrs. Dutch's scarf. She'd grown quite attached to it, apparently.

As they walked, Hana glanced to him, and noted *his* nose in the air. "Alvin, do not gawp. What are you looking at?"

He pointed up. "Them old tramrails up there, ones that spiral from the Heuridium down to the modern line. Hasn't run a tram since the tower was closed, but they're just so … *high*."

"Why did they close it?" she asked. "The tower thing?"

"Obsolete. It was suspended like that to draw current from the atmosphere during the storms."

Around the tower, the sky smoldered through Orphan's paneled glass with a closing, golden thunderhead.

"Something wrong?" Alvin asked her.

The first peel of thunder rang and made Hana jump as if she'd been shot, even yelp a little, but the thunder drowned her out.

"Can the storm get us in here?" she asked.

"No. Do you get a lot of damage in your ... where you're from?"

"People die in storms," she said. "Especially if they leave the Rift. Going to be bad. Look at it."

It did look ominous, and was slowly surrounding the towne on at least three sides, a deep wave of rolling black that broke around Orphan's glass walls and spilled around its base, dark as pitch.

"I ask you something?" he said.

"Huh?"

"Why do you never say 'I'?"

"Huh? Never thought about it," she defended. "Nobody really does, back in the Rift."

They waited until a crowd of Scholars was heading up the bridge for their night's work, and ducked in at their rear, settling among the chattering waves of frock coats and frequently consulted timepieces. Hiram Lorecroft appeared up ahead on the bridgeway, in hot conversation.

"Oh no..." Beside him strode Inspector General Hartchild, Ellery at his side. "Oh ... that's bad."

A yank to his arm pulled Alvin from his trance, and near off his feet. Hana jerked him through the thick of the crowd.

"They'll still see us!" Alvin insisted, and he was right.

They would be back in view within a moment.

"Uh uh. Down there."

"Down ... what?!"

"Your turn to trust *me*," she insisted, and when the Scholars' attentions were elsewhere, she bounded over the bridge railing—several stories' high over Bellamy Park.

"Hana!"

She landed on the tension beam that ran alongside the bridgeway's framework, established her footing, glanced favorably up to Alvin, and offered her hand.

"Are you—you can't be serious—"

"You saw me do it," she reminded him.

Alvin's head spun dizzy at the height, his body stilling, frigid and hard at the vision of plummeting to his death. He couldn't. It'd kill him. All the lights would go out and there was nothing that would make him do it.

"Esker?"

Except one.

The sound of one's name in the unhappy tones of Ellery Hartchild could make anyone's skin crawl, and it certainly did Alvin's. A sharp glance told him Ellery was near, but not in sight. So Alvin looked to Hana, squeezed the images of his own death out of his mind, held a big breath, and leapt.

The landing was painful, but at least there was one. His hands frantically snapped about like caught fish. Hana chuckled, and helped him hang on.

"You're mad, is what!"

"Shh! Up there."

The booming outrage of the Inspector General's voice sounded over their heads. "What in blazes did you think you saw, boy?"

Then came Ellery Hartchild, leaning over the edge of the bridge but apparently not thinking to look down. Alvin and Hana pressed themselves into the rafters a little deeper, but still beneath the noses of anyone overhead. Hana put a finger to her lips and Alvin tried very hard to not fall and die. The top of Sir More's marble head was under him. A pigeon angled his bobbing little head up to look.

The Inspector berated Ellery, "Well if you're done with your little game of pointless delusions, may we please carry on our way? Go back and catch up on your work while we're out, boy."

"Gracious, Alec," said the Professor. "The stew shan't disappear in two minutes. You'll have your bacon bits but let's not have ourselves an embolism on the way, shall we? You have your heart to think about—"

"Don't lecture me about my blazing heart, Lorecroft. A man asks for few pleasures in life, the least his offspring can do is avoid getting between him and them. Now let's knock off for lunch."

Their voices trailed away, and Ellery's oscillating face went with.

"That was piker, yah?" Hana whispered.

"That was him, yeah. All-around stooge, you ask me."

"His hair is like feathers. He looks like that thing in that gloomy place. Duster! He looks like a duster."

"Uh huh. Now what?" Alvin asked, rather angered once his shock melted off. "We can't climb back up and somebody would—"

"Through here," said Hana, nodding toward the rafters.

"*There?*"

Hana pulled off her boots and stuffed them into her pack. She must've seen the face he made. "What? Never liked things on my feet. Better for balancing, too." She clung to the overhead beams and hopped on bare feet to the next foothold along the framework while Alvin tried to not throw up.

"Hana, it—it's so far down. We'll die if we climb across this. Doesn't that bother you?"

"You mean, is it scareful? Course it is! Gonna let a girl beat you?"

She winked and taunted.

"Let a…" Alvin was incensed. It raised his hackles, and he slammed one foot onto the next beam and kept his eyes on her. Then another.

"It's like hiding from the Istlund Faldins," she mused.

"Those—" He gripped the overhead brace so hard his fingers ached, but swung round to the next footing. "—those crazy nomads you told me about?"

"Hmm hmm."

"You've had to hide from them?"

"Twice," she returned, with a hop to the next beam. "Once in Jalóheim. Once in Svaraheim, on the way here. Did not want to die like that, you know? Like you do not want to fall."

"*Inside* your village?"

"At night," she said. "They came in the north wall. Had to hide." How easily she vaulted through the framework! Alvin had his arms wrapped around a beam.

"Where'd you hide?"

"Somewhere," she told him, landing, finally, on the Heuridium's under-balcony. She gave him a hand. "See? You made it!"

"You taunted me!"

"It worked, yah? You have to stop being so scareful of heights, if you want to fly."

"Want to fly!" he protested. "It's just a fancy, Hana, just a fancy. We don't have flying machines, and they'd be no good in here anyway!"

"When you drove that carriage thing, you were like flying. Now where?" she asked, as if *he* knew! But she clearly had exhausted her expertise for the moment, so it was on him, now.

"Um … around the southwest quarter that faces Calumbria," he said. "It's less traveled and there should be a way up on the far side." The outside skin of the tower was little more than levels of open peristyles, like something out of a painted Roman forum, but the inner chambers were walled and windowless.

"What is this?" Hana asked.

"Construction lift," he told her. "Once the tower was finished, these were lowered out of sight and left."

Its gears were rusted and older than he realized, the funicular tracks behind them looking less than operable, but Alvin didn't tell her this.

"What does it do?" she asked.

"It's a lift. It lifts."

Alvin spun the dials on the locking mechanism, squeezed the clutch on the lever, and pulled. With a hard yank, the platform snapped free of the rust and years, and clanked its way slowly upward.

"How can you do that?" asked Hana. "How do you know all these things?"

"Someone once gave the codes to my sister, and I saw the list when she almost left Orphan with Uncle Otto. She finally chose not to leave, but Otto never hesitated."

"But how do you remember the numbers?"

The counterweight descended as the lift rose, and Hana had to graze her hand along it in passing. Before long they could see some of the great arches and inscriptions that adorned the Heuridium. Its main entry archway was marked with the words: *There Shall Come a Day.*

"Someday?" he went on. "All them perimeter windows will be gone, and we'll breathe free air again. Somewhere in Orphan is the means to blow them all open. They're made to. It's the last stage of the Initiative."

"What is Initiative?" she asked.

"It's the final task of Orphan, to terraform the Expanse and make it so we can live there again, once the air's clean enough. Then them windows around Orphan can blow off and we'll start building *outside* the walls."

The lift rose until it came near the second level, then ground its way to a screeching halt. The gears were far too rusted to continue. Alvin had to stop the lift there.

"Bugger. Ruddy thing's broke." he said.

"Those statues look like we can climb them," she observed.

"You want me to *climb* onto Newton?" he objected.

"Will it bother him?"

Alvin dropped it. He rubbed his sore arms and took a good hold on Newton's robe. He apologized to the great Scholar when he jammed a knee in the crook of his neck. Hana glanced out at the great distance visible through Orphan's panes from this incredible height, at the constant glow of the vanished sun.

"Alvin?" she asked. "What happened to this land?"

"You don't know? What were you taught?"

Hana hoisted herself hand-over-hand up Newton's chiseled form. "We found it like this. The Clans left our own homeland and followed the Call of Jalós until it brought us here. The Clans settled the land but it is hard to live here. Some fought each other. Some left. Only us from Jalóheim in the Rift and Faldin in Istlund are left ... at least we think."

Alvin's foot slipped, but he managed to jam his knee against Newton's neck. "So ... why stay?"

"Same reason we came. To find our way home."

"But you *left* your homeland."

"We left *a* land. Agarta is our home, where our ancestors came from. There is a way that will open to where Jalós is."

Over the railing between the great ivory pillars, Alvin scrambled, pulling Hana up behind him. He breathed easier once they were again on solid ground. Hana gazed at faces in the reliefs of figures like Archimedes, Pythagoras, and Porphyry. They paused long to catch their breath.

"What do they teach *you*?" she asked him again.

"Wars," he answered, as if it were obvious. "And lots of 'em. Countries and giant weapons and the like. The atmosphere was scorched and diseases broke out until there was nothing left at all. This land was once called Angland, but we're all that's left."

She looked at him funny and he realized how silly he sounded. "Well obviously that part ain't quite on, but you get the idea."

Hana turned her face to the Heuridium. "And this," she said. "This is *real*. Now. This place. Never thought this would happen."

"What, you thought you'd die before you found the towne?" he said.

Hana did not laugh back. "Yah."

Over the second level's arched southern entry stood the words:

Let our eyes correspond to the knowledge of eons.

All his life, he'd seen this place at the high height of Orphan Towne, a tomb of its early days, sealed off since long before Alvin's time, or even his father's. He put his hand to the coded dial lock aside the door, each brass cylinder marked with a number. The lens of his mind, he spun to the list of codes Agnes had once accidentally let him see.

"Is there a Proving Tree? If we are caught?"

"A *what?* We'd be arrested, is what will happen. And if they catch you? *Really* don't know. Ain't you gonna put your boots back on?"

"Nah. This is better."

The great inset gears came alive, the door turning like the movement of a fine timepiece, until the door came in two, and turned outward along curved tracks. And when Alvin and Hana stepped through the door, between the shadows of the great men of ancient science, Alvin was prepared to witness almost anything *other* than what actually waited for them.

ENTRY 13: "A TOWER, A DOME, A VISION"

Early in Orphan's history, atmospheric problems in the Expanse multiplied, as did temperature instability (which some called 'winter'), and as happened whenever anything worth discussion arose, a symposium was called. Propositions from iron-skin houses to fashionable filtration suits were both considered and insulted. One geologist suggested geo-thermal drilling, because of course he did. This angered the Engineers, who reminded the symposium that no such drills existed and they didn't want to be bothered to invent them. The punching began shortly after. Amid the ruckus, Cornelius Erasmus Hicker arose, cleared his throat, and proposed the construction of both an iron lattice and glass dome over Orphan Towne (which was rejected), and the Heuridium Tower, (which was loudly ridiculed). The math was beyond anything the whole of the Scholary could conjure; despair ensued. Later, while on his nightly constitutional, Hickter experienced a vision, in which reconciled algebraic formulae appeared atop a mountain, alongside a message: *In hoc sine vinces*, ("By this sine, conquer"). Hickter attributed the revelation to his own magnificent brain, since no observable cause could otherwise be located at the time. He arrived back at the symposium the following hour and declared not only the mathematical solutions to Orphan's dome quandary, but also the advent of Hickter's Law: *Nothing Unobservable Exists*. The phrase and the mathematics so beguiled the scholars that a spontaneous parade erupted from the assembly, and Hickter was carried on the shoulders of the Scholars across Orphan amid shouts and clamour all the way to Bellamy Park, where a statue was commissioned, though it took fourteen years to complete and resulted in a readdressing of the pigeon breeding ordinances passed ten years prior. Heuridium and dome construction began the following day.

in which various laws of physics are carelessly bent

THE ONLY WAY TO THE FUTURE is through the bending of today. With those words, Agnes Esker resolved to expand her mind enough to comprehend all she craved to understand, moments before her final experiment—her own Great Initiative—laid claim to her life.

Her obsession with star-patterns and their parallel to some grand unified equation of the universe had been on the boil for long enough. The sun must eventually reach its zenith; the great bear must advance through the heavens. So it was with Agnes Esker, though the fatal gravity of her desire apparently didn't dawn on her until those final seconds, when she tried to force her eyes, her mind, to understand the patterns she believed lay writ across the endless stars.

The last place on earth Alvin Esker expected to see them was in the heart of the Noble Sciences of Orphan Towne.

Yet, Agnes's star-patterns were everywhere. Strings of constellations, equations, and planetary models adorned blackboards, glass dividers and even stone rubbings.

A loud *snap* struck his ears, followed by the sizzle of lectral incandescents. He found Hana at a nearby switch.

Row after row of lights came on.

"What?" Hana asked. "You love glass stars."

"They didn't have incandescents when this was shut down."

The hall was dim everywhere except its center, a glassed-off column, a window into a great atrium that, from Alvin's glance, extended the entire height of the tower. Light poured down from above, around great conduits of machinery and piping and insulators.

"What is wrong?"

The great hall was empty, old and lustrous in its scarlet-carpet way, but there were no spiderwebs, no piles of dust, no old machinery. They could hear noises from the many adjacent halls, and they could hear the sound of voices.

Most curious of all, frequencies scribbled alongside the patterns, aligned to fractals of particle physics—the same alignments at interstellar level as at microscopic. He became lost in the nearest blackboard:

The constancy of these proportions manifest not only at the macro-cosmic level but at the micro-cosmic. Molecular patterns reflect their macro-cosmic counterparts with no measurable loss of fidelity, but a lack of a finite resolution microscopic apparatus sufficient for observing these patterns rules out that method of transnumeration, making it an untenable avenue of pursuit until such an apparatus might be perfected.

"Alvin?"

Alteration of the micro-cosmic level should then be tenable through cymatic induction using the macro-cosmic patterns as standard...'

"Alvin!"

"What?"

"People!"

She pulled him back behind the blackboards. Along the western wall stood one of the old trams that ran along those lofted tracks, and nearby it opened a door and let in two men, Scholars, by their look. Alvin and Hana held their breath until the two men drew out their pipes and fitted some tobacco, apparently taking a break.

"What is wrong?" Hana asked from their hiding spot. "Alvin Esker. You are being stupid. Do not be stupid."

He grabbed hold of the lens of his mind firmly enough. He glanced around for the Scholars again, who paced their way out to the balcony, their back turned to the hall, obviously enjoying their pipes. The curled rings puffed up and away.

"We … we keep looking for books?" she urged.

In spite of his whispered arguments, she went for the trolley, keeping herself crouched below its wall while plucking anything the Scholars had carelessly left there for herself. As if some hunting instinct took over, she stalked, sniffed, surveyed and rummaged the trolley over until she found two old frock coats draped over seats, flinging one hard against Alvin's chest.

Ornate stairs led them to Third Level, where an outer arch over fat columns announced its intent:

Atoms vibrate according to the world's ascending current.

Hana turned to him. "Are you ready for—"

But he was already on the march, spinning the locks open and boldly stepping inside. Something unseen bore him terribly forward now, into the halls and branching laboratories and workshops, the same feeling Hana drew out of him, as if all his anchors came unmoored.

What if?

What if what? He would ask himself. *What do you even wish was here?*

He didn't know.

At the sound of arrivals, Hana pulled him, and they flung themselves under a wall-length window into one of the laboratories. Two Scholars went in and tossed their frocks over the backs of chairs and talked with the one already in there. They couldn't hear them, but peered over the edge anyway.

Along the far wall behind the scientists were design schematics and a table of experiment logs. Notes about the apparent "improbability of return bindportation" seemed to be the main focus.

"What are they doing?" Hana whispered.

"'Entanglement Bindportation Test *one-one-three-eight*,' I'd wager."

One of them set his timepiece on a mechanical platform in the middle of the room, next to a cylinder a little smaller than Alvin's lectral lantern. He pressed a switch on the cylinder and all three stepped behind a glass partition. Hana turned and put her back to the low wall, apparently bored from lack of mystical books around the place.

Then all the hairs on her arms stood up.

She tapped Alvin and showed him, and he shrugged, turning back to the view inside. The air around the timepiece warped and swirled in a loud sphere. Ribbons of haze appeared, around the chair and the dais, arcs of distortion and energy in a perfect sphere, overlapping like a gyroscope. Hana gasped, still facing away from the laboratory, smacking Alvin's arm and pointing, but his own astonished gaze was fixed on what was happening inside the room. It all only lasted two seconds before the waves collided with one singular *boom* as space over the platform folded over and in on itself, then exploded in a pulse of air.

Alvin then felt the boom. *Behind* him.

He turned slowly and found the dais, the timepiece, and the cylinder all sitting there in the middle of the atrium. Hana was gasping, flicking her eyes between him and what just materialized in a duplicate pulse of—whatever.

He turned back to the lab. The objects were gone.

The scientists, meanwhile, nodded, and headed for the door, bickering something about 'returning' portation problems, but Alvin paid them no mind. Compared to what Alvin was seeing in here, the rest of the Academy's accomplishments were little more than ha'penny tripe.

Three other cylinders like the first one were tabled on a rack. Alvin inspected them, but they didn't have time.

"All of that came from this little … *thing*," he whispered, then turned his frantic mind to getting out of there before they came back. "Come on," he muttered, dread about the amount of trouble they were in gradually swelling.

At the far end of the hall, they came to the next stair to the fourth level, and then to the next archway and set of lustrous doors, these, like the others.

Let the polar ends of this Confluence balance us on its fulcrum.

The higher they climbed, the stranger things became. There on Fourth

Level his mouth hung open, for the machines inside the laboratories floated over the ground, suspended on nothing at all. Like the last floor, the Scholars seemed focused on their work, and few in number, all hunched over tables, charts and graphs, blackboards of numbers and traces of what Alvin knew was the constellation-patterns. Hana searched for this enigmatic book of hers—or any book, but there were only thousands and thousands of papers.

Alvin took a long look at one of the hovering machines in a laboratory. Some kind of spinning ring beneath it lit and hummed, hollow in the middle. They didn't appear to *be* or *do* anything, other than levitate.

"How does it do that?" Hana asked him.

Alvin drew close, open-mouthed and with his eyes ringed with dark lines and disbelief. His mind circled with visions of flight, of soaring over the Expanse or, or anywhere else—*everywhere* else. He thought of all his books of flying machine designs, and all his ruddy little models. *Toroidal Gravitic Field Governor Operation*, he read on the papers scattered across the table. With shuddering hands, Alvin snatched his notebook from his satchel and frantically sketched what he was seeing, along with every important-looking note he didn't understand.

"You draw good. Alvin?" She had to shake him, hearing Scholars coming up from the level below. They were running out of floors.

Let the current of the skies tune our minds to one harmony.

They stopped before going in when Hana had to shield her eyes. Near constant, blaring light sparked from massive lectral generators, larger than any of the enclosures used for constant power distribution.

Great glass tubes hung between porcelain insulators on tabletops. Coils stood as tall as men in the corners of the room, and everywhere great arcs of lightning bolted across the room while gauges wagged their needles. They ascended to the sixth and final level of the Heuridium tower, and stood small before its doors with their backs to the bottomless, wild, and golden sky.

Let the ageless cause of light yield the effect of a coming future.

"It has to be here," she said. "It *has* to."

The gold from the west broke through the thundering clouds in long streaks against the doors of the Sixth Level. This time, the little ivory dial spun and clicked into position, but nothing happened. Over the dials it read simply:

"Clearance Level Zero?"

But there was no such thing, not then nor ever.

"We can't get in?"

"Just *wait*," he said. "Let me think. Just a minute … okay. Okay, that's a good idea, sure thing. Let's use the lift, instead."

"The what?"

Alvin pulled her back, pressing them both into hallway walls while Scholars argued by, until they found a clear path to the funicular around the far side of the central shaft. The two great lifts carried one another up and down until it clanged to a halt on Fifth Level, amazingly empty. Alvin ushered her past the little gate.

"What're you doing?" she inquired.

Alvin pried off the dial panel.

"In for a penny, in for a pound. It might need another numeric for clearance, but it still runs on simple lectral signals that drive the motor down under the floor of First Level."

From his satchel, Alvin drew his lectral lantern, twisted off its glass casing until it came apart. Two little prongs stuck out of the induction end.

"What's that?"

"These deliver the current into the incandescent. I'm just … using them for other purposes."

He slit the casing on the Sixth Level control and on the Fifth, and crossed them together with the live and ground line of his lamp's leads. A single spark was enough to send the signal to the main generator. Hana yelped when the lift ascended.

The funicular halted, and when Hana gasped again, Alvin assumed it was because of the jolt.

It wasn't.

She slammed herself into the wall behind the front walls of the lift, beside the door, and once he realized why, Alvin did the same.

"I don't see why we can't do more trials, Sir," said the sharp voice of Ellery Hartchild. "It seems the least we can—"

"After the last one? No. No more of your testing."

It took a moment to place the voice of the responder. Who was it? Only when he turned his lens to his many trips to the bank with his father did he realize it was Viscount Hawthorn Pike himself. What was a banker—*the* banker—doing in the Heuridium? Or Ellery Hartchild? He was nothing more than a Junior Engineer, Second Class, hardly above Alvin himself.

And hadn't he been on the way *out?*

Pike wasn't alone with Ellery Hartchild. Chancellor Finch was there.

"It might be wise to delay further testing until after the hubbub of the electorate is ended. Don't you think?" he posed, a statement made to sound like a question.

How could the Chancellery know about this place? With the elections looming, they couldn't possibly hide this.

Could they?

"Nonsense. Elections are an ideal time," said Viscount Pike. "Everyone has his nose in the business of Parliament."

Finch paused. "Did one of you summon the lift?"

Alvin and Hana sucked in their stomachs, held hard breaths, and Alvin distinctly felt her hand grip the cuff of his sleeve and twist it.

"I certainly didn't. Hartchild, did—"

"No I didn't call the lift."

Ellery offered, "It's probably malfunctioning again. Would you like me to look at it, Sirs?"

Alvin's heart was bound to rupture clean out of his chest. Slowly, he snaked his arm up toward the dismantled dial controls, and tiptoed his fingers behind the plate, to the wires.

He had to do it by feel alone, and was left-handed in the attempt, but he found the constant wire—he hoped—and pulled it down to the post of the Fifth Level call.

"I'd be obliged," said Chancellor Finch.

With a spark, the doors drew shut.

"Oh," said the Chancellor. "Well it seems fine now. Someone must've summoned it."

The gate closed over the doors, and the lift descended.

Alvin let go of the wire when it was half way between the floors, and the lift hung, stalled in the nowhere of Fifth-and-a-Half.

Light from Sixth Level still bled through the paneled glass, the shadows of their ankles casting over Alvin's head.

But Hana finally breathed, and looked faint for a moment.

"Are you okay?" he asked.

She nodded. "Thought Duster had us."

A little laugh burst from Alvin. "You can't keep calling him that."

They laughed together, quietly as they could, until "Father!" sounded from somewhere else on Sixth Level, and they could still hear them just a little. It was a voice Alvin knew without mistake from many hours in the Esker home.

"Who is that?"

"It's Albany Finch," Alvin answered solemnly, and left it at that.

"Viscount Pike. Inspector General. Listen…"

"What is it, young man? You're positively winded."

"I've just collected witness reports about those stolen clothes, and related incidents throughout the city."

"And?"

"Well, I've taken the sequences of Orphan's routines and the positions of the people within standard limits of variants, and the numerics of these events account for the standard complement of Orphan's citizens."

"Of course they do," Pike bellowed, a hard and forthright man. "Why would you bother in the first place, man?"

"Plus one unaccounted anomaly."

"Unaccounted?" Alvin turned to Hana, who simply looked confused.

"What's he mean?" she whispered.

"He—he knows you're here," Alvin answered quietly.

"What?!"

"Not *here* here, but in Orphan," whispered Alvin.

"That's ludicrous," said Chancellor Finch. "Your calculations are off."

"I've run it through three times. I'm quite certain we have someone unaccounted within the perimeter."

"Albany," said his father. "If you're wasting our time—"

"I do not waste time, Father. It's unbecoming. I'm quite certain."

Alvin muttered out low, "Traitorous cad!" though even as he said it, he didn't really mean it.

A moment later, and the light through the upper portion of the door came clear as the ankles disappeared. Alvin leaned against the side wall and slid a little.

"How?" asked Hana.

"I don't know. Orphanites brag about how we're so precise the whole towne is like clockwork but—but nobody actually *believes* it. And I don't understand. Lorecroft and the Hartchilds and the others, they were on the way *out* when we came."

"Well we can't stop," she said. "It *has* to be up there!"

Alvin shouldered up his courage one more time, and told her, "Okay."

He returned the lift to its rightful lock on Sixth Level. The doors cranked open to a thankfully empty landing atop the highest level of the Heuridium.

Alvin and Hana stepped into the light, scarlet carpet under heel. They awed at the vast enclosure, halls and ornate arches branching everywhere. There *were* books, shelves upon shelves of them, a whole archive of volumes in topical libraries, dense rows of hickory shelving and lamplight.

"It's here!" said Hana. "It *has* to be!"

Her face lit with hope. She spun, pulled Alvin further into the hall, and rushed to find the closest shelf, just in time for Albany Finch to step around the corner and stop dead on seeing the two strange youths.

in which rash words lead to switches rashly thrown

A DREAD MOMENT OF ARRANT SILENCE passed between them as Albany Finch slowly let his jaw fall open. "What in blazes?" he muttered, shock twisting his face. "What—what's the meaning of this?"

"Albany!" Alvin said. "I…"

"What in blazes are you—*Alvin?!* Do you understand where you … did you steal your father's *badge?* And—and who is this?!"

"My—my cousin!" Alvin blurted. "Miss Hana … Cavendish. That's my mother's family, the Cavendishes, from the south concourse. Norberia, actually, but my father always told me that's no reason to judge them, and he obviously didn't because he married one and all, but Hana is my aunt's oldest daughter—well, hers and her husband's, obviously. She recently joined the Engineers—Hana did—because my aunt wants her to contribute to the Initiative and since she never had any sons she thought it was Hana's duty to try her hand at it, and wouldn't you know it? I thought she could learn a thing or three and I needed the extra hand anyway so…"

Alvin was unaccustomed to lying, and did not much care for the stress of it and was, frankly, poor at it.

"Your mother's family are the *Heinrichs*," Albany corrected. "There are no Cavendishs left in Orphan because Lawrence Cavendish had no sons." He crossed his arms. "Try again, Alvin."

86

"Oh! Um …" What was the lie? What was Alvin doing there? "Uh…" It wouldn't come to him! The best he could do was, "She's adopted, not actually blood relation."

"Lectral lines," interrupted Hana in her raspy tone. "Along the fanways. Something wrong with them. Orders from the crew chief. Esker here's teaching me."

Alvin's heart beat so fast it made his ears numb. "It's not a big deal, Albany."

"You understand that you have destroyed your future by doing this? You don't bring a *date* into the Heuridium, Alvin!"

Alvin almost blurted a denial of Hana's relationship, but there was an obvious advantage to the assumption, and he motioned for Albany to lean in. "You never did anything brash to show off to a girl?"

Albany did not look amused, but then, he *had* done brash things to show off to a girl, and Alvin bloody well knew it. So Alvin marshaled his meager nerves, cleared his throat, and answered, "But I understand. We'll go at once." Hana didn't seem to like that but he dismissed her with a sharp wave. "I'm sure there'll be questions—"

"Bloody right there will be."

"Especially about how we managed to break into the most secured building in all Orphan Towne."

"And how exactly did you?"

"They'll want to hear all about how I knew the dislocking codes to open the doors, sure will. I could figure *one* out, they'll assume, but *all* of them? There'll be lots of questions about *that*." Hana's eyes flashed between them, while Albany Finch turned ghastly white. "They'll want to know where any kind of security breach came from, and who would have leaked—"

"Al—alright. Stop it," Albany Finch defended. "Blackmailer. I will forget this *once*, understand? And I won't let you hold this over me again."

"I won't, Albany."

"But you and your *date* have to leave. Now. And you can't ever come back or talk about what you've seen in here—which I hope wasn't much." He turned Alvin around by the shoulders and took off for the sound of voices down the hall.

87

"Albany?" Alvin called after him, and Albany Finch paused with an irritated look back. "Did you know about this? That her work…"

"It's not what you think it is, Alvin. Look, I'll—I'll come round the brownstone for dinner tonight. You and I will talk then. Agreed? Now I'll give you two minutes, so clear off!"

A long silence passed between Alvin and Hana, until she finally cleared her throat, and asked, "How did that happen?"

Alvin breathed until he could collect his wits enough to go on. "I know where the bones are buried," he said.

"Oh! Okay! Yah, that always makes trading easier," she answered with an understanding nod.

"How do you even know what lectrics is?"

"You say it every minute or so," she answered, turning her attention to the legion of books. "Lectrics this. Lectrics that. Not stupid, you know."

"I see."

"Are we leaving like he said?"

"We certainly ought to!"

"Alvin!"

"Well this ain't what I signed on for, is it? This is getting big, and Author knows what we've gotten ourselves…" Something in her face sank, and stung him. "Alright, fine. Come on. We're here among the books, ain't we? No turning back. No sir. I mean, Miss."

Hana beamed, grinning her teeth at him, and started climbing shelves.

"I thought you couldn't read."

She pulled many a volume out and glanced it over, sometimes flipping through some pages, usually holding them upside down. "Have to try, yah?"

Many of them were illustrated and Alvin would have given his right eye to know what lay within their collective depths. Fast as he could, Alvin ran his eyes over the spines. Some of the names, he knew, works of Orphan's greatest minds. Most, he did not, nor did he have any real idea what he was even looking for.

"What did you call this book you're after?"

"<u>Dark Illumined Eye</u>," she returned.

"Aye but, is it actually titled that? You've an author, year, *anything?*"

She only returned a shrug.

"They sent you all this way, crossed the Expanse, broke into the Heuridium, and you don't even know if you've got the name right?!"

"You did not ask."

"I didn't think I needed to!"

"Then that is *your* fault!"

"Then how are we supposed to blazing find it?!"

"By looking!"

Over the immaculate hall, a cold silence ruled as both intruders thumbed and fingered and eyeballed their way across the spines. Somewhere in the minutes that followed, he happened to stumble across: *Lorecroft, Hiram A.*

He had read them all, of course … or thought he had.

"<u>The Intra-geometrics of Harmonic Field Resonance</u>"? he read. "Never even heard of … '<u>The Heterodyning Ultraviolet Properties of Cellular Luminescence</u>'? What *are* these?"

Between these two volumes, someone had apparently misplaced a book, which bothered Alvin. <u>Sandcastle</u>, it was titled. Inside the cover some sort of odd library note lay tucked: *The Pleasant Draft: CVI 42.4, Section 7, Shelf 4611.* He'd never heard of any of it, and the book looked rubbish, too.

"You'd think they'd at least organize these."

"Hmm?"

Hana followed his hand as he pointed to the misplaced text. Curious, she tried to pull it off, but only the binding pulled off, but just a little.

"Oh…"

"What?"

"It broke."

"What broke?"

She showed him. "It just broke."

"Wha—how?"

She shrugged.

"Hana! Fix it."

"It will not come off. Stuck on..."

The binding spun in the middle, perfectly and smooth. Alvin stepped over and peered between the binding and the pages. The book itself was hard-mounted to the shelf. Under the binding were gears and pins, both top and bottom symmetrical and matched. He clicked it back into place, then pulled it out again. It spun on smooth bearings, and for curiosity's sake, he rotated the spine upside-down, and it clicked perfectly back into place that way—and then it happened.

Something shifted inside the wall. Gears turned, clanked, and started a deep reaction. New lights sparked as the central bookcase parted in two. A hiss of pressurized air vented around their ankles, and the trespassers peered into to a dim interior of the central shaft. They both jolted when the overhead lectral lamps flared into low light with a sizzle, lighting a dais.

"What do you suppose *that* is?" he said out low, and didn't say the rest of what he was thinking.

Above and below it stretched more lectral conduits, ceramic insulators, and pistoned machinery than Alvin had ever seen in his life. They came from spaces in the ceiling and linked with the dais, then extending down into the great shaft farther than they could see. She ran to it first, probably certain to find her book, but there was no book, only the dais, with a descending tube clamped tight over it, hiding whatever lay under.

"You think it's the book?" she asked.

"No," he answered truthfully. "Something I don't think we're supposed to see, though? That, I don't doubt."

Hana circled it, fiddling with anything her hands could grasp, tugging, turning, and getting nowhere. Mounted on its horizontal seam sat the dial lock, which Alvin knelt to, and touched. This had ten places, but unlike every other dial lock in Orphan, this one was *lettered*, not numbered.

All of it seemed off, seemed *wrong*.

The Heuridium felt more a *temple* than a laboratory.

The dials were sharp under his touch, cold and dusty. "Ten places," he muttered to himself. *Ten places.* Little squares. His fingers started turning dials until he came upon:

V – A – T – E – R – L – A – N – D

But it was one short.

F – A – T – H – E – R – L – A – N – D

Steam vented, Hana yelped, gears clicked and spun, lamps illuminated, and the seal separated, drawing up and down in two portions by way of the alongside slotted tracks.

"I think … it's an incandescent?"

It was not large, about the side of a fist, a lens set into a gold radial housing. Its depths were black, and looked like starlight, but in its murky interior hummed a ring filament of amber haze. The radial edge of the thing was inlaid with several small tracks, marked with tiny numerics. Below the incandescent curved a little silver plaque, and on it was inscribed:

WHAT IN ME IS DARK, ILLUMINE

WHAT IS LOW RAISE AND SUPPORT

"There … should be a book," she said. "Why keep *this* here?"

"It's probably a prototype of some kind, nothing more. Incandescents don't give anyone knowledge unless they're using them to read in bed of an evening."

"Well maybe this one does!"

That's when Alvin said a stupid thing.

"You don't know what you're talking about."

Hana bristled. "Then find out!"

She reached for the ornate throw switch aside the incandescent, but Alvin caught her hand. "Hey! We don't know what this does!"

"You can go, if you want."

She reached for it again.

"Wait." He caught her wrist. "This ain't the book you're looking for! Which obviously doesn't exist."

"It does!" she insisted, her raspy voice cracking ever so little. "It's … it's *got* to…"

"Look … magic books don't exist. Alright? Neither do your gods or—or this Agarta place, alright?"

"You … you take that back."

"I won't! I ought've known better, too!"

Anger boiled in her reddening face. Her shoulders and nose and hair rose, mouth quivered, but nothing came out. And in her hurt eyes, some deep part of him reflected through the lenses of her goggles, and wondered what would happen so badly it hurt him to not pull the lever.

What if?

"Ugh. Fine!"

So he gripped. He pulled. A high whine sounded, rose for a second. The bulb flashed, but Hana's gasp struck him before he actually realized that it had done anything at all, or that static had made his hair stand on end, or that the deep hum of lectral power suddenly surged through the wiring in the pedestal.

"Ah!" He rubbed his eyes and growled at the sting of it, though it was only a flash. "You feel that?"

"What?" she asked.

"Like everything just jolted a might? Stung, didn't it?"

"Nah. You feel something like that?"

An amber sheen lingered around his peripheral for a second or two "Yeah, scalded retinas, that's what. Maybe something weren't set up correctly or—what's happening?"

A set of bulbs overhead illuminated a simple flickering message:

Reconstitution Program Initiated

He felt it before he heard it, a rising hum of power. This time, Hana screamed, and dropped back. Hot sparks crackled from the pedestal, and the room turned dark. While the deep yellow hues from the outer windows still glowed, all the lamps in the room shorted, and burst.

"Alvin?!"

"Oh no…"

The whole Heuridium lurched under their feet, and Alvin wondered if the tower would drop.

Generators blew amid shouts and clamor as they stumbled through the bookshelf door and back into the archive.

"What have you done?!" Ellery Hartchild had found them, now in full view of both, his face twisting into shock. "Esker?!"

Hana grabbed Alvin's sleeve. "Duster! Should we—"

"Run!"

"Esker come back here!" Hartchild shouted.

Hana's wrist in his grip, Alvin ran.

They found level five frantic. There was no hiding from the Scholars and Engineers now. Alvin and Hana flung off their frock coats and ran. The Scholars all screamed orders at each other, disconnecting this and clamping emergency throws on that while the beating hearts of the Heurdium's power burst into arcs of current.

One of the funicular lifts plunged down to the atrium and smashed itself into a twisted heap.

"What happened?" Hana yelled.

"I don't know!"

There was no way down to the atrium, so Alvin, gripping Hana, flew to the only way he could imagine, onto the aged tram. He squeezed the clutch and threw the drive lever over hard enough to take Hana clear off her feet when the car jerked itself into life.

"Stop the tram!" someone cried, but it was too late.

The carriage soared through the gate. Alvin knew little about academic protocols, but he knew a lot about trams. The sickening height they were at dizzied him as the car emerged from the Heuridium, and the floor dropped away. Alvin clung to those controls like he'd never clung to anything.

The wind soared through his collar and hair as the old car banked and curved along suspended rails. The motion was almost planetary, poetic as it smoothly made its way down around the Heuridium's frame, out over the forested rooftops of Orphan Towne. Had it been any other moment, Alvin might've wailed with delight like he'd never felt, controlling that machine through Orphan's interior sky.

But everywhere flickered with bursting substations and lectral relays, flashing their last as if the storm had made it inside the walls of towne. With the substation dead, there went power for the rails. Over the rooftops of Harchester, the tram rolled to a stop. Tanno's Landing was some hundred yard ahead still. Out the tram door was simply a drop-off, which seemed to be Hana's intention.

"What in blazes are you doing?!"

"Getting off this!" she confessed.

"Down there?"

"Rooftop. Just jump."

"This is like the bridgeway earlier, ain't it?" Alvin's heart raced, and it already was racing, but when Hana bounded, skidding down the slope of the Songbird's roof, there was nothing else for it. Alvin edged his toes to the lip of the door, shut his eyes, and bounded. The landing hurt, spilling him sideways onto the roof and sliding him down almost over the edge. Attention came loud and swift as they all pointed at the two fugitives, helping each other off the Songbird. They landed hard on the stone floor of the patio.

"Alvin?" called Cleveland Dewitt. "What in blazes are you doing?"

"We have to run," Hana muttered to him, and he would have. He would have bolted from that place and taken Hana wherever he had to take her, but he never got to answer.

His name sounded loudly over the crowd. "Alvinheim Lockwilde Esker!" it called, and the voice was his father's, who must have heard Dewitt call to him first.

"Father?"

The chapel.

Alvin missed it.

Hugo Esker shouldered his way through, marching upstream against the flow as he pushed them off one side or the other.

"Alvin!" he called.

"Father!" He could not let Hana be found. So Alvin pulled her to a side alley behind the café, and made it half way there before he stopped so hard he almost bowled them both over.

Alvin spun on his heel and tried to run the other way, but his father's grip caught his arm. "Stop!" he yelled. "Boy, what the devil's going on?!"

"Father, let go!"

"Please let him go!" Hana shouted.

"What? Who…"

Hugo Esker quieted, tilted his head to eye the strange girl.

His father's hand let go of Alvin and took Hana's hat, pulled it off, and all her great shaggy mane of golden hair spilled into open light. Blind astonishment washed over him, and over everyone else.

"Please let go," Hana pleaded, and his hand slipped off.

Then the last of the power failed. All of Orphan Towne dimmed to the blackest state Alvin had ever witnessed. Alvin yanked free, and reached for Hana to run.

He caught her wrist.

Then her palm.

Then her fingers.

And then nothing at all.

Alvin spun. "Hana? Hana!" The whole of the towne lurched again, knocking even Hugo Esker over onto his side.

Alvin was already running.

There was no sign of her in the thick of the boldly darkened crowd. He spun, but she wasn't there. She simply was not there.

"Father—"

He only caught one fleeting sight of his father as he called out to his son, before a strong hand coiled around Alvin's mouth and pressed a kerchief into his face among the thick of the crowd, plunging Alvin into blacker darkness than he ever knew possible.

CHAPTER 10

ON THE EIGHTH OF APRIL, THREE WHOLE YEARS before Alvin discovered Lofthana Engindaut cín Jalóheim fra Sóholdt through the lens of his sister's spyglass, at exactly four twenty-eight in the afternoon (it was a Thursday), Agnes Esker tried to illuminate her mind so she could finally understand her star-patterns, and change the world forever.

They later called it heart failure.

The last drifting words he ever heard her utter: *It … it goes on forever,* struck his ears before her life evaporated.

But in the present, the lens of Alvin's mind swung freely on its axis, and maybe its gaze happened to land there. Maybe it was the restraints holding his wrists against the arms of the chair.

Alvin Esker?

"Hana?" he answered, still trying to reach for her arm as if he'd only been in that alley an instant before. Out of his stupor he roused, and the eyes that greeted his soggy senses were certainly not pretty.

"Yours ain't the kind of face I hoped to wake up and see once I'm dead," he told Ellery Hartchild. "Or ever."

"That's what you've got to say?" said Ellery. "After—" He stalled, collected his livid self. Dark rings circled his eyes. "Where's the blonde?"

"Fetching to land yourself a date, Hartchild?"

"Don't talk like a tough guy, Esker. You're not your father."

Hartchilds famously carried their words with the precision of a surgeon's knife.

"That's enough, Ellery," demanded Inspector General Hartchild. "We are not thugs."

Alvin spoke up. "Inspector Hartchild—"

"And you," he said, no happier than Ellery had been. "Do you have any idea what you've done?" The broad man paced his weight around the room, wiping his nervous face more than once. "I'll get to what you've done to Orphan later. Now. How many others are there?"

"Others?"

Inspector General Hartchild touched Alvin's jaw to turn his head a little. He opened Alvin's left eye wide, then his right, tilted his head up to see him better, and glanced at either temple. "Other Galó, Esker, other Galó. Blighters like your blonde creature."

Alvin's fire was far dimmer under the Inspector General's gaze. He shuddered in his stomach and chest, but tried to keep his mind on Hana. *She* was the one in danger if he told them too much.

"None."

"Are they surrounding the towne?"

"What? No."

"How did they know about the Oculix?"

"The what?"

"The *bulb*, Esker! A bloody Engineer should understand!"

"I'm only Third Class, Sir. And we didn't know *what* it was. Neither of us, Sir, not me nor Hana did."

"'Hana'?" Inspector General Hartchild repeated with disgust. "Ugh, naming the bilge, now. Bloody parasites, is what they are. Orphan was not ready, Mr. Esker." He wiped his face, tried to steady himself. "It simply … wasn't ready. Too many systems linked with too many others and none of them bloody *ready!* The harvesters aren't even working yet, and Author! The toroidal field's anything but stable! And … *Author*, the doorway into your fool mind."

"Father?" said Ellery. "What are you talking about? The Halo Program wasn't likely to…"

Hartchild drifted into himself for a long moment. "'There are more things in heaven and earth than are dreamt of in our philosophies,' Ellery. That's Shakespeare. Not that anyone reads Shakespeare anymore."

Alvin turned to Ellery Hartchild, of all people, but Ellery looked more confused than Alvin felt. He shrugged at him.

The door on the far end blinded Alvin, outlining a tall, narrow frame Alvin had come to know. "Alec? Are you quite finished vaulting threats at the boy?"

"Professor!" said Alvin.

The Professor held up a palm, and gave Alvin a little wink.

"Hasn't told me anything," said Hartchild. "Blasted youth never shuts his mouth for the paying but now I can get neither word nor wit out from him that's any use!"

"Well, spitting in his face continually is sure to illicit cooperation, isn't it, Alec?"

"This isn't one of your confounded word games, Hiram!" Hartchild barked. "What he's done—"

"You think that I fail to understand our situation?" His voice fell deep. "Or what comes next? Go see to them, won't you?" The Professor put a hand on Hartchild's shoulder. "Or are you still harboring the delusion that you're going to do any good here, old friend?"

Hartchild stood himself as tall as he could. "If anything happens to Ellery or Tabitha because of this little—"

"Go and help Hawthorn and the old man before they worry themselves into a tither. Or *you* do, for that matter. And make certain to keep Chancellor Finch out of our hair, while you're at it."

Chief Hartchild took a last long glare at Alvin, and a short one at Lorecroft, demanding with a shout that Ellery follow, before leaving the two of them alone.

"Professor, you've got to tell me what's going on!" Alvin insisted. "Chief Hartchild wouldn't say and I—I'm afraid something's happened to Hana."

"The greatest likelihood is that your little friend left you to your fate, Master Esker," he said, and so coldly, though Alvin wasn't about to believe it. "I had an ill feeling you two would attempt some addle-minded thing, but you even surprised me. Anyway, give no mind to Alec. His personality lends itself to hysterics ordinarily. Most people's do. Don't you think?"

"Sir, Hana didn't do nothing wrong! It were *my* fault, sneaking into the Heuridium like that—probably ought've told you."

There was nothing in Orphan that Hiram Lorecroft couldn't make right, and Alvin knew it better than most. While Alvin's father preferred the 'sleeves rolled and fists balled' method of sorting things out, Hiram Lorecroft never needed to resort to such matters.

"Yes, well. You were telling me about speaking with the Inspector General."

"He called her a creature! Can you believe that?"

With one swift inhalation through his nose, Lorecroft spoke frankly. "Yes. Her kind is a somewhat 'mutt' race of old Nordic nomads and settlers across the Expanse, Normans and Danes and the like, as backwards as they likely are inbred. They are partly remnants of the people who were once believed to originate from Hyperborea."

"Hyperborea?"

"Yes, Master Esker, Hyperborea. The Miocene Continent. It's a somewhat mythic landscape at the northern axis of the planet. It had many names. Your uncle Otto believed it was the gateway to Thule, if I recall. These nomadic noridcs believe the same, though they call it Agarta."

He spun the dial locks that held Alvin's restraints, one by one.

"You knew about them. All this time?"

"Please, Master Esker. It's my job to know things, remember?"

Alvin's lens drifted to all the things he'd seen in the Heuridium, even the incandescent itself. "Sir?" he asked. "Why is the Heuridium filled with my sister's work?"

"It would be more accurate to say your *sister* was filled with the *Heuridium's* work, but we'll deal with that by and by. Did you play with blocks, as a boy, Master Esker?"

"Sure I did. Father used to machine them out of the square bar remnants at his work. We had lots."

"You built houses and such?"

"Yes, Sir, and forts and boats and the like."

"What if you had trillions of those blocks? You think you could build Orphan Towne?"

"Maybe in a thousand years," Alvin laughed.

"Did you know that the universe is made of sound? Vibration, more like. They govern the nature of every little particle. Change the vibration, and you change the wavelength. Yes? Everything in the universe vibrates. Vibration is simply a matter of frequency—of numerics."

"I'm not sure I'm following, Sir."

From his overcoat, Professor Lorecroft drew a silver pen. "This pen's outer casing is nickel. There are vibrations that govern its mass, its weight, other elements, just as there are within my own hand. All the vibrations in the universe coalesce into a world where the pen is in my right hand. The pen is in my right hand, Master Esker. You can observe it, yes?"

"Begging your pardon, I don't see what that's got to do with anything."

"Don't you? What would happen, if we were to discover the very last thing there is to know?"

"And what's that?"

"If we could—hypothetically, of course—perceive and manipulate the most fundamental *blocks* of this universe, could we not alter it?"

"Begging your pardon, Sir, but that ain't … actually possible. Right? I mean, you sound like my sister…"

Lorecroft rose, and put a finger to the side of his nose. "'*When to the new eyes of thee. All things by immortal power, near or far, hiddenly, to each other linked are, that thou canst not stir a flower without troubling of a star.*' Never read Francis Thompson, have you?"

"Haven't, Sir."

"No, suppose you couldn't possibly have. Take your satchel and coat. We're leaving."

Alvin found his things in the corner, and swiftly pulled on his Tramrunner jacket and flung his satchel on as Lorecroft opened the door for

Alvin in his most mannerly way. Only then did Alvin see how bad the storm had gotten. Smoldering golden clouds boiled along the near horizon.

He was back in the Heuridium.

But Alvin didn't keep his eyes on the horizon. He turned them downward where the customary energy of towne had twisted into disarray. They wove in scattered formations, no pattern, no rhyme, no method.

"Sir? Is my family…?"

"I was only a few years your senior when I engineered the first incandescent, yet I understood so little of how life actually works. And then it struck me, one day. You know when? It was when I stood over the grave of my boy."

Alvin turned to his mentor, but his face changed. A deep fierceness lay beneath those hawkish eyes.

"Come, Alvin. I'd like to show you something. I think it'll help explain a great many things."

"But … did I really do all this?"

Lorecroft circled the tower's outer stairs, as Alvin and Hana had. "What struck me as I stood over William's grave was that scholars need not learn to balance equations, or corral themselves *within* the rules of the universe, but to *change* them. My wife never understood that, but where I found fire from William's death, she only found solace in a bottle."

"What fire did you find?"

"Always we fight the tide of decay and agromatic yields, food shortages, preservation to feed the mouths we breed. But what if we could simply rearrange those numeric building blocks until they added up to a universe wherein man is immortal to starvation? Or there is simply plenty of food?"

He glanced back at Alvin and held the pen high enough for him to see it.

"These are lofty, of course, but imagine we start with adding up to a universe where the pen—" He tossed and caught it in his other hand. "—is in my *left* hand."

Up to level three they went.

"But this is all theory, right, Professor?"

Lorecroft stopped on the steps for a moment, and turned to him. He narrowed, inhaled slow, selecting words like drawing cards for play. "Once you threw that switch, a program was initiated, systems upon systems upon systems. It is too late to stop it now. Isn't that delightful?"

"Sir? What's a program? Like a play? Was in a play, once, I was. Christmas pageant—"

Lorecroft laughed. "A program is a series of operations linked together, following a directive, like your trams moving because you adjusted the throttle. Transporting Orphanites is not unlike a program."

"Sir, can't we just flip the switch back? Like this never happened? I'd no idea what we were doing, honest!"

"Alas, no. It doesn't work that way, Master Esker. Sadly, systems were not prepared yet, which is what's flustering Alec so." Lorecroft turned and kept on his way. "First thing you ought to know is that Orphan is not so much a *towne* as it is a *machine* that people live in."

"A machine?"

Orphan shook, not that Lorecroft seemed to notice. He marched on, up through Level Four, which was as abandoned as the last, through Level Five, and finally onto Level Six. This is where Lorecroft stopped, his focused eyes scanning the walls of books. The Professor led them between the shelves, passed the open door where the strange incandescent had sat enthroned in the hidden room. It was gone, now.

"Sir ... what was that thing?"

"Hmm? Thing?"

"The incandescent."

"Oh. Well, you're close enough in calling it an incandescent. Young Master Hartchild insists on calling it the *Oculix*, fitting enough, if a little dramatic, but Ellery likes his Latin ever so. For now I will say that it is very old, older than you might imagine. We didn't so much invent these things as discover them, at least some."

The Professor gazed up at the seven hanging lamps over their heads, each bulb just inches above them.

"Sir? Where are you taking us? We're already on the top level."

"Oh Master Esker, there is *always* another level."

He went to the first lamp and grasped a flat, golden ring near its bottom, and spun it. It clicked. The shape of the glass changed, and made the light warp. "So convenient, being tall," he said. "Poor Alec always needs a step stool." He went to the next lamp and did likewise.

"Sir? What was it supposed to have done?"

One by one, he went to the seven lamps, and each time, something clicked into place like a combination lock.

"Supposed to have?" he said with a wry smirk. "Woolgathering again, my boy? The 'Bequest of the Ancients,' it's called, among other things. The pedestrian phrasing is simply that it is a light which grants knowledge, but there is far more to it than that. Have you ever looked at a foreign language written down?"

"I … guess?"

"You cannot comprehend it in spite of the order within the pattern. The Oculix Infuses the recipient with *itself*, transmuting ocular nerve tissue with its own filament substance—it shapes chaos into order, translating the most obscure patterns into ones that the mind comprehends. That is Phase One. Phase Two is far more interesting…"

Alvin's head hurt, and he certainly didn't feel any smarter—dumber, in fact. The last lamp clicked. The ceiling plates lowered one by one, forming a circular stair. With the sound of the machinery gone, a new noise struck Alvin's senses. It was unmistakable—a girl crying out in anger. Or in pain.

"Hana? Professor? You said she'd got away!"

He started up, and might've even attacked his mentor at that moment, had he not raised an open hand toward Alvin, his underarm braced with machinery, something like a tuning fork, coursing with a golden glow that implied to Alvin that any movement would mean his death.

"Master Esker, you really must learn to listen. I said that her escape was the most *likely* event. Now, what you're about to see? It's not likely at all."

in which high winds make for lousy friends

AT THE TOP OF ORPHAN'S GREAT ARCHES, in the apex of industry, the Heuridium was mounted, the shining hope for a future born of the great Noble Sciences. It had six levels. Everyone knew that. Alvin ascended into the dark recesses *above* it with with a well in his stomach and a weapon in his spine. They reached a landing, and Lorecroft drew back a long throw lever. The stairs beneath them ascended up like tucked legs to allow whatever great machinery was above them to move freely.

"This … this is all so unbelievable," muttered Alvin, feeling smaller and smaller in this suddenly vast new world.

And as if the Professor sensed his feelings, he asked Alvin, "Do you know what we are? Cosmic dust, to be scattered by the winds of Confluence, that is our lot." Alvin didn't know what 'confluence' meant, but it wasn't the time to be inquisitive; still, the gravity with which Lorecroft said it lingered in his mind for a long while. "We are here and we vanish in a turn of the world. Your sister was deeply unsatisfied with life in Orphan. What was it she called it? A 'prison of the predicted,' that was it. But what truly haunted the girl was an inability to reconcile that we are nothing more than what we are—slates for the hand of time to inscribe."

Alvin stepped onto a floor that hung in the center of the sphere, a tremendous Fabergé egg of limeiron and brass and geometric panels of shimmering glass and great lenses mounted on turning trackways, and greater than he ever imagined it could be. The galactic plane, the tropics and equatorial ring, even the zodiac ecliptic each had their own set of orbiting tracks and lenses on the glass eggshell of the immense sphere.

Alvin's head swam, but maybe it was all the spinning machines.

Even the floor spun, or turned, more like. It lay in great, black circles, concentric, like the rings of Saturn turning around a central disc, each ring several strides across, and each rising inches higher than the last, while the machinery from above descended in the middle, making the whole center of the machine like a great hourglass.

At the narrow, open center of it knelt the girl, teeth gnashed and grinding in a constant low roar.

"Hana!" The rest of Alvin's shouts died when something hot stunned his spine in sharp and sudden waves that stiffened him and left his mouth open in a silent yell until he dropped hard.

"Kindly settle down, Master Esker. Hysterics will help no one, least of all your little friend. Status, gentlemen?"

Alvin's head blared with a cold and constant ringing, shuddering his skull from the inside. He couldn't move, couldn't see, and could hardly hear anything but disembodied voices.

"Half the towne's in a blazing panic," said Inspector General Hartchild. He had Hana's wrist in his hand and seemed to be poking the back of her head. "And this Author-forsaken Halo will not work!"

"You are the last of us to judge a machine, Alec, and I'll speak with you later about clasping that device on her wrist. Waste of rare equipment."

"Well I had to try something!"

Someone else's voice caught Alvin's ear. "These ticker machines of yours seem discontent also, Hiram! I take it your fancy machine is not up to the task." *Viscount Pike?* Alvin turned, but nothing came into focus. Pike was there indeed, standing with Inspector Hartchild aside suspended gauge panels hung from the trackways around the perimeter of the dome.

A professor.

A banker.

An inspector.

What in blazes was going on?

"My 'fancy machine' is hardly the problem, Hawthorn," Lorecroft called over the turbulence. "And I might just resent the remark if I weren't so civil. You should be well aware that the harvesters *and* the toroidal alternators were not even near completion, not to mention a plethora of other 'fancy' components of the Initiative. Now, no need to ruffle your plumage. The Initiative Program has begun whether or not you or I like it."

"Well then," said Pike. "If the Halo will not function, and she cannot affect the Program, there is only one way to stop it."

"Hawthorn?" said Lorecroft.

Alvin shook the blur from his eyes. From under his frock, Hawthorn Pike drew what could only be a weapon. It was shaped like an old flintlock pistol, but growled with a crackling shine that sounded from across the hall, dark rings cradling Hana's big, blaring eyes when he put it to her head.

"Do you really think it's prudent to go blowing apart the girl's brains?" asked Lorecroft.

"No!" Alvin yelled, pulled and crawled, his arms shaking to lift him from the ground until a hard fist hit him clean in the stomach. Of course it was Ellery Hartchild. He didn't even say anything, nor did Alvin. They just glared at one another, mutual disdain boiling beneath their skins.

Pike pressed his foot into Hana's calf to pin her still. She hit his shins as she could, but he was a pillar of a man. "We have six minutes—"

"Six and twenty. Seconds matter, Hawthorn," Lorecroft reminded him.

"Liminite becomes inert once the Infused is dead. Did you not tell me that? If Orphan isn't ready, then there's only one way to stop the process!"

Baron Lorecroft's voice came louder than the rest, clear and calm and focused. "Killing a girl who *isn't* Infused will do nothing but cause a frightful mess on my machines, and give you one more thing to answer to your Author for, Hawthorn—not to mention *me*. Now you will put that weapon down immediately, lest I forget myself and remind you *all* what my 'fancy machines' are capable of."

Then from over the voices and the arguing came a graveled, old voice: "Viscount Pike?"

Alvin rose again and readied himself for a full-on brawl with Ellery

Hartchild, but no one said a word in the presence of the rickety old man who could be no one but the Academy's great living patriarch, Solomon Day.

"The rule of order!" spoke the old man.

Hana knelt still when he strode over, his bright copper cane tapping the floor. "Hiram, you're certain the Infused is not this wasteland creature?"

Hana growled. "My name is—"

The old man jammed the tip of his cane onto Hana's hand with a sharp jerk. She yelped loud and would've slammed the old man to the ground if Pike hadn't stepped on her other wrist.

"What'd you do that for?!" Alvin yelled instinctively, but whatever bravery he felt quickly withered under the old Duke's still shadow.

There she lay on her back, one hand pinned under the cane and the other under Pike's boot. Solomon Day bent to look at her wrist, the one he pinned. "And the band did nothing to help?"

"The problem I believe we're having is that she isn't Infused at all—the *boy* is," Lorecroft explained. "See for yourself, if you'll examine her scalp."

The old man bent Hana's head forward and forced his fingers under her hair. "Hiram is right, Alec. Alas. The boy will have to be inducted, or candlesticked."

Hawthorn Pike called for Ellery to, "Fetch a hatchet," and he would see to the bangle.

Hana panicked and jerked and pulled, but could get nowhere.

"Hawthorn, have I ever told you, you have a *gift* for frightening children? Gracious, even if I *were* to tolerate such macabre solutions as a 'hatchet,' it would do very little good. By now, it has already tuned itself to her signature. Besides, I believe the young lady may still have need of that hand at some point—assuming you don't aim to candlestick *her*, as well."

"Ought to," Pike argued.

"Candlestick?" said Alvin.

Pike took her by the hair and dragged her down the pedestal. He finally released Hana's other hand and she clutched the cane-crushed palm.

The old man stiffened, looking to flake apart like old bread at any moment, but he settled back into shape, and strolled past. "I trust you will settle this nonsense, Hiram."

"Doubtless, good Duke." *If I might suggest, it might be a good time to reassure the commoners.* Your warm and grandfatherly voice on the Broadcast would be quite comforting to the masses, I'm sure." He then turned to Hartchild. "Alec, why don't you make yourself useful seeing to the clamor, as well?" Lorecroft then turned his attention onto Alvin. "*Your* turn, Master Esker." He led Alvin to the center, passing Hana, where she and Alvin shared a long and silent exchange of dread. "Young Master Hartchild," Lorecroft continued. "Kindly hurry to the Sixth Level, to my office. In the third drawer on the left, you'll find a small device, silver casing. I believe I shall need it shortly."

Ellery Hartchild hurried down the stairs.

Under Alvin's feet, machinery spun, magnets and lectral coils through the darkened glass. Overhead hung a lens, at least six feet across, bending the whole of the heavens into an upside-down dome above his head.

"It's ... it's full of stars," he awed. Agnes's favourite recitation of Virgil drifted across those stars:

Above my head, a boundless sky I see...

Orbiting him in slow concourse went Hana and Viscount Pike on the great glass rings of the floor as they turned, pinpoints of light erupting on and off from under the dark glass.

He looked to Hana, Hana who had her own eyes fixed on the now-unguarded stairway. She glanced to it, to Alvin, and back.

She wouldn't...

No, he assured himself. *She wouldn't.*

"What ... does the machine do?" asked Alvin, fascination overpowering his fear.

"Many things, but for our purposes: think of Orphan's Armillary as a great observatory, one aimed at more ... distant coasts, and its lens bends the *patterns* of stars seen above into *new* ones below," said the Professor, strolling 'backwards' along the floor ring as it spun so he kept his place just over Alvin's shoulder. "You'll notice that it is currently focused on the Pleiades." Sure enough, overhead, those cloudy blue stars looked down on him. "Now then. When young Master Hartchild returns in a moment, I'll need you to finish transcoding the new pattern into balance."

"Trans—what? Professor, I don't understand." Alvin was understating it. He understood nothing of what Lorecroft had said.

Transcode stars?

And into *new* patterns?

What patterns?

And *what* needs to balance?

That's when Orphan Towne rumbled. The floor lurched beneath their feet and vented steam from somewhere under the panels.

And then Hana bolted.

She tore over the floor for the stairwell and bounded over the rail, but didn't make it far. The scuffle was loud, down below the stairs. She appeared again and landed hard against the floor at the hand of Ellery Hartchild. He dragged her back into the dome and threw her down.

Hawthorn Pike eagerly took over holding her by the hair.

She ran.

She actually *ran*.

She would've left him there.

But Alvin had little time for the sudden sting to do anything but mangle his meager courage all the more.

"Continuing," Lorecroft noted, taking whatever it was Ellery had brought him. "We'll need to execute the Halo Program in your brain now, and you can decipher the—"

"This—this is banging mad! You want me to translate stars, do you?! Land's sake, I don't even speak good Anglish! Ask Mum!"

"Then open your eyes, Master Esker."

When Alvin finally looked at his mentor, the Professor tapped his temple a couple times, with an easy smile. "Like this," he said. "Just behind your ear."

He still didn't understand, but Alvin tapped as the Professor showed, and when he did, something impossible happened.

Bands of amber light erupted into space around his head, floating lines and rings and markers for degrees and angles. His heart raced and he tried to push them away as more bands formed in front of his eyes. They shimmered and glowed, and when his hand struck the light, the bands spun and turned.

"What...?"

A great wall of wind struck the dome as a crashing tide against the hull of a ship. The limeiron groaned and bronze warped, and all the geometric panes rattled in their settings.

"One minute forty before we have a very big problem, Master Esker. Kindly concentrate."

The amber band ... could they see it too? It all came clearer, as if he could not only see the stars, but the precise distance between them, the depth of their alignment, and every angle, line, and ratio among the cluster simply ... became clear through the 'eyepieces' of that light. Interconnecting lines appeared to link the stars in micro-constellations, anywhere he looked at the stars.

"One more tap," the Professor added. "Then look to your hands."

"What?" Alvin did so, and in the palm of his right hand, more light spread into being, like a hand-sized dial, intricate and complex.

"Delightful. Touch the central trigger on the rim twice, if you please."

If he thought of protesting, his curiosity got the better of him. The dial 'hovered' just over his palm, and when he turned his hand, it went with. He tapped it as Lorecroft said, and all around his body, more light erupted in a single flash, shaping itself into hovering bands, rings and marks for degrees and thousands of markings he didn't know, all forged of warm luminescence. How the great machine made light hover in the air, he couldn't fathom. There wasn't any place that it came from, either.

What was it? *How* was it? A projection?

"Now, reach out your free hand and rotate the view until you see the Pleiades, just like our own machine, here."

Alvin stretched out a shuddering hand, and touched the light. He touched it—could *feel* it. It tingled his skin. When he pushed against it, his hand finally broke through. The light under it scattered to dust, and then reassembled itself.

"Kindly play later, Master Esker," the Professor chastised.

Alvin gave a little pressure, and the rings rotated around his body. Floating dials and rings of the light went with it, until one largest came in front of his face, and through it, he found the Pleiades.

"Now tap the cluster," said the Professor, stepping right up to the rings. "Then turn the outer dial on the control in your hand."

"Tap the—"

Against all established sanity, Alvin put his hand to the hovering amber lens, and tapped thin air where he could see the Pleiades on the other side, up in the great dome. The star cluster flashed, and a ring like a lens appeared around it, and when he turned the 'dial' in his hand, the cluster appeared bigger, as if a lens was extending.

"That's it, Master Esker. Now fiddle with the control in your hand until you manage to realign the cluster."

"'Fiddle'! You want me to fiddle?!" Alvin objected.

"I've little time for a more detailed explanation, so yes. Fiddle."

"Professor I don't understand anything that's—"

"We already transcoded some of the numeric matrix within that cluster," Lorecroft continued, ignoring Alvin's plight. "But that Final Sequence, we need your help to decipher and execute. The Gate shan't open fully until the final sequence is finished, and executed."

"But I don't—

"Look *closely*. If you don't finish this, we are *all* in trouble, Master Esker. Now then: *three nine four nine seven one four two, two three six eight—*"

The Pleiades did look wrong, though Alvin couldn't possibly have said why. He slowly adjusted the dials in his hand, and with every move, the stars of the Pleiades shifted around. More, the thousands of incandescents under the glass floor followed what Alvin was doing, lighting and blinking out to match every alteration he made. Through the band of light around his eyes, he could see the way the stars interacted, lines appearing and disappearing as they moved in and out of places, rings of their movements, depth measurements.

But there was something more, something deeper, *under* the numerics of their positions and distance and mass and gravitic measures, like if he tilted his head a little he would see through a mesh to an image.

And something in those patterns *emerged*, to Alvin's sight, and it shook him. What he saw within the details of those random stars couldn't be there. No, not an image. Words. *Language.*

What he saw could not possibly be there.

Hickter's Law said it could not be there.

The prior arrangement of the Pleiades had previously said **The Gate Stands Shut and Sealed**, but when he realigned them, it so obviously wrote **The Gate Stands Open**.

"Now when you've got it, initiate the new waveform pattern by executing the program, the key in the middle of that dial in your hand…"

What was he doing? What would happen if he did what Lorecroft wanted? Flipping a blazing switch was destroying Orphan Towne!

"Professor—I can't do this."

Ellery Hartchild could stand it no longer. From Hawthorn Pike's hand that *wasn't* holding Hana's hair, he snatched the arc pistol, and marched over to Alvin before Pike could do little more than shout at him.

Lorecroft shut his eyes for a short moment. "Master Hartchild!" he demanded. "Give me that gun."

"It's not going to work!" Ellery Hartchild called. "He isn't ready for this! No training, no understanding! He's a child playing with a loaded gun!"

"And what then are you, Master Hartchild?"

"I won't let something happen to Tabby because of this blighter!"

Alvin heard two things, then—the shrill and clear whine that he'd heard just before Lorecroft discharged that weapon into his body, and the voice of someone calling *hello?* from down below the steps.

Stepping up into the Armillary came Tabitha Hartchild.

"Uncle Hiram?" she'd called, but stopped suddenly when her eyes met the glassed tempest. "Oh *my* … what is … what's happening? What … is all this?"

"Miss Hartchild," said Lorecroft, but that's all he got out.

"Ellery!" she cried. "Miss Sóholdt!"

The scene had to be incredible, and was enough to cause her to run at her brother. "I—I found the Heuridium open and—and all this is—Ellery stop that! Put that down! For land's sake, what's going on?! What *is* this?"

"You oughtn't be here, Tabby," Ellery insisted. "Go…"

"Why are you holding a—a *gun* on Esker?"

"Alvin run!" called Hana, struggling against Pike's strength until he slammed her on her back against the floor. She reared back and kicked him in the groin.

Tabitha cried a pleading yell for them all to "stop it!" She dove at her brother's arm as a crackling *CHANG* echoed off every plate and beam.

Alvin stumbled, his hand so accidentally 'engaging' the button in his palm. A pulse of golden light flowed through the shapes, and they vanished. Tabitha Hartchild slumped to her knees.

"Miss Hartchild?" called Lorecroft.

"Ta—Tabby?!"

"Ellery?" Tabitha whimpered.

Tabitha doubled over as Orphan Towne's aching limeiron beams all screamed and bent against whatever force was ravaging it. Ellery Hartchild caught his sister's fall with pale horror. The hissing pistol fell from his hand and cracked the glass ring, his LIT Corps. jacket splattered with dots of his sister's blood.

Panels of the glass dome burst and let the storm rage against them.

Tabitha's shocked and pained eyes met Alvin's.

"What are you going to do, Master Esker?" Baron Lorecroft perched where he was, but around him swirled a golden light, like the light that had just surrounded Alvin, though now a solid sphere that dissolved the raining bits of glass that rained on it.

Hana cried his name, tugging on his hand. "Come on!"

Alvin rose, blinked away the haze, tore his old satchel from the floor, gripped Hana's hand, and soared over that black glass floor with all possible speed toward the western hatch on the far wall. The sudden gusts nearly took him off his feet.

Pike cursed, yelled for them to *stop-or-else* something.

Alvin and Hana slammed against the locking wheel on that old hatch, and shouldered their strength into it until it creaked open, letting all the more wind and sand flow in.

"Master Esker, wherever is there for you to go?" called Lorecroft.

Alvin and Hana pushed their way through, out of the finest towne at the end of the world, out of the only possible hope of survival, out of the only home Alvin had ever known. And the two ran out onto the roof of Orphan Towne for their sorry little lives.

ENTRY 17: "A SPIRE INTO THUNDERHEAD"

Among the landmark work of the mind of Cornelius Hickter, his second-most impacting legacy—behind Hickter's Law—was surely the concept, design, and erection of the great Heuridium Tower. Simultaneously an Atmospheric Lectral Collector (ALC), observatory, museum, laboratory, and research station, the Heuridium represented all that Orphan Heights aspired to be … pun intended. It was the great achievement of Orphan's first century of life, and that is saying something, the crown jewel of the Academy, overseen by the rumoured Fifth Marquees of Orphan, but nobody knew who that was.

Once the time of Baron Hiram Lorecroft came, and Orphan knew lectral lighting for the first time, the Heuridium was posthumously lit as a splendour of the Expanse, a public relations stunt to raise taxes for the Academy, but it worked. The papers made a big thing of it. By the time of the relevant Sub-Variant Shift of 12473, the Heridium was closed to all public access, except for the Museum of Science & Fabrication on the first level. The upper levels were used only for housing prototypes for terraforming machinery for the Great Initiative, but this was mostly bunk. Orphan's laboratories were very much in use, and the new apex of the great spire housed an observatory-like Armillary mechanism, used for mapping astral patterns and generating a Cymatic Induction Wave, apparently for the purpose of shifting Sub-Variants … or Major ones, since why else would one want to generate Cymatic Induction Waves?

Regardless, this is a troubling prospect for any occupant of the Expanse, past or future, or of any other continent, for that matter. Let the reader consider himself warned.

– PART II –

Expanse

CHAPTER 12

in which Alvin goes outside for the very first time

IT WAS AS IF A GREAT GATEWAY HAD BLOWN OPEN. The heavens themselves opened before his senses and all hit him at once—freezing, roaring winds and bone-shuddering thunder and unfiltered, undiluted light.

Uncle Otto claims that, in Agarta, death itself was unwritten, Agnes once told him, the very day before he lost her. *It wasn't magic, or immortality, but they had learned to alter the Metarcanum itself—to alter the building blocks of the universe that they learned from the stars. Transmutation of matter, Al! But you know your uncle. Still. Imagine a future free from the doom we see in the Expanse.* Cynically she added, *but that was before Hickter's Law.*

She set the book in her hand back on the shelf, and her finger stayed on it. Agnes would do that sometimes, just stop whatever she'd been busying herself with and be suddenly still, looking to a horizon that nobody else could see. *Can you picture it, Al? I don't mean Uncle's legends. I mean if we could make a future without iron walls? Or iron minds?*

Over the roof of Orphan Towne, Alvin and Hana ran because their lives depended on it, yanking each other along with anchored grip.

"Where can we go?" Hana called over the winds that threatened to scoop them up by their clothes and fling them headlong into the abyss that lay in all directions. They were atop the world, after all, his old shoes clanging off the great beams that held Orphan's dome aloft.

117

No suffering? No death?

The transparent panels Alvin had gazed up toward all his life, so small from far below seemed now big as houses. Somewhere under them both, his father probably wondered what had happened to his boy.

Without hunger and want?

They ran over airways, past angled vents and ailerons tilting the winds in Orphan's favor. Great lightning rods rose in spires and collected the lectral rage from the clouds above. Hana yelped and clung when the great columns of lightning came.

A place where our thoughts are free again?

The wind tore at them, tugging at their hair, their sleeves, their chests, trying to pull them in all directions at once. And when their speed picked up, and the dome sloped, it was too late to stop—they soared down the slant.

The place we all see in daydreams?

They couldn't stop, or even slow down.

The wind came so hard it bowled them both over, flinging Hana right over Alvin's tumbling body. His fingers grazed her arm, her wrist, her palm, fingers, then nothing at all.

They spun on their backs, called out for each other, but there was no slowing down now.

Where we could live happily, forever without end?

They caught pipes, braces, but couldn't hold on. They reached for arches and ailerons and beams, but couldn't hold on. Finally they came to the rim of Orphan.

Hana flew over it.

Alvin flung himself headlong for her plunging body until he felt something that wasn't metal or glass, and gripped it as tight as his fear would let him. His satchel had caught hold of a protruding grate, and Hana's leg wrapped in the strap aside his hand, twisting his wrist against her weight. They hung together over the long fall to the Expanse below.

Where the ones we lose...

"Hana!"

"Can't reach!"

Something came free from her coat—a cylinder. Hana grabbed for it. "Hold on!" she cried, but it came apart in her grasp.

One half hurled down into the depths.

The ones we love so dearly...

Alvin grabbed her by the arm and yanked her into him, but he was slipping off the bag's strap, too. When whatever held them gave way, they plunged, tumbled and rolled into the open air, grasping for each other, yanking at loose clothes or hair or arms until Alvin's hand took hold of hers and felt the chill of metal in her palm. All they could do was grip each other's hand.

But it was enough.

A bursting ripple of cosmic wind enveloped them, and together they vanished clear out of space.

Could hold onto us always...?

At the very bottom of Orphan Towne, down even lower that the west gate, down the slope on which the towne rested, a spherical bubble swirled momentarily like a gyroscope of rippled air around two young people, and dissipated after it deposited them hard to the ground.

For a long while, they gasped and moaned and twitched while their bodies fought to understand that they weren't actually plummeting to their deaths anymore.

I'm sorry, Alvin. Just woolgathering. Want to knock off and have lunch?

"Hana I think we're dead!"

"This is not death," she panted. "This is outside. What just happened?"

"I think ... I think I have a headache."

Alvin slowly caught hold of his own breathing, and took stock of the previous moments. "Tabitha," he said. "You don't think..."

"Dead," said Hana. "Has to be."

"Hana!"

The storm struck the far end of Orphan Towne, currents of mist coming off of Orphan's dome above like drifts of ghostly snow.

They were outside. Yes. He managed to pin that much down.

And they'd fallen, yes, but ought've died, by his count. His mind tried to pull his memory of falling with the one of the teleporting cylinder in the Heuridium like two wires that wouldn't quite reach one another.

Alvin Esker was outside.

Immediately, he regretted it.

He fell to hands and knees and crawled. That sky! There wasn't any roof! Not anywhere! No walls. No protection. No echo or railing or glass. There was *nothing* and so much of it.

"Alvin!"

"What?"

She was stark white, clinging to the cold ground like she might fall right off of it. What stunned Alvin was the fact that she might. Rocks and dust and mist levitated around them in a wide circle, turning this way and that in the air as more peeled themselves from the ground and ascended.

"What s happening?" Hana asked.

"I don't—I don't know," Alvin panted.

White streaks of lightning lit up the land behind them. They came down in violent ribbons and left rings of scorch across the ridge lines.

Hana pulled on Alvin's arm. "We have to go! Come on!"

But his father … and Alphonse and his mother and his home all orbited the lens of his mind.

"Alvin?" she called.

But he couldn't move, and didn't hear the shrieks of lightning as it came roaring over the land in all directions.

"Can you hear me?" Hana pleaded.

And finally he did. Alvin lifted his eyes toward Hana's own, cast so wide he could've seen her racing heart if he'd looked close through them.

"Okay," he said, nodded, and repeated, his eyes falling on the cylinder beside him. "Did you steal this from the Heuridium?"

"Yah."

"Good girl," he laughed, and slipped the thing into his pocket. "Where'd the other half go?"

"Do not see it."

"Whatever. Can you move? We—we ought to run."

Hana's mouth pressed shut and twisted a little, but she nodded.

She would. *Could* didn't matter.

"You said there are buildings over the ridge. That way?"

"Elder ruins. West. Over the rise there. But the lightning—"

"We'll make it."

So they ran. Again. Alvin wasn't nearly so good on his feet as Hana proved, but this was her world. Even in her new clothes, she soared over the ground. Her ankles found their balance like a mountain goat.

On the leeward side they panted, and Alvin Esker finally saw the old ivory-toned ruins he'd seen through Orphan's glass so many times, now up close. He stared at the bowing stones in what was left of a roof, and thanked the Author they were still alive, running hands through their hair and uttering the occasional ironic laugh.

Alvin slumped his satchel on the floor.

— —— — —— — — —— — — —— — — —— — — —— — — ——

Somewhere in the later hours, Alvin woke, having not known he'd fallen asleep. Hana was snoozing against the wall, and outside, the storm was past.

Alvin rose on sore legs. It was dark. It was dark*er*. It was the darkest thing he'd ever seen, so dark he had to rub his eyes to know his eyes were working. No glare separated him from the night, no reflections of lights or walls or faces, no echo off the perimeter glass.

There was nothing between him and starlight.

Alvin stepped up the incline, coming to the crest of the little hill, and stood exposed beneath the clear canopy. The long arm of the galaxy stretched across his southern view, from one end of sky to the other.

He'd no idea it could look like that.

Fingers splayed overhead, he bent and turned them to let the starlight beam through, and a little laugh rose in his belly.

And something else.

From the north, a breeze came up cold. Far harder gusts hit him atop Orphan, but this was different. He wasn't running for his life, now.

121

The wind flowed between his fingers like from a spigot.

Alvin tossed off his jacket, neverminding how bad it made him shiver. Sleeves rolled and boots kicked off, Alvin Esker walked further into the open air. It was open air. His toes throbbed from the cold of the rock. No matter where he looked, he saw horizon, except where Orphan Towne's immense silhouette broke its line. No beams, no braces, no arches or limeiron anything.

It was the greatest thing *ever*. He turned, jumped, and bounded. He gave running a try.

Never did much running, had Alvin. Nobody ran in Orphan, after all. The schedule … but there *was* no schedule out here, no time to keep, no work whistles, no perimeter.

Before a few moments passed, he ran with arms wide, voice wailing into the un-echoing sky, head back and fingers coursing in wind, hair snapping and teeth chattering.

He ran anyway.

One great and wild *yeeeeeaaaaah!* cut into the night from his cold lungs.

"You have lost your mind!" Hana yelled through cupped hands.

"But you can feel the air *move!*"

"You mean *wind*?"

"Look how clear the sky is—*everything* is!" He twirled like a dancer. "Land's sake, my feet hurt! Now I understand why you dislike shoes!"

Hana laughed, watching him make a total and utter fool of himself, running like an idiot under bare starlight for the first time in all his small days, climbing onto every rock and ledge for any view he could muster, wondering how he could've possibly ever lived without feeling something as wild as this. Alvin Esker finally slumped against the stone wall, gasping cold air into stinging lungs.

"Never been outside?" Hana asked.

"Not really, not past the door you came in by. Felt some wind back then —and when you came inside—but nothing like *this*." Alvin rested his head against the cold wall. "We're just so … so *small* out in this. You know? Does it even notice us?"

"Does what?" Hana was fiddling with the band on her wrist.

"The universe. The world. The Author, anything. We just come and, you know, you blink and we're gone. Orphan's been standing for hundreds of years, and how many are lying at Chapel Hill?"

"Huh?"

"Buried."

"Out here, Svaraheim buries things by itself. We live and we die and that is that."

"Probably right. It's still new to me, you know? All this is … so *different*." He meshed his hands behind his head. "Well, there's nothing for it. Suppose we'll have to make for your village, then."

She wasn't listening, too busy digging her nails at the band on her wrist.

"Hana?"

"Huh? Why won't it come *off*? Oh. Nah, cannot go to Jalóheim."

"Well we can't very well eat here or … you know … survive in this rocky wasteland."

Hana shook her head hard. "Uh uh."

"Why?"

Hana grit her teeth digging at the band, nails cutting into her skin. "Come *off*! Alvin it won't come off!"

He went to her and took her wrist. "You're cutting your own skin."

"There has to be a clasp or hinge!"

But there wasn't. "Let me see what I can do. Keep talking."

"Talking?"

"About the Expanse. Jalóheim. Your home. Any of it."

She seemed disinterested, but humoured him. "Cannot go home. We, we got droughts and—and food is scarce. Daily rations." She held up her waterflask. "See? Everyone in Jalóheim has one. We go to the wells twice each day. No more." She tucked it away. "You trade for everything. For food. Blankets. Clothes. Sometimes other things. That is life in Svaraheim."

"What else is 'life in Svaraheim' to your people?"

"What else?" she answered, and fumbled, kicking the dirt around at her feet. "It is a lonely place. You put down your things and find them gone.

What is yours is what you can take. Your Chieftain is lord. And your life is
... waiting."

Alvin tried prying the band apart where he thought it should separate. It
didn't. Nothing helped. "Waiting?"

"For the Last Journey Home. Lifetime after lifetime. Waiting for Jalós
to see you. To bless you."

"Something must've changed," said Alvin, sliding his fingers under the
edges of the band, trying not to hurt her.

"Hmm?"

"For them to have sent you now. They must've wanted that book—or
incandescent."

"Oh. Yah. Things have changed. But it is cold, out here. And the
Istlunders watch all land east of Jalóheim."

"I'm sorry, Hana. It won't move."

"What is it?"

"I don't know, and I don't want to hurt your arm trying."

She cocked an eyebrow at him. "What does it matter if it hurts?"

"What's it matter? It's wrong, is what. I won't let you get hurt if I can
stop it, I won't."

Hana laughed a little. "You are so strange, Alvin."

"Ain't nothing strange about it!" He stood to proud feet. "I swear I will!
Might be nothing but a Third Class Engineer but Orphan fellows, we know
how to be gentlemanly, unless you're some git from Wesbeldt." Alvin sat,
and made himself comfortable ... sort of. "Anyway, I'll get you home to
Jalóheim. You've my word as an Esker."

"Alvin..."

"You'd prefer staying in this hovel?" he reminded her. "I tell you, we
can't very well make a posh estate out of this wreck. How would that work?
We start farming all the rock, then?"

"Fine!" she snapped. "Cannot stay here, but the Rift is bad. It is." She
started pacing.

"You mean other than not dying out here of starvation or thirst or
lightning or falling rock or whatever else there is that's likely to kill us? Are

there wolves in the Expanse? Probably wolves."

She pointed to herself. "Survived all the way from the Rift to Iron Hollow, remember?"

"Who did?" he asked, goading her just a little. "Because if you mean that *you* did you might say 'I' did."

She arched back, as haughty as she could manage. "Don't do that."

"Won't you say 'I did'?"

"Stop it."

"Try it."

"*I* did!" she barked at him. "I did! *I* survived. *I* did not live *my* whole life in a palace! I – I – I – I – I! Happy?" She leaned against the opposite wall and wouldn't look at him.

"Suppose I had that coming…"

"Stupid idea to go to the Rift."

"Stupid?" he defended.

"Yah. Stupid."

"Well … you didn't think breaking into the Heuridium was stupid," he reminded her.

"Maybe it was."

"Well next time, I won't!" he snapped. "I oughtn't have even done that! Maybe then none of this would've happened, and Orphan wouldn't be dead on the Expanse!"

"Then maybe you should have listened to Tabitha and sent me back where *I* came from!"

"Well next time, I might!"

"Good!" She plopped against the wall and heaved an angry breath.

The wall was harder than Alvin's fist thought it would be.

He cursed at it under his breath, and rubbed his sore neck, rolled a pebble over with his foot a time or two. Hana rubbed her arms and shut her eyes to herself for a long moment.

When some minutes had gone by, long enough for Alvin to get a lump in his throat over how horrid he'd been, he reminded her, "We still gotta go to your village. Unless you know somewhere else." Alvin went to the entry and looked west. The land was dark, and full of rolling, veiled hills. "You called that place the Shift," he said.

"Yah. Ground goes this way and that, can swallow people up whole, but we can go around it. It only takes two more days."

Alvin faced a sky without glass between him and it. Jupiter just barely showed itself over the horizon, and there hung Capella further up.

The storm rolled to the south.

He sat down beside Hana, closer than he'd originally meant but then it was too late to move without being obvious, but she didn't seem to notice.

"Listen," he said with a hard swallow. "Today's been—it's been rough. Real rough. Tabitha. We fell from the sky. You sort of got tortured. Light burst around my head, I think, but it's all sort of fuzzy. I turned my ankle on a rock out there. And I'm hungry, but we—we'll be alright. I know we will."

She leaned her head back and eyed the ceiling, laboring to eek out the words, "I am sorry," especially on the 'I.' "You are not stupid."

"Not stupid," he said, tossing a rock. "I missed my own sister's memorial. *Twice.* I hid you from my family when I ought've asked father for help. Flipped the switch on that blazing incandescent because my own curiosity got the better of me, and I couldn't protect you in any of it. And I let Tabitha get herself shot. I think I earned 'stupid,' today."

Hana eyed him funny. "You do not need to protect me."

"Still ought've."

She kept eyeing him funny. "Why?" It was his turn to look at her funny, but he didn't answer. "The Rift is no help," she insisted. "We turn northeast once we circle around the Shift. Atí lagi?"

"Atí lagi," said Alvin, still unsure what it meant.

She got up, and within moments, had drawn some old kindling from around the ruins and perched them in its center. Alvin had matches, and the fire was welcome. He'd made plenty in his time, but always in stoves, or in the hearth. He discovered a darker side of wind, then.

For the first time since they'd discovered their little hovel, Alvin inspected the curious ivory stone. He felt a hand along its smooth surface— too smooth. It was cut so perfectly as to have no real texture to it, but somehow wasn't shiny. And when the firelight it hit it, it made shadows of hundreds of shallow etchings of circles, lines, runes, and other marks. He'd never seen anything so intricate and perfectly fit together. Even Orphan's best engineering couldn't product mason work like this.

"Hana? Do your people know where these ruins come from?"

Hana, nestling herself into a rehearsed position, tightened into the best knot she could, her hands tucked between her knees and her scarf rolled into a pillow. "The Elder days," is all she had to say about it.

Alvin, meanwhile, couldn't rid himself of the memory of her running for those stairs. *She would have left him there.* She had every reason to, he reminded himself, but it was an unpleasant conclusion. She wouldn't stay still. Eventually, her scratchy voice whispered to him in the dark of the hollow, just when he would've usually been asleep.

"What did they mean by all those things?"

"Things?"

"Up there," she clarified. "They thought there was a … something inside me. In my head? And that light around yours…"

"Something projected from that machine, I guess," Alvin finished. "Bollocks if I know." The lens of his mind kept tilting toward his father, and brother.

She shut her eyes, and lay still with her shadow draping against the wall from the crackling fire. "Your sister. Did she believe in Agarta, before she died?" she asked. "Like your uncle?"

"Don't know. You're asking the wrong Esker," he reminded her. He stared into the fire, talking to it more than Hana. "She'd have liked you, a lot. Would've thought you were terrific. Did anyone in your village ever…"

Hana was deep asleep. Her mouth parted. He watched her, and with no one to observe him, he kept on watching, the shape of her face, the stray hairs that would drape over it, the tiny movements of her breathing. Meanwhile, his entire world—everything he thought he ever knew about anything—slowly and methodically disassembled itself.

Just like the real one was about to do.

in which not all lost ones keep wandering anyway

THERE WASN'T MUCH TO DO about the solitary waterflask they had to survive on, other than blink at it. Which they did a lot of. Both Alvin and Hana sat in their little den and took inventory of how doomed they were.

"You brought … the spyglass…"

"Telescope. What of it? Look, it's a little much to ask me to predict that we'd be exiled from the towne nobody's never left! I mean, Uncle Otto did and Agnes almost—"

"But why is it *in* here?"

Alvin contemplated admitting that he put it in his bag because of his plan of taking Hana to the Agromatic Gardens, but decided, no.

"Thought it might be handy."

"Only the girls carry this much stuff, in Jalóheim, but most do not own this much."

"It's an explorer's bag, I'll have you know!"

"You have never gone anywhere," she reminded him. Alvin swallowed what he wanted to say. "Cannot eat it, either. Leather, maybe on a fire…"

"You try to eat my bag and give you what-for! It'll prove itself useful."

"As food, maybe. Leave the spyglass. It will weigh you down."

"It won't. Besides, we can spy the distance with it. And I weren't thinking we'd find ourselves—you stole that thing?!" he hollered when Hana causally produced the Oculix from her coat and sat it on the hard ground.

"Yah?"

"Why—why would you steal that?! How did you even do it?!"

"Good at it."

"Good at—at *stealing?!*"

"Yah. Took it when all that stuff went boom." She gestured with her hands. "Boom! Nobody was watching it."

Alvin rubbed his forehead. "You're banging on about my spyglass and you brought that rubbish thing!"

Hana flushed, right eyebrow twitching a little. "This is what brought me here. Cannot go home without it—"

"You thought it was a book!"

Hana displayed her wristband. "*This* stupid thing could stay if it would come off!" Alvin grabbed the Oculix, but Hana wouldn't let go. She inhaled to shout at him, but had nothing.

"And that fool thing didn't do nothing but sting my eyes and set off whatever in blazes happened back there!"

It was the first time he'd thought of it in so many hours, and it drew his mind elsewhere. Light that just—just *hovered* in the air like that...

"What is wrong with you?"

"Hmm?"

She'd pulled the Oculix from his hand and he hadn't even stopped her. "Keep it, not like *I* want the fool thing. But I'm taking my spyglass."

"Alvin!"

"Ain't leaving it out here to rot in this barren rot! It—was hers and..."

Hana sighed and snarled at the same time, a habit of hers he was picking up on. Then she huffed, paced around the tiny ruin before planting herself firmly in a folded huddle with herself against the wall aside what they chose to call the door.

"If you don't mind me saying so," Alvin broached, "you seem doomful."

She glanced up. "Any food?"

"Three of Mum's rolls. Why did they send you?" Alvin asked, abruptly.

"What?"

"I mean, why *you*? A girl your age? Did you volunteer?"

"Yah, volunteered," she said. She stood again and crouched over the pile, gripping her thick hair in her fists. "Look, we can—maybe if we had…" She held herself still, passing over deep, long breaths to still her body. Finally she asked him softly, "Say we can do this."

"Pardon?"

"You called me doomful. Stay out here long enough … yah, you become doomful. Jalóheim is doomful. They sit. Linger. Wait for the Sign. Always barely enough food. Yah, it makes you doomful. So. Say … we can do this."

"I don't think I understand what—"

"Just say we can do this, Alvin!"

"We can certainly do this! No question. None at all, and nothing like it. We'll survive, and won't die, neither. We're champions! You and me."

But he felt sick inside. He chose not to tell her.

It seemed to switch something on inside her, pathetic as the attempt was. She nodded to herself, repeated it under her breath a few times, and got up. "Atí lagi. Let's go."

They packed their things mostly in Alvin's adventurous satchel, and the two travelers assured each other that they weren't going to die. Probably.

Hana sucked in a couple quick breaths. "Alvin?"

"Hmm?"

"To the end of the earth, yah?"

"I think I might throw up."

"Oh come on, Alvin!"

"No it's not what you said—that was lovely—it's just all a lot to take in. I'd say hang it all and let's knock off for lunch, but there ain't any Songbird out here, most likely." For once in his life, he didn't say anything else at all, and it seemed to worry Hana, who kept stealing troubled glances at him. He shut his eyes and gripped to the strap of his satchel like a tether that held his life.

Hours and hours they walked in silence. Alvin started counting the number of "orphans" they crossed by evening. These two shelterless youths, they were phantoms, swept on iceward winds toward a precipice they didn't understand.

--- --- --- --- --- --- --- --- --- --- --- ---

Alvin sat opposite Hana with her inscribed waterflask on a stone between, and she insisted, "Hit me, if I touch it. Hard. Got it? Goes both ways, too, so watch out. I swing for teeth."

It had come to rationing, and so the dark little bargain was made.

Alvin smirked. "You're saying 'I' now."

The final hour of the sun had come and gone for many weeks, and now came only rolling, perpetual twilight and the high aurora to light the way. They'd made camp along a ridge with some backing, so the wind wouldn't hurt so much that night. Alvin pulled his notebook from his satchel and started sketching something in the dim, green glow.

"What are you doing?"

"Didn't you make a map when you came through?"

"Nah. Why?"

He paused. "So you could make it home easier."

Hana blinked, several times, and tried taking her goggles off, apparently having trouble again. "Not good with maps." She fiddled more with her goggles but got nowhere.

"Here." He reached behind her ear where the metal piece hid beneath the thick head of hair, and freed it for her.

Hana eased it off, and rubbed her face. When done, she looked to him, rings of indented red pressed along her cheekbones and forehead. Alvin choked on his half of roll when he saw her.

"What?"

Soon he erupted in hilarity at the ridiculousness of her face, almost crying (if he'd had any hydration) from laughing so hard and so sudden.

"What?!" she yelled.

"You look like war paint! You've got this … from the goggles…"

"Well you look like a girl with that girl bag!"

That made him laugh harder. "I'm sorry. I am. I don't mean to laugh at you! You're just funny."

"Ugh!" Hana got up, and busied herself with pulling in some kindling from the many broken husks of what used to be trees. Alvin lit it, only losing three matches. He would need to improve, but they weren't as sheltered that night as the one before.

"Hana? You said you found out all about Orphan from somebody in your village," he said. "The people who sent you? I'd like to talk to them when we get there."

Hana shook her shaggy mane. "Nah. If we are caught, let me do the talking, Atí lagi? Any of your mother's roll left?"

He tore off a hunk of a roll and tossed it to her. "Hana? What aren't you telling me?"

"Nothing. Drop it, please."

"There's something more that—hey! Don't walk away from—"

"I *failed*. Alright? I failed." Hana was cornered and there was no escaping it. She slumped to the ground. "I cannot *go* home, Alvin! I *failed*."

"Well it's not like it's a law or something." She turned furtive eyes up at him. "Is ... *is* it?"

After a long and stolid moment, her guard withered, and she sighed. "I had to bring back the book. I have no book. I cannot go home like this. But there is nowhere else, either! Faldin would kill us. Even if other clans exist, I do not know where they are. And we have two rolls to survive on."

He sat down too. "Still don't much understand why they'd send a girl your age, alone, on a mission like that, but what do I know? Look, you forget you're not empty-handed? You *do* have the—light-eye thing."

She held up the Oculix. "You think they will believe *this* is the <u>Dark Illumined Eye</u>?"

"Then why take it?"

"I was desperate. Atí lagi? But you said yourself, it did *nothing*. 'It *is* the book!' I'd say. A liar. That's what they'll call me."

Putting her back to him, Hana folded up on her side, head on her pack, and tightened up the neck line and sleeves of her simple Orphan dress as snug as they would go. He should say something. That much was obvious. But what? Meanwhile, Hana shivered. He almost had something, when her raspy voice said out low, "Always so cold," the last thing she said that night.

Alvin watched her for a time, wishing he could jump to his feet, fight the monsters, and make it all right. But he couldn't. In some ways, he *was* the monster in this little affair. He couldn't even stop her shivering, though he imagined wrapping his arms around her and taking the brunt of the wind, but he knew better.

He thought about it, though.

Alvin and Hana perched on the precipice overlooking her fabled Shift, looking the wrong way. They faced Orphan Towne. The pink clouds to the far south were serene, but Orphan Towne looked like the End of Days.

The path behind them was gone. The great stone plates that comprised the Expanse were breaking into husks, levitating into air, currents of thin lightning streaming between all the pieces.

All of it radiated out from Orphan.

"Getting bigger. How far will that go?" Hana asked.

"I don't know what that *is*."

Neither one needed to explain: *it was spreading out from Orphan.* Alvin pictured it as a great shockwave, but it was too slow for that. The Shift lay before them to the north, miles of lurching and churning silver sand and rocky masses, a great lake of desert without safe purchase almost anywhere.

"It'd be pretty if you were only here to look at it," Alvin noted. "What … did we *do?*"

"You think *we* did that?" Hana questioned.

"Seem to have. It'll go down that way in the *High Times*, and no mistake. 'Boy from Harchester Opens Orphan's Gates, Then Blows Up Entire Towne,' except it won't get past the headline because Orphan will be blown up by then."

Hana suddenly started, as if she'd puzzled out a riddle.

"What?"

"Nothing."

"No, you looked like you'd an idea."

"Nah," she said. "But you were right. We will go to Jalóheim. The Chieftain will know what to do. Come on. Boulders move, if you put weight on them," she explained. "They turn and sink and rise somewhere else."

"We have to go through, don't we?" he asked.

"If we do, we probably die."

The earth beneath them quaked in one sharp jolt. The crack of ancient stone motivated both. They bounded from the precipice, sliding down the slope of sandy incline and tumbling end-over-end until they rolled onto solid rock.

It wasn't really solid.

When it lurched side-long into the sand, Alvin grabbed her wrist and bolted up the incline to the next, and it did the same.

"Hana? Who is your Chieftain?"

"Eaorn," she yelled back. From stone to stone they leapt, darted, yelled and pulled and stumbled.

"And he's the one who sent you?" She didn't answer. "And told you about the tower?" Again, no answer.

Each huge fragment of the Shift listed and rose and fell with the smallest turbulence, keeping them moving without any hope of rest. Their tired legs carried them up and down newborn hills and ruts and slopes, and each time they landed on a new piece, they wished that it would be still. It wasn't. None of them were.

"There!" Hana yelled.

Atop one of the higher ridges stood an old dead tree, rooted in what passed for soil in the Expanse.

It wouldn't have survived on shifting earth, Alvin noted.

Alvin pointed, and they made straight for it. Up another slope, they bounded off the rim as the whole plate sank and turned. Hana's gait was agile and fast, but even she was tiring.

The last plate pitched forward as they landed, grinding against the solitary ridge that wouldn't move. It was too high to jump.

"Now what?!" Hana yelled.

"Alley-oop! Let's see how high you can jump!"

Alvin slammed his back against the wall and cupped his hands for her. It wasn't much. Alvin wasn't used to tossing girls about, but the few inches of boost was enough for her to grip one of the spiraling roots of that old tree. With a few steps back and a run of his own, Alvin caught her hand and jammed his foot into a cleft. Both travelers fell hard against the old tree at the top.

"Here." He pulled the waterflask from her side. "Drink."

Hana scrunched her brow at this but took up the flask anyway, and as she raised that last swig to her mouth, Alvin relied on the experience of brotherhood and lifted the bottom of the flask with a finger, dumping it all down her throat.

"Hey!" she gagged. " What are you doing?!"

There were no more than a few drops left, now.

"Father would strangle me if he found out I didn't give the last to you."

"Why?! I can handle being thirsty!"

"I'm sure you can," he said. "But now you don't have to."

"That is stupid," she panted. Hana weakly got to her feet and surveyed the land. "We are lost," she concluded, plopping back down with her face in her folded arms. "Lost and dead."

Alvin sat behind her, and for a few breathing moments, they rested their backs against each other. "You say that like it's nothing," Alvin noted.

"Say what?"

"That we're going to die out here!"

She shifted against him in soft heaves of hard breaths, his neck tickled by her hair. "I do not understand. We will live or we will die, like everything."

"Sure everything dies but … don't it do something to you? To imagine it? Everything just—just winking black? No coming back?"

"Death is part of life, yah? Do you know what my name means?"

"Actually, no. Well, the 'Jalóheim' part I suppose is your Clan, and Sóholdt is part of the village? That's what Tabitha thought."

"Yah. You know what 'Engindaut' means? Means 'nobody's daughter.' *Lofthana the Fatherless.*" A long moment of windy quiet passed between them before she spoke again. "You will die someday, but you have family now. So you will bury them someday. Would you rather escape that by having nobody at all?"

Alvin swallowed hard. For the past several years, he was the boy-who-lost-his-sister, an identity so obvious it never once occurred to him to see himself as the boy with a loving father, mother, and brother. He wanted to cuss himself, cuss the whole blazing mess, but fat good that would do anybody, which is precisely what his father would've told him.

What would his father tell him now?

Examine the problem instead of getting his cottons in a knot.

He tilted his head back against the tree. The low sky still glowed, but the brighter stars shown overhead.

He angled his head, and found the Pleiades, though he could hardly see them for the horizon's haze. The strangeness of what happened last time he looked into that cluster flashed in his mind, but so did something else.

"The Pleiades," he muttered.

"Huh?"

"The Pleiades," he repeated. Star cluster in the constellation Taurus."

"We are out of water. Unless there is water in Taurus and you can bring it here with that stupid spyglass, what does it matter?"

"There's Gemini, so that's northward, so…"

"We are *lost*. Stars do not give water…"

He hopped to his feet. "No, but they do give direction."

Her face contorted into baffled annoyance. "Huh?"

He knelt and pointed so she could trace his arm. "You see that bright star? The one to the right, and up a little."

"Yah?"

"That's Aldebaran. Now, if you follow—"

"They have names?"

"Didn't I just say the one was called 'Taurus'?"

"That was a constellation, not a star."

"I—but—it's really the same…"

One little laugh burst from her, and after a moment of weighing making a point against Hana's mood, he wisely chose the latter, and laughed along with her.

She caught her breath, and sighed a few times. "I have been mean to you. All day. You do not deserve it. Go on about the stars. I want to hear."

Cautiously he continued: "If you follow straight up from Aldebaran, you'll find Capella. That's the star I was watching when I discovered you."

"'Discovered' me?"

"What would you call it? Discovery, that's what, and no mistake. Now, follow Aldebaran diagonally, up and to the right. See that bright hazy spot?"

Hana angled her head and tried to look straight down his arm. Her hair tickled his jaw.

"Yah."

"That's the Pleiades. It's actually seven stars. If that's northeast, then we should see Jupiter over … there! Just over the horizon. See how you can see it even through the pale light? And there's Ursa Major above it. That's the great bear."

"Above that old wall, there?"

Alvin's eyes fell to the northwest, to man-masoned stone protruding through the Shift, arches and an open circle for a roof.

He squinted to see it clearer, and looked down at his own feet again.

Then up.

As he captured the sight of that dark sky, untold trillions of those cosmic sparks, he found that if he focused on any of them for more than a moment or two, it would strain his eyes, like what it normally felt like when he tried to see the dimmer stars behind the bright ones.

Only that wasn't it.

Something about the way they hung there, the shapes they made, pulled at his eyes and mind. One last time, he looked at the rock under his feet, then straight up overhead. "Draco," he whispered. "Hana, this ain't a rock! It's one of them ruins! Look! That's another. They wouldn't survive any more than this tree would if they weren't stable. They're patterned after

Draco!" Alvin took her chin and lifted straight up. "See?"

Hana looked at him like he was mad.

"The—the dragon. Constellation?"

"Already know they're stable, but getting to them? There are old tunnels under us, a maze. But nobody gets through them."

"What do you mean?"

"Too dark, and the paths all branch. Most lead into the Shift's currents again, and you get swallowed. It's why I went around."

"Can we get into them?"

"Yah. Think so." Hana slid down the side of their little hill just enough to find a gap in the stones, like an old ventilation window. "Here!"

Alvin followed, and squeezed his larger self through. They landed in almost pitch darkness, sand at their feet, but the ground felt stable enough.

Alvin drew out his lectral lantern, and shone it down the corridor. It was a strange place, massively wide and ornate arches and curves and reliefs along the walls of beings that looked inhuman, gods and planets and wars and villages, but he took little time to examine them.

"Could fit a small army in this place," he mused. Ahead, the path branched, but never stayed straight. Knowing which way to go would've been madness—if he hadn't thought of Draco. He quickly drew out his notebook, found an empty page, and sketched every angle of the constellation from memory. "Come on. We ain't lost anymore!"

Standing inside the dragon's 'head,' a great pavilion at the northwestern end of the Shift, Alvin and Hana found themselves scrambling up through a mostly caved-in gateway. Just to the west of them stretched another low ridge line, this one solid, like the rim of a titanic basin—the Shift's end, Hana assured him. Alvin swore he could see buildings where the land descended away beyond it into a deep canyon.

"The Rift," she said. "And … Jalóheim."

They last stretch was back to open sand. They bounded from the ruin to the highest rock, and immediately felt it angle under them. It was his turn to grab her and pull, but something was wrong. She dragged, stumbled here and there, and her usually bright eyes were glazed.

"Hana?" The rock they'd been walking on buckled in half, sinking into the earth, her leg sinking with it. "Hana!"

She panicked, gasped and pulled and dug at the rock but the larger plate sank down against her shin. She screamed, but it wouldn't move. Alvin pulled, but it wouldn't move. He jammed his foot against the rock aside her leg, wrapping an arm beneath hers, but he couldn't lift her free.

She was about to lose the foot.

"Alvin, the machine—the little one—hurry!"

Alvin understood. He drew out the little cylinder from his pocket.

"We left the other half at Orphan!" she said, clutching his hand that held it. "Push the button and take us back!"

"Hana? Hana stop!" He pulled it from her grip. Her small hand clutched his arm, fear washing over her face. He needed something to pry the rocks apart, but there was only one thing he had.

Alphonse, after all, was a craftsman.

"Agnes forgive me." Alvin jammed the eye end of his spyglass down into the crack, and pulled, pried against the weight of the rock.

The metal started to buckle but he pulled harder. One of the side mounts snapped clean off and the center shaft cracked down its length until Hana's battered leg scraped free, and they fell together onto firmer ground on the northwestern rim of the Shift. Alvin flung her arm over his neck and ran, pulling and dragging her up the slope of the rim as the land sank.

He jumped, and didn't make it far—but far enough. They landed and rolled onto the rock of solid ground beyond the shift, lay on their backs and breathed.

That's when the men came. Hana tried to bolt, but stumbled and pitched to the ground. Two of them came skidding at the awestruck sight of the Shift, at the churning land, at the lectral sparks flowing among the levitating rock and dust and earth.

"Jalós!" the younger muttered.

Like Hana, these men were golden-haired and lean. They seemed eager to come no further, their wide eyes turning from the horizon to Alvin and Hana and back. They exchanged a few words.

"Hey!" Alvin called. "Hey! You two! She's hurt!"

The younger glared, but when he looked closer at Hana, his face faded to horror. "Lofthana?" he muttered, and lifted the wounded girl off the ground. "Lofthana!"

Alvin watched him hold her carefully. He seemed near tears at the sight of her fainting eyes, but the other didn't, and would hardly look at her.

"Her leg's hurt!" Alvin explained. "Look, she needs food and water! She's the one you sent! We came all the way from Orph—from Iron Hollow."

The older one was busy scooping up Alvin's bent spyglass from where it lay near. The younger was still ghostly white, holding Hana. He would look long at her face, then up again at Alvin. "You … you cross the Shift with Lofthana," he said.

Alvin could only nod.

"How?"

"There's a safe way through."

"Where?"

"Where—what does it matter?! For land's sake, she's hurt! Can't you just help her?"

The older man came back to them, holding the telescope. The younger looked sick, and handed Hana gently to the older man, nodding his thanks. He came over to Alvin. "You. Her friend?"

"Wha … yeah? I'm her friend. Sure. Yes. Wha … ?"

"A way across the Shift. To Iron Hollow. Where?"

"I—look, if you'll help her, I'll show you. Here."

Alvin produced his notebook, and opened it to the map he'd made of Draco overlapping the Shift's ruins. He didn't understand the wait, or why any of this mattered now. Every second she draped in their hands made him more pensive and agitated, but this young fellow before him wasn't about to do anything without examining the map.

"Well?"

"Loftin?" said the older one holding Hana. Loftin…" He nodded to the notebook and said something in their native tongue that sounded like a command to Alvin. Loftin (apparently) shut his eyes. His breath quickened, and even his companion seemed worried, calling to him. "Loftin? Loftin!"

But Loftin clenched his teeth, and as Alvin himself succumbed to exhaustion, Loftin ripped the pages of the Draco map from Alvin's notebook, crumpled them, and flung them far into the churning mass of the Shift.

ENTRY 6: "THE SHIFT & OTHER UNMANNERLY ACRES"

Giving proper heed to the crucially somber tones of such mysteries, this entry will feature many words like "eons," "cryptic," and "non-euclidean." The reader has been warned.

Littered throughout the continent stand dark ruins of some ancient and cryptic people from the darkest eons of the world's forgotten days. Impossibly formed and forged of megalithic components (bricks, in other words), these ruins often align with astral patterns, particularly those in the Zodiac, though others get to join the party as well. Some in other Confluences and locations have come to call this exterior anomalies "Outcroppings," for whatever reason. Regarding the Expanse, many of such ruins exist, some in better or worse states than others, and one apparently erected in one of the most unmannerly and difficult pieces of land, commonly known as the Shift among the Galó locals.

The Shift is a region of land surrounded by high ridge lines. Unknown geometric forces beneath the surface keep it in a continual state of churning upheaval, resulting in constant overturning of the dry, crystalline sand, doing the labour of ten trillion earthworms every half hour or so. It's quite deadly. Long since viewed as a treacherous place by the Galó, the Shift is avoided by most settlers in the Expanse, though it has been used in times past for various and unpleasant initiation rites.

It is in this place that, of all things, major constructions of eldest days seem to reside, intricate and sprawling and majestic, though now mostly under the watery ground, making excavation not only impractical, but less than desirable. However, the mysteries beneath the Shift have intrigued many curious adventurers over the years, but most simply became examples to others.

Orphan's earliest scouting parties quickly decided that it wasn't worth the effort, and turned their attention to researching more useful things, and then produced proper book binding.

CHAPTER 14

in which strangeness multiplies aplenty

AT LEAST HANA WAS IN GOOD HANDS, and that cosmic wreckage was behind them, though Alvin worried anyway. It was the Heinrich in him. He found himself on what had to pass for a bed, in a ruddy little room in lamplight and low beams. Meanwhile, the headache was one for the ages. One day, minstrels would pen ballads of his headache, he figured, but it didn't make him feel any better. The cold cloth did, though. He tried sitting up, and failed.

"Shh." someone answered. An old metal cup was put to his mouth, the sweetest taste of busted-up tin he'd ever known, or maybe ever would.

"Thank you," he said. "Might kind of you, and no mistake. Is this Jalóheim, then?"

"Yah. Sóholdt." She spoke like Hana, poorer Anglish, but with a clearer voice than she ever had. On her head she kept goggles like Hana, old and battered.

"So dizzy. Are my fingers supposed to tingle?"

"Old Galó medicinal elixir. Calms nerves, eases pain, rests body."

"What's in it?"

"Do not know."

"Reassuring. Is Hana alright?"

His eyes cleared, and found her cheery young face shadowed in the thin blue hood of some ruddy ornamental robe, lit by flickering oil light. Stitchwork designs circled her face in white rings. Her eyes weren't different colors, either. Both blue. But the hair was unmistakable. It wasn't so ridiculously bright as Hana's, but still many shades lighter than *anyone's* in Orphan. She kept it in braids.

"How long?" he asked.

"Hmm?"

"How long was I asleep?"

"Ah. Sixteen hours. You are strange," she said. "Hair is so … *dark*." She ran her fingers through it. "You are rounder, too." She patted his stomach.

"Hey, kindly don't damage the gear, Miss … I don't actually know who you are. Should I?" He gently pushed her off.

"Sigrie Arnardaut cín Jalóheim fra Sóholdt," she returned.

"Author! You people have long names," he noted. "But listen, Hana—"

"Nah, '*Sigrie*.' Actually, it is 'Sigrieya,' but everyone calls me Sigrie."

"No—not you. I heard *your* name. Listen. A girl was with me."

"Oh, that is nice."

"No I—I mean a girl from *here*. From Sóholdt. I have to find her. Her name is Hana—or, wait—Lofthana, I guess."

"Guess? Are you not friends?"

"Well she has this long name, like yours, and (begging your pardon, Miss) 'Hana' is easier to say, but I'm pretty sure it's Lofthana. Lofthana Engindaut something Jalóheim something Sóholdt?"

He could pronounce it all fine, but was too lazy to bother.

She rolled the name around a few times, nodding passionately. "Oh! Yah! Lofthana! She lived in the Orphan Lodge up the hill. Mended coats for the stitchery. Not seen her for weeks…"

"Well she's the girl I'm after!" he asked.

"Oh yes. She is pretty."

"No, I don't mean—look, could you find out if she's here?" He couldn't rest in bed without knowing what had happened to her. "Please, miss, I mean. Sigrie. I've perilous need to see her."

"Wait! Do not get up—"

Rolling onto the floor was probably the most painful thing he'd done, ever in his life.

"You must rest!" she insisted, helping him to extremely shaky legs.

"I'll be alright," he explained. "I'm an engineer. I get hurt a lot."

"Nice to meet you, Anengin. You should get hurt less." Her warm face welcomed him as she laid him back to bed. The girl stood, saw to the lamp, cooled and wrung his washcloth, then tended a modest pot on the fire.

Alvin rubbed his eyes, and tried to fathom where in blazes he was. Spirals of blue and white and brown adorned old moulding. Sigrie crouched over the modest pot. She was dressed nothing like Hana, wearing some oddly ornamental drapery in blues and greys. The hem of her simple robes crumpled about her feet, but on its back was stitched an odd emblem, a red serpent, or dragon, or something like it.

Peering into the rafters, he found it carved into the main beam overhead, and elsewhere. It was a ramshackle place, old stone and misaligned wood, running over with dark, bitter drafts and musty stink.

"Listen, Miss? I hope you don't think me rude for saying so but … what am I doing here? Are you a physician? An undertaker? (Hope not…)"

"Nah, am an Arnardaut—*Sigrie* Arnardaut cín Jalóheim fra Sóholdt. Your memory seems bad. Here. Eat. Maybe it will make you think better."

Alvin's eyes widened to eager growl in his stomach, and it overcame his worry over the smell of it—for a moment. Once the bowl was in his hands, he bore in, and promptly stopped. Elise Esker, this girl was not, but the joy in her face stopped him from returning it to its bowl—took three tries to swallow it, and now it was a war between taste and hunger. Hunger won.

"She has to be here somewhere," Alvin mused.

"Hmm?"

"My friend," he explained. "She needs rest and food and we can…"

They can what? he himself wondered. What on earth *were* they to do? They couldn't go back to Orphan, at least not as things were now. Maybe there were answers here, maybe not. If he could find the man who sent Hana, maybe. *Someone* in Jalóheim knew about Orphan, and the tower and even that incandescent.

A sudden draft erupted interrupted his thoughts, and it carried a thin, old voice. "Sigrie?" He cast a long shadow, was unsurprisingly blonde, and eyed Alvin suspiciously. Despite his age, he was broad, and strong, weathered in beaten furs and wools and scars. A scarf hung around his neck, and he wore eye protection that he quickly pulled up.

"Would this be your house, then?" Alvin said around the spoon in his mouth.

"My father: Arnar," Sigrie told him.

He lifted himself again to stand. It took as many tries as swallowing the stew. "I'm sorry to invade what I take as your house, Sir. Sigrie was kind enough to feed me. That's really all I know. Name's Esker, Sir. Alvin Esker Um … Hugo's my father. Is that—is that how this works?"

He offered the old man an open hand, which was eyed, and ignored.

"Sigrie, why is he here?"

"Forgive me, Father. Priestess Tevir instructed me to take him to our—"

"She cannot. He is too many. He will eat from our stores, and eat too much. Drink too much. Look at him."

Alvin glanced down at himself.

"Father, the Priestess said—"

"Then it can come from her own stores! There is not *enough*, Sigrieya! Would you go thirsty for *him?*"

"I didn't mean to be a burden, Sir. I don't suppose you know what's happened to the girl who was with—"

"Speak when *asked*, Hugoson." Arnar slumped to a log bench, and rested his face in his tired hands. He looked nothing like Alvin's father, but when he sat, his body spoke a language Alvin knew well. "Have you seen it, Sigrie? The horizon?"

Sigrie brought him a bowl of hot stew and took a seat beside him on the log bench. "Yah." Gently she rested her head against his shoulder. "It is terrible."

"Horizon?" Alvin said to himself. "Oh no."

Alvin leapt to his feet and left his manners behind as he bolted through the door. Even when Sigrie called after him, he ran, not even conscious of the thrumming ache in his legs. He found himself in a broad and winding street, thatched houses placed aimlessly on either side. Alvin figured which way was east and ran for the nearest hill. The locals backed away from him or called out to others, but Alvin ran. Up the incline he rushed until he came to the lip of the cliff edge and scrambled high enough to have a vantage.

Ahead was the great arch at the entrance to Jalóheim.

"How?" he whispered aloud. "How is it still *there?*" But it was worse. The cosmic ripping-up of the world was stronger now, not lesser, a field of celestial rubble. Hunks of rocks and curls of crystalline sand turned in the air, broken and weightless. Whole mountains hung fractured in space. *Could they even be alive in all of that?*

His chest beat and the strangling ache in his legs caught up with him. It hurt to strain his lungs that much to breathe.

In laboured breaths came Sigrie up the hill, panting against her knees. "Too fast for me, Hugoson!" she said, and slowly rose to standing. "Nobody runs here." She looked for a long while at his face while Alvin's eyes locked ringed and tired on that horizon. "Does it frighten you?"

"I don't understand it," he answered.

"It is the Sign, maybe," she said. "Do you know?"

"Me?"

"You are from Iron Hollow. Iron Hollow is somewhere beyond *that.* Do you know what is happening?"

"Not enough."

"Come. You need more rest. It is my job to look after you. Priestess Tevir said. Come."

Sigrie snatched up her own small leather shoulder bag and put it on.

Alvin glared at it and sneered to himself.

Hana must never know.

She took his arm and turned him back toward Jalóheim proper, into Sóholdt on its eastern edge. It was a village built into the walls and floor of a canyon among the low mountains and foothills of the western Expanse—old timber and steep roofs meeting cliff dwellings like he'd read about in ancient history. The browns and blues of the buildings against the grey stone of the Expanse made the whole place drab, though splashes of aging color came in the form of pennants and decorative tapestries. Everything looked too old to be cared about by anyone alive there, though.

At the foot of the hill, someone watched them from the shadow of a building. They wore a robe like hers, sprigs of blonde hair jutting from it.

"Ha—Hana?" Again, Alvin bolted.

"Hugoson, wait! Not again…"

He stumbled and ambled his way back down the incline, and found it harder than the climb, and when he reached the edge of towne, whoever it was had gone.

Alvin held himself up on his knees and gasped for air. Used as he was to feeling it move and change temperature around him, it was thinner than Orphan's air, and he strained to fill his lungs. Sigrie again joined him, gently scolded him for running off, and invited him back to the house.

"She was right *here*. I saw her."

"Your friend?"

"She—she was dressed like you."

"Like me?" she asked. "Do not think so. There are no Lofthanas in the shrinemaids."

"Shrinemaids?"

"Yah. See?" she showed him her robe, as if he hadn't seen it. "Shrinemaid. There are six of us, but Lofthana is not a shrinemaid."

"Well that was before somebody sent her on a mission. Your chief, maybe? Priestess? Sigrie, who could've sent her? She said somebody here in Jalóheim told her about Iron Hollow, *details* about it."

Sigrie shrugged. "Don't know, Hugoson, but maybe now you can find out—the Serkers are coming."

"Pardon?"

Sigrie nodded to the lane up ahead, where a young warrior-looking fellow marched his way straight at Alvin. A weathered powder gun hung over his shoulder, and some battered old Nordic sword dangled on his belt, and weathered goggles on his head like everybody else. He was like a costumed viking, muscular but centuries behind Orphan's time—could still kill Alvin, though, by the look of him, so his antiquity didn't help.

"You," he said. "Come. Chieftain Eaorn wants you."

"Esig!" Sigrie returned. "He is not strong enough—"

"Enough, Shrinemaid. Chieftain summons him. He will come. Or I can kill him now."

In the shadow of Sigrie's front door stood her father, arms folded, scowling with a nod to his daughter.

Esig didn't even draw his sword or a powdergun. Alvin supposed he wouldn't need to. He'd been in more than his share of scrapes in his years on London Row, but wasn't fool enough to start a row with a viking, or what amounted to one by his look.

"It's fine, Sigrie. This fellow looks amiable enough, I'm sure. Just doing his job, and no mistake. I'd be delighted. A fine constable you'd make, I'd wager! I'm Alvin, by the—"

"Come. You waste time."

The chieftain of Jalóheim was an odd one. In his younger days, he might've been a warrior, but like most in Jalóheim that he saw, the old man seemed withered, his strength aged and unused, but he was still several times Alvin's size, great grey beard and ornamented furs and wools. His leather breastplate was emblazoned with the same serpent sign. It was only the young men who looked muscular enough to fit the clothes they wore.

149

"You are the stranger?"

"Alvin Esker, Sir. Oh, uh—Hugoson, I think you prefer. You'd be the chief of this—"

"You come from Iron Hollow?" he pressed. "With the—with one of our Clan, yah?"

Alvin squinted. Didn't he know? He had to. Who else would've sent her into Orphan Towne? The chieftain sat in a battered old chair that probably once looked almost kingly, but not anymore. Beside him stood an old woman, proud and piercing. She reminded him of Lorecroft with her hawkish nose and searching eyes, watching everything he did.

"Answer." Esig hit him hard in the back, and Alvin was just about to bark 'Hartchild!' back at him when he remembered what he was dealing with, and who.

"Esig, be kinder!" Sigrie snarled quietly.

"Why are you here, Arnardaut?" the chieftain pressed.

Sigrie bowed. "Forgive, Chieftain. Priestess Tevir asked me to look after the stranger. He is my charge."

Tevir nodded assurance to the chief, and Alvin answered the question before anything went more wrong. "I left with Hana—with Lofthana, Sir. It's just we two."

The old woman watched him down the length of her nose. Her robes were like Sigrie's, only far nicer and more elaborate. "Iron Hollow is supposed to be impossible to leave, Hugoson. You must have the faith of your chieftains."

"Don't know about that, Miss. Ma'am?"

"Priestess," Sigrie whispered.

"Priestess, Ma'am."

"Impressive that you crossed the Shift," she noted. "Nobody crosses it."

"Weren't easy, if that's what you mean, Ma'am. I mean Priestess."

"And what do you do in Iron Hollow? Are you a warrior's son?"

"Heavens, no, Priestess!" he clarified. "An Engineer, actually. Junior Grade, Third Class. Father's a tramrunner—a railroad man."

"Engineer. A *tinkerer*," she noted. "Do you *read* much, Tinkerer

Hugoson?"

"Re—read, Ma'am?"

"'Priestess,'" Sigrie reminded him.

Eaorn erupted from his chair. "Enough *nonsense*, Tevir!" He marched almost clear over Alvin. "Has Iron Hollow attacked us?"

"S—sir?"

"Is this their way of ending the Galó? Are you a criminal or a spy that you are here now? Perhaps the Proving for you…"

"Sir I—no! No I brought Hana—Lofthana back to you! She … she is alright, isn't she? Her leg—"

Esig hit him again.

"He is a boy, Eaorn," the Priestess noted.

"A boy of the Hollow!" he reminded her.

"And why send *him* as a herald to attack us? And he who so easily crossed the Shift? And so valiantly returned one of our own to us? I suspect he is a boy of many … hidden talents."

"One of our own," Eaorn scoffed.

"She is alright, ain't she—"

Esig hit him again, harder, and Alvin almost lost his head.

"Let the boy ask his question, Esig Ganikson," Tevir insisted. "Go on."

Alvin took the opportunity to sneer a little at his bully and straighten his jacket. "Lofthana, Priestess. Is she alright? Her leg was hurt pretty badly. Could I see her?"

"Soon, Tinkerer Hugoson. She is resting. Sigrie will take you to her when time is right. Chieftain?"

Eaorn studied Alvin closely, and the smell made Alvin's eyes water a little. It made him fear looking like crying in front of this tower of a man. "The Proving would—"

"We cannot put anyone to the Proving who has not broken Jalóheim Law, Chieftain, as you well know. The Law of Jalós is chiefest."

"He drains our waters."

"Yes, and has not Jalós been faithful to keep us at waterline? The boy has broken no law."

He spun, and returned to stand at his chair. "*Yet.* Then if not an attack," he asked Tevir. "Is this the Sign?"

"You will have your chance to conquer foes, my Chieftain. Patience—"

"Patience!" he snarled, dropping back into his seat. "My father was patient! *His* father was patient! And *his!* You ask for patience while we wither on, and on, and on, and now Svaraheim dies. We are people of the land, Tevir. Foes? There is a time for killing. Faldin has drunken deep from that well. We are Jalóheim! Where is a *land* that we might conquer? Yet Jalós asks us linger."

"The Oracle will tell us, after the Proving. Then we will know—but, my Chieftain, it might be best to have the people gather to leave."

"For Niavellir? And have them anxious for a Journey, only for it to be pulled from us again? Why torture them?"

Tevir touched his arm. "Perhaps we *have* been patient enough, my Chieftain." Then she turned to Alvin, Sigrie, and Esig. "Tinkerer Hugoson, return to the Arnar home, for now. Sigrie, you are awarded an extra water-right for his presence."

"Thank you, Priestess!"

"Esig, get Sigrie a tag, and escort them home."

The great doors of the Chieftain's Hall opened, and Alvin found himself again outside in the cold wind. Sigrie chattered about how well that went, about how exciting even the inkling of hope was that the deadly horizon might actually be the Sign of all Signs. She went on and on about it as they descended the long stairs back into the village lanes. Esig said nothing.

From that height, he could just see what he'd come to call the Upheaval in the eastern distance, and a lump in Alvin's throat welled up from the pit already widening in his stomach. There wasn't any way he could be responsible for this.

Surely there couldn't be.

But the device in the Heuridium *must* have started all this.

And whose stupid fault was that? He asked himself.

Alvin swallowed, and chose to focus on finding Hana instead of putting himself on trial for the end of the world. Where were his things? His satchel, and along with it, all his gear, including the crippled spyglass?

He slid a hand into his pocket, and found the little cylinder that landed them on the ground outside Orphan, that they almost set off when Hana's leg was caught. Alvin thumbed it, but couldn't use it without Hana in tow.

He chose not to ask about his other things with Esig present or let him know the cylinder existed, and so walked on northward while the meandering, thin and aimless people of Jalóheim gave wide berth and watched him pass. Way up ahead, a shape rose into the sky, but Alvin couldn't make it out in the dim light.

There was something odd about Jalóheim. Under all those buildings and huts and crude stone shrines rested something far older, and far, far greater. "Sigrie, how long as this village been here?"

"Many generations," she said.

Black stone ruins dotted the village, sometimes spread among the houses and sometimes under them, same kind as he found in the Shift. These were all cut to perfection with skill beyond rational explanation. There rose ivory columns and colonnades and peristyles and archways here and there, yet nowhere in the Expanse itself was any such stones to be found except in these kind of remains. Where did they get it? All of Jalóheim was like a vagrant shantytowne laid on the bones of Atlantean glory.

"Is water that scarce, here?"

She nodded. "Since the Yedak dried up, many years ago. Niavellir stopped its flow. Only the Three Wells are left, now. Come, we can stop at one!"

She led Alvin and Esig through Jalóheim until they came to a heavily-guarded well, with three young Esig-looking men around it. They gripped their powderguns as they approached.

"You have had today's ration, Sigrie," one of them warned.

"Priestess Tevir gave me another ration for keeping the boy from Iron Hollow," she explained, and handed over a small wooden tag.

They didn't seem to believe her until Esig nodded to them.

"Is water so serious, here?" he asked.

"There are few crimes more serious than watertheft, here," Esig gladly informed him. "Test it, if you wish to find out."

"I'll take your word for it."

They wheeled a bucket up from below and scooped what passed for water from it. "Shrinemaid, he has no waterflask."

"Oh. Yah. Forgot. Um. Esig?" Esig didn't answer but eyed her with distaste. "Oh give him yours!"

"Let him get his from the Priestess!"

"She has enough to do, today. You can get another easier than we can. If he dies of thirst, she will not be happy."

Esig snarled, took out his waterflask (exactly like Hana's), drank the last of his own ration, and shoved it at Alvin's chest.

"I—thanks, mate. Terribly kind of you."

"Get your water and keep walking."

Alvin left there with a flask of his own, marked *Esig Ganikson cín Jalóheim fra Issel* on its leather wrap, and they strode on through Jalóheim until they came past a spot Alvin had noted on the way there—a risen hill to the north, wide and flat and open, stone steps cut across is rise, but what made him notice was the great bronze spire thrusting from its top into the sky. Instead of a tip, the spire branched into various rings and arcs, like a great ornate trident. It was the shape he'd seen rising from the doors of the chieftain's hall.

Around its base, five shrinemaids in robes like hers worked on something, gathering rope and sweeping.

"The blazes is that?" he asked.

Sigrie's voice went low. "The Proving Tree," she said. "Come. Do not think about it."

"But what's it for?"

"Please, Alvin Hugoson. It is not good to think about—"

"It is where Jalós tests his people," Esig proudly interjected. "Accused are bound to the Tree. Jalós may spare them."

"And if not?"

"The Heavenly Spear with strike them." He said it with a grin that gave

Alvin worry, especially since that chief seemed eager enough to have Alvin put to that thing.

"And … what are they shrinemaids doing there?"

"Esig, please!" Sigrie objected. "He does not need—"

"Tonight is the Proving Rite," he said. Some sick part of him wondered if the next grinning word wouldn't somehow be 'Lofthana,' despite Alvin knowing better, but Esig continued with only, "For Loftin."

"The fellow who carried Hana?!"

Sigrie couldn't bring herself to look at the Tree. "For … for throwing your map into the Shift. It was a crime against Jalós."

"Crime? I'll admit, my notes and stories *were* legends back home but…"

"Your things belong to Jalóheim, not to Loftin," Esig corrected. Alvin was all set to demand to know what happened to the rest of it, but decided, *no*, not with this git on his heels. They passed a granary, a textile workshop, crude ironsmith, and even something like a meat market, though what meat they had out here, he couldn't guess. Esig started barking instructions to both of them that Alvin not leave the house unless summoned, and he said it in a way that made Alvin sure that leaving would mean dealing with Esig's gun, or sword, or both. But while he was talking, someone up behind the Arnar house darted away into the alleys between, someone in a priestess robe, hooded—the one he'd seen before.

"Sigrie?" Alvin asked. "How many shrinemaids are there?"

"We are six."

Five had been at the Proving Tree. He said nothing about what he'd seen. Arnar, thankfully, wasn't home when Esig left him and Sigrie there. Glad as he was to be inside again, it was no Esker brownstone, and his mind could do anything but rest. There was Hana to think about, and what in blazes they were to do now. It was obvious that Jalóheim would give them no help, nor even time. He'd set off more than just an incandescent, and this sank into his bones as he settled onto the cot where he'd woke up before.

His mind turned to his father, mother, to Alphonse, and even some of the gits on London Row, to the Songbird and the Lager than Life, to his room and books and notes and smell of Elise Esker's cooking, and never felt more the foreigner than now.

Was this what it was like for Hana, coming into Orphan?

Sigrie excused herself to fetch a wood ration for the fire, and Alvin turned his attention to the window above his bed. It faced west, and on *that* horizon hung a wicked storm, billowed blackened rolls like those that hit Orphan the day they left it. It would be there by night. Alvin didn't have time to watch through his window for long. The earth beneath him shook and trembled. Walls of his room cracked from the bedpost up into the corner, raining chips down into his hair. People stumbled in the streets, and dove for support. They cried out. Others bent in prayer to Jalós.

Oh Author, he realized. It wasn't stopping.

When he turned away from the sill, he found a little stone outside the pane that pinned a folded bit of paper. From Hana, he figured. Who else could be the mystery shrinemaid? It took some doing to open one of the panes, but he managed it, and reached around to snatch the little message.

You can't stay in this place.

You are in more danger than you know, here. A long time ago, Orphan's ancestors found a lot of secrets in the Expanse, especially in the North. It's where they found the way to bend the world like you're seeing now, and it's just the beginning, and these people know it. Don't expect anything except treachery and theft. But in the western side of the village is a temple, where you'll find some answers, and me. Only the Priestess and her shrinemaids are allowed into the under-chambers. But you're clever, aren't you?

Find a way. I'll be waiting.

—A 'shrinemaid' of Jalóheim

in which various hearts skip, with or without help

ALVINHEIM LOCKWILDE ESKER WAS MANY THINGS, but none of them were particularly strategic. It wasn't like he knew what he was doing, or had set out on some clandestine quest. What he actually wanted was to go *home*, to his (wishfully) waiting bedroom, his models and books and notes there around him, his thick blankets and Orphan's finest cooking, with the west-facing window where he could just see the stars through the dome over the neighbor's rooftop.

The letter was from Hana. This, he knew, but it still didn't make sense. And what danger? Was Sigrie…? She snoozed in a big chair across the room. *No.* Not her. Her shrinemaid robes lay across the arm of the chair. Itchy things, by the look of them, she'd shed them quick as her duties of the day were over, and lay there in her more Hana-like clothes, half under a fur blanket on the chair.

Until the earth quaked again and pots fell from the hearth with a *clang*.

"Hugoson!" she started, and ran over to him as the house trembled to its beams. Dust and bits of the roofing spilled to the floor. Biting her lip didn't seem to help, but finally she muttered lowly: "Will we live?" The girl seemed as if, at any moment, she would fall to his chest and cry. Why did she think *he* knew anything?

A plea pooled in her misty eyes.

"Sigrie…? What are you talking—"

"It comes closer. Doesn't it?" She fumbled for his hands and gripped them. "You know. You have to. Iron Hollow is a wondrous place, we've heard, the great city alight. The place we cannot go. Surely you know…?"

"I don't know what's going to happen, Sigrie. I don't. I'm only an Engineer, I am, and a Junior one at that. Third Class, actually."

"Some are saying it is the Sign," she said. "It never seemed *real*. What … what if we are too slow to outrun it? What if Jalós hasn't opened the gate at Niavellir?"

"Gate?"

She nodded. "There is a book. We were supposed to have it before the Sign came, but nobody knows where it is. It is the only way to open Niavellir's gates into Agarta. We do not have it. If this is the Sign, we are not ready. If it is *not* the Sign … then what?"

Alvin's stomach sank into a pit. Whatever he would do, whatever the letter meant, he had no more time to plan. There was no time left. But the *surrender* approach was never in Esker blood, nor even in Heinrich blood. They were railway men, the lot of them, builders, fixers, tinkerers. Men of tools. Give an Esker a clamp and spanner and he'd build Orphan Towne, but Alvin *had* no tools.

"Will you stay with me, Hugoson?" she asked without looking at him. "You … you are not like men here."

Or did he?

Her robe draped across the arm of the chair across the room. And Alvin saw—there was something he could leverage there, a tool in the making. He *had* to. He would. "Sigrie, I don't know much of nothing, but it'll be alright. It will. Don't give up hope now."

"Nah?" Alvin awkwardly set his hand on hers. "Why not? There is never hope in Jalóheim, only year after year of waiting, withering, dying."

"Hope—hope is the thing that shapes what you dream for. Ain't it? It's the thing that stands up taller than all those things, like a mountain you can always see, if you look up at it. Least, that's what mum says. What do *you* hope for?"

Her brow furrowed. "Nobody has ever asked." She paused, thought a moment, and started to speak before stopping herself. "You are kind."

Alvin swallowed. He found he had to pull away from the sudden gaze from her blue eyes. What was he doing? His gut told him it was something horrid, but his thoughts demanded, *go on.*

"Sigrie, what kind of meat did I see at that stall, earlier?"

"At the Swap Market? Goat jerky."

"You keep goats?"

"Many, mostly in Issel, not much in Sóholdt. For milk and fur and fat. Old ones are killed for meat. You like goat?"

"I'd love to know how well you can cook it!" he beamed.

Sigrie nearly bounded off the cot. "Yah! Father loves it, too! We have enough ration tags, too! Uh, wait a little?"

"Of course."

She flung on a scarf and strapped her goggles back on top of her head, yanking her boots onto her slender feet. "Be back with meat for dinner!"

She hurried out the door, and Alvin swallowed the sick feeling in his stomach. Once she was gone, he swept up the shrinemaid's robe and made for the window into the alley swinging one leg over the sill.

"Sigrie, we have—"

The front door swung open, and Arnar stalled on his heel. So did Alvin.

"Oh bollocks…"

"You—what—" Arnar leaned out the door, calling loudly, "Sigrie!"

"Oh no…"

"Yes, Father? Was just bringing some goat for…" She stopped in the door, swallowed, and looked at him with bafflement.

"Let him run, Sigrie. Keeps him out of this house. Let Svaraheim deal with him."

"But—but it is my job to—"

"No, Sigrie. Chieftain had just told us. Priestess says this is the Sign. Time to leave."

She couldn't take her misting eyes off Alvin. "But…"

"Pack, Sigrie! The cart will be ready soon. Leave him to his fate."

Arnar slammed the door, and left Sigrie alone with Alvin, who slumped back to the cot. Silence lingered over them both for a long, long moment.

"You … do not like goat, do you?"

"Never actually had it," he said, and tried to laugh.

Sigrie was not amused. She noted the empty armchair and Alvin's sudden luggage. "You wanted my robe. Why?"

"Listen, Sigrie—"

"Tell me *why!*" she yelled, louder than he thought possible, an almost Hana-level outburst.

He hadn't thought of it as a matter of truth or lies but of life and death, until then, and now it made little difference when he thought of saying it aloud. "You're right. I weren't interested in dinner, or in staying."

"You lied?"

How he wanted to back up the world thirty fool seconds, but nothing he knew could revert her innocent face to before it twisted into its present anguish. It had been a long time since Alvin knew what that kind of shame really felt like. He would've traded a limb to be free of it.

"I lied."

She put a hand over her mouth, and drew back. Her eyes welled.

"Sigrie, I can't explain everything, but I have to…"

A quick shake of her head, and she was gone. Door shut. That was that. The absence of her cheery voice settled like dust. Her crying came to his ears from outside, though. Alvin hit his head against the nearest beam some eight or nine times before perching on the bench against the back wall, and gripping his ragged brown hair in his fists, pulling against his own scalp.

"What are you doing, idiot?" he muttered to himself, certainly the most contemptible Esker who ever blackened the name. All of it came onto him at once—*he'd lost his home, his family was probably dead already, Tabitha too, no word from Hana but a cryptic letter and impossible mission.* After these thoughts came every stupid, brash, or immoral thing he'd ever done in his fool little life. It all circled his horizon until he wept.

Until the door opened again.

Sigrie's face was painted in shades of red still. She leaned against the door. "You were crying," she said.

"Uh…" He couldn't hide it. "So were you."

"Everybody lies in Jalóheim," she said frankly. "Thought you were different. Prove you are. Tell the truth, now," said Sigrie, red around the eyes, but composed. "At least tell me that much."

A deep crack, like the sound of thunder beneath the earth, sounded across the valley. "I'm the reason all of this is happening. Hana came to Iron Hollow looking for your magic book, and I—I helped her find it."

Her eyes broadened. "You have the book?!"

"Not exactly. Hana does, but I don't know where she is, and it ain't no book. Don't see how it can help. But listen, she contacted me, left this letter on your window." He produced it and handed it to her as proof. "She's waiting for me in the Temple of Jalós."

"My robe," she said. "Alvin Hugoson, you cannot go in there. Even the shrinemaids are only allowed to watch the entrance to the lower chambers. Only the Priestess goes past that. If the Serkers find out, they will kill you."

"I didn't have any other way."

"But how did *you* cause what is happening?"

"Mucked about with a machine I oughtn't have. Look, it weren't supposed to be a weapon! It was an accident, but if there's a way to stop it, I'll do it! That's why I … tried to nick your robe."

"I'm sorry," he told her. "I used you. It … it were wrong of me."

"Been used before," she said. "What other way is there?" She sighed, and turned her eyes to the rafters for a long moment. "You love her. Lofthana. Yah?"

"She's my friend."

Sigrie laughed to herself. "This is not the Sign, is it?"

"Can't say."

She nodded, at first to herself, and to him. "Give me my robe." When he handed it over, she swiftly slung it on. "You cannot be seen without me. You will take it when we get past the storehouses."

"I don't understand. You're doing this?" Alvin asked her. "But I—I was horrid to you."

"Yah?"

"Isn't this a crime?"

"Treason."

"Treason?! If this gets back to you, you'd be put to that tree-thing?"

"Yah. Exile is for lesser crimes like watertheft. It would mean the Proving. Take Mother's old dust lenses. You will need them."

"Didn't know your mother lived here, too," he noted.

"Dead now. She doesn't need them."

"Sigrie, you can't do this. Let me go alone."

She cocked her head. "You would be caught without me, and they would Prove me either way for letting you escape."

"And if *you're* caught?"

"You asked me about hope. What better thing to die for than somebody who made me feel it? Somebody who needs me."

Alvin's stomach sank into a pit. He just stared at her innocent face as she straightened her robe. Her cheeks were still ruddy from crying, and when she noticed him looking, she flashed a fake smile.

Sigrie acted like she was giving him a tour as they left Sóholdt, despite the massive storm rolling in. She showed him everything there was to see—*everything*. She first revealed the Cleansing Room, which Alvin assumed was some ritual chamber, but turned out to be where they kept the mops.

At his request, she even hurried him through the Orphan's Lodge up the hill, and in its dark recesses, he found Hana's home. A cot, a few personal trinkets, and a tiny trunk of clothes. Her immersion into his little world seemed far less surprising, then. They went on.

"Sigrie?" he asked. "What do you know about Istlund? Are they another village from your tribe? Hana mentioned them a lot."

"Another, yah. Our tribe, nah," she returned. "Istlund is where Clan Faldin settled."

"And they're the violent lot?"

"Yah. Faldin kills wanderers. They *give* life to the land to *get* life from the land. Growing food is not easy, here."

"And, did you all migrate here together? You and Faldin?" he pressed.

Sigrie shrugged. "Jalóheim. Faldin. Ormisson. Farasson. Maybe. Four tribes in Svaraheim, only two left. Truthfully? Never listened to history much. Probably should, but didn't."

"What does the symbol on your robes mean? The serpent or whatever that—"

"Uroboros," she answered. "Jalógander—the Seal of Jalós. Jalós is without father or son, beginning or end. Serpent eating its own tail."

Aimless, the people of this village might've been, but not slow, not now that the Upheaval was closing. The ascension of the great stone plates of the Expanse was visible even over the walls and rises, as if gravity itself had been dismantled like a tram engine. A gathering had begun up ahead, just past the pavilion Sigrie told him about. People clamored to watch, but kept low as the sky overhead lit with bolts of light and raging thunder.

"What's happening there?" he quietly asked Sigrie.

"The Proving." She pointed. "Even now, they will test Loftin. Jalós must judge his heart, now."

"And if Jalós judges badly?"

"Then he dies. It is quick, at least, the Heavenly Spear. You have no law in Iron Hollow?"

"Sure we do but … I guess I just can't picture this."

"The law is everything in Jalóheim, Alvin Hugoson. *Everything.* None are above it, not even the Priestess or the Chieftain."

Alvin couldn't help but gaze up at the highest steppe of the hilltop. The base of that strange spire, someone stood bound to it by his wrists. It had to be Loftin. Near him, the Priestess bowed and prayed and chanted some strange, foreign song. Many of the masses joined them.

As usual in the Expanse, no rains came, but raking, merciless wind and rage struck the towne like a wall.

Sigrie took Alvin by the hand. She lacked Hana's speed and boldness, but certainly knew her way around. Together they wove and slipped through the masses, between shoulders. When the people of Jalóheim weren't gazing at the Proving Tree, they were rushing to gather carts and packs and meager livestock. A small herd of goats ushered past them as they hurried westward, keeping out of the wind. Only a few labourers were still rolling carts from the granaries, when they came to the largest structure in Jalóheim.

Alvin gazed up at its height through his eyewear, where a singular shape of that serpent sign rose from its peak, like an old cross on a churchtop, but the serpent was a poorly made as most of Jalóheim. The temple's base, however, was another story, cut with impossible, enormous perfection from that ancient ivory stone. Something about its angles gave his eyes a struggle. Sigrid pulled him into a dark recess past the granaries near the Temple's entrance, and pulled off her robe.

"Here, Alvin Hugoson."

"You're sure about this, Sigrie?"

They had to yell over the wind.

She nodded, and fitted her robe on him as well as she could, drooping the hood over his face as much as possible. It almost blew away. "Your dark hair might be a problem, but it is dark, inside, and Priestess Tevir is at the Proving—"

A single volley of blinding light plunged down from the sky in the east, and as Sigrie pulled herself to his chest, he didn't need explaining. "Heavenly Spear," he mused.

Sigrie nodded against him. "Loftin was … he was nice," she said.

She shook her head, then looked up at Alvin one last time. "Speak *Ilonef kirin aldistan* to open the door into the lower temple. Never been past that, so know who knows what you'll find? Hopefully, your friend."

Now, Alvin Esker hardly had the feminine figure that suited the normal wearers of those robes, but he tried his best. He'd hardly been immune to observing the gait of the young Orphan girls as they strolled in groups through Bellamy park of a weekend, and fumbled his way through moving like they would, not thinking about what his father would do if he'd seen it.

Six Serkers like Esig stood guard, but gave him no pause as he went by. They didn't even look carefully at his face, which made him wonder if they ever had reason to expect intruders in here. Apparently not. The hall was like others in Jalóheim, but at the far end stood something different—a rise in the floor made of that same ancient stuff he'd seen in the foundation. Altars and torches and tapestries and statues stood all around it, but *it* was the heart of this temple. All the age and decay of this village was unknown on this deeper architecture; it looked as perfect and new as they day it must've been made. Strange symbols adorned its face.

Alvin took a glance back at the guards back at the entry, and said out low, "*Ilonef kirin aldistan.*"

With hardly a sound, the floor in the platform recessed, and vanished, leaving a long and massive stair. The warriors still hadn't noticed, and when Alvin stepped down inside, the door shut behind him.

How he wished he had his lantern now!

But soon it changed. A golden-amber glow struck his eyes. From within the strangely-angled, non euclidean walls, shapes were alight, strange constellations and similar forms. He knew the stars, but not in these patterns, and the way the walls angled bent his perceptions of everything, even made it hard to walk. This place was different from the others, deeper in its atmosphere of age and weight, and the very seconds in which he waded seemed to slow down, like wading through knee-high tides.

As he tiptoed through the long hall in search of Hana, he held out his hands along either side in utter wonder, and let his fingertips graze the carven stars—but none that he knew. Five moons passed under his hand, and strange stars of stranger skies.

He came to a vast and empty circular hall, constellation-lights casting the place in some astral golden glow. Which way? Something sounded from his right, a voice or something low like that, so he crept his way along the wall, drawing closer to its source.

"Hana?" he whispered.

Was that her answering? His heart raced. It had to be her! But it came from behind him. Alvin paused, craned back to see shadows coming into the great ring hall, and knew it was not Hana's voice.

"Last chance to settle the question of the gate," said the Priestess. Alvin caught only a glimpse of the three warriors behind one, but one was Esig.

"Oh bollocks!" he whispered, and bolted on his toes as fast as his legs would take him, further into the ring. Past a shut black door he hurried (couldn't possibly move the thing himself), all the way around the great ringed hall of astral lights, but he could still hear them coming—rushing.

They'd heard him.

He was halfway around the ring hall when he passed another great door, this one just open. He wouldn't stop, but did when a strong hand snatched him by the arm and jerked him into the opening. The door shut itself quietly, and Alvin held his breath.

"Shh!" someone whispered in his ear.

He could just make out the sound of rushing feet on the other side of the door, and Alvin leaned against the cool wall, and breathed. It was black as pitch, until the lights came on, and he found himself face-to-face with his rescuer as he was letting out the breath he didn't know he'd held.

Then he sucked it back in as their hood came down.

And Alvin immediately took a swing at 'em.

CHAPTER 16

in which many expectations are carelessly fractured

IT FELT SO, SO GOOD. MAYBE IT WAS THE RUSH of his making it all the way into this forbidden place, but once Alvin saw that hood come down and the ridiculous blonde wig along with it, and under it Ellery Hartchild's obnoxious face, he chose to belt him one, right across the mouth.

His hand throbbed but Ellery held his jaw and doubled over. "Ow! Corking *idiot!*" Ellery barked, and rightly so. Alvin hit him *hard.*

"Blighter! You tried to kill me!" He may've broken his hand. "Wait. *You* wrote the letter? Oh, why did it have to be *you?* I thought it was Hana —Hana can't read." Idiot, he told himself. "Uh! Could've been Mrs. Dutch or even Pike for all I care but anyone else except you and your *stupid ugly face!*"

"I just saved your arse, Esker! Ungrateful—"

"You put. A gun. To my head! What I ought've done is I ought've smashed your fool head into the rock and seen what *you* thought of it. What ever possessed you? And where'd you get a wig to—is this a mop?"

"Was," Ellery corrected. "*Was* a mop. Well I had to get here somehow!"

The two postured and glowered at one another in girls' robes, a contest both seemed equally matched for. They heaved hot breaths and showed their teeth and squeezed their fists until they both got bored. "What in blazes are you even doing here? Is Orphan—"

167

"Well it was standing when I left—no thanks to you—but I left right after your theatrical exit so … *ow…*" Ellery occupied himself with his face.

Alvin's next question was more reserved. "Is Tabitha…?"

"I don't want to talk about it."

"But is she—"

"I said I don't want to talk about *Tabby*, Esker!"

"Then—then what are you *doing* here?" Alvin kept his fists clenched, and Ellery certainly did the same.

Ellery eyed him up and down. "Think I'm here to hunt you for sport or something?" He reached around beneath his jacket, and drew out the arc pistol he'd had before, and before Alvin could react to it or even trip over himself (which is what he nearly did), Ellery spun it around and offered it.

"What…?"

"Take it," said Ellery.

Alvin did, to have it out of Ellery's hands. He was no stranger to dangerous tools but pondered where to put it or how to keep it secure without fear of the thing going off—he'd never seen such a weapon until that day atop Orphan.

"Here. Take the spare cartridge, while you're at it." He tossed the pistol's battery to Alvin, too. "Those have enough power in them to light your ruddy little brownstone for a week, so don't go waving them around. I won't lie and pretend I like you, Esker, nor any of your greasy brood. I think you're a tosser, but I didn't come to have it out with you. I'm here to bring you back"

"Why?"

"Your Infusion is—it's needed back in Orphan. You smart enough to understand that?"

"Smart enough to keep away from you, I'll wager. Wait—how'd you get one of these robes?"

"Nicked it."

"You nicked it?"

"From the stichery. Well? They do make new ones *sometimes*."

"How did you even know about any of this? You tell me what you know. *Now.*" He still had that pistol in his hand.

"Alright—fine!"

"What's happening to the Expanse? Will it keep spreading from Orphan?"

Ellery rolled his eyes, then pinched them. "Blazes," he muttered. "Where to even begin with you. Ugh. Esker, this isn't spreading from Orphan. It's spreading from *you.*"

"What?"

Of course Alvin trusted Ellery as much as Sigrie's cooking, but even the astral chance anything he said was true, it was the worst of what Alvin feared: "It's following you like a zipper across the Expanse. Anywhere you go, it'll come with you."

Alvin braced himself on the wall. "Me?" he mumbled. "I'm doing this? I *did* this?"

"Like a tosser."

"How? Why? What sort of fool experiment was this?"

"One that wasn't ready! And you had to stick your fool head into it. Look, the wave coming off you is trying to re-shape the Expanse. That's what it does, reshapes things."

"Reshapes?" Alvin patted himself for show. "What wave? Do you see a wave? A little smell, maybe but ain't nothing else to it except the wave of nausea your face causes me!"

"You're tearing apart the Expanse and reshaping it to a new blueprint."

What Ellery was saying made Alvin sicker than he already was. All he wanted was to take a curious girl on a harmless little adventure not far from his own brownstone—and then *this.* Go back and do more? He couldn't even entertain the thought.

"How can this happen? How can lights tear up a continent?"

"It's complicated—"

"Then simplify it for me!"

"And expect you to understand it? Ugh. Look, the wave changes particles. Or something. What? It's like a transmutation wave, changes matter from *one* design to another."

169

"You've had one too many widowmakers, is what I think. You sound like my sister, and all her theories were decades away from being anything more than a fever dream, and probably never would. You expect me to believe it's all up and running here you all are, just faffing about in the Heuridium, transmuting matter easy as you please? Just like assembling a sandwich, turns out! What'll we transmute next?"

"Esker, it's the truth. I didn't come here to fight with you!"

Alvin backed away from Ellery, and something in the hall changed. More lights came on, more of the inset astral shapes, but now they illuminated all the way down the long, ancient hall.

"But you know what this place is. Don't you?"

Hartchild swallowed, and nodded. "I think so."

"What's down there?"

Ellery groaned, turned his eyes to the ceiling for a long moment, and rubbed his eyes. "Fine. You want to see? Hoping it wouldn't come to this but—"

"But you asked me to meet you *here*."

"I did. Knew you wouldn't believe me and I've no time to dally around. Down that hall is one of the things we found out here. See for yourself."

Alvin tucked the pistol into the back of his belt, but it was uncomfortable with its weight pushing against his spine. The dark was near sightless, wind moaning through the hollows as it banked around the bends. It made Alvin's spine shudder, but it might've just been Ellery.

"All these years in school … 'nothing left outside,' they said. 'Nothing can survive in the Expanse,' they said."

"They had their reasons, like most Scholars. We reveal what we can."

"What's this 'we' balderdash? You're my age, Hartchild. What made you special enough to let into the club?"

Ellery's practiced expressions folded aside just long enough for something else to come through, something timid like a child peering out from beneath the covers, afraid of the shadows along the walls.

"Absolutely nothing," he returned, "but a family name."

Alvin felt in his pocket and drew out the dark little cylinder. "The

Academy's got plenty of its secrets, seems."

"You … where did you get that?"

"Heuridium. Where else?"

"That's a bindporter! Give here." he snatched it from Alvin's hand and looked it over. "Where's the other half?"

"We left it just outside Orphan."

"You left—Esker! This is perfect!"

"What?"

"We can bindport back there! Stand here and hold your breath. It's a bit of a kick—"

"I know it is."

"You … know?"

"That thing's how we survived the fall from Orphan's roof."

"You already used it," he said—but not as a question. Ellery's face faded. He'd handled the arc pistol like it was nothing more than a pencil, but this little thing, he cradled like a live bomb.

"What in blazes is wrong now?"

Ellery carefully closed the cap over the trigger. "Esker? Whatever you do, don't touch this thing. Get rid of it."

"Why?"

"Because—because a bindporter draws anything in a two meter sphere back to its other half—*once*. It only works *one* way, *one* time. Try to reverse it? You won't reappear at all. It'll obliterate you and anything else in its range."

Alvin too flashed over with horror. "We almost used it! When Hana's leg was caught in a rock! You're telling me she—"

"Would've been vapourized, and you along with." He slipped it into his own pocket with caution. "Leave it to a Third Class…"

"Enough," Alvin snapped. "Hartchild, I've lost my home, probably forever and likely won't see my own mother and father again, and I've had to travel all this way while the road is obliterating under my blazing feet. These people have kept me locked away and already executed this one blighter just because of a little property damage and they've got Hana somewhere and my spyglass is broken and the only sad excuse for an ally in the whole blazing world I've got out here is you! Stop playing. What did that thing do to me?"

Ellery fumed, and Alvin readied himself for a fight. It was coming. He was sure, but Ellery cooled himself off, and sighed. "It's called Infusion."

"Yeah, I heard that one. Infusion with what?"

"The mineral in the Oculix filament is ... different, like nothing found in nature. Liminite, it's called. When lectral current runs through it, it has this way of emitting energy that *overwrites* the matter around it. If it's channeled just right, it'll infuse a person's optic nerves with its own particles. Spreads through their brain from there. Molecules in it act like—like mail being delivered, information traveling at light speeds. It assimilates. It replicates. And all of it's connected—*everywhere*. That's part of how bindporters work."

"You're telling me this tripe turned me into a walking antenna?" asked Alvin with rightly-angled brow.

"More like a *lens*, bending the world around you like it's bending the Expanse. *It's* the lens, Esker, not you."

"Why put it into a human at all?"

"I ... I don't know. Lorecroft understands this stuff better than me, alright? But there's a danger to it. More current means more light. More light makes you see more, *understand* more as your brain fuses with its processes. The information it processes is linked with your own mind. It's like a cosmic-smarts ray. Physics, gravitics, time, space, no limit to it."

"So what's the danger, then?"

"Because you'll never reach it. *Too* much current and it—it burns out your brain. Like it gives you the mind of the Author himself, for a few moments, only it costs you your life."

An old, icy fear twisted its way around Alvin's chest, but he didn't have time to dwell on it now, and turned on his heel further down the hall. "This is bollocks, Hartchild. Total codswallop."

"Just tap behind your ear. Just like you did in the Armillary. Go ahead."

Alvin grit his teeth. He wanted to punch Ellery again, not tap himself like keeping a beat, but his old curiosity tugged at the collar of his mind, again, and so Alvin lifted a shuddering hand, and—*tap. Tap.*

The hall glowed with the vibrant amber hue appearing around Alvin's head in rings and figures and he near fell over. "Gah!" he yelled, losing control of his breath and trying to bat it all away. "I thought this came from that machine!"

It stayed fixed around his head as surely as a hat, no matter what way he turned.

"Tap it again," Ellery prodded.

Alvin did, and the luminous dial of light came into being in his hand, and as in the Heuridium, when he touched its rim, more and larger rings erupted around his whole body. Over it all came Ellery's orange-lit face. Part of Alvin was awed, let his fingers glide through the light, watched it dissipate and reform after he'd touched it.

"You've got a program in you, Esker, *Halo*. And before you ask, no it *can't* be removed. Tap the dial's bottom edge with your thumb twice."

When Alvin did so, all the lights vanished into luminous dust, and then into nothing.

"That incandescent put this in me? Why didn't it do it to Hana? She was standing right beside me!"

"I wasn't there! How should I know? These people love their goggles. Was she wearing hers?"

"I—yeah, she was."

"Well, that's it, then. Any kind of glass or barrier diffuses the process. Won't even work through spectacles, I'm told."

"What's this business with the back of my head?"

"It's just the activation point," Ellery told him. "You'll find you have markings on your scalp, like a tattoo, there."

"I've a tattoo?!"

"Pray you never bald."

"How could even Orphan create something like this? Three weeks ago the incandescent was the height of industry…"

"You really want to know? Go on down that hall, but you should know, it'll do to your mind what you're doing to the Expanse."

Alvin tugged his girl's robe straight. "Had plenty of that, lately."

"No you haven't."

When Alvin approached the dark mouth of the tunnel, a sound enveloped their senses, a deep, mechanical trilling like distant thunder. Threads of thin, amber light awoke from more the etchings in the walls, and spread out slowly, giving shape to nameless things.

"You said I'm tearing apart the Expanse to a new blueprint."

"And?"

"Couldn't we just use the original blueprint to put it all back?"

"I don't think it works like that, Esker. And I can tell you, any of those records still in the Heuridium are likely destroyed."

Alvin and Ellery both fell back when the lights illuminated two forms on either side of the last arch, something like statues set into alcoves. They were not human, and too dark to see clearly.

The lights swept on, opening from the chilling hall into a great rotunda. Four of the great, inhuman statues kept watch over the room from alcoves in the cardinal compass points. He thought he saw corridors, maybe sealed entries, maybe collapsed portions of the caves, but deep shadows fanned across from among the statues. The whole rotunda descended down shallow steps, ring after ring of them, until they came to the bottom, and rose back again until they formed a great central platform, at least forty feet across. In its middle stood a single tapering dais with a sphere mounted on its top.

"The program in you? Things you saw in the Heuridium? It's old, Esker, *very* old. We didn't invent it. We refined it. A lot was buried in the Expanse."

The rest of the lights came on in the rotunda, and on the far wall, a shape came to Alvin's notice. Moss and roots grew down through portions of the walls of this ancient place, but especially on the far side. Some of the wall lay crumbled, and there against the wall lay the remains of ... *something*.

"Hartchild ... what is *that?*"

It was human in its shape—or once was. Hints of arms and long-fingered hands and joints lay there in the rubble of the shape. So much moss and ruin lay on top of it, there wasn't much left.

At first, he thought it nothing more than a statue, but this was no rock. Pearlescent casing, mechanisms between the joints, it must've once stood seven feet tall if it was an inch. But its body hung in pieces. There was no face, only a single hole in its triadinal head.

"You ever have nightmares about things looked like that?" Ellery asked.

"Who hasn't? That's a real monster-under-the-bed affair."

A flicker of light trailed around the etchings of the rotunda, and swept in and up to the sphere atop the dais. There it burst up into brilliant rays into a domed ceiling they couldn't see before, and cast a million stars against its surface. So vivid and clear, whole galaxies and clouds of colour and shapes among the stars shone down at them.

"Hartchild?" said Alvin. "You can see this, right?"

"Of course I can!" said Ellery. "It's observable, ain't it?"

The lights around the rotunda flared, the ones on the floor orbited faster, and all the lights birthed new ones that collected, floated in the empty space of the room, until they coalesced into letters, into *words* that repeated across the great hall, audible within the trilling and written across everything.

Containment failing

Gravitic mass imbalanced

Why do you open the breach?

ENTRY 16: "THE GALÓ & CULTURAL RELATIONS"

"The Galó are a soiled lot of half-rabid reprobates with both violent and thievish tendencies when not otherwise engaged in sloth and rampant gluttony. Tribal, undisciplined, and prone to outbursts of foul language and even fouler odours, they seem fit for little more than eventual artillery testing, once we invent it."

—Calgotten Barclay, 1st Lieutenant, Orphan Survey Regimen

The assessment made by 1st Lt. Barclay remains unfortunately accurate when describing early encounters with the Galó. Nevertheless, it is known that on first contact, Orphan's scouting teams noted their likeness to portrayals of Viking clans, but most of those came from operas the scouts had attended in their youth. Still, the similarity was noted, if less impressive than their theatrical counterparts. Attempts to trade with the Galó resulted in gained furs and lost provisions, and the furs turned out to be poor quality and poorer stench.

At that time, the Expanse housed at least eight different clans in settlements from Istlund to Sordun Valley. Most were believed by Orphan's Scholars to originate from a single group of settlers that later quarreled and succumbed to killing each other. This would prove to be correct, though the Orphaners would never know that. The Galó arrived on the land mass more than two centuries prior in three longboats.

In comparing accounts, the Galó seem to have regressed to a more superstitious and barbaric way(s) of life as time went on, becoming cult-like, dwindling in numbers, intellect, manners, dress, and, tragically, culinary skill. Hygiene remained unchanged. Curiously, the Jalóheim Clan splintered farthest, shifted religious practices, and became matriarchal in structure. No one knows why, and nobody has cared enough to ask.

in which stargazers prattle on about things esoteric

As the light formed itself into shape, and those words formed across the wall before dissipating into vapor, Alvin and Ellery both fell back over one another. Stars erupted out beneath them as if they were giants broader than suns atop the galaxy itself, with still more overhead in the dome.

Alvin scrambled, tripping to his wobbly feet.

"Did you see that?" Alvin and Ellery looked at one another and got up slowly off the floor. "Can … can you hear us?" Alvin asked. "Who are you?"

"I hardly think it's a 'who,'" Ellery insisted.

"Thought you knew about this!"

"Well it's another thing to actually stand here, ain't it?!"

An echo

"It *can* hear us!" Alvin loudly whispered. "An echo of what? Are—are you what the Galó call Jalós?"

No

"Then…?"

Keeper

Installation 04

Koah'riel

"Well that answers everything," Alvin muttered. "Okay, *what* are you?"

The words dissipated, as if nothing but a reflection in moonlit water, and someone splashed their finger through the surface. In their place came a succession of words, one after another, fading in across their vision, spreading over the "stars" and walls.

Keeper of this installation

"Begging your pardon, Sir," said Alvin. "I don't think I understand."

"Don't call that thing 'Sir,' Esker," Ellery insisted. "It's some kind of synthetic neura-matic. A stereopticon."

"Stereopticon … did the Galó create you?"

These ones create nothing

But more of themselves

They devour all

"Then what *is* this place?"

A long pause of darkness followed, long enough for them to wonder if whatever-it-was had gone.

Installation 04

"Zero-four, yes, got that, for whatever in blazes it means! Bloody helpful. Who built it?"

Purveyors

Alvin turned instead to Ellery. "The Scholary knew about this thing. They had to if—" Lights were beginning to dawn in Alvin's meager mind. "The Galó's Oracle. This *thing* is their seer or mystic or whatever, ain't it?"

The pieces were gathering in his mind, a constellation he couldn't quite string together through the lens of his mind. All he saw were similarities— patterns. "Keeper," he posed. "These Purveyors. They built this. Created the program in my head, too, I'd wager."

"Then maybe you'd know. There's a way to stop all this, ain't there?" He didn't add *other-than-me-dying* out loud, and hoped he wouldn't have to.

"There's got to be a way!"

"That … that's very helpful, thank you. I'll get to that immediately."

He glared at Ellery. "*That's* why you were going to kill me? That's why Pike was going to kill Hana when he thought she was…"

"The one Infused. Look, Orphan wasn't ready, Esker. A thousand preparations needed to be made still. Some of us—some didn't have time. You brought it all on too early, and anyway it wasn't meant for you."

"Then who in blazes *what* it meant for?" Alvin's chest fluttered. Ellery Hartchild seethed, and put some distance between himself and Alvin, turning his back to him. "*You?*"

"I'm the one who was supposed to use the Oculix," Ellery admitted. "It was supposed to be *me*, Esker. Me. *I* was supposed to be Orphan's deliverer, not you, not some grease-stained louse from a Tramrunner's hovel!"

The pain in Ellery's voice kept Alvin from even being angry. He didn't understand what he possibly robbed Ellery of, but it was obviously something to *him*. He said nothing to him, but turned back to the stereopticon.

"Alright, but is there a way—dying aside—to turn this back? Is there an *original* cymatic pattern? A way to still read it and bring us back to how things were *before* I was Instilled with that spinny light globe or whatever?"

Time is not eternal

The stars once were

Present confluence variant of prior

"That—okay that's a little contradictory but—but I'm asking if the original pattern still exists somewhere? Like written down or the like."

Seeking reference: original pattern...

The pillar of everlasting stars

The founders column

First confluence enshrined

"Right," said Alvin. "And where is it?"

Installation 01

The axis gate

The breach is opening

Containment failing

"Containment of ... *what?*" Ellery asked, apparently losing his nerve to curiosity. The words dissipated, swirled and spun in rings around the mirrored floor and overhead dome until they erupted again into tangible meaning.

The anomaly

Ilós

"What does that mean, Hartchild?"

"Blazes if I know!" he defended.

"You knew this thing was here, didn't you?"

"Look—Orphan discovered it a long time ago, discovered a lot of things in the Expanse. Yes, I knew it was here, but hardly knew anything about it, and I don't know what this Ilós thing is, either. Sounds enough like your girlfriend's god."

Alvin rubbed his head, tried to take all this in, but none of it seemed to change anything. All it did was leave him with more confusion than before. He needed clarity. "What'll happen when the Expanse *is* reshaped? When the current sequence is finished?"

Ilós awakens

This confluence will end

The cycle will continue

This time the lights formed more than words. Rings and planets and whole worlds erupted above and below them. Alvin knew them—Venus and Saturn and Jupiter and the others, and it moved to show him the ring of asteroids around the sun, closer, and closer until hunks of a once-spherical world were clear among the debris. Even Ellery stood closer to look.

"Confluence will end?" Alvin whispered.

Civilizations do rise and do fall

And many now never have begun at all

"What?" Alvin posed, but the stereopticon did not answer, or elaborate. It didn't seem like its own voice, but like it referenced famous words that Alvin had never heard of. "There ... there has to be another way to return to the old pattern."

"Well there ain't, Esker!"

The whole of the rotunda shuddered. Bits of rock and dust and shimmering amber light spilled around their feet. Again the lights dissolved and shifted, for the last time they would wait for.

"Esker, we're out of time. Especially if you're insisting on rescuing your invasive strumpet from this place. Come on!"

"But…"

Back into the hall they ran, and it was longer now than even what it seemed before. They came to the door, and as its insides lit with patterns, it opened almost silently. No sounds but the rumbles came from the ringed hall. They made it all the way back to the stairway up to higher halls, when Ellery shoved him back against the all opposite the stairs, and shushed him.

"Chieftain Eaorn knows what to expect," said Tevir, and Esig followed after. "Departure is at dawn. Make certain you have all the arms loaded for light travel."

"They're coming!" Ellery mouthed.

They couldn't go back toward the Keeper's … *place* without being seen, so darted quietly back into the ringed hall, hoping the Priestess would choose to visit her Oracle again. Beneath their feet, the rotunda trembled, steadily and quick. The upheaval was creeping into Jalóheim Village.

They backed farther and farther away as the voices of Tevir and Esig grew quieter, until Alvin stumbled into a threshold.

"Quiet, idiot!"

"Weren't like I was trying to … wait. weren't this door shut before?"

"Who gives a curse! Let's get to the surface before—"

"But wait. You hear that?" Alvin peered into the dark hall behind him. It was long, like its opposite.

"Esker, we don't have *time*."

But Alvin went anyway, into the now-open door, down the long, long hall, strange as the others, angular and just as optically upsetting, all amid Ellery's ringing protests. It was a *scraping* sound, metal on stone, and as they came into the opening chamber, he found its source—the chains that bound a young girl's ankle. Her face lay buried in her arms as she sat folded up.

She lifted mismatched eyes to them, but they still wore their robes.

"Oh!" said Alvin, and pulled his down, and Ellery did the same.

Hana's face washed ghostly pale. One eye was blackened, and her lip bled from a rip in the corner.

"Oh no," she gasped. "*Anyone* but you…"

"What've they done to you?"

Hana kicked back away from him. "You can't be here, Alvin! Go *away*."

She tried to collect herself, rub her face dry with her sleeve.

"Blast if you think I'm going anywhere without you. I look all over this blazing village for you, expecting to find you in some alien somewhere and … Hana … what are you doing here?"

"Alvin please. You should not have come!"

"You know what I had to do to get into this place? Look at me. I'm dressed like a girl! There was more, too but I'm not ready to talk about that ruckus."

"Please leave," she begged him. "Forget me."

Alvin knelt. He tried to draw near, but she'd have none of it. Her wrist still had the bangle, but her arm was far more wounded around its edges than he'd left her. "I'm sorry I wasn't here to stop this," he said.

"Don't! You cannot say things like that!"

He lowered his eyes to hers. "Did they do this because the book wasn't what they thought—"

"Oh Alvin, for Jalós' sake!" She hollered. "There *was* no mission! I wasn't *sent* anywhere except *away*."

"I don't … think I understand."

Ellery stepped up beside him. Hana recoiled more, but said nothing.

"Esker, they exiled her. She's a criminal. Can't you understand? She was never *supposed* to come back."

She lowered her eyes to the floor.

He couldn't believe it, not of her.

Of Alphonse on a bad enough day.

Even of Professor Lorecroft, after everything.

Not Hana.

Never her.

No.

There was too much color in her for that. Too much light. Too much spark. Too much energy. He had wagered on her, risked his home and life and (ultimately) the fate of his towne on her.

"Hana…"

"I lied. I'm a *liar*, Alvin. I lie to eat my fill, to trade in alleys, to get what I want. There. Now you know."

Alvin's heart settled within him. "I—I don't believe that."

She sat back on her haunches, and in her raspy voice, told him, "People will let you down, Alvin. Always."

"But … why?"

She unwound the wrapping on her arm and showed him the branded mark. "This does not mean *mission*. Means *waterthief*. Takes only one sip from someone's waterflask to be exiled, and I stole *lots*."

"But…" Alvin's heart strained like it wanted to pull itself from his chest. It was hard to breathe. "You told me we were meant to—"

"Oh come on, Alvin! Never meant any of it! I *lied*. No different than Jalós or—or whatever Author or fate! All we have is us. That is a sorry lot."

"But … *why?*"

"Because she *can*, Alvin—"

"He is right," said Hana. "That—that is how life is. When you let me into Orphan? It was my only way *home*. The only way out of exile is to return with a great gift to Jalóheim."

"The book." Alvin shut his eyes. "That stereopticon was the one who told you about it, weren't he? You once had to hide someplace secret. He knows about Orphan, and the Oculix. That means the Priestess knows, too."

"Well? Was it worth it?" Hartchild asked.

Hana got up and marched at him until her chains stopped her. "Do you know what it is *like* here? Every year the water dries up. The food shrinks. People die, and die, and die. The boys are docile. Girls are stupid. And I … I never saw it until *you* came into my life. Your home and … and your family. But what do any of us even matter?"

"But … we *do*," he defended.

"Really?" She straightened up a little taller. "'We are nothing but dust and windsong,' Alvin." All the pain that coiled around her chest couldn't diminish the color that shone from her eyes, though it lay under murky fears. "Why are you not angry? You are supposed to be angry."

"Okay," he said. "So you made some bad choices. Make better ones tomorrow, and I'll forget today's."

"What?" she said. "What is this?"

"What you've done. I don't care about none of it. You hear? It's forgotten. I'm just glad you're alive."

"That—nah, that is *not* how it works."

"Well it is today."

Hana marched as close as her chains would let her. "Stop that! You are supposed to be angry! Hit me."

"What?!"

"Hit me!" she demanded.

"Ain't gonna hit you none!"

Hana shoved him. "I said *hit* me! Be angry. Hurt me—*something*. I used you. You are supposed to be furious! Are you that naive?" She swung, tripped over the chain, and dropped.

Alvin knelt. "I'll find a way to get you out of there."

"You cannot forgive this, Alvin."

"Blazes I can't. Now never mention it again! I'll get you out of this chain, and no mistake. Understood?"

"You do not understand. You can *not* forgive this!"

"Why?"

"I told about the book—that golden thing, but even if they believed me, what good is it? I had nothing else to offer." She choked on her words.

"Oh Author," Ellery breathed. "Esker..."

Footfalls sounded from the hall. Alvin turned, and might've run, but they'd already seen them. There wasn't anywhere to go.

"—I only had one thing left," she confessed.

They came and aimed their guns at him and Ellery. Esig Ganikson took Alvin by the collar. Hana didn't need to tell him what she offered. She gave them a boy who could open the gates of Iron Hollow.

in which lives are coldly pitted against each other

ALVIN USED TO VISIT A FRIEND DOWN ON Lowry Lane as a boy, and his house, the last one on the right, stood by the freight line that ran from the Ironworks to the mines. The house shuddered continually from the passing trams, and Alvin used to imagine that house was alive and suffered from extreme fear of railways, and that's why it shook. Jalóheim Village shuddered like that now, every hut and temple.

The thunder didn't help, still booming overhead. Whatever the Priestess had been planning, been waiting for, been preparing, the spring was ready for triggering.

"They're going to kill you, you know, if you don't do what they want. Likely kill me too, for the lark of it," Ellery muttered. "Blighters."

"Don't much care for these folks, do you, Hartchild?"

"Orphan dealt with them a long time ago. Thieves, brigands, and crooks, the lot of them. They've been after a way into Orphan for *ages*, and now they've got *you*, the uneducated boy with the freak memory."

"Well they ain't figured out yet that their pilgrimage won't be worth a tinker's toss without ships to sail to the north pole. Can you believe it? Not a ship or sailor in sight."

"Oh. Um. About that..."

"What now?"

"Look, this'll take longer to explain but you should know that this—the Expanse—it ain't exactly … Angland." Alvin blared his angry eyes at him. "It's … well, this *is* Hyperborea. We're *on* the Miocene Continent."

This gave Alvin a migraine. He blinked a few times, glanced over at Ellery, but he didn't seem to have anything to say. Alvin rolled it around in his mind, but his mind was sick of being torn to pieces and rebuilt so many times. "Okay," he accepted. "Why not? At this point, I'd probably believe the moon's made of a nice, supple brie."

They knelt in the hall of Jalóheim's chieftain, hands bound behind their backs, guarded by Esig Ganikson and two others like him.

Ellery had some questions of his own. "I don't understand how you knew how to open the gates in the first place. Nobody knows them except the Chancellery!"

"Up," said Esig.

"Huh?" Ellery returned. "I don't take orders from—"

Esig threw a fist into Ellery's stomach, enough to drop him over in bursting coughs.

"Hey!" Alvin started. "Get your hands off him!"

He rose at Esig, paused by the drawn blade the young Serker held against his shoulder. He surprised himself, sticking up for Ellery like that, though perhaps only an Orphanite streak of camaraderie.

Eaorn swung open the doors of the aging hall and marched in with Priestess Tevir at his back, gusts blowing sand and cold against the boys. "They will not take this change of plan well, Tevir, and now that it is upon us, I care little for it too." The chieftain and the Priestess pulled off their goggles.

"It is the will of Jalós, Chieftain."

The chieftain stopped where he was. "Will of Jalós?" He raised his voice. "Jalós also willed the death of that young man on the Proving Tree! And look what happened there. Are you sure you are not losing your touch, Priestess?"

The old woman glared at him.

Ellery leaned closer to Alvin. "What's he mean?"

"I think—I think Loftin *lived*. Poor fellow was struck with lightning."

Ellery's eyebrows vaulted, and a rip of thunder shook the hall.

The old Priestess assured the chief, "The way lies before us, Chieftain. Do not reject the hand of Jalós now." She strode closer to the boys. So did Eaorn, but he stayed behind enough to watch carefully. "We have a saying in Jalóheim, tinkerer. 'Calamity is the forge that tempers the faithful.' Seems you bring both calamity and salvation, and so temper us all."

"If you think I'm giving you the keys to Orphan, you're out of your mind. Ma'am. Um, Priestess, Ma'am. And don't think about hurting this blighter because I can't stand him."

"Nice, Esker."

"Esig? Get them up. Come. Walk with me. Eyes over, everyone." As they pulled their eye protection down, Esig and the other Serkers escorted Alvin and Ellery behind the Priestess. Eaorn watched carefully, straying behind them farthest. Through the great doors of the hall she led them, into the streets of Jalóheim, and into the raging winds. The churning of the Upheaval was up to the east gate, now, and covered half the sky. Gigantic husks of rock and stone spun and hovered across the distance. Arcs of current webbed between them and the winds careened across the village.

Tevir raised her voice easily over the winds. "We have waited a long, long time for this, tinkerer. You will forgive my trickery, but it was necessary to confirm what the little waterthief told us."

"What?"

"Did you believe you made it into the Temple of Jalós without any problem with just some stolen robes? You were helpful, and will still be in the road ahead." She marched with a gait of a man, tall and proud, her avian nose angled ahead.

"I don't know why you want into Orphan when *that's* between you and it, and when your pilgrimage is supposed to take you the *opposite* way."

Tevir halted, turned, and could hardly contain her rapture. She leaned down, close to Alvin's ear. "Because the Blind Oracle has told me something about Iron Hollow," she said lower. "Something even *you* are unlikely to know."

"Even if you *did* have the gate codes, there's no way to get there."

"Of course there is." From her pocket, she produced the torn and battered map of the Shift that was once in Alvin's notebook.

"Wha—how did—"

"It took great doing, and we lost three men obtaining it from that ruin out there, but your map will be very useful. You understand why Loftin had to face the Proving. It is only a miracle of the great god that he was spared."

"Like blazes it will. There won't be nothing left of—"

"Are you aware that there are some materials *immune* to what is happening in the east? No? The Astral Stone is one of them. The ruins you came by will be the needle's eye through the storm. Would you like to know something else? In my youth, part of the initiation of Priestess was journeying to Niavellir. The place where Jalós once imbued his people with the Harmony of Creation. With it, he forged the world as it is."

A strange thought came to Alvin, then, a coalescence of many things he'd heard and learned. He feared he was beginning down the way of Uncle Otto. "Did *you* learn the song, then?"

"No," she confessed. "He has given his song to no one in eons, but Niavellir was a sight to see." Tevir took her waterflask from her robes and indulged a long drink, the red serpent glinting in the storm light on its side. "This village shall die in this calamity, and forge us our road in the Last Journey Home," she continued, and drew something else from her pocket— the Oculix.

Ellery's whole body seized up at the sight of it. "Esker?!"

"Our little waterthief has assured me that this object *is* the <u>Dark Illumined Eye</u>." She held it up in front of the boys. "Of course, there is no sense in her words, is there? Or is there?"

Ellery fidgeted in place.

"You need to understand something about Jalóheim, tinkerer Hugoson. Here, you are either valuable to the Journey or you are not. Right now, you are of *immense* value to us, and we need only two more things from you."

"You want Orphan's door codes."

"Indeed. And the way to open the gates at Niavellir, in case *your* people fail." She held up the Oculix and peered through its lens. "I believe you have already read the book, yah?"

"I won't give you what you want, Priestess."

"Of course you will," said Ellery.

Alvin shot him a look.

"What? You haven't figured this out yet?"

They came to the central crossing of the village. The east gate stood far in the distance, already starting to break apart. The people gathered in panicked throngs. Alvin scanned the crowd for Sigrie, but found none of the shrinemaids.

"Chieftain," said Tevir. "Seems the people need their chieftain."

Eaorn came up among them, and stood at the base of the mount to the north. His voice bellowed even over the storm *and* the Upheaval. Hundreds of goggled eyes watched. "Jalóheim!" he began. "Your wait is over. This is no hour for fear or cowardice. Your grandfathers died on this rocky soil that you might see this day."

He went on, gathering the crowds to him while Tevir kept her attention on Alvin. "Eleven generations, we have occupied this land. Today we take our Last Journey Home. It was difficult to believe that the way *north* would come through a road *south*."

"I don't understand."

"You will," she said.

Eaorn paused, and called to his Priestess of Jalós. She addressed the people. "The hand of Jalós is often strange. Just yesterday, Loftin survived the Proving, a great mercy from a great god, but we have one final evil to put before the hand of Jalós before we leave this ancestral home, for a truer one."

Tevir gestured toward the mound behind the chieftain, even as he stepped down, and Alvin's lungs seized. The impossible winds nearly took Hana off her feet, but then, she was chained to the great bronze spire.

"Hana!"

"Told you," said Ellery.

A rage swelled within Alvin, burning his throat and chest even as he screamed and hurled himself at Tevir with all his feeble might. Two of the Serkers slid trying to hold him back, and only the blunt end of Esig's blade slamming into the base of his neck finally dropped him.

Alvin gazed up at his assailant. "He is not ready to fight," Esig snarled.

"Because he is not ready to die."

"Bring him to the Tree. Young Lofthana was expelled from Jalóheim for her crimes," Tevir explained. "Her welcome might have been regained with a worthwhile offering, but it seems her offering has amounted to little."

"Leave her out of this!" Alvin yelled. "Can't you see how crazy this is? Because everyone else can!"

"Lofthana violated the sacred laws of Jalós, and so must face the Proving. If her offering of the keys to Iron Hollow were to come to us, Jalós might show her mercy still…"

"This is dirty pool! It's indecent! Politician!" Alvin threw out every curse and spiteful scorn he'd ever heard his father utter to machinery, and then some.

His and Hana's frightened eyes met in the center and wouldn't break hold. Their lives flowed across that momentary tether.

"See, tinkerer, souls are either valuable for the Journey or not. Right now, Lofthana is immensely valuable to us, but for only one thing—for gaining your obedience. Without that, she is no use to us, a waterthief, and bastard child of a dead mother, and unknown father. In a way, you are *giving* her value." Tevir then shut her covered eyes, spread out her hands, and began the same chant Alvin heard at Loftin's Proving, but now the great trident spire began to *turn*. Slowly it rotated, arcs of threaded light sparking among the tines and rings. The black clouds rolled thicker over Jalóheim. Wind carried up the dust and crystalline sand.

Around the edges of the pedestal knelt the shrinemaids, Sigrie among them, tears pouring from her eyes. She was the only one (save Hana) without her goggles, and could look at nothing but her clenched fists on the ground.

And in the midst of that ruin, a peaceful stillness fell upon Hana. Her face wouldn't break its hold on Alvin, and though no one seemed to notice it but him, she whispered, mouthed almost without sound at all:

No, Alvin.

He wanted to avenge her. He wanted to rip those chains apart and scoop Hana up and run. But she just shook her shaggy head. The world would drop out from under her and send her hurtling into the bottomless void, and he would be there to see it.

And then Tevir stopped. "What was that?" she asked. "Didn't quite hear you, tinkerer."

"I said: seven, three, three—"

"Alvin no!" pleaded Hana.

Ellery could only shut his eyes.

"—two, one, four, zero."

"There. Was that so very difficult?"

"Let her go," Alvin demanded.

"Esig," called Tevir, and the spire slowed its turning even as her chant had broken.

Reluctantly, he unlatched Hana's chains, holding her by the arms still, away from the spire, and all the Chalices rose and moved aside, holding themselves against the wind.

"Very good. Thank you for your offering to Jalóheim, young Lofthana!" the Priestess yelled. "Jalós has chosen to spare your life. You are free to go, a citizen once more."

Esig let Hana free, and tossed her waterflask to her, and her little knife. She stood, no longer able to look at Alvin even when he tried to get her to.

"We will honor this gift for a long time to come," said Tevir.

When Alvin reached for her, Hana bolted into the thick of the crowd, and was gone.

"Now we embark," said Tevir. "Our Last Journey Home."

in which old crimes are happily repeated

ALVIN ESKER RARELY FOUND HIMSELF OUT OF WORDS, but he had none left, no ideas, no ways out. *A chatterbold*, his father often said, surely and (as his mother often noted), *mouthy as a lark*, but today he waited in silent dread. So when all of Jalóheim gathered at the southern gate, he found himself utterly despairing of what to do.

"So Alvin Esker's finally run out of things to say," Ellery taunted. "Never thought I'd live to see this." Alvin still said nothing. "Wow. You really are the worse for it, eh? And all because of a skirt. You know she just—"

"No, Hartchild," said Alvin. "She ain't 'just' nothing. She—don't much care to hear any further of your opinions, neither. Alright?"

"I was about to say, she's just escaped death because of you. Isn't that *any* comfort, even with everything else as it is?" Alvin eyed him. "What? Look, just because I loathe these blighters don't mean I'd take joy in watching the poor girl fry! Author, she's even an orphan—a *real* one. Couldn't get more pathetic lest she were blind, could she? Author help me, can't believe I'm saying this to the likes of you. Esker, you took a hit, today. Bad one. Your girl betrayed you. You know you're responsible for the death of … well, *everybody*, including you and me and—"

"Hartchild, you ought've been a counselor."

"If you'd listen: I'll tell you something I ain't ever told anybody." He took a long breath in through his nose. "I've always hated you."

"Wow. Revelations! We should get matching tattoos, maybe?"

"I hated you … because for all your commoner's blood and horrid education and brownstone hovel, you were always so bloody *happy*. You were the one everyone looked to for the sunny side of a lectral burn, because for all your idiocy, you *could*. You had no reason to be, but always were. Obnoxious, is what it is, but seeing you like *this*? It's like watching someone kick a puppy."

"Are you done? This mess ain't so simple, Hartchild."

Ellery laughed. "Of course it is! Idiot. That's what you proved. No matter how complicated it all gets, it's as simple as how you answer it. Now *fix* yourself or I'll smash your face into this gravel."

Alvin shut his eyes, and could only regard Ellery with a thought. What thought it was, he wasn't sure. Meanwhile, Priestess Tevir led the way with lanterns hung from staves the shrinemaids carried, golden stars among the twilight of the sunless days.

So many people…

A clean line of separation appeared down the length of the east gate, and the entire quadrant of the eastern side lifted into the air, disintegrated into a dozen pieces, and spun itself into the mass of levitating rock.

Then the people ran. Some were trampled. All cried out and prayed and wept and pulled on each other.

They rushed the two Orphan boys up among the chieftain and the Priestess, the tip of the spear that would impale Orphan Towne … assuming there even *was* an Orphan Towne anymore.

"You found her," called Sigrie's familiar voice among the shrinemaids. Alvin shut his eyes, and could only answer with a single nod. "And she survived the Proving! We were so *frightened* for her. You look so … wilted."

Sigrie's sad eyes waited for an answer.

And what could he give her? Her world was crumbling. His own was crumbling. Ellery's and Hana's and his family's and…

No matter how much he wanted to bolt into his room in the old brownstone, slam the door, and read a book, he was the only one who could change this. He caused it. He carried it.

There would be no hiding.

"I'm—I'm sorry, Sigrie. I don't know how to get where I need to go."

She looked at him sideways. "Did you not tell me that hope gives shape to things? Is there nothing left to give shape to?"

Tevir came alongside Alvin. "You will stay beside me, tinkerer Hugoson," she said. Esig gripped his arm as they made their way through the gate.

She held the arc pistol in her long fingers, looking it over. "Incredible, how your people have advanced," she said. "I look forward to finally seeing what wonders await within Iron Hollow's walls. Though they won't compare to where we're going after that."

Nowhere could Alvin find Hana, neither trace nor sound nor hair. He stole glances back over his shoulder as the village slowly tore itself apart. One particular lurch was stranger than the rest. When the ground cracked, the crowd around Alvin shifted and fell, and even Priestess Tevir toppled.

"Get off of me!" she yelled as some of the young landed on and around her. They pushed and tugged until, one by one, they righted themselves into standing and helped the old Priestess to her feet. She limped.

"Are you hurt, Priestess?" one of the shrinemaids asked.

"Fine," she claimed. "It's time to set this pilgrimage to the march."

"People of Jalós!" she began. "We make for Iron Hollow. There, the way to Thule will be open to us."

Alvin knew the Orphanites outnumbered the Galó, but all his eyes would see were the rifles, the litany of powder gun barrels aimed at the sky over the shoulders of the men.

But then a sound caught his ear, a sound over all the deafening roar of thunder and Upheaval and marching, a raspy call he knew better than all the sounds in the Expanse.

"Priestess Tevir! Does this belong to you?"

"What is she doing?" said Sigrie, pulling down her lenses for a moment.

There in Hana's hand was a gilded waterflask. The old woman searched herself, but found her pockets empty. Hana took the flask and lifted it to her lips, and drank it there before the sight of the whole village.

"The stupid girl," said one of the men by Alvin.

"Stupid?" he repeated, but the confusion didn't last.

When she tightened the cap on the flask, she flung it toward the crowd, yelling Alvin's name at the top of her voice.

Alvin bounded onto one of the old wagons, and off its frame, plucking the spinning flask from the air and landing hard on his shoulder, swallowing what he could before throwing it to "Ellery!" between the people.

Ellery downed the last of it before they tackled him to the ground and tore it from his hand. A moment of silence fell on the Galó as Ellery and Alvin got to their feet, and the crowd parted around them.

"Begging your pardon, Ma'am," said Alvin. "But we can't rightly go with you. Jalós law says something about exiling thieves, I think."

There wasn't time to argue over it. Another seismic lurch rippled through the Expanse and brought the southern wall crumbling.

Most of the people took to their heels by then, seeing as how the world was coming to an end, and all. Tevir ground her teeth, and might've called for their deaths, if Eaorn hadn't taken the old woman by the arm.

"Come, Tevir. They have made their choice. As you would say, their lives are in Jalós' hands. Leave them to Svaraheim."

Without another word, Priestess Tevir turned her back on the boys. The sea of villagers swept around them.

"Alvin Hugoson! What did you do?! What did you both *do?*" It was Sigrie. "You—you're going to die out there! Why are you doing this? Why would Lofthana—"

"Yes," said Ellery. "Why *did* we, Esker?"

"Sigrie," said Alvin. "Listen. When you get to Orphan Towne—Iron Hollow—you look for someone, see? You find Alphonse Esker. You hear me? You find him and you tell him Alvin said to look out for you. Warn him what's happening and he'll look out for you. You do that, promise me?"

"Alphonse?"

"He's my brother. You find him. You find *anyone* with the name Esker, understand? Tell them Alvin sent you."

"It is promised. You are really going to do this?"

Someone else took Alvin by the shoulder and spun him around, and he found himself looking up at a large, chiseled, familiar face.

"A—Loftin?" Was he going to kill them? Down his left arm and across his neck and the part of his chest that Alvin could see, he was painted with deep scarring, a tree-like white shriek of ruined skin. "You *did* live!"

Sigrie cautiously told him, "Loftin is the *only* one to live through the Heavenly Spear. Jalós showed him mercy, seems."

"Forgive, boy from Iron Hollow. Did not want the map to take us through the tunnels to your village."

"You knew about this plan?"

"Overheard. Sometimes … eavesdrop."

Alvin laughed, and so did Loftin. Hana was making her way along the southern wall and clamoring down the inclines toward them. Loftin watched her for a long moment. He watched her *fiercely*.

"You leave with Lofthana?"

"That—that's up to her, suppose."

"What can *you* do?"

"I've one hope left." He looked to Sigrie.

"Name?" said Loftin. "Your name?"

"Alvin. Hugoson."

Loftin nodded. "You protected her in Svaraheim? Yah? Saved her leg? Alvin Hugoson, you make promise. You protect her. Understand? You keep her safe."

The crowd gave Hana room, not out of any kind of reverence, but revulsion, though it was convenient enough for her. She limped on that bad leg, now, but not horribly.

"Swear it," Loftin insisted.

Ellery could only shrug at Alvin. "Don't ask me, stupid git. I've no idea what you're doing."

"Al—alright," Alvin told him. "I swear. But listen, you do something for me."

"Hmm?"

"See that girl there? The shrinemaid behind you?" Loftin glanced carefully, and gave Alvin a knowing nod. "You do the same for her. She's on a mission to Iron Hollow. See to it that she accomplishes it."

Loftin nodded with all the seriousness of a Tramrunner, and slipped back into the flowing mass of faces before Hana came near.

Sigrie handed Alvin a wrapped little parcel. "Goat jerky," she said. "I think you will like it, if you try. Do not die," Sigrie told them, and kissed Alvin on the cheek.

"How many girlfriends did you *make* in this bilge towne?!" Ellery yelled.

That was when Hana came through the crowd, and her coloured eyes went wide. Sigrie chuckled, and made her way along with the crowd, turning lastly to Hana to advise her to "Take care of them, Lofthana. They need it."

For a long, long moment, Alvin, Hana, and Ellery waited, and said little as the caravans left for the middle of the Upheaval. They couldn't remain there, of course, but for a moment, Alvin and Hana stood near, there on the slope outside Jalóheim. Hana rubbed her arms a little. Two or three times she even tried to say something, but not much came of it.

"So," Ellery finally said. "What's the plan, then? Now that we *can't* go back to Orphan, even as prisoners."

"We reverse all this," said Alvin. "All of it, go back to how things were. There's a way—"

"Reverse!" Ellery scoffed. "There's no *reversing* this!"

"Not without the original pattern, no, but what if we had it?"

"It took Uncle Hiram and his team years just to bang out the first sequence change. If there *were* a record … oh, Author, you're going where that stereopticon said. What makes you think anything is even there?"

"Installation Zero-One," Alvin reminded him. "Look, all this stuff, this —this Halo Program, the Purveyors who made it, they were some kind of brilliant civilization, yeah? Uncle Otto's Thule and—and Jalóheim's Agarta, all of them are at the Axis, along with this record of the original Confluence. It's got to be all the same place."

"You're starting to *sound* like your uncle."

"Maybe, but I don't see as there's anywhere else to go. Nobody has to come with me, but I have to—"

Hana shoved him so hard he flipped, and landed on his shoulder. "What is wrong with you?!" she yelled.

"I—I'm sorry?!"

She leaned over him so she could more easily shout at him. "Why would you let them into Orphan? And for what?"

"I think for you, Miss," tried Ellery.

"Well it was stupid! You were supposed to be angry at me! Not give up your family and any hope for your towne! How could you *do* this?"

Hana spun, and found Ellery in front of her. Once she'd had a good long look at him, she promptly belted him one, right across the mouth.

"Ow!" he yelled. "Stupid—"

"And why are *you* here?" Hana barked at him.

"That's a rotten thing, hitting a fellow like that. Ain't like I can hit a girl so you get off easy."

"Go ahead," she dared. "Hit me."

"Hartchild don't you—"

"I'm not about to hit her, Esker! Author, what sort of Wesbeldt ruffian do you think I am?!" He pointed a finger at her. "Don't ever hit me again."

Hana kept her distance from him but looked sure enough like she wanted to hit him again, or worse. Alvin breathed, and waited. Hana fumed, shook her shaggy mane, and huffed off several yards with her back to them and arms folded.

Gingerly Alvin got to his feet. Ellery stood beside him, rubbing his mouth. "I'm glad she's on *our* side. Where'd you find her, again?"

"Window shopping. Took her home with me. Wonderful violinist, turns out."

"Really?"

"No. Hartchild, there's one more thing."

"Oh what now?"

"The Halo Program was meant for you. Means you—you can teach me how it works."

"The blazes I will. Esker, you realize the power you're messing with?"

"Maybe I ain't the genius like you or your friends, but I can't change the fact that I'm the one who's carrying it. Would if I could. Can't turn this damage back unless I know how it works."

Ellery chuckled to himself, bitterly. "You know that's why Uncle Hiram chose *me* for Infusion, Esker?"

"Why?"

"Wasn't because I'm smart. It's because I ain't smart at all."

"Rubbish," Alvin insisted. "Your marks were top of the school's—"

"Tabby dragged me through schooling, Esker. Uncle Hiram said they needed someone with a 'wandering mind.' He picked me because I'm just bloody *stupid* enough to make it work. Until you came along, anyway. Seems you're even stupider."

"Right," panted Alvin, cracking his neck and rubbing the arm he'd landed on, and turning his eyes to the aurora-clad northern fields, marching up past Hana. "There's nothing for it. Off to—"

Hana caught Alvin by the arm, and pulled him to her, coiling her wrists around his neck so tight he could hardly breathe. She buried her face in his shoulder. For a long moment, he stood confused, very confused, and eventually lifted his arms and folded her up in them. Silvery mist flowed around their ankles from the northern winds.

"I will never lie to you again," she whispered. "Not ever."

"For however long that is," Alvin answered. "Might've lived a longer life if you'd gone with your people."

"Better a short life with hope than their road." Then she whispered, "But what is Duster doing here?"

"I can hear you both!" Ellery reminded them. "And if you two don't stop mooning over each other, we'll all be swallowed by that maelstrom!" Ellery came between them, yanking them back to their senses. "Probably a long, long walk, and we've got bollocks for supplies."

"Well we've some jerky, at least," Alvin reminded him. "We can share, make a meal of it."

"Would this help?" asked Hana. She rushed to one of the abandoned wagons and and tore off its cover. Under it lay Alvin's satchel, her pack, and more. "There are a few things," she told him. "And—and your spyglass."

Alvin paused. "There's what? You actually saved the spyglass?" He could hardly contain laughing, but Hana only shrugged her shoulders without even a glance. "Hana!"

"There is more," she said. "Found this. What is it?" She pulled the arc pistol spare cartridge from his satchel.

"It's for a gun we don't have. Thing's just a supercharged battery, now.

"Yah?" she added, and she produced the infamous eye of light.

"How? How did you manage this?"

"Thief," she reminded them. "But at least I am a good one, yah?"

Entry 49: "The First Astronomer"

Of this strange place and its stranger ... (occupant?) little can be said. Actually very much *could* be said if anybody knew *what* to say. Alas, nobody does, and those who do are annoyingly silent on the matter. Scattered reports from the towne of Orphan Heights in its early days make mention of the Galó from Jalóheim referring to a "Blind Oracle" of sorts, when no such belief existed prior to their settlement in the Rift, and corresponds to no known parallel in earlier Nordic folklore, fraudulent or otherwise. Furthermore, there is little to link these sparse accounts to that being encountered by two particular Orphan boys generations later.

What they encountered—or believe they encountered—wholly defies reason, and so their claims were dismissed by all competent historians out of hand. What they allegedly observed was an intelligence, luminary interplay of language, and knowledge of ancient astral events that, if true, would rewrite cosmic history as known by pretty much anybody. Neat.

One could easily still dismiss the claims of the boys, though the presence of such a being would help explain the Jalóheim Clan's choice to settle in one of the worst locations in the Expanse that otherwise makes one question their judgment, or even sanity, if not their basic competence. Still, if real, if ancient, if intelligent, if (somehow) disembodied ... if indeed he ever had a body, then his existence and relation to the present Confluence would be ... frustrating.

— PART III —

Upheaval

in which wandering children bicker, hike, & read

HANA SÓHOLDT SAT AGAPE AT ALVIN'S LIGHT SHOW, while Ellery would repeatedly tell him he was doing it all wrong. At some point she took a bite of goat jerky from Jalóheim, but forgot to chew it. It dangled from her teeth as she stared at the rings of amber light, almost without even blinking.

"Look how this big one in the middle's got directional compass points!" Alvin marveled. "What'll they think of next?"

"You've no idea what it took to translate that text into Anglish. You'll find it keeps itself level, too. The markings on your head follow where it aligns with points in your brain."

"That—that sounds charming. Why not?" Alvin tilted his body this way and that, and sure enough, the largest equatorial ring around his body kept level, and when he turned, the directional markers tracked properly. "So how does this big ring translate star-patterns for me?"

"No, the *first* phase of the program is the astral translator! You know, the two-tap one? Around your eyes?" Ellery lectured. "It's the *second* phase that reprograms the waveform."

"But I don't understand how it works."

"Neither do I! That's Lorecroft's world. They only taught me *how* to work the bloody thing. Look, the dial in your hand is the primary control interface. It's got three main rings around its edge that shift depth and X/Y axis position of whatever you're analyzing, while the other shapes it to—"

"But how's it a light without an incandescent, is what I want to know."

"Can—can I finish? May I finish, now? If it's not too disruptive to your commentary? Author! No wonder your brother calls you *chatterbold*."

"He doesn't!" Alvin defended.

"I heard him."

"You haven't. You ain't heard nothing of the like Hart … child…"

"What?"

"What's *this?*" When Alvin fiddled with the fourth dial, the Halo flashed red, and reset.

"'Temporal positional analysis functions—*locked*'? The blazes did you do to it?" asked Ellery.

"I didn't do nothing!"

"You did! It's not supposed to do that!"

"Maybe it's temperamental, just prefers the sole company of Harchester folk to you uppity types. How do I shut it off again? Weren't listening when you told me before."

"Esker, if you don't … what's the matter with her?"

"Hmm? Hana? You alright?"

Jerky hung in the breeze from her still teeth.

"I think she blew a fuse."

Alvin almost choked, and the amber projection dissipated. "'Blew a fuse.' Brilliant."

Hana took the jerky out and finally blinked, and in her usual way, tore it to ribbons. "What is that? Thought the machine in Orphan made it. Did you have *that* in your girl bag?!"

"Girl bag?" Ellery questioned. "I knew it!"

"But what *is* it? Magic glass or something?" Hana pressed.

Ellery kicked his feet together, put a finger in the air, and did his best possible Hiram Lorecroft, complete with tilting head: "Actually, dear child, it's what we eggheads refer to—scholastically, enthusiastically, and grammatically—as a Stereoptic Tangi-Light Interfused Projection!"

205

Alvin and Hana exchanged gazes of disbelief.

"Did you get quite all of that, now?" Ellery finished. "I so dislike repeating myself, and if you didn't understand, I'm afraid I shall have no choice but to use even *longer* words in the future!"

Alvin fell over laughing, and even Ellery couldn't finish without succumbing himself. "I'll—I'll do it! I *invented* words, you know! Patent-pending, of course…"

"Brilliant!" Alvin gasped. "Sounds just like him!"

Alvin leaned back on his hands, and took a long, long breath of the cold evening air. The aurora shone so bright overhead he didn't even need his lantern. White peaks on the eastern ranged glowed under the raining light from above. It was the first time Alvin had laughed, *really* laughed, since he could remember. The three had huddled by a rocky rise they used as a windbreak, and surveyed the meager gear that would hopefully keep the three of them from dying. They all agreed that it was insufficient for the task.

It was the only time Alvin Esker and Ellery Hartchild found themselves agreeing.

Without warning, fingers dug at Alvin's head. "Hey!"

"Hold still," Hana demanded.

"What're you doing?"

Callously she bent his head down, rummaging through his hair. She was not gentle. "Want to see."

"What," said Ellery. "The markings? Should be visible by now."

"Aha!" Hana pulled his hair taut. "You *do* have them!"

"This is a little invasive, you know."

"There's a ring here where you tapped your head. And lines spread up. One over each ear. And others. You sure this is new?"

"Course it's new! Now kindly release—"

"In a minute." She kept rummaging, and he came to tolerate it.

"Any water, Esker?"

"Sure." Alvin pulled open the flap on his satchel and tossed Ellery the waterflask he was carrying, still Esig's from the day at the well. It seemed to bring Ellery intense relief, tossing it back to Alvin when he finished.

"Everyone in your village had one of those, didn't they?" he asked Hana.

She nodded. "The flask is mine. The water is not. Everything in Jalóheim is ... *was* for the Last Journey Home. Had no purpose other than that. The Yedak dried a long time ago. So little water."

Ellery heaved a long sigh, and quietly put his attention back on Alvin. "What's that there?" Ellery asked him.

Alvin drew out the manuscript and ran his cold fingers over the dimpled, hand-stitched lambskin cover.

Metarcanum:
A Theory of Linguistic Constitution
of Matter & Energy
by
Agnesine Elspeth Esker

"It's Agnes's book."

"Didn't know she published one."

"She didn't," Alvin corrected. "She tried, for eight—ow! Pulled a hair!"

"Sorry."

"Eight months or so."

"Why?" asked Ellery.

"*Altruria Publishing House* is owned by old members of the Academy. *Bellamy Standard* is funded by it. And *Freeland Press* has graduates on its board of directors. Nobody would print it without the Academy's say-so. So she printed it herself."

The manuscript pulled away in Hana's thievish grip, apparently bored with Alvin's head.

"Can I see? You found this in her office-place, yah?"

Hana opened its cover and once she was passed the illustrations, she eyed every letter, every mark, as she'd eviscerated the dinner he brought her in his bedroom, the night they met. She couldn't read it, but seemed to enjoy puzzling out the markings. Mostly she skipped to more illustrations.

207

"What's it about?" asked Ellery. "Rather dull title, if you ask me."

"It's … well it's her idea about … matter and all that."

Ellery sat up straighter. "Wait. You haven't read it."

"I have."

"You haven't read your own sister's book!"

"I have!" he barked. "Well—well it ain't like I had a copy! Only found it since Hana came to Orphan. Why do you think I've got it in my bag?"

"I like the pictures," said Hana, sparkling in awe of all the illustrations the book contained. She smelled one of the pages.

Ellery added, "I hardly know why you brought half of that rubbish. A spyglass? Honestly? Don't forget you brought the bindporter that would've killed you both."

"What?" asked Hana.

"The little handle thing?" said Alvin. "Would've killed us both, turns out. Apparently it only works once."

"Well, it's always *possible* it'll work again, but it's not worth trying. Only happens one out of every hundred tries, at best."

Hana's eyes bugged out, but in her way, she shrugged it off quick enough and didn't seem to care anymore, her attention back to munching jerky and looking at pictures. She handed back the book, open.

"Alvin?" she said around the jerky. "Teach me."

"Teach you?"

"If he can teach you to make magic lights, you can teach me to read."

"You can't *read?*" asked Ellery.

Hana tightened.

"Leave her be," Alvin insisted. "She ain't stupid, I'll have you know. Hana, I'll teach you, if you want."

Hana nodded excitedly, and swallowed her food.

Once Alvin had stitched his mood back together, they surveyed what little had to carry them to the ends of the earth. Alvin had only the few things in his satchel, including the spyglass.

Hana kept her knife tight to her hip, where her hand could quickly reach it. Her goggles, the ones with the rusty clasp, nested on top of her piles of bright hair, and her waterflask sat inside her jacket. In her pack she found a rope, wraps and bandages. She still wore Mrs. Dutch's scarf and would fold it and use it for a pillow.

"Oh, this is all very useful," Ellery remarked. "We're buggered."

Hana tried to argue with him, as politely as she could manage, how she'd survived to Orphan without so much as a map or a prayer, and while they argued the sanity of the northward plan, Alvin found the manuscript still on his lap, and for the first time in his life, opened its cover.

For Alvinheim,

whose stalwart company kept me sane, all those long,

lonely hours in the vaults of my strange imagination.

His insides twisted up within him. Surely she'd have dedicated it to Albany Finch; he was her fiance! Or to their father, or mother or Alphonse or—or *anyone* but Alvin!

It shouldn't have been him, *no.*

Anyone else.

He swallowed hard and hurt his throat. He choked on those words. He wanted to erase them, expunge them from the pages or tear the page clean out of the manuscript, and if he could've marshaled the power of the designs within him, he'd have wiped them out of existence all together. Rolling around in the observatory of Alvin's mind were memories of Agnes, of these past days since leaving Orphan, and a lot of other things.

"Alvin?" Hana sat a little closer. "You are acting strange. Moping."

"Ain't moping," he insisted. "Never were an Esker who moped. Ask anyone on London Row and you'll hear—"

"*Alvin.*"

Who knew she could sound so much like his mother?

"I mean, I'm still hungry and it's cold as bollocks out here and there are nomads coming to kill us and I might have—allegedly—and inadvertently brought about the end of the world, and I barked my foot on a rock about an hour ago, but if you look past all that, things are alright. Atí lagi, and the like."

"You say so many things."

"So I'm told."

"I am sorry about your spyglass."

"What?"

"You damaged it, yah? Trying to save my leg in the rocks?" She leaned forward and gazed skyward with him. "*Was* she the last one? Maybe she was, but I think you are a—hey Duster! What is a name for someone who goes to the stars?"

"How can there be a name for something that doesn't exist!"

"'Dream' is a word, yah? Can you show me a dream?"

"I…" Ellery fumed. "*Stellarnaut* or some such, I suppose."

"Good." She turned back to Alvin. "You are a stellar-nut."

"What?" he laughed. "Hana, we can't even go to the stars—"

"But you would," she insisted. "You do not want to see them. You want to go there, to that and other places, I think."

"Rubbish, is what that is. I'm perfectly content to keep to my things. A good story now and then's all I need. Agnes was the wanderer. Ain't so adventurous as you think, Hana. I'd give just about anything to be back in the brownstone … probably ain't even there, anymore. Bed. Books. My desk. Mother's cooking. And I will! If we can reverse this all."

A troubled look came over Hana, but even when asked, she didn't voice it, instead going back to Alvin's room. "You'd also have the window you stared through," she reminded him. "Maybe they are gone. Don't know. Your bed *is* nice. So warm."

Alvin was afraid to see the face Ellery was probably making, and and he regretted looking once he did. Ellery mouthed some horrid accusations, which Alvin silently waved off and denied, thankful that Hana didn't notice their quiet argument.

"But you are always dreaming, yah?" she continued. "When I came to Orphan's window, you did not go home. You opened the door. Alvin?"

He turned back to Hana, and found her almost nose-to-nose with him.

"Um … yes?"

"Read to me."

"What?"

She pushed the manuscript into his hands. "Read," she said. "Please?"

"You know how hard it is to read in this dim light?" he mused, but she said nothing of it and he didn't bother to argue further. He turned swiftly past the dedication page and opened to the preface:

> Before beginning, I must address the coming consequence of the publication of this work, that it will entail the end of whatever career might have otherwise stood before me in the Noble Sciences, for which I have nothing but admiration.

"What does that mean?" Hana asked.

"Means she admitted that this book would be the end of her life with the Academy ... which she never even had anyway." He went on.

> I am about to propose that the universe itself is comprised, at the atomic level, of a pattern which governs all Newtonian and axiomatic laws, a vibrational pattern that is both numeric _and_ linguistic.

Alvin blinked at these sentences a few times but couldn't really understand them, and this was just the forward. He was no Agnes Esker. Thankfully, Hana didn't ask what they meant.

> This pattern, which I shall explain in the coming chapters, I have named the Metarcanum, the Mystery of All Mysteries, a grand unified equation.

Hana was asleep against his shoulder, or mostly so. She mumbled half-there, "Keep reading?"

> However, the implication of this pattern, from the atomic vibration of every particle that governs its nature, all the way up to gravitic mass of planets, having any kind of _linguistic_ nature is obvious. Bluntly oversimplified: the universe is more mysterious than we are willing to accept. It is this implication I cannot deny, and the great

Academy of Science cannot currently accept.

There was the sentence that ended her career as a scientist forever, and he remembered the day her letter of dismissal came. She'd been at her 'laboratory' for more than a week stretch, but she came home that day more chipper than any Esker ever expected. It was the last time he'd seen her peaceful.

It was after that day, her attentions focused heavily on trying to understand this pattern, and the link to his own circumstance was not lost on him.

In the quiet of that moment, he remembered what he saw emerge through those astral patterns—language. The patterns said something, a language not just of shape but of depth and time, cutting meaning out of space, a thing that should not, *could* not be there, yet it was. He'd read the language the universe itself was woven from, and seen how it could be rewritten. It made his mind spin with possibilities.

Hana was mostly asleep, and slipped her hand beneath his arm. The book seemed to lull her.

> If the reader will indulge a moment of less-than-academic confession: since I was only a little girl from Harchester, I would walk past the statues of Newton, Kepler, Copernicus and others on my way to primary school, and were taught of their great minds. These men were brilliant because they opened their minds to any and all possibilities. They and many naturalists through the ages have sought to unify what we know of the universe under a single, perfect equation. I believe it is before us, now, but it cannot be understood without acknowledging the linguistic elements within it.
>
> One final indulgence: what if man is not merely a blank slate onto which time inscribes us? The beauty of this world is that, for all its majestic complexity, it is so vividly simple. Dust might very well be what we are made of, but I am now convinced that it is not what we are.

His eyes left the page, and trailed up Hana. She so scarcely rested, yet she sat aside him now with such stillness, just breathing, in and out, and for all her temper and trial and choices and lies and endeavours, there she was, just a girl, breathing in and out.

His silence roused her. Her eyes fluttered a little and glanced up. "What?" she said, her mouth drawing back like a curtain on the one side.

"Nothing," he said. "You fell asleep."

"Oh. Sorry."

"Don't be!" he said, a little too enthusiastically. "I mean, it's alright. weren't no bother to me, and no mistake."

"Agnes sounded smart," she said as she rubbed her eyes.

"I think she'd have—"

"Get up!" Alvin found Ellery standing behind them, kicking him in the leg. "Come on!"

"What is it?" Even Hana roused and got to her feet with a little help from Alvin.

Ellery turned to show them the southern distance to the east, beyond the coming Upheaval. There in the distance, a single glimmer of light moved northwards, tightly on the trail of Alvin and Hana and Ellery. "I think someone's following us."

"Who?" Alvin posed.

"Spyglass," Hana asked.

"Oh so *now* it's useful!"

"Just give it, Alvin."

He drew it from his bag. It was hard to extend the thing, bent as the eye end was, but he got it working. Hana put it to her eye. "They're from Faldin Clan."

"They're what?" asked Ellery.

"Violent tribe, east in Istlund," she explained. "Must have seen us."

"Is this a problem?"

Alvin answered, "They'll kill us if they catch us. I'd prefer to avoid that, if possible, though I can't speak for you."

"You're not serious. Listen, girl…"

"I have a name."

"So do I and it isn't 'Duster.'" She didn't seem to care. "Ugh. Fine. *Sóholdt*, how can you tell who they are from this distance?"

"Red furs," she returned. "Easy to know who they are. We have to go. No sleep tonight."

Within a minute, they gathered their things into their packs, shouldered them up, and were ready to press on. Hana dusted over their tracks and erased all visible trace of their little encampment before they left it behind and followed the dry riverbed further north.

Nobody said anything for most of the night, though 'day' and 'night' at the top of the world meant little. It was early days of the months of daylessness, and for three lone adolescents in the barren Expanse, it was disorienting, timeless sort of journey, and it was nearly 'morning' (at least by clocked time) that they came to the edge of a rise, where the riverbed wove through the flat and empty distance beyond. They climbed over the great jagged plates that buckled like colossal pottery shards the size of limeiron foundries. Hana kept having to brush messy strands of golden hair from in front of her eyes, for the wind came up stronger from the north.

"What is that?" she asked, though obviously Alvin couldn't know.

He stopped suddenly, his eyes fixed on the very edge of the steppe far ahead of them. He had to rub his eyes free of their sleepy haze, his breath catching in his chest as he tried to make out what it possibly was that he was seeing, and finally did.

"What is that?" asked Hana.

Ellery caught up a moment later. "What are you both on about?"

"That," said Alvin.

Two immense objects rose in ghostly form at the distant rim of the steppe, perched on the plateau's edge before the land dropped low out of sight.

Whatever they were, all three travelers swore they were moving.

in which Alvin happens upon a decaying history lesson

"SHIPS!" ALVIN SHOUTED FOR HIS COMPANIONS, over the wind. They listed a solid ten degrees or more on their keels as rotting husks of prior glory, like the bones and armor of fallen warriors. "Wooden sailing ships! How in blazes could they end up here?"

Hana marveled, as he knew she would, mouth open as she gazed up at the masts, but Ellery only raised his collar to the wind. Only two still stood, but fragments and ribs of many others lay broken across the plateau's ridge.

"You knew about this too. Didn't you?" Alvin asked.

"They're us."

"Us?"

They exchanged a long, long look at one another, Alvin trying to puzzle Ellery out. Ellery didn't handle the cold, in spite of the coats Hana managed to procure, and shivered to himself even as the hull of the nearer ship started to break the wind for them. Some deeply buried part of Alvin's boyhood surfaced, reading of high adventure and lost civilizations, and here before him stood two great ships, moored forever on the edge of the land.

"Must have sailed up the Yedak," Hana guessed. "Before it dried up."

The first ship was long and slender, low and sleek, with three masts (or what remained of them) and what once were fore-and-aft rigged sails. Her oak was grey, and the mainmast lay broken like a great felled timber.

The dry river opened into a vast lake bed, and dropped off into further depths. The bottom lay covered in silvery, sandy mist that flowed from the northern landscape and poured into the basin. From its murky shimmer, the hulls and bones of many more ships protruded, phantoms in a sea of the dead. Both surviving ships apparently beached upon what once was the southern bank. Something about the agelessness, the specter of the towering apparitions gave Alvin the sense of stone temples. He squinted up at the dim shades of the plaque mounted high over them on the stern.

"'Catch'," he read.

Hana turned and put out her hands, apparently assuming he was about to throw something.

"No! That's its name! Up there. The ship's name is the *Catch*. See? That's … that's what it says."

"They name them?"

Alvin put a hand to the old ship's hull, feeling the knots and wear on her timbers. Even in the dilapidated state she lay in, half way on her beams, the mastery of her craftsmanship was evident.

"Come on!" Ellery shouted. The wind picked up. "Inside!"

Along the port side of the *Catch*, the ship was torn open beneath her keel. Her beams protruded like splayed ribs. Alvin peered into her bilge hold and found most of the ship long since hollowed out. Ellery found a place to rest his laurels and breathe, while Hana immediately occupied her gaze with scavenging for … well, anything.

As for Alvin, he strolled along what was left of the beams of her keel, soaking in the ages, imagining the men who once sailed her, the cargo they kept, the sound of boundless waters slapping against her hull.

"Hartchild?" he said. "If this ain't Angland. If it's really a polar continent, is Angland…?"

Ellery, exhausted, lifted his eyes like it was work. "Still there, far as I know, Esker." He rolled his eyes, heaved a thick sigh, and went on. "Alright, since I know you're going to ask: there was never a war that killed the world. This place is not the remains of Angland. It's a wild and savage land. That's all. Oh, and it is not the year you think it is, either."

"Of course."

At this point, Alvin had come to terms with the fact that he didn't really know anything at all, most of all the things he thought he knew for surest. Those were the first to die. He leaned against the bulwark.

Ellery talked on, a preemptive strike on Alvin's curiosity. "A flotilla of ships sailed from Angland in 1609, bound for the New World, along with a host of other Anglish vessels," he began. "The *Sea Venture* led the fleet, but these ships of the flotilla had other orders. They faced a hurricane in the Atlantic, and these ships slipped away as planned. They turned north for the Arctic Circle. They're almost three hundred years old."

Alvin lifted his face from his tired hands. "Why, Hartchild? Why?"

"They were sent to look for something, something they knew they'd find —I don't know how—and with enough iron and supplies to build so they could study it for as long as necessary."

"Even three hundred years?"

"Even for three hundred years. Or three hundred more."

"Wow," said Hana. "You all are *patient*."

Alvin got up, and walked over to Ellery. "It's this, ain't it? This thing Infused into me? This is what they came here after."

"Partly," he confessed. "I know there's a lot more to it, but Esker, I don't know everything. Alright? Look, if—where are you going?"

"Alvin?"

But Alvin didn't stop. He marched himself outside, and rested his weary body against the hull. He held his head, and squeezed his eyes shut.

"Alvin?" Hana approached slowly.

"I watched her suffer for so long," he said. "Wishing for any future but the one inside those walls. And she weren't alone! And all along, all this time … it was all a *lie*."

Hana only listened, her mouth in a crisp line.

The other ship, the grander of the two, lay perched just ahead, her long bow protruding past the edge of the drop-off. Alvin stopped beneath the ship's great and swaying shadow, a shrill wind coming up over the crest of the plateau like a charging cavalry. His eyes adjusted to the twilight against, and read the plaque between the lamps, arching over her aft cabin windows:

"They're us, Esker!" Ellery shouted over the wind. "Can we please stay inside?"

"I want to see it," said Alvin, rushing along her starboard side until he could reach weathered shrouds. When he found them reliable, he handed the lines to Hana. Alvin planted a foot on the hull of the ship and gripped the lines. He spun and faltered, but once he and Ellery were up, they pulled Hana over the bulwark.

An Orphaned Hope breathed like an ancient woman dying, waking just long enough to see their faces, her braces creaking and deck sagging into rot. She listed on her starboard side so they had to hold themselves against anything they could find. Alvin quickly found the chart room at the stern of the ship. The door cried, and one of the hinges snapped in two.

"Don't like this place," said Hana.

He found incomplete charts of the Arctic Sea, charts of the Azores, of the Channel and Cape Horn and Good Hope and many more, all laid up in rolls.

Left on purpose?

Not taken to Orphan for evidence of their source?

The cabin was otherwise largely bare. A few tattered sheets lay in a corner, but there were no chairs, no table. Didn't these things always have a table? Hana cautiously examined every crack and cabinet and loose board for anything to salvage. She moved around the room, prying off this and that. Most of the ship had long since been stripped of any excess timber, any useful metalwork, like the *Catch*.

Beside the helm, a copper plaque still hung aside the door. Most of it was unintelligible but he could make out *1591* and *An Orphaned Hope*. Alvin picked a bit of gunk from the corner of the H, and when it fell, it landed in a wooden box.

"What is that?" asked Hana.

The bare papers cracked when they lifted them out, and most were only shipping records or navigation charts. He hoped for a captain's log.

Didn't captains always keep logs? They did in all the stories. There wasn't one, but he did find one bound book, and pulled it free of the rubbish.

"The manifest," he told Hana, because he knew she would ask. *The year of our Lord, Sixteen Hundred and Nine, in the month of June,* read the heading of the voyage, and after it, pages upon pages of names and tables for every ship in the flotilla.

"'Alcot. Alanstein. Abernathy. Becker. Barclay ... Comstock ... DeWitt ... Dutch ... Erskine...'" He paused on one name in particular, once he sounded it out in his mind. "'Escher.' There were four of them. 'Werner Escher, wife: Elspeth,' That's Agnes's middle name. 'Sons: Reitz and—and *Lockwilde*'." He looked up from the manifest. "Old family name..."

He followed across the grid to Werner Escher's home and vocation. "He was a brazesmith from Eilenberg. Wherever *that* is. Look here: 'Matthew Finch – Captain.' He was captain of the *Catch*. Like Chancellor Finch. And Albany ... 'Herschel, Faust, Freeman ... Leonard' and—and no Lorecroft?" When Ellery shrugged, he turned back to the H table. "'*Heartchild*,'" he read. "'Hallisburg, Hale ... Martin,' all these people. I *know* these people. Their families. What *did* they find here? Exactly?"

The north wind howled through the broken bridge windows at the stern.

"I don't exactly know," he said.

"You don't ... know?"

Ellery stepped away, turned his attention to the walls, to the rotting curtains along the back windows, to anything else but Alvin's gaze.

"Tell him," said Hana. "If you don't, he will never let it go."

"Why do you say that?" asked Ellery.

"I know him," she answered, as if it were a stupid thing to ask anyway. "What? You won't! Like the tower in Orphan," she said, clamoring onto the slanting starboard wall to reach the overhead cabinets.

"What are you talking about?" Alvin asked.

"Why you agreed to take me to look for the book,"

"I took you because you asked me to."

"No," she said, and flung an old shelf brace over her shoulder. Alvin had to dodge it. "You hoped I was right. You hoped there was more out here than dust. You hoped there was still magic somewhere." She snatched up an old can and shook it by her ear. "Like when you found me again. It hurt you, when I said there is nothing but us. You wanted to believe in *anything*. So just tell him, Duster."

Alvin didn't respond. He let what she said rest on the floor of his mind.

"You don't understand," said Ellery. "Neither of you. No one outside can know about any of this."

"Outside?" said Alvin. "Of what? Of the Academy?"

"No. I mean, yes. None of the rest of Orphan, anyway."

Alvin stepped closer. He didn't know what he was looking for, but something in his chest started to hurt, a lot. He couldn't get his breath, and from somewhere down so low he didn't even know it was there, a few feeble words erupted. "Hartchild?" His voice cracked. "Did they kill my sister?"

Ellery's mouth tightened. Hana's fell open. She looked from one to the other, back and forth in the silence.

Alvin pleaded. "Hartchild!"

"I don't know! I don't bloody know! At least not if it was on purpose."

"On purpose?!"

"Agnes was part of the project when she was still Lorecroft's student, alright? She knew a lot of this. She'd been in the Heuridium. Lorecroft treated her like an understudy."

"You're lying—"

"I am not. I know that the thing in your bag that flashed in your eyes is the same thing that killed her. That's all I know. I swear. It's all I know."

Alvin had to sit down. His knees needed to bend. There was nothing to sit on so he opted to plant himself on the slanted floor.

But Ellery couldn't stop. "I'm only a stupid initiate, alright! My job in all this was supposed to be years away! Maybe decades! You think I wanted this? I'd have been happy enough as a chef at the bloody Songbird, but there are … *expectations*. You've got to 'live your potential,' you know? And I had one purpose. *One*."

Hana's gaze went back and forth between them, but both just shuddered in silence for a long, long moment. "I will look through the other rooms while you two quarrel," she told them, making her way carefully down the stairs and leaving the boys to themselves.

Alvin and Ellery sat in silence for some while, Hana's rummaging around sounding through the ship for a time. Narrow rays of dusty light painted the walls in red splatter.

"Who are these people? Initiated into *what?* Hartchild, I understand Lorecroft being a part of all this, but Pike? Man's a banker, and a tosspot. And *your* father? An inspector?"

"It's always been that way," Ellery told him. "It was a fraternity, back in Angland, started a couple decades before the flotilla sailed, I think. Like-minded men, ties to government and the sort. And it was always in three branches—scholarship, finance, and law. The League of Rook Fellows."

"Stupid name," said Alvin, with no better criticism. "What do these people want? This re-writing Halo thing?"

"They want a different future. What that means, I don't know."

"How many?"

"About three dozen, in Orphan, but they contract a lot of lesser work."

"I'll never heard the end of this from Alphonse," Alvin mused. "Him and his constant conspiracies. Author help us if Newkirk at the *Hilldiver* gets a hold of this…" He didn't add 'if he's still alive,' but thought it. "Hartchild? Is Tabitha…?"

Ellery's hands shuddered and rubbed together. No words. He could only shake his head, and back away.

"Hartchild!" But he was gone. Ellery stormed out and went on deck. He meshed his hands behind his head, turned this way and that, then screamed, long and loud, into the cold Expanse, with all the rage and anger that only an adolescent boy could summon. Alvin shut his eyes while Ellery cursed, kicked and smashed whatever his hands could reach.

It took Alvin a moment to realize that the Upheaval had caught up with them. He leapt to his feet and went after Ellery. "Hartchild, the ship is—"

Alvin flung himself against the wall. He didn't move, but his heart did.

There were six of them, all in hooded red furs and leather, powderguns and blades, dragging Ellery into a clear spot and throwing him hard to the deck. The ship listed and roared as the land around it all fragmented into flaking husks as the men aimed their guns at their captured prey.

CHAPTER 22

in which horrid things are done to antique sailing ships

HANA. WHERE WAS HANA? THE FALDIN HUNTERS gathered by the iron gate over the deck's cargo hatch. The hooded one who shouted the most was obviously the leader. He put his knee on Ellery's chest and held him pinned while the others stood on his arms, and the others kept their guns on him. Ellery panted hard, winced under the weight of their boots on his arms and the leader's knee in his chest.

"I—I don't know where they went."

The leader drew his dagger and pressed the tip to Ellery's cheek. Alvin held his heart in his mouth. "Where?!"

"I don't know, alright! I'm telling the truth!"

"Where is the mouthy one from the Hollow?!" the leader yelled.

"Alvin run!" Ellery screamed.

And Alvin did. He could've bolted through the broken windows and let himself down the stern, but no.

No, Hana was in here somewhere.

He ran for the stairs, vaulting between the floor and the wall, zig-zagging across the bridge. Down he went into stowage, stumbling past casks and crates. It was even darker within the belly of the ship. He bounded over the empty tables of the sail room and found the armory door. No guns left.

Never was Alvin so thankful for the Upheaval as then, for the bottomless noise outside the ship made for silent running. But finally, he ran out of room. Crossing the open floor was madness, so he huddled himself down behind the empty cargo as two of the Faldin men searched the room.

He made it three steps before someone caught his arm. He spun, swung, and nearly hit Hana straight in the eye.

"Shh!" She pressed a hand over his mouth and watched the ceiling. Once the men's steps sounded overhead, she led him into the forward hold where the ship's cisterns were housed.

"I thought you were—I thought—they've got Hartchild."

The ship rose along her starboard side. Alvin caught Hana as she stumbled, bracing against one of the cistern tanks hard enough to hear water sloshing inside the tank that still—somehow—wasn't entirely dry.

"I think we can—"

Someone hit him across the back so hard he dropped straight to the floor. Hana yelped and called his name but he was too busy hoping his spine wasn't broken.

He couldn't move.

Hana bounded at their attacker before Alvin even understood what was happening. She slashed with her knife, bounded off the cisterns and rammed her shoulder into him, but he was so much stronger. He caught her once in the stomach and that held her enough for him to hit her across the face.

Alvin rolled on his back and found one of the Faldin men over him, aiming his rifle butt at Alvin's face. He dodged its edge one, twice, and managed to kick him in the knee and roll on his side behind one of the cisterns as the powdergun swung, and *boomed* in his ears. The corner of the cistern burst, and water sprayed over the hold.

Alvin's head still swam, bleary and aching. Sounds of Hana and the man fighting came to his senses.

"Take her!" the man yelled. Though Alvin couldn't see her, he could hear her struggling, screaming, fighting. "Will bring last one." Within a moment, all turned quiet, only the striking of the man's boots against the floor. "Come out," he demanded. "Come, and they live."

Alvin crawled his way around the cistern. At the far corner lay his bag splayed on the ground. He knew nothing of powderguns, but even he could tell the sounds of loading one.

"She is pretty," his attacker taunted. "You think?"

And Alvin's blood burned in him. His fingers raked the boards, dragged himself forward, and reached for the bag.

"Think maybe we should…"

Alvin rose, and marched around the corner. The rifle rose. Alvin dove, wrenching the cover off the pistol cartridge in his hand, ramming its exposed poles into the man. They slammed to the ground together, the Faldin man convulsing and heaving until Alvin rolled off, gasping. Never had he harmed so much as a fly, and there lay a dead man's body. He held his mouth and tried to keep from being sick, but when he heard Hana's cries of struggle through the ship up above, it went away.

He held up the cartridge in his hand. While he knew little of weaponry, Alvin Esker knew lectral power. He'd discharged a *lot* of it into that man.

"One of you," he said to the cartridge. "Five men. *Bollocks.*"

Of course there was the powdergun on the ground, but he had no ruddy idea how to load it or even use it. *Think, Esker—think!*

Two decks down from topside, he could hear them threatening Ellery and Hana. They would kill them to get to him—why they wanted *Alvin*, he could only guess. His hands shuddered. They'd kill him, too. Five men, warriors, hunters, killers.

They would. Whether a bullet in the head or sword in the belly, it would end fast, and all the lights would wink out.

Alvin shut his eyes, slumped to the floor, leaned his head against the cistern, and breathed. And his mind went to another moment like this in his life, a moment when he also sat with his head against a wall.

And did nothing.

But now, this time, something *else* came into his mind.

I am tired of living like this. I don't want to believe that all we have is us. I—I want to believe you were meant to discover me. That there's a reason. That we—that we matter. Somehow.

And if that was true…

And if it were even possible…

Then what he did now would matter even more.

Alvin Esker opened his eyes. What was he? Third Class Junior…

"*Engineer*," he whispered to himself, and looked at the cartridge in hand.

Then he turned to the cisterns, and the cargo net still under the middle one. He found a halyard tied to the netting, spun it from its cleat, and loosed the line. It worked like the funicular lifts in Orphan—counter-weighted so handling weight was easy. With little effort, he quietly raised the cistern to the next deck, and from here could hear them clearer.

"Call out to him," their leader demanded. "Call him!"

"Leave her be!" Ellery cried.

One of them was struck, maybe both. "Call him!"

As Alvin readied the lines just under the open cargo hatch, there was a fury in him he'd never felt before. He loosed the top latches on the cistern, coiled the line around his arm, and braced.

And then he heard her cry in pain, and she didn't stop.

For one last second, Alvin strapped the empty powdergun on his shoulder, shut his eyes, let himself hope, and loosed the rope from the counterweight. The cistern tank shot up with him on top of it, sending him straight through the hatch and into the air above deck, where four of the men spun. The fifth had one knee on Ellery and his hand on Hana's throat.

"Esker?" Ellery called.

"Come down!" they laughed. "And we let them go!"

"Bloody likely," said Alvin, and with one feral kick, snapped free the lines holding the front of the cistern up. It swung down hard, slammed against the deck, Alvin aloft and hanging by his one arm.

The cistern's lid burst open and poured its contents in a wave against the four men, sweeping them nearly over and pooling several inches at their feet. Somehow, Ellery must've understood. He took the surprise to shove the leader off, grab Hana's wrist, and fly back as fast as possible.

The drenched men stood with ankles in water, looked up at Alvin in bewilderment, and broke into harder laughter. "Was that supposed to hurt us?" they taunted, and drew their blades.

"No." From his hanging line, Alvin took the arc cartridge in hand, and flung it to their feet. The four men screamed, convulsed, and fell, bolts of white arcing over and through them, between them, and all through the water pooled two inches deep at their feet.

The leader reached for his rifle, but stopped when Alvin spun his own rifle off his shoulder. "Don't. Drop it." Alvin knew it was unloaded, but his enemy didn't. "I said *drop* it, Esig. Throw it over the side."

"Esig?" Hana coughed, still holding her throat.

The cartridge thoroughly discharged, Alvin landed on deck. "The fella you sent after me, I'd seen him in Jalóheim."

Esig Ganikson flung his rifle over the side of the ship, and pulled down the red hood of his Faldin uniform. Slowly he lifted fierce eyes to Alvin. "Finally ready, Hugoson?" Then at his dead men: "How?"

"Don't quarrel with an engineer," was as tough a thing to say as he could come up with. "Why, Esig? Why chase us all the way out here?"

The land lurched again. Cracks in the great slope already appeared, and the plateau itself was entering the time of its disassembly.

Esig eyed him, carefully glanced back to keep track of Ellery and Hana, too. "You have something Priestess needs. Tell how to open Niavellir."

Hana rose to shaky feet. "Esig … how? Were you always Faldin?"

Esig grinned with whatever secrets he was keeping.

"Is that how Jalóheim does it?" Alvin pressed. "Pick off people now and then when the numbers get too high? Or people get too old? Always just enough water?" Esig only glowered. "Does Faldin even still exist?"

"You—you kill your own Clan?!" Hana rasped, still holding her throbbing neck. "That was *you* who hunted me that night?"

"The people abandon the Journey, if too much want," he defended. "The Journey is *everything*."

"That's twisted, mate," said Ellery.

But Esig's attention was on Alvin. "Hugoson, finally, you are ready to die." He grinned a sick, wanting grin with a glance back at Hana. "Found something to kill for—"

As if someone had snapped a great carpet beneath the earth, the

Upheaval rippled near even as the great plates beneath the *Catch* and *An Orphaned Hope* cracked away from their ageless foundation, throwing Alvin straight into Esig.

It took Esig all of a second to twist the powdergun from Alvin's grip, aim it, and *click*. "Should always check that," said Alvin, and ran his shoulder into him.

End over end they tumbled across the deck as the ship crested the edge of the plateau through surf of silvery mist, dust, rolling rock, and lectral streaks, her prow rising to a ghostly zenith before bearing into the slamming wind.

Hana clung to the deck and held on, while Ellery dove for the rail and held fast.

The bodies slumped off the edge, and into the swirling chaos.

Esig and Alvin wrestled, kicked and swung as they tumbled across the deck. With a war cry worthy of opera, Hana flung herself onto Esig's back, trying to stab him with her knife, with little success. She pulled him off Alvin and the two twirled to gain footing before Esig flung her off his back. The girl hit her head hard, clutching it with clenched teeth. Esig reached for his battered old sword and raised it over Hana.

With nothing else to stop Esig, Alvin thrust his hand into his satchel and pulled out the old spyglass with one hard swing. It flicked open to full length against Esig's blade, and rang over the lake bed.

With a hard shove, he pushed the blade off, the two clanging together again, and again, and again, until Alvin swung the spyglass's end hard across Esig's head.

"Candlesticked," said Alvin. "Now that makes sense."

All around them *An Orphaned Hope* soared through the empty space over the lake bed, listing further and further on her starboard beam.

Esig Ganikson wiped blood from his mouth, seethed at Alvin, and flew, charging him clear across the deck and into the broken base of the mainmast.

"Tell me how to open it!" he yelled, spat in Alvin's face, and Alvin couldn't hold him off. He gripped Alvin's skull.

He would've lost his grip and strength, if at that instant, Esig hadn't fumbled his hand on the wrong spot, and the Halo Program hadn't ignited and flared into luminous being around Alvin's face. Dial appearing in his palm, Alvin sparked the full program into life, rings of light flowing and breaking against Esig. Panicked and wailing, he swatted at the light as if it bound him, tripping and flailing, until Alvin hit him as hard as he could.

Before he could retaliate, Ellery slammed a deck plank over Esig's head, and it was over. Alvin's lights vanished. He shuddered, and sighed, pulling Hana gingerly to her feet as she held her head.

An Orphaned Hope shed her bones. Whole hunks of hull and bulwark broke way and hurled, spinning and spiraling faster than the eye could track. But then the ravages calmed. They didn't stop, but came to a balance. For a long instant, the ship crested a zenith of its climb, and became almost still.

Ahead of them rose the steep side of the lake bed. They careened straight toward it.

"Can you steer this thing?" Hana cried.

"Are you serious?!" yelled Alvin.

Hurling up behind them came the wreck of the *Catch*, spiraling through the air but coming almost upright as it crashed into *An Orphaned Hope's* starboard side. The rim of the lake bed was no longer higher than they were. The hulk slid down the great plate of rock it rested on and was now aimed straight for the wall, but the *Catch* was rising.

"We have to jump!" said Alvin.

Alvin gripped Hana's hand and shoved her to the edge. She bounded, and he was about to follow when he heard Ellery's cries. He'd been flung over the port side, and held on only to a cracking stanchion.

"Ellery!" Alvin yelled.

Alvin gave a last pleading look to Hana, and ran the opposite way, bounding over Esig and diving to grab Ellery's hand.

"Alvin just go!"

Alvin wouldn't. He yelled, pulling, tugging, and dragging him onto the deck inch by inch.

"Alvin! Just run! Don't leave Hana alone here!"

"Stop bellyaching and *climb!*"

The ship beneath him pulled itself apart at almost every seam as Alvin dragged Ellery Hartchild's surprisingly heavy frame onto the deck of the ship, and the two boys ran.

They bounded, tore through debris and wind and haze, and finally planted feet hard on the edge, and launched over the gap.

A vicious shout hit Alvin's ear, and he turned one last time to see Esig where they left him. *An Orphaned Hope's* bow bored into the side of the lake bed, breaking and bursting forth into a volley of hewn oak and mangled iron.

Then it was the *Catch's* turn.

She listed sideways as her rudder caught the edge of the land. Alvin knew nothing more than the spin of that fateful impact. He felt himself slamming into things, and things slamming into him, into arms and shins and fingers and forehead as the remains of the *Catch* slowly blew to pieces against the northern bank.

ENTRY 4: "SLEEPING GIANTS OF THE HEIDEKKEL"

There is an old Galó myth of the Ghost Gallies of the Expanse, a fleet of long ships which once sailed from the frigid wastes of Niflheim when the world was new. The tale was told only once, by an inebriated old man in the drinking hall of the Faldin Clan, and was thereafter forgotten by everyone (except for this fine volume). He told how the great clan leader who was known by his comrades at the time as Erik the Daft had gathered a crew to sail for the land of gods, a venture that earned him the title. To everyone's surprise, they found it. Into a wild country they went, encountering a god that Erik knew as "Jalós" ('Ya-loce'), who would seal them within the land for many ages, so said the old man in the drinking hall. The sailors would marry wild women and have adventures chronicled in following chapters, and spend many ages sailing a sea that never found shore, before losing both their way and the mythic country. They sailed until their ships faded into mist, the bones of their timbers settling into the sea until the land arose and lifted them into daylight. The preceding tale went on to be heard by as many as six drinkers in the hall, none of whom committed the story to memory. It would go on to be forgotten by the universe itself, due to its connection to a continent that would come under the distressing strain of non-existence, which would bugger up absolutely everything. Curiously, there is no recorded origin of the ships among Orphan's Archives, but there does exists a legend in Orphan Towne of the Sleeping Giants of the Expanse, two great skeletons of ancient enormous travelers that would come to life and devour any poor approaching souls; this myth has been disregarded by scholars as having been derived from Orphan's mothers, persuading their children to remain within towne, with the additional bonus of frightening them into doing their chores.

in which odd companions make fools of themselves

THE ALVIN ESKER OF ALVIN'S MIND OBSERVATORY rubbed off the filthy eyepiece of his inward telescope. The lens wasn't cracked, at least, but it would take him years to tidy the place up after that much ruckus. His papers lay everywhere, not to mention all the fittings and wires and insulators he'd horded over his brief time as a Third Class Junior Lectral Engineer.

He peered through the eyepiece. Saturn was upside down.

Maybe it was the lens.

No, it wasn't the lens.

He breathed on the eyepiece and rubbed it again. What was happening out there? He angled his scope groundward and saw … timbers? He swore he saw a mast out there, staked at an angle into the ground like a javelin.

Is Esker awake yet?

He mutters. Mostly about soups at the Songbird, but no.

That water thing was bloody brilliant. Don't ever tell him I said so.

Alvin spun his lens to recent memory but quickly dismissed what he saw as nonsense. Sailing a ship through the Expanse, the very idea! Dueling with a spyglass. Absurd.

Why would he do that? He shouldn't have come back for me at the end.

Maybe he did not want you to die.

It's never that simple.

We lived. Yah? He still will not wake up.

Have you tried hitting him?

Think I should?

I would pay good money to see it.

How much money? And how hard?

Whatever that racket was, it was interrupting Alvin's cosmic dusting, and there was plenty of that to do. There was still Saturn to deal with. The wreck of the *Catch* was bad enough to knock a whole planet on its end!

Hard. Hit him hard. Half a crown.

That had better be a lot. Open your eyes, Alvin!

Alvin opened his eyes in time to see Hana's palm coming.

"Ow!"

The first thing he knew was that he (likely) *hadn't* died. The second was that his face hurt more than the rest of him, suddenly. Hana's stern eyes spread into a beaming, open mouth drawing back like a curtain.

"Alive!" she hollered, throwing herself on top of him. "The boat, it went to splinters, like this." Hana gestured an explosion, and even made the noises with all the exuberance of a toddler. "*Ker-foom!* We made camp under its bones," she explained.

"Did you tell him?" Ellery called.

"I'm talking to him!" Hana snapped, then turned back to Alvin. "It's nothing. We're fine. Don't listen to him."

"Did you tell him or not?" asked Ellery.

"Tell me what?" asked Alvin. "Did I lose a leg? Oh blazes, I've lost a leg! You probably already amputated!"

"Alvin."

"I—how can I possibly be an Engineer without a leg? What'll I do? *Wheel* myself on top of gatehouses and garden pergolas? I should've tucked and rolled when the ship hit…"

"Alvin! Your legs are still there."

"It's an arm then, is it?"

"Actually, we lost the bags, Duster's and mine. Yours is here—"

"Oh thank heavens!"

"—but ours are gone. Means we've lost the extra water. Food, too, and blankets."

"You're—you're hurt," he said, once she propped herself on her hands over him. Hana's upper left arm was bandaged from just below the shoulder with thick fabric.

"Didn't die." She shrugged. "Just a gash. Found bits of sail to make this. Duster helped."

"The gash is deep," Ellery added. "But Sóholdt here handles pain better than a smelter." Her lower arm was still stained muddy red from whatever wound lay under the wrapping.

"No," said Alvin, pressing his aching body up sitting. He took her arm in his hands. "You got hurt. Is it bad? I mean, it ain't to the bone or something because you could die from infection or the loss of blood. We should—"

"Alvin, I will heal!" she assured. "No stranger to injury."

They were under the carcass of the *Catch's* stern, which lay splayed upside down like a great oak ribcage. The northern lights shone in curtains overhead, currents of green and pink and cyan ripples.

Alvin's head swam.

"Don't touch." She slapped his hand. "You got gashed too. On your head. Not bad but leave it alone."

Then Ellery came into view of Alvin's hazy sight. She had him reclined up against a piece of the ship, his arm in a sling, head bandaged, and right leg bound to a bit of lumber as a splint. His whole body was dotted with blood.

"Hartchild!" said Alvin. "Blazes! What happened?"

He seemed to wince every time he so much as leaned his head, but he never answered Alvin. He watched him for a moment with narrow eyes, like he was trying to puzzle something out. His leg had to have been ravaged.

"Can he walk?" Alvin asked her quietly.

"Don't know," she said. "Arm's broken. Had to set it. Legs seem okay, but pretty bruised."

"You set his arm?"

"Mmm hmm." She tucked a truss behind her ear. "Done it before."

"Oh?" both Alvin and Ellery responded.

"Harchester is not the only rough place." She winked. "We have to rest. Duster needs some time."

"You think he can—"

"Alvin. We need to rest," she insisted.

"Hana?" Ellery interrupted.

She and Alvin exchanged a grin. "He called you 'Hana,'" he whispered, and she nodded. "Don't punch him this time. Be nice."

She nodded again. "Yah, Duster?"

Alvin groaned in a long sigh.

"Tell me about the Expanse, will you? You've been out here. What are we headed for?"

"Never been to Niavellir," she admitted, not that it was any secret. "What do you want to know?"

"Anything you can tell me about it. Esker's not the only one who's never been out of Orphan, you know." He breathed hard, and slow. Hana looked so tired, but humored them without complaint. She sat by him, and shared what little she knew, some of the stories she'd heard about Niavellir as a little girl. What was folklore and what was true, she'd no idea.

Then she asked him what he knew of the Galó.

He proved no expert, but regaled her with the little bit of history he knew, how her people had sailed to that land hundreds of years ago, how they were once a fearsome and vibrant lot among the northern places of the world, how operas had been written of them. His folklore was quite weak, but his recounting of heroes like Sigurd against the dragon Fafnir or Tyr's trickery with the great wolf Fenrir was enough to broaden her eyes, and bring a zeal to her heart Alvin rarely got to see. Then he told her of Beowulf.

And while they talked, the cool glow of the northern lights grazed her face, and lit a few strands of hair. Alvin found himself lost in the simple clarity of her shape—the smooth curve of her expressive mouth, her ears, the freckles across her nose, her stunted eye teeth. If one thing were out of place, she wouldn't be Hana, not even the grit in her voice, nor mismatched eyes.

Then she caught him looking. "What?"

"Nothing."

"Don't mind him," said Ellery. "He's always drifted off like that. In school, the tosser would doodle designs for flying machines instead of taking notes in Agromatics class."

"Was the class bad?" asked Hana.

"Agromatics," Alvin interrupted, "is where learning goes to die. If I'd an enemy—truly vile one, and the like—I'd wish him a fair sight better fate than ending up in one of Erskine's lectures on symbiotic lichen, I don't mind telling you. Flying machines was a better use of class time."

"No, no," said Ellery. "Heaven help me, Esker's right. Pretty sure Erskine's mosses weren't over-watered that year. They committed suicide."

Hana, for whatever reason, belted into harder laughter than Alvin had ever heard from her, so hard she couldn't stop herself, and near fell on her back—and then she did. Alvin laughed and helped her up.

Ellery chuckled, but couldn't move much yet. "Poor plant-life. Only grows now in the hills of the Undiscovered Country."

"The what?" asked Hana.

"Undiscovered Country. It's from *Hamlet*. Act Three. Father has me and—and Tabby read Shakespeare every spring. Means death, the unknown future on the other side."

"Oh. Yah."

"Well," he said when finally they settled. "It's the end of the world as we know it. And I'm facing it with a tosspot Third Class Engineer and a thieving makeshift viking berserker maid ... *Author*, I need a widowmaker."

They laughed a little at this, too, and then Hana asked what it meant. Alvin explained what a pub was. Then he tried to explain why the workmen were so fond of them, and she didn't need it explained to her. She eyed them both for a long moment, then reached into her coat.

"Oh thank heavens," said Ellery.

"What? I miss something?" said Alvin.

Hana drew out a vial from her pocket.

"You thirsty, Hartchild?" he questioned.

"Nah," she said. "This is *not* water. *This* is for pain, old Galó elixir. Calms nerves. Rests body. Gave Duster a little while you slept, for his leg, and I had some, too. Arm … arm hurts. Just a sip."

She tossed it to Ellery, who happily drank a little, blared his eyes at the heavens, and leaned his head back against the beams of the broken ship with a deep sigh. "Cheers to what ails ya, Esker … or however it goes."

He tossed Alvin the vial, and he took a meager drought, coughed hard, and handed it back to Hana with watering eyes.

"That there stuff," said Ellery, "would give the *Lager Than Life* a run for its money."

"And no mistake," Alvin added. "What's in it?"

Hana shrugged, and took some herself. "Nobody ever told me. 'Good for the soul,' is said in Sóholdt. Lots of things said in Sóholdt." She took a long breath, and added, "Most are stupid, though."

This made Ellery and Alvin laugh all the harder.

Over their fool heads, the aurora rained down its colours. The Upheaval was coming, and they all knew it, but they also knew their bodies were exhausted beyond measure, strained beyond ordinary breaking, and something unspoken among them said their spirits needed to laugh at the most pointless and ridiculous things, for no reason at all.

"Does it seem like it slows down, sometimes?" Alvin mused.

"What, time? Only after a pinch of that stuff she gave us…"

"No! I mean the Upheaval. Seems to me like sometimes it comes crashing in and others it lollygags about for long stretches."

"I have an idea about that," Hana proclaimed.

Both Alvin and Ellery stopped everything, even breathing. "You?" they both said in unison, but the shocked glower she gave back averted their eyes.

"I think," she declared. "It slows down when you are sleeping. Or weak. Or hurt."

"Might, actually," Ellery mused. "If the liminium draws energy from the body. Might be true. You're not as dumb as … sorry. That's not how I mean it. Hana?" said Ellery. "Tell me something. Why do you call me

'Duster' all the time?"

Alvin held back laughing again, but when Hana's face shaded red, he looked at his countryman and explained, "Because you are in extreme need of a haircut, Hartchild."

"In need of a…"

It went on like this, every little thing bringing them back to a point of idiocy, and nobody complained at all.

Eventually, Ellery lifted an imaginary glass in his hand to the sky, and made his toast. "To the Undiscovered Country, fellow strays! Whatever it may look like. And however near it may be…"

<hr>

"Why are we doing this?" Ellery asked, shivering as he stood (as best he was able to stand at all) on a small outcropping, staring down at a modest pile of rocks on the ground.

"It is important," Hana answered. She dropped a large rock in place, heaviest she could lift with her bad arm, and went back for another.

"Why?" Ellery stood perched on the makeshift cane Alvin made him from rubble that was once a ship.

"It just is," she explained.

Alvin dropped a rock down in its place, panting between trips. One by one, he and Hana collected rocks and stones and planted them over mangled remains.

"But why," continued Ellery, "are we having a funeral … for a *spyglass?*"

"Because we are," Hana insisted.

"We are all likely to die, you know."

"Exactly," she said. "But nobody can give us one."

There wasn't much left of it. It limped broken from its telescoping joints. Its lens was broken through and missing half of it, and its eye end was buckled and cracked. Not even Alphonse could repair it now. Alvin went to it, unscrewed the aperture lens, held it up, and looked at Hana, skewed into mismatched warping through the broken glass. Then he set the final stones.

"Won't it just be torn up when the Upheaval comes for it anyway?"

Alvin hadn't thought of that.

"Do not ruin this!" Hana insisted. "It is important."

Alvin stood formal and stoic, hands folded, and Hana pulled off her goggles. "Should I say something?" he asked.

"It's a bloody spyglass!"

"Oh noble telescope," Hana began, her word choice pleasing Alvin. "You were a good telescope. Your mounts never creaked. You made the moon a little bigger, and you gave your master happiness."

All of them shivered in the steep wind, but Alvin thumbed his eyes.

"He's getting emotional over a tube of brass…"

The winds rose. Hana drew a little closer and shivered harder. "And in the end, you saved our lives," she continued. "What other telescope has ever faced single combat, and won? None."

Ellery pinched his eyes hard. "What was *in* that stuff you gave us?"

"Don't remember, but there is a *lot* of it," Hana admitted. "Spyglass, you died bravely, and even the great … somebody name an astronomer…"

"Galileo," Ellery told her.

"Galileo himself would have honoured your sacrifice! And hired sculptors to make a statue of you. If spyglasses have souls, may your spirit rest forever. In space or something."

"Amen," Ellery sighed.

Between all their gathered work, they managed a ragged little camp for the night, even including a crackling little fire, thanks to the aged splinters of the *Catch*. They had its skeletal bow for a windbreak on one side and a rocky rise on the other. Whether or not Hana's theory was true, the Upheaval did seem to slow itself some. It was easy enough to hear coming, at least. The fire meant *hot* food for once, and all three agreed to 'go out like kings' on the last of the rations left in Alvin's satchel. Now and then, Niavellir was visible in the distance, and wasn't far now.

"You thought it was a ruddy *book?*"

"Yah," she defended. "The stories in Jalóheim said so." Hana took the meat from the fire and gave some to the boys, both of whom burned their hands on it immediately. "Oracle told me it was in the tower but nothing more about what it was."

"Bloody stings," Alvin grumbled, perched on a rock he used as a stool, sketching something in his battered leather notebook. "Would un-flip the switch, if I could."

"Would you?"

"Of course! Ain't that the whole point of this? Everybody's got things they'd undo, don't they? Turned left when we ought've turned right, and the like. Leave it be."

Ellery tried to peer at Alvin's work. "What are you drawing?"

"Hmm? Oh. It's nothing."

"Spill it, Esker."

"It's just … I had this idea. For flying."

"There he goes again," sighed Hana. "He loves his flying machines."

"No it—it's the Halo Program. It's almost like a gyroscope, ain't it? The way its rings measure direction and astral positions and the like. Keeps itself balanced. And I thought, when we were hurling across the lake on them ships, how much easier that'd make flying? You could use it like a guidance tool. So I were just sketching it out."

Alvin showed them. On the page adjacent to where he'd drawn the hovering object from the Heuridium, he had sketches of the Halo Program and how to use it for that purpose.

"Esker," Ellery said slowly. "That—that's brilliant. Author help me, it is."

"It's nothing," Alvin assured him.

"Bollocks, it isn't. To adapt something like that for that purpose? You're not quite the rubbish engineer I thought."

"You're so awfully kind, Hartchild. They'll put your words on greeting cards, one day. You wait and see."

"So," Ellery pressed. "What would you do different, if you could unwrite the choices?"

And when he asked it, all the focus went out of Hana's eyes. She tilted her head slightly, and stared into the fire. Whatever rolled through her mind, it shaded her face redder. At first Alvin thought it was the light of the flames, but no.

"Hana?"

"Can I think?" She tried to hide it in a forced laugh.

"There's one thing I still don't understand," Ellery continued. "Esker, how in blazes did you come to know the security codes for Orphan?"

Alvin finished his bite, and swallowed. He knew better than to tell anybody about it, but Ellery wasn't stupid. The curious mood of that lone evening seemed to be a quiet acceptance of whatever lay ahead for them, so if there was ever to be a time, it seemed the one.

"Agnes was engaged, before we lost her."

"To Albany Finch, I know. Everyone knows that. Poor blighter's not been able to set his sights on a single girl since."

"She and Uncle Otto were close," he explained. "Otto's interests weren't in physics. He was too obsessed with legends of Agarta and *anything* of the like, but he also didn't treat her like she were cracked. Otto wanted to leave Orphan and find his lost kingdom or whatever's out there. Talked year in and out about it, he did. Hated Orphan almost as bad as Agnes. Then Albany fell in love with her. Father gave his blessing. Closer Agnes and Albany got, the worse her hate of Orphan got. Said it made her feel like a piano key, just there to be played. No freedom, for her. Like a happy life with Albany and one still stuck Orphan couldn't work together."

"I know about your loony uncle. Half of Orphan did, before he died. What's it to do with Orphan's gates, is what I'm asking?"

Ellery was obviously in pain. Hana had given him the vial of her elixir, and he helped himself to a little more, but passed some on to Hana next.

"Otto set his mind to leave, few years back."

"Can't just leave," Ellery noted, chewing on his dinner.

"Right. Well, happens that his grand-niece was engaged to the son of the Chancellor."

Ellery stopped with his teeth in the meat, and drew back. "You don't actually mean that Finch—"

"Gave Agnes the door codes. I was there when he left."

"Left? The papers said he'd keeled over of a stroke!"

"Weren't no stroke. Set off with his huge pack and cane and cap and all. Said a hardy goodbye. Don't believe the papers, Hartchild."

Alvin didn't need to angle the lens of his mind to that day; it was often there. It was the first time in his life he'd felt moving air like that, when the great gate ascended.

"There was this long moment when … when I thought she was leaving, too. She just stared into the sun, hanging there northwest, like a lamp calling a moth. Minutes went by and she just—just stood there after he'd gone. Asked me if I'd ever thought about it. She talked about it to herself. Worried me sick, she did. Finally I grabbed her hand, and she snapped out of it. Didn't realize she'd dropped the code list, though. Being the helpful chap I am, I picked it up."

"Nicked it, you mean," said Ellery. "Fellows do mad things for a dame. Lovesick mutton-head that he is. How that freak memory of yours works, though is more than I'll ever know, gave you too much the edge in engineer training, it did."

"How *do* you remember things?" Hana added.

Though he'd been the one talking, he suddenly felt under a spotlight. He got up, stirred the fire, and tossed on another plank. "Everybody thinks its a gift," he said.

"You realize how rare it is to be born with a mind—"

"Weren't born with nothing," he insisted. "When I was little? Couldn't remember nothing. Forget what I was doing half the time. Forget my own house number. Mum wanted my brain tested, but father said no."

"Then how…?"

"Agnes would sit with me, teach me exercises. Taught me to picture things I'd seen in a way I liked, so I started thinking like I was looking through an observatory at my own memories. Somehow that helped them to stay, well, *focused* when I thought about 'em. She'd work with me for hours until I got it right."

Ellery had no answer to this. Hana didn't seem to either but she was still staring into the fire, even as Alvin stirred it.

"I would stay," she finally said, and broke the quiet.

"What?" said Alvin.

Her cheeks flushed again. "That is what I would change. I would go to Orphan, to Harchester and your house, with your mother's cooking and your father's lectures and your brother's kindness, and your—*your* ... and nothing at all would pry me from that place, not *ever*. Live in the attic if I had to.

"Esker, better take that elixir back from her, now."

"Right." Alvin chuckled, and plucked it from her.

"I am serious!" she insisted. "Haven't you ever wished *you* could undo something? Besides *that?*" She gestured to the pulverized continent behind them.

Both Alvin and Ellery grew quiet. Alvin shut his eyes, and he did something he never normally would.

"There was a Thursday," he began. "When she told me not to come to Cavendish after school. She'd said she had an experiment to run, a way to understand her 'language' of stars, the key to transmutation of matter. Course, now I know what she was after. Anyway, I went. I got there and she was in that back room, through the windowed door and there was this—this awful light. It blared so bright I—I couldn't even see. There was all this noise of generators. She kept muttering about 'more current,' and how she could 'almost see it.' I called, but she didn't hear me."

Alvin's eyes dampened. Hana seemed to notice, brow tight and leaning in to watch him closer.

"And then something went wrong. Whatever was happening, it was killing her. I didn't—I didn't know what to think. If I opened the door, it would've killed me, too! That's all I could think about. Agnes, she called out for help. What could *I* do? What could—so I ran. I ran home, and got Father."

Alvin swallowed the last of the elixir down. "'Heart failure,' they called it. She died in her chair, just ... just *slumped* there. Couldn't understand what killed her—none of us could. Do now, of course."

For one long, unguarded moment, he looked up at Hana, and stayed there. "She needed me," he said. "And I ran."

Hana happened to glance over to Ellery, then nodded for Alvin to do the same. Ellery's eyes were wet. "Tabby was in a coma, when I left," he said. "You ran? Let her die? I probably killed mine, Esker."

Long silence fell on them.

The fire crackled here and there, but it was Hana who finally got up, belched, and informed the boys, "Well, don't *we* all have our ghosts? Enough sulking. You cannot change it. Any of it."

"What if we can?" Alvin whispered to himself.

"Come. Time for sleep, boys. Tomorrow, Niavellir." Hana had to rest her leg, and Alvin was glad of it. She didn't complain, but he reached his tolerance of handling the sight of her limping and clutching her own thigh when she thought they couldn't see.

"Suppose you're right," yawned Alvin. "Can't speak for you all but I'm quite finished with all this 'being awake' business."

"Likewise," said Ellery. "Anyway, just need a minute on my back. Then I'll help clean things up…"

Four minutes later, they had to move away from his snoring.

Alvin slid himself back and sat against an inclined rock, just under the protection of the overhanging bow, and he started when Hana marched over toward him, plopped herself down between his knees, and shouldered herself back against his chest.

"Um…"

She made nothing of it, just flopped her shaggy head against his shoulder. "Tell me more," she said.

What was he supposed to do with his hands?

He needed his father.

Or Alphonse in a pinch.

No, not Alphonse.

"Uh—of—oh. What do you want me to tell?"

"Hmm … what happened to the uncle?"

"Otto? Never saw him again. Nobody did. I wondered if he'd been seen in Jalóheim but seems he wasn't. I wonder about him often. He was a nutter, but a great one. He would've loved you, and no mistake."

"Oh yah?"

"'Feisty,' he would've called you. 'A lass with spirit!' or the like. Then he would've slapped me on the back."

"Why?"

"Because … he just would've. That's all."

If Agnes had been there, she'd have put a hand to her mouth to cover a giggle, and whispered for him to not panic, and just be kind to her. Alvin stroked her head a few times.

"Alvin?" she said softly. "What will happen if you undo everything? How—how much will go back how it was?"

"I suppose it'd be like before any of this ever happened." She grew darkly quiet. "Hana?"

"Nevermind," she told him, and settled herself more comfortable. "I like this," she said. "Talk more?"

Alvin put a hand on the crook of her arm, and used the other to point out stars. Hana settled and relaxed while she listened to him nervously explain the heavens.

"Well, that there's Orion," he began. "He's half below the horizon so he looks like he's drowning in the Upheaval right now. Funny, huh?"

"Mmm hmm."

He pointed out Gemini, Auriga, and Perseus, explaining in brief what these images were. A minute later, she took his arm and wrapped it over her waist like a quilt, which made Alvin's pulse triple. While she slept, drooling on his shoulder just a little, it settled on Alvin that there was nothing he would not do for her.

Nothing.

And something about that frightened him. He happened to glance to Ellery, who shuddered there, fumbling with his hands, and when Alvin called to him, it startled him more than it ought to have.

"Hey. Hartchild?"

Ellery couldn't look at him. He seemed so *strange*, all of a sudden. "Esker … there's something I haven't told you. Haven't told anybody. I left … I left Orphan for a lot of reasons. But there's one more."

"Besides Tabitha?"

Ellery nodded. "Besides Tabby. I—I had my own jobs for the Initiative. I were in charge of one of Orphan's major systems, training to operate it, get it working. But. I couldn't."

"What's so awful about that?"

"They don't *know* I couldn't. And—and Orphan's going to fall. Look, I thought I'd more time! Years! Thought they'd never know that I—I mucked it up. Couldn't face them, then. Even Lorecroft doesn't know. That—that's why I found you, wanted to bring you back. I thought maybe you could…"

For a long moment, Ellery just looked at the ground, letting the wind sting his face as it stung Alvin's. Hana, at least, quietly snored against Alvin.

"Mind telling me what the problem was? Which system?"

"It's in the Toroidal Field Governor. It's a system that—well without it working, Orphan *can't* survive this."

"Ain't there no way to fix it?"

"The field just won't yield enough force like it ought've. I don't understand why. I know the system was too fast for what Orphan could handle, but slowing it wouldn't do enough. No matter what I did, it was like something was *blocking* the field."

"But what's it do?"

Hartchild chuckled. "I don't think you'd believe me if I told you."

"Really? After all this?"

"Maybe. Don't matter now, anyway. He glanced up just long enough to catch Alvin's eye, then looked down again. "See? You're not the only one who doomed Orphan, are you?"

Alvin knew the feeling, but had nothing to say, no words of great comfort beyond, "Condemning yourself won't help anyone, you know," to which Ellery said nothing.

They sat for some time like that, until Ellery finally looked over to Alvin, and to the ragged thief girl sleeping against his chest. A little smile lifted his face. "You're not getting rid of her now, you know."

"I'm what?"

"She's hitched herself to you. Like a stray dog." He must've anticipated

Alvin's response to that because he put a hand in the air and added, "I don't mean that how it might've sounded. I only meant … her loyalty is really quite fierce, isn't it?"

He heaved a long sigh, worn and sore, and was shortly snoring again, himself.

"Would've stayed forever," Alvin breathed, looking down at the wild creature that had come so abruptly into his life and broken it into shape, a stone hurled through the window of his future. He would've given his eye teeth to see her safe in the Esker brownstone, nestled beneath one of his mother's famously comforting blankets.

But she wasn't.

She was here, and here with him, in this frigid wasteland that might as well have been the moon. What could he do but let her cocoon herself between his tired arms? Alvin was no Agnes. Orphan was anything but ideal, but he had no such lofty wishes as her.

Then how did you end up here? he asked himself, and had no answer.

For the first time since leaving Orphan Towne, Alvin Esker's heart lightened. In the days to come, he would often return to those hours through his lens, and linger. With the bare stars overhead and Hana held snug in his arms, he was utterly and fully content beyond anything he'd ever felt even in the brownstone.

It was, sadly, not to last.

in which three fool kids are on the top of the world

ACROSS THE STEPPES, THERE WAS SOUND, but none from living things nor any sense of them, only the unfettered winds down the spines of the stone plates. It swept currents of silver mist where they parted around Alvin and Hana and Ellery's feet, only to merge again a few steps beyond, as if they'd never been there at all. It was the silence that chilled them, the cosmic stillness of what seemed a dead and ancient world, with old stars burning slowly to embers. Hana, as always, clamored over the rocks and plates far easier than the other two, though her leg still gave her a hefty limp.

And when they came to the city, the miles-thick, crumbling, rotting, dry bone and hollow and wailing city, they strode its avenues as the only phantoms to have disturbed the dusty mist for ages. It circled the axis as a great and empty ring, only now waist-high columns and former walls and corners.

And at its center—at everything's center—rose a great pyramid, a great and monolithic structure, at nearly a mile wide and rising to a truncated top maybe midway up the height of what it would have been if it rose to a peak.

"Is that Niavellir, then?" asked Ellery.

"Has to be," said Alvin. "We're at the axis." Alvin pointed up. "The stars," he explained. "They only move like that at the axis. It's called 'tholiform,' like turning an umbrella over your head."

"But Agarta is supposed to be *past* a gate at Niavellir. I see no gate. And if this is the pole, isn't 'past' it just down the other side?"

"Maybe it's on top?" mused Ellery, but as they came near its base, he winced far more often, and harder. He slumped. Alvin caught him, and they sat him on a stone. "I'm sorry," he said. "I don't think I can climb that. Least not without a rest."

"Hartchild, we'll help. Here, put your arm over my neck—"

Ellery buckled. "I'm telling you to leave me here!"

Hana slipped his arm over her neck, and Alvin did the same on the other side. They limped along with him in tow.

"Esker," he said. "Listen. This is idiocy—"

"Think of the stories you'll be able to tell Tabitha!" said Alvin. "What do you think she'd say about that stereopticon? Or saving Hana from lightning? Or—or sailing a ship across the air! Or seeing the north pole?"

"Don't you want to tell her about it?" added Hana.

But Ellery stumbled, and plunged to the ground. His leg bled through the bandages, and he shuddered at every joint.

"Esker. I can't. I—I'm sorry. Take Hana, and go up there. Relax. I don't aim to sit here and die. Just need to rest. Go ahead and come get me when you find out … if you find anything at all." He put a hand on each of their shoulders, and forced a smile at them both. "It's alright," he promised.

Alvin and Hana would help each other up the damaged and ageless steps of the great silvery pyramid, give hands and "alley-oops" to clamor over the great breaks in the rock and stonework. The stars still hung over their heads in turning sheets. When they came to a hollowed-out chasm in the stairs, Hana gasped for breath, her arms shaking to hold on. Alvin momentarily turned his back to the rock and rested his head back against in inside 'wall' long enough to breathe.

Hana touched his arm. "We will make it. Yah?"

He panted, but gave her a nod, at least. "Hana?" he asked, trying in his way to ask if *she* could make it.

Her mouth drew back as it bared her short eye teeth through a forced smile of her own. "Ends of the earth," she told him.

"I think we're there, actually," he mused.

It's supposed to be like a great wheel in the sky, Agnes once told him. *According to your uncle. He says many ancient cultures have a 'myth-memory' of an origin at the axis, but I suppose he says a lot of things.*

A hard wind surged over the rim of Niavellir like a wave at its crest, blowing dust in their faces at first, and taking Hana full off her feet.

"Hana!" He grabbed for her wrist, and caught her palm, her fingers, then only the strap of her jacket in his hand and held to an edge of stone with his other.

Then he lost the strap.

Why does it fascinate me? You're right. Physics is more my interest, but I admit, there's something about being at the center of all things that strikes a chord, doesn't it? I'm idealizing, I know, but I imagine it would be like touching the face of the Author himself.

"Alvin!" Hana screamed, sailed over the edge above a rupture in the slope, where her jacket caught a stone. "I can't reach!"

With only the cyan light of the aurora overhead, all he could do was try to reach her, pulling against the currents of gale-force winds.

"Give me your hand!" he yelled.

She hung over the drop and flailed for him, dangling from her shredding coat. "It's ripping!"

And then it tore clean. He grabbed her hand, his body and arms unwilling to let her go again until she found the footing she needed.

I'm sorry I'm like that. I know. I know I should just be happy here. And Albany … but that's just it, Al. I want to marry him, but I want to give him a better life than sitting out his days in this—this iron prison. This isn't about rewriting the world in a day. It's about a keyhole glimpse to a hopeful tomorrow, nothing more.

Hana's coat soared off the edge and vanished in the distance, but they found solid enough landing, and breathed together for a long moment. Alvin pulled off his own jacket and swung it over her. "Just take it and don't argue!" he demanded.

In the moment of that breath, they gazed back down at the world below. Ellery wouldn't have long, down there. Nothing would.

We're nothing but cogs in a machine here, Alvin—not just in Orphan but in the minds of men who guide it. Their brave new world is an age of pre-written destiny. Aren't we more than a blank slate that time inscribes us on?

As the last grasp pulled him onto the top of the ridge, Alvin helped Hana up and they both slumped to a heap. Alvin Esker rolled onto all fours, faced the heart of the world, the top of the great pyramid and the center of the axis of the world, and beheld with the eyes of an astronomer.

"Alvin?" Hana asked, her voice thin and quivering.

"I don't understand," said Alvin.

There was nothing there at all. A few ancient columns circled the great top of the structure, but most of those stood broken and low.

The center of the great plateau housed a curious flat tile in the floor, several feet across, intricate with inscription and symbols, an almost mirror-finish to it. Alvin felt it, knelt, spoke to it, tried to pry it up, and even smash it. "Maybe this … maybe it's …"

Nothing. There stood no gateway, no stairs, no Jacob's Ladder, no laboratory, no inscription of any pattern of any kind. Alvin turned, and turned again. He ran a hand through his hair, wiped his face, stamped and stammered and spun and cussed under his breath.

"Alvin?"

He started gasping, holding his chest. And he ran to the other side to look over the far edge of the pyramid. On the far side was only the other side of the corpse of the great city, and to his horror, the Upheaval. It had circled all of the Expanse. Hana tried to take his arm, but couldn't catch him.

He didn't mean to pull away.

He didn't mean anything.

He didn't mean for this to happen.

He didn't mean to abandon his father and brother and mother.

He didn't mean to deliver his friends to their doom.

"Alvin, please," Hana pleaded. "Calm—calm down. Alvin!"

He gnawed on a thumb when it itched, rubbed his neck when it hurt, grabbed at his heart when it tore itself to ribbons in his ribs.

Alvin plunged to his knees and hollered, a long, piercing, furious yell that made his ribs throb and mouth burn. Hana threw herself in front of him, taking his face firmly in and shouting in her best Elise Esker.

"Alvinheim Lockwilde Esker! Listen to me! Don't give in now!"

"Hana, there ain't no record, no column, no anything. How do I undo it now?" He grabbed her wrists as she held his face. "Hana, there's no way to undo what we did—what *I did*. There's no 'Installation' here."

Alvin's fragmented heart became a terrible weight within his chest, a pile of mangled limeiron. "I thought there would be a way. It seemed so *fated*."

"It *was*. Are you going to lose hope so quickly when it doesn't happen like you want it to?"

"I am so sorry," he told her.

Hana took his head in her hands and pressed her forehead against his. "I am not. You discovered me, Alvin. Even when you lose hope, I will not."

"How?"

Hana's coloured eyes smiled so wide, it brought light to that darkened hill. "Because I choose to have it. Like you did."

She held him there, breath warming each other's faces. Alvin let his heart beat, his lungs breathe. The lens of his mind had angled down where there was nothing to see at all.

That's when somebody shot him.

The bullet bore across his forearm like lightning before the boom. He let out a silent cry and toppled.

"Alvin!"

He gripped his arm where his skin was torn and rolled until he could lift his face enough to see what had happened.

Broken, bloody, and gasping, Esig Ganikson stood at the edge of the summit with smoking powdergun, his body seething in hot agony. One eye was bandaged over and his left arm hung with a plank strapped to it.

He growled, reaching for the blade on his hip. "Open it!" he demanded.

Hana flung herself against Esig before he could draw the weapon, trying to push him off the edge with her weight, but it wasn't enough. They rolled, wrestled and hit ground and ruin, but Hana was not enough. Esig slammed her into a column and hit her head hard enough to drop her like a sack.

"They are doomed," said Esig. "If you do not open it!"

He stumbled to his knees as he drew the machete-like sword, coming for Alvin across the summit of Niavellir. Alvin kicked himself to his feet, still holding his bleeding forearm. He swung his bag out at Esig who glanced it away with a slash, and it soared from Alvin's neck with a severed strap.

Alvin could only watch in horror as the wind caught his sister's book and pulled the pages apart, fluttering, spinning, and then gone. His lectral lantern spun, plunged to the ground, and broke into pieces.

"There's no gate, Esig!"

"Then we all die together," Esig cried, but he never got his chance.

Ellery slammed against him with all his weight and strength and sent them both tumbling across the ground.

"Hartchild!" Alvin yelled, but it was so hard to move.

The sword fell and clanged. They rolled until they came to the edge.

"Ellery!" Hana shouted, crawling towards him.

Esig put his weight on Ellery at the edge of the summit, stalling as they came close to toppling over the edge. Alvin scrambled to his tripping feet and ran for him. Ellery held Esig's arms with one of his own, both pressing against each other's strength. He tilted his head to Alvin, and to Hana.

"It's all alright, Alvin," he said, while he reached his damaged arm and grabbed something from his waistcoat pocket.

"Ellery? What are you doing?!"

As Hana and Alvin stumbled and rushed to help, as Hartchild wrestled with Esig's strength, he smiled at his friends with joy. "Same thing you did for me." Then he flicked the button on the bindporter.

A spherical maelstrom enveloped Ellery and Esig with so much force it held Alvin and Hana back, and almost flung them away.

It circled, swelled, then folded upon itself.

Ellery Hartchild and Esig Ganikson vanished into nothing, leaving a shallow crater where they'd been, and a billow of dust to catch the wind and scatter over Niavellir's empty height.

C H A P T E R 2 5

in which a great many atoms gather, and then don't

ALVIN ESKER KNELT BESIDE THE LEGACY of his friend, a crater in the floor of Niavellir's summit, still gripping the wound on his arm. Hana came up behind him and fell to her knees, fists to her mouth. She had no words. He looked past her, to the Upheaval. They sat in the eye of the greatest storm that ever had raged across the planet. It would be only minutes, now.

"Woolgathering, Master Esker?"

Hana turned in horror. "Nah," she said. "Nah it—it *can't* be you!" She stumbled to wobbly feet and backed away. Alvin's dread and disbelief rose within him, but he couldn't look. He didn't need to look. "How are you here?!" Hana yelled.

"Kindly calm yourself, Miss Sóholdt. Hysterics are of little use to anybody. Don't you agree, Master Esker?"

Alvin stood painfully to his feet. Slowly he turned, and faced him. He was exactly as he'd last looked, same tight brown waistcoat, bright cravat, ivory coachman, and self-assured calm. Lorecroft offered his most disarming smile. "Now now," he said. "Relax. You both seem quite the worse for wear. Gracious, Master Esker! You're wounded. You'll sully your clothes, like that. Miss Sóholdt, you're not fairing much better. Come let me tend to you."

"Don't you come near us you—you blazing gasbag!"

253

Lorecroft kept his hands open and out. "I did not come to harm you, Master Esker, nor you Miss Sóholdt, and it might surprise you how much effort it took to be here. Now, let me see to your wounds. We've only about twelve minutes, twenty seconds, by my estimate, before we're swallowed by that atmospheric agitation out there."

Baron Lorecroft planted himself on a fallen column and gestured for them to gather like children for a story. The pain was motivation enough. He invited Hana first. "One must be mannerly to the fairer sex," he reminded Alvin, who didn't ask. "Come now, Miss Sóholdt. I shan't hurt you. You've my word."

Hana looked to Alvin first, but when he didn't stop her, she went to Lorecroft and knelt cautiously so he could see her face, one hand ready to grab her knife. Lorecroft tilted her head this way and that, pulled her cheeks down to inspect her pupils. Every time he reached to touch her, she recoiled, but gave in. He examined her bruised head, and bandaged it as best he could with the few things he had in the valise at his feet.

"I want this off," she told him, holding up the bracer on her wrist, but knew the answer from the length of the sigh the Professor heaved.

"I regret, Miss Sóholdt, I haven't a way to remove it." Hana swore through her teeth. "As it was meant to bond with the waveforms of its wearer, it was never *designed* to come off."

"What *is* it?"

"It is best known as a Refractor. My colleagues (in their fret) applied it to your own gentle self, assuming it was you who'd been Infused, rather than Master Esker, here."

"Then why give it to me?" Alvin asked. "That was the idea, weren't it?"

"It was, indeed, but such explanations are best kept for later. You know, Miss Sóholdt, you've really very pretty eyes, in spite of heterochromatic colour. Mind you, I'm no physician, but I do believe you've a concussion, judging from your eyes and the knot on your head. I can do little else here."

Niavellir lurched, and cracked. In all directions, the Upheaval drew tighter, a noose about the neck of the earth, and about theirs.

Lorecroft turned to Alvin, and seemed quite horrified by the wound. Alvin reluctantly gave him his arm. While he and Hana exchanged a worried, weathered glance, Lorecroft went to his own bag. He drew out a bottle and ball of cotton. "It's a numbing agent, not strychnine," he defended. "Now sit."

Alvin kept careful eye on Lorecroft, but sat where Hana had, beside him. He winced and yelped when the old Professor touched the wound, but it did numb quickly. "You know, you're not exactly convincing me in favour of your fraternity, Professor."

"The Rook Fellows?" he remarked. "Pity. You're already set to be inducted, you know. Good story behind the Fellows, there is, again for another time. Would've called us the 'Diver-Gents,' myself, but my compatriots lack my generous sense of humour."

"Were they always keen to ruin a continent, then? Or is it a newer hobby of theirs?"

"The Rook Fellows are purposed only to nudge the wheels of the present, Master Esker, in order to guide the future. Gracious, who did this to you?"

"Jalóheim soldier," said Alvin. "Old rifle, just a moment ago. Professor, there's something else. The Galó, they're all on their way to Orphan Towne. They're going to invade. Also they—they may know how to open the gates."

Lorecroft raised a disappointed eyebrow. "And how did they learn that, I wonder?"

"I—"

"No no. Let me guess. All it took was threatening the freckled skin of your little gold maiden, here. This is unfortunate, I must say. A violent lot, barbarians—present company accepted, of course, Miss Sóholdt."

She snarled under her breath.

"Once such a sturdy people," he added. "Shame what's become of them. Even since Orphan's first encounter with them … my how they've degraded. How did you survive your attacker? Or did childhood in Harchester make you that effective a pugilist?"

"Wouldn't have, without Ellery."

"Ah yes. Young Master Hartchild. Went off after you without order. Gave us quite the headache, I don't mind telling you. Where is he? His help is quite overdue and necessary."

Hana turned away and covered her mouth.

"He—he's dead. Professor."

Lorecroft stopped still. Twice he blinked, turned his eyes from Alvin's arm up to look at him, but said not a word.

Alvin's mouth shuddered, and when he thought of Ellery, of that crater over there, he wanted to throw up, scream, kill someone, or all of them. He would've erupted into tears if he weren't swallowing his grief so hard to keep Lorecroft from seeing it, or any other weakness in him. "He saved our lives," Alvin told him. "Used a bindporter for a second time." Lorecroft shut his eyes. "He *knew* what it would do, but he—it was the only way he could…"

"Hold pressure on this."

Lorecroft rose, and turned back away, walking to the center of the plateau. He lifted his hawkish face to the aurora, and held his eyes shut. "Oh no. No, not Ellery. Oh Alec. You poor bastard." He inhaled sharply, and gazed at the raining colours. "'Above my head, a boundless sky I see, and seem to scent the odorous west-wind's kiss. The soft rough grass seems pressing on my feet.' Your sister so loved Virgil, as I recall. You must think me a monster, Master Esker."

"A monster?" Alvin dragged himself closer. Hana kept her distance but watched cautiously. "You lied to everyone in Orphan. You let Tabitha get shot, tried to pry our brains apart, and you killed my sister! You *are* a monster, Professor."

The Professor thought for a moment to himself, and sighed aloud. "I suppose I deserve that," he said. "But I did not murder Agnesine."

"Why should I believe you?"

"Because she meant a very great deal to me, probably the finest pupil I ever had."

"Then…"

He put his hands in his overcoat pockets, but kept his clear eyes on the heavens. "I let her into my confidence to the point of showing her the Oculix. She wished to be its test subject, but I would not allow it. She begged, pleaded, even *after* leaving the Academy. She was so consumed by her need—curiosity and hopelessness are a frightening combination, I assure you—I finally relented. I brought it to Cavendish. She ignited it, and at first it seemed to work. But she wanted more current, kept crying for more vision, more sight. There was no satisfying her want of more and more understanding. I would go no further, but when I had my back turned, she raised the current herself, to fatal levels."

"You … you were there?" Alvin breathed. "I never saw…"

Hana could only watch, eyeing Lorecroft with distrust.

"Of course I was. When I realized it was too late for dear Agnesine, I could do nothing but take the Oculix, and return it to the Heuridium. How is your arm? Seven minutes and forty." Lorecroft sat himself back down and examined the wound closer.

"Professor. I thought—I thought the Axis Gate would be here."

"It is, Master Esker. Surely you've realized by now, the Expanse itself *is* the Gate. Why else would opening it destroy it like it is?"

Alvin and Hana exchanged horrid realization for a long moment while Lorecroft bandaged and bound the wound.

"What's it opening *to?!*"

"Now *that* is the question, isn't it? I shall explain when there is more time. I am curious, though—" He tightened the bandages, and clipped of the loose ends. "—why did you come all this way, just to discover a gate?"

"We didn't," Hana interjected.

"Oh?" Lorecroft rose.

Alvin rolled his arm a few times, and clutched where he'd bandaged it. "We came to undo all this," he informed him. "We were told we'd find a record of it here, of the First Confluence. That we could use it to reset the Expanse as it was. But … there's nothing."

Lorecroft set his glasses higher up his nose. "Oh there is such a record, Alvin, or at least legend of one, but it would've done you little good if you *had* found it."

"Why?"

"Because this is not the Second Confluence. It is one of *many.*"

Hana drew close to Alvin, standing close, as if she sensed he would need her somehow.

"But—but wouldn't that mean—"

"The world you inhabit was altered, engineered, Master Esker. You do know this.”

“I know.”

“No I do *not* mean Orphan Heights. This universe as it is now, as you said, is what we call a *Confluence*, a ‘Gathering of Atoms,’ one of any number of alterations made in ages past. The world you and I and Miss Sóholdt know is *hardly* the original Confluence. Far from it.”

Alvin grit his teeth. “I don’t ... I don’t understand how this is even possible. How can some mineral in my brain *do* all this?”

The Professor sighed. “Every particle in the universe vibrates, Master Esker, from this rock to the trees and stars and even the strands of young Miss Sóholdt’s bones. Their pattern of vibration is what makes them what they are. In essence, the universe is made of sound. Isn’t that lovely? The Halo Program simply emits a cymatic frequency—like a sound wave—that *alters* the surrounding particles according to its program, reconfiguring matter and energy alike. Master Esker, your sister did not invent these ideas. She worked with them, but as I said, curiosity and hopelessness ... anyway, the transmutation effect works best, of course, when standing at the epicenter of the change, which in this case is ... well, *here*.”

“But why?”

“That is a longer answer than I’ve time for, Master Esker, but for now, to forge a better future.”

The Upheaval came to Niavellir. Violently, the pyramid quaked and cracked across its middle. Two of the arches tumbled and broke in stone hunks.

“I’m afraid we’re out of time.” Lorecroft raised his voice over the maelstrom drawing up the structure. “Come with me, both of you. I’ve one last bindporter to take us to safety.”

“But I can’t let this happen!”

“It already has.”

“But there has to be a way!” All he could think of was how to *reverse* it all. If only he were smart enough to understand. The continent wasn’t only coming apart; it was disappearing altogether now, and the Upheaval orbited at impossible speed, whirling into new shapes, violent lightning arcing between the plates. The great stones lifted and rose and joined the vortex.

"Sooner or later, Master Esker, you'll have to face the sum of your fears."

"And what's that?"

"That we are all we have," he answered. "That there is nothing at all beyond this. That there is no grand plan, no destiny, that you and I and she are nothing more than dust and windsong. Our fate is in our own hands. It's time you preserved your lives instead of wishing thinking."

The places behind them cracked apart. Hana clung to Alvin's hand as the plate under her feet started to rise. Hana pulling into the Upheaval behind him, Lorecroft before him, holding up a bindporter, Alvin stood stupefied between.

"I'm afraid I've only one way out of here, Master Esker," said the Professor. "And it's now or never."

The Professor eyed Alvin as if the maelstrom wasn't even there, his hair and cravat snapping in the wind. How long would he wait? And what else was there to do? He had all the power to alter matter at his fingers, but couldn't understand how to stop it all from happening.

How to put right everything he'd done. How to go *back*.

He simply didn't understand enough, and that's when the answer came.

"No human mind could conjure…" he muttered.

Alvin turned, took Hana's face and smiled at her vivid eyes. "There's one way left, Hana," he said, and with one jerk, he pulled her goggles down over her eyes and locked them tight.

"What—"

"I'm sorry."

Niavellir split down the middle and blew into pieces. Hana suddenly braced her feet wide as the the one beneath her lifted into the air, broke apart, and left her with little to hold as she drifted out of his reach, crying out his name. Yes. There was only one way.

"Master Esker?" asked the Professor.

When the temple lurched, Alvin spilled to the ground, where he scooped up the remains of his lantern, and flicked the dial. The leads sparked with current. From his pocket, he drew out the Oculix and set it in front of him.

"What are you doing, son?" Lorecroft pressed.

Even if it wouldn't give him the knowledge to undo this … then at least the emitter would be terminated.

"Facing them, Professor."

"Alvinheim!"

He let out his breath, locked gaze with Hiram Lorecroft, and rammed the exposed poles against the device.

*Who ... who are you? Oh, you're new. Hmm. Haven't had anybody new in ... wait, what is this, I wonder? You've opened the Gate, haven't you? That means someone reforged the Axis Gate. Oh! You didn't realize, did you? You thought the Gate was the opening at the pole, didn't you? You did! How tragically pedantic. Already mucking with reality, are you? Couldn't resist the temptation more than, what? Thirty seconds, could you? Oh, don't feel too bad. It's a terrible temptation, after all. A terrible temptation. I'm curious, though. You're not really ... impressive. I mean no offense! It's just unpleasantly true. Suppose you don't have to be. Who is there to impress, anyway? Your brain seems familiar, though, just a little. Though I suppose everybody's does, after while. Well? You lose track, don't you? Wait a moment, now. Wait just a moment. I remember. You're with that girl, aren't you? The one who also over-shone the Blessing of the Ancients. Terrible headache, I'm told. And there was another one before her. Compatibility problems, if I remember. So sad. Oh, you poor boy. You're about to perish, aren't you? And so young. Well, at least it's your life, not your existence. Existence is where things turn interesting, isn't it? Where it turns ... **meta**. Give it a moment. You'll find out. Anyway, don't mind me. Please, carry on.*

For the moment, I'll just watch how this all—plays out...

in which Alvin Esker's mind pretty much explodes

ALVIN'S MIND FELT LIKE A BALLOON SURGING FULL WITH WATER, with no way of shutting off the spigot. As he gripped his head, he fell to his knees—but it wasn't his knees. It was the knees of the Alvin of his mind, the Thought-Alvin he imagined who kept his Observatory.

"What in Author's name was that?" he gasped, but obviously, it was nothing, because Alvin remembered nothing of it. In fact, he didn't even know what he meant by 'that' or even 'it.' In reality, Alvin stood with the amber rings around him and the Oculix boring its fatal gift into his eyes. In a moment, Thought-Alvin's head settled. He peeked between his fingers like a child beneath the bed.

He missed his bed.

All the wonders of the cosmos lay bare beyond the glass, far and near, ancient and current. Trillions of sights, sounds, patterns and histories and orbits and laws and things Alvin couldn't even begin to classify opened inside his mind, unfolding, expanding, resounding, and bending it at the seams. It forced its way in and would not stop—*could* not stop now. All possible information came flooding back against Alvin's consciousness, barrages of equations, histories, proportions and numerics, all patterned in starlight and all overwhelming his already frail mind. They burst against the glass of his observatory.

He would not live long.

It was his only chance to reverse what was happening, so he got up, dusted his thought-self off, and set to work.

"Gravitical mass of elliptoidal sphere in at 6 x 10^{24} kg, angular dispersion of major heptal-numeric planispherical objects 1.61803398875 … there has to be a way!" he strained, raking chalk against a blackboard, and trying to force his mind to see any way to quickly re-tune the program.

His mind had only so much room, so as it all came in cascades against the dome—waves of equations, gravitic fields, quantum entanglements—he would spin his lens around, find a void in his cosmos, and run to the blackboards at the base of the spyglass to chart it all out. All the formulae of existence emblazoned itself in the astral planes of Alvin's mind and memory.

And it just kept coming.

It just kept coming.

"Al? Don't you think it's time you opened your eyes?"

"I can't, Agnes," he insisted, snapping a piece of chalk, only to find another in an open box. "Have to undo what's happened."

"You can't possibly understand *everything*, Al. You do see that?"

Agnes Esker stepped over the spilled papers, boxes, crates of telescopic components that lay everywhere on the furniture of Alvin's mind.

"Why not?" he said. "You did."

Alvin grappled with possibilities, causality, as more and more of the physics of the universe spilled into his mind and overflowed it. He understood gravitics, so impossible that even Hickter himself seemed a blithering idiot to Alvin's senses, yet a child could understand it.

But no matter what he did, he couldn't see a way to reverse it all.

"And it killed me, didn't it? Al. Won't you listen to me?"

The whole of the dome shuddered as the tides kept coming, a storm ravaging the panes. They began to rattle and crack.

"*You* didn't even listen to you."

He went back to his blackboard.

"Guess I deserved that. I know what you're going through. Better than you do. Remember?" When he wouldn't stop, she took him hard by the arms. "Al, you cannot control life and death."

"I *can*," he said, the panes breaking apart along the edges of their mounts. "It's all just matter and energy and—"

Agnes put a finger to his mouth. "I mean *this*, Al. You cannot change the past."

More and more and more and more flooded into Alvin's mind, and of course he saw a way. "I've been so stupid, Agnes! That's all there is to it! I'll make it so this Infusion mineral doesn't *exist* in the first place!"

"Al, *no*."

He pulled away from her grip and set his attention on the amber light in front of his very real hand, adjusting the view to the astral patterns that detailed cosmic attributes of particle matter. Spinning the whole device around was easy. Finding the right star-pattern wasn't, but everything in his mind was so clear. It would've taken him lifetimes to figure it out otherwise. He looked closer at the patterns, and saw the language beneath them.

But when he tried to alter the patterns, nothing happened again but the red flash. The dials would not luminesce; the program would not obey. He tried again. Nothing.

"What's the matter?"

"Al. It won't let you."

"Why?"

"It's the one part of the program I was able to affect before it killed me. All temporal shift functions are locked out."

"Locked out? What's that mean? 'Temporal shift'? This thing can travel through *time*...?"

"No, but I'm sorry, Al. I can't tell you more than that."

"Well it might've stopped me a moment ago. I'll find a way around it..."

"And have you ever thought of what'll happen even if you *were* able to turn it all back? What would happen to Hana, Alvin?"

"What?"

"Think about it. Will you ever have even met her? Will she ever have found you? Or will she have died in the Expanse? What about everything you've learned and done? Maybe I *would* be alive, and Ellery too. How many others dead? Alvin … who has the right to play god?"

"But if *I* don't put this right, it'll all go bugger-up!" Alvin flung the eraser across the room. "You're *dead*, Agnes. And now Ellery and—and Hana's—"

He pulled away from her grip and bounded up to the higher level with the great telescope. Everything came against his mind, every piece of information from the dawn of known time to that instant, all laying siege to his cracking soul. Two of the panes at the top of the dome fell and broke across the floor. The rage of it all howled through the opening like wind through a cave.

His papers went everywhere.

Agnes bounded on top of his desk below and took his head, pulled her forehead against his own as the panes shattered and burst.

"Alvinheim Lockwilde Esker, you listen to me. What I hoped for? The better life I wanted to have with Albany outside those iron walls? Those were good hopes, Al. What wasn't was how I tried to catch them. You cannot control life and death. Nobody can. Who are any of us to wield power like —like *this?* True hope never asks you for your soul. "

"It's the only way to go back."

"Al, sometimes you become so afraid of death, you can forget about living the life you've been given. Your life is like someone you love: you can grip it so tightly you forget to cherish it, or even live it. You will *not* do this."

"Why?"

"Because I'm your big sister and I said so."

"Then what *can* I do?"

"You remember who you *are.*"

"And who is that?"

Her mouth quivered, her face wet and running. "A good man. A man unafraid to face his future. A man who won't let his mistakes consume him. And … you're a beloved brother. A beloved son. And to that ragged girl out there? A savior."

"I … I'm not that person."

"You are. But if you forget, learn from Hana. Comes natural to her.

That girl would march through Hell with you, and no mistake. That's how much she trusts you."

"Hana puts *too much* faith in me."

"Does she?" said Agnes. "Don't you have any in her?"

"Of course I do. But it's different. She's *earned* my faith."

"Oh Al..." Agnes looked up at him with her big eyes and pulled his heart in two. "Hasn't your life? It ain't different at all."

Alvin gasped in heaving sobs, squeezed his watering eyes shut, and in the real world, tapped the back of his head, and the program died. Here, he gripped her wrists as quiet sobs rose up from his lungs and and breathed feeble words into the breaking air: "I miss you. So much."

Agnes wept with him, pressed her forehead hard against his. "Do you believe we'll see each other again?"

"I don't know if I can. I don't know if ... I'm strong enough."

"That's the beautiful part, Al. You don't have to be." She spoke softly. "'Above your head? A boundless sky you'll see, and seem to scent the odorous west-wind's kiss. And soft rough grass will seem pressing on your feet.'"

She kissed his forehead, and her words became a vapor, dissipating as they wrapped around his collar and his ears, warming his face and his heart. There was nothing for it now but face what ever lay on the other side of existence. Alvin stood his ground as all the force of the Metarcanum collided with his mind, a terrible east wind that came to wipe away anything as minuscule as a Third Class Junior Engineer.

But Alvin met it with eyes open.

In that instant, he let himself imagine that, in spite of being nothing more than he was, having no answers, no understanding of much of anything, it would all be alright.

Because his life, like his sister's, was part of something more.

He chose to believe it with all the force his heart had left within him, and a deep, immersive calm came over him. Muttering a silent prayer to the Author, Alvin released his balled fists, released his want of holding Agnes and Hana and even Ellery's life in his hands.

Alvin Esker let go of his fear.

And by doing it, he finally found rest.

That's when the light dimmed.

Something shook his body, took his arms in trembling grip.

His senses came back to him and he opened his burning, physical eyes. Someone pressed between Alvin and the shining Oculix—an angel, glowing, streams of luminescent hair, luminous eyes, and face he knew, yet had never really seen before.

His hands rattled and body convulsed, but she held him.

His mind burned and warped, but she held him.

"You look at me, Alvin Esker!" Hana yelled over the violent chaos. "You hear? You look at *me!*" Through the lenses of her goggles, she shone out her eyes at nothing else but him.

He saw her, saw *through* her, every molecule of her colored irises streaming from her tight pupils and every split strand of golden hair rolling as the tides—even the rate of her racing heart. It all wrote itself upon his consciousness as an open book. He knew her intimately as he never knew possible, her birth, growth, every lost tooth and skinned knee, every atom of her flesh and bones and body and every electron in her cells, the atomic weight of the oxygen flowing into her blood stream as she breathed.

The way she would age.

The year of her first grey hair.

The instant of her death.

Tides of light shone out from behind her hair and lit it like flame. His feeble hand reached up to hers, and grazed his fingers against her cheek as her eyes swelled. He saw what she was *made of,* and he saw what she *was.* And when he dropped to his knees, she went with him, holding his face up to hers. And for all the impossible complexity of her, there she was, as simple as a girl he'd met in a window.

"Alvin? You're crying."

Alvin's whole and utter being fragmented apart from the inside out, but he pressed his voice up from his chest to answer, heaving the words against the strain of his broken body.

"I—I can see your soul."

"Yah? What does it look like?"

"Green," he told her. "And it's blue."

Her grip never relented so long as the light burned, but it was different, now. Without the light against his eyes directly, the pain eased, and the flow subsided, just a little.

"I'm sorry," he said. "It was the only way to…"

"Goat-skid it was!" she barked through her tears. "You swore you would not leave me. You *swore!* I thought you were going to make it all like it had never happened!"

"I thought—I sort of like it this way better."

As Alvin Esker kept his eyes on green and blue, the power in his lantern exhausted, and the light died.

Dark.

He collapsed.

Hana spun, took it in her hand, and smashed it on the ground as hard she possibly could.

Then she stomped on its remains.

Alvin's mind scrambled and burned, but he still breathed. All the chaos and images and knowledge in his head faded, and blurred like waking from a dream. He couldn't even remember how he circumvented Agnes's lockout of the program's functions. Lorecroft, like all of Alvin's vast understanding was long gone. Hana grabbed for the remains of Alvin's lantern as the rock beneath them angled and rose, but couldn't catch it. It rolled into the tumult below them.

But Alvin and Hana sat on the central chunk of Niavellir as it hurled through space with the rest, surrounded by the swirling, thunderous reconstitution of the top of a planet.

"Are you scareful?" she asked.

He held her hand with lacing fingers. "Not anymore."

"Because you know everything, now?"

Alvin shook his head. "Because I don't know *anything.*" She smiled at him, her mouth drawing back like a curtain, crooked and showing off her slightly stunted eye teeth. "Except that we're probably still going to die. I mean—I do sort of know that."

Hana lifted her eyes to the distance. "Nah. I do not think we will die."

Alvin laughed. "Become an optimist, all of a sudden?"

"Nah. If we were going to," she mused, "I think we already would have. Also because of *that*."

Alvin angled his head back, and when he saw what he saw, he spun himself over onto his stomach to be sure his mind hadn't destroyed itself after all. The great, smoldering clouds rolled themselves into shape, swollen and bursting open across a misty seam. From those mists something emerged, so immense it made the great stones tremble.

Orphan Heights came sailing upon the wind.

Landing on the rim of Orphan's great dome, together they breathed, and laughed. Hana turned to him and threw her arms around his neck, laughing and laughing and laughing. Alvin held her with shuddering arms and tried to keep his body from utterly folding into an exhausted, crumpled mass. Then the two travelers turned their eyes to what became of Hyperborea.

Orphan jolted hard, lurched and listed, but they could see *everything*.

The distant seas churned. The rock and remnant of the whole continent reshaped itself now into a ring—into an *opening* in the earth where a continent once had been, now a great maw, miles and miles and miles across, gently curving inside. Great tides came from *within* the planet to merge with the northern Arctic Seas. It was all so vast and so wide, Alvin's eyes couldn't take it all in.

"Alvin?" Hana yelled. "Is … is that really Thule?"

How he wished that Agnes could see this now. Alvin and Hana glanced skyward, and how the aurora magnified! Its cyan and jade shades—its radiant blue and green—shone down on them as daylight, mingled with whatever light shone out from within the planet. Clouds formed around them as all the Upheaval settled into new and settled form.

And then Orphan lurched again, its great beams yawning and groaning against the strain. How the two-mile-wide Orphan could even stay together was beyond him.

"Hana, something's wrong," he shouted.

"You think?! The planet just reshaped—"

"No! I mean with Orphan. Doesn't feel right, and…"

Suddenly Ellery's fears came back to him. "Hana, we have to get inside! Ellery said there was something wrong with Orphan, with its systems. I think he meant it wouldn't stay in the sky long enough!"

Even Lorecroft didn't know…

Hana did not seem ready, but put on a strong face.

Alvin swung a leg over the edge of Orphan Towne and found his footing on a beam. They climbed until they found themselves against the windows where they'd met. She laughed when she found her hand print.

They came to the side of Westgate, and Alvin reached for the dial lock.

"Alvin, wait. Look!"

It was already open. They exchanged a worried glance, and climbed inside and into the Recess. The wind was deafening through the open door, so once they had their footing, Alvin threw the lever to close the gate.

The doors out of the Recess were sealed.

"Odd," said Alvin, but luckily, he knew Orphan's codes well enough.

Once the lock gave way, they pushed the doors open and ran up the stairs and into Orphan's main dome level, running to find anyone they could, until they burst into the promenade not far from Bellamy Park.

But no one answered.

Orphan Towne was utterly deserted.

Entry 9: "Rule of the Finest Towne"

As with all other times, places, cultures, and of course, Confluences, the dominant news media in Orphan Heights was characterized by questionable management, state narratives, dull editorials, moral bankruptcy, typos, and mostly conveyed things everybody already knew. It was an overnight success. The media primarily consisted of the *High Times*, a weekly paper, and was long rumoured to have once begun by Orphan's first Towne Crier, Phineas Rill, who eventually tired of his job and his sore throat, and so founded a newspaper as to more efficiently yell at the whole of the populous without rendering him incapable of performing with the towne choir. This has never been substantiated, though a bust of Rill was once found in a drawer in the *High Times* archives.

It is also known that, upon settlement of Orphan Towne and during its early phases of construction, the settlers enacted their chartered form of peerage rule. Nobody liked this, especially the Barons, who insisted that, since Marquess was the highest noble rank among the settlers, and absent a proper Duke, the whole system was rubbish. The Marquess promptly disagreed. Democracy erupted.

Unsurprisingly, this led to bitter infighting and both escalated and concluded with the Hour-&-Quarter War, in which one man was winged across the ear, and the skirmish subsequently ended with drink. A rudimentary republic followed. It was based on both Plato's Laws and Republic, and so the smartypants among the settlers insisted they be elected the much-ballyhooed Philosopher Kings. For the commoners, this smelled too much like a monarchy, and for the nobles, this didn't smell enough like a monarchy.

And nobody liked the smartypants anyway.

in which brinkmanship becomes an art form

THE TRAMS OF ORPHAN TOWNE NEVER RAN SO FAST, or so numerous. Alvin and Hana paused at the railing over the western bridgeway to the Bellamy Park and awed at what they saw. Every tram car in Orphan must have been assembled, running in *two* complete rings around the central circle, end-to-end, one track clockwise and the other counter. Under the cars, blue glow emerged and mixed with lectral arcs. Alvin couldn't fathom the amount of power he was seeing.

But everywhere else? The kitchens were cold on Rosewater Way. No palms were greased on the Merchant Circles. The factories produced dust, and naught else. Pike's Central Bank and Trust hoarded shadows instead of everybody's wages.

"Nobody is on them," Hana noted.

"I don't think they're doing that for transport."

"You don't think they're all…?"

"No," said Alvin. "No they—they've *got* to be here. Somewhere."

They followed the promenade curve as trains were zooming by. Actually, they never *stopped* zooming by. Alvin and Hana came up the stairways into the north Merchant Circles, and stopped at the landing.

The buildings were moving.

"The—the *buildings* are moving."

All Alvin and Hana could do was look at each other. All the Merchant Circles were turning together in slow rotation, like great gears in a timepiece. Now that Alvin noticed, *all* the central circles were turning. *Orphan is not so much a towne as it is a machine that people live in.*

But nowhere that Alvin looked had any people. "I've got to go home," he said, and Hana didn't argue, for once. They jumped over the seam onto the north circle and sped themselves up by running the same way it was turning.

"Shh, Alvin. Hear that?"

It was the Broadcast coming through the copper horns mounted around Orphan's arches, the unmistakable, hollow voice of Solomon Day.

...THAT WHEN THIS CRISIS HAS COME TO PASS, ORPHAN HEIGHTS SHALL EMERGE THE BEACON OF THIS NEW AND SHINING FUTURE THAT IS YET TO COME UPON A HORIZON BROUGHT CLOSER BY THE TENACITY OF THE HUMAN MIND.

Among the scattered litter and fallen leaves that dusted the streetways, a discarded edition of the *High Times* leaned against the leg of a nearby bench, his own face there across the front page. He stooped and picked it up. It was dated three days prior.

From Orphan Sterile to Orphan's Peril

He muttered his way through it, all about possible contaminants this and momentary disruption that, and promises by the Chancellery and the Academy to reset Orphan to its former clockwork regularity. And then more.

"What?" asked Hana.

"'Accounts regarding the involvement of an unknown interloper within Orphan's walls continue to increase. Eyewitnesses report observing a young lady with golden hair on the run with alleged accomplice, one Alvinheim Esker of Harchester. Though details of their relationship and operation are still speculative, tensions and even alleged sightings of the fugitives continue to gain ground as the situation around Orphan escalates. The Esker family has refused to comment on the matter, compounding rumours about their son's involvement in—' Load of rubbish, the lot of it."

"I do not understand."

"Folks will be on the lookout for you and that hair of yours."

"Should I hide it again?" she offered.

"No," he said firmly. "No you will not."

Alvin crumpled up the paper and eagerly flung it into a rubbish pail. They took the walkways over the speeding trains to Tanno's Landing, where the Tramrunner's work car was still where he'd left it. Two rows up, he found the street he knew so well, and a familiar brownstone, however cracked in places, with only a few missing bricks.

And even Hugo Esker himself never flung that door open so fast, or so hard. "Mum!" Alvin hollered. "Father! Alphonse!"

Nothing. Broken plates lay where they'd fallen from the cupboards, and one of the hutches lay at an angle against the kitchen table.

Hana checked his bedroom. "Your little models are broken," is all she had to report. Alvin called and called and called. Finally he had to let himself breathe, and shut his eyes at the front door. "Hana … what if …?"

She drew closer, as Alvin almost let go of his hope; that's when his ear twitched. Something sounded from upstairs.

"Alphonse? Is that…"

At the top landing stood Elise Esker, a little worse for wear, her hair spilling into frizzled mess, apron dirty, and eyes swiftly swelling red, and wet.

"A—Alvinheim? Is … is that my *Alvinheim?*"

"Mum?"

She almost threw herself down those stairs at speed he'd never seen from her before. Her arms found their way around his neck so fast it near pulled a muscle, sobbing and calling out praises of motherly joy. She held his face out to look at it, then pulled him in again. He hugged her shaking body for a long, long time. "I thought—we all feared…"

She held him out, and laughed through her trembling mouth.

And then her eyes fell to Hana, who visibly seized.

After all, wasn't this all *her* fault, really?

And wouldn't the woman have every right to despise her for all the misery she'd brought to their home?

"Oh you dear child!" Elise pulled Hana in, this time, smothering the poor girl in her chest. "Oh Alphonse told me—and—and then Hugo saw you when it all went dark and … oh gracious, you could use a bath."

"Never … had a bath."

"*Author help us.* We'll see to that, soon as we can, won't we? Supper and a scrub and—and some clean clothes. Yes. Yes we'll do that."

"Mum? Are you alright?"

"I never caught your name, dear," she said.

Alvin suddenly felt a streak of formality well up in him, despite his legs wanting to buckle and die. "Mum, this is Hana, Hana Sóholdt. Hana, this is my mum, Elise Esker."

"You cook really good, Mrs. Esker."

"Aren't you a sweetheart? You could learn from this young lady, Alvin."

At the risk of his mother embarrassing him (more), Alvin returned to the pressing question. "Mum, where's father? Alphonse? Where *is* everybody?"

"Of all the questions…" She shook her head. "Not 'why is Orphan flying, Mum,' or 'what happened since I left, Mum,' or—"

"So I oughtn've asked about Father first?"

"Well put," she said. Elise straightened her apron, and as was her habit when worried, tidied the room. "Truth is, I don't *know*. Warning came through on the Broadcast for everyone to stay indoors, except for some of the Engineers, Tramrunners, too. Well? Had to report to the yard, didn't he? Broadcast kept promising that everything would go back just like it was, soon enough. 'Trust the Academy,' they said, because of course they would. Finally had to turn the blooming thing off. And don't even *tempt* me to think about what the *Times* has been saying! When all this is done I'll have that editor emasculated, I will."

"Mother!"

"Well somebody's got to hold them to account!" She fluffed the pillows. "Most don't even realize Orphan's in the air at all! Gives me a whanging headache just to think about it, I don't mind telling you."

"How do *you* know, then?"

Elise's worry washed across her face again while she straightened the knickknacks on the mantelpiece. Orphan wouldn't stop shaking so everything she set right immediately jittered around or fell over, but she straightened them anyway. "Alphonse," she answered. "Went to the door to leave last night, going to look for your father with 'and damn the Chancellery,' on his lips. Foul language aside, he never made it. Opened the door to find this young girl in braids standing there, along with this—this big strapping fellow. Both looked a lot like your friend Hana, here."

She and Alvin exchanged a curious look, until it dawned on him. "Sigrie," he said. "Her name—"

"*That* was it!" his mother exclaimed, dusting some glassware on her apron. "Alphonse thought she was *you*, Hana, at first. Only got a quick look at you. She told us what had happened."

"What *had* happened?"

"That they were invading. Most courteous invaders I'd ever heard of, I told her, but then said Orphan had just taken off and their leaders were marching off toward the tramyard, for some reason. And she said—she said *you* sent her to warn us. What were we to think? She knew who you were, didn't she? So we went outside (yes, against orders), and it was easy enough to see. So Alphonse, he—he left with them. Haven't seen him since."

"You're taking all this well enough, Mum."

Elise brushed off her apron and tucked a truss of frizzled hair behind her ear. "I've been married to your father for twenty years. Nothing rattles me, these days."

"Mum, listen. There's something wrong with Orphan's flight. Do you know where the Chancellor is?"

She heaved a long sigh. "I'm afraid Chancellor Finch died, Alvin. Heart gave out from all the strain, about a week back. Albany's acting in his stead until Parliament can meet—"

"*Albany* is Acting Chancellor? Well where is *he*, then?"

"I—I'm sorry, Alvin. I..."

"It's okay, Mum. I'm sorry I—I have to … let me think a minute, is all."

Alvin stepped outside onto London Row, for a moment to catch his mind up to where his breath was, which wasn't good. His whole body was strained to breaking point, but there was still no time for rest.

Who even knew where the control systems for Orphan's flight were?

And where was Lorecroft?

Was he even *in* Orphan?

Every question circled Alvin's mind with the tick of each second of the clock at the end of London Row. It was so quiet. There was noise, the distant thunder of all the trams and machinery running across all of Orphan, but the constant cacophony of its people was utterly silent.

It was almost like being in the Expanse, again.

Alvin walked to the end of the street row, just to where he could see the trams circling in their glowing course, between the buildings. Orphan groaned, and lurched again, angling enough to make the rubbish cans roll along the street, and the whole of it shudder without end.

"'Too fast'," Alvin said to himself. "'Orphan's going to'—oh bollocks."

Alvin breathed, and spun his very cracked and busted lens around to the last night with Ellery and Hana in the Expanse. He swallowed the sharp pain that came with thinking of Ellery, and remembered his wounded confession.

It's in the Toroidal Field Governor…

Alvin focused on the trams, their speed in that endless circle. *Toroidal. Torus.* "A ring," he said aloud. Alvin knew little of that degree of lectric engineering, but even he knew what *a superconductor* was.

It's a system that—well without it working, Orphan can't survive this.

"You were talking about flight, weren't you?"

The field just won't yield enough force like it ought've. I don't understand why. I know the system was too fast for what Orphan could handle, but slowing it wouldn't do enough.

"Too fast … but slowing it ain't enough."

No matter what I did, it was like something was blocking the field.

Alvin spun his lens to the Heuridium, to the levitating machines there, the hollow ring at their center, and his eyes lifted to the great dome around the tower that covered the whole of the city.

"'Orphan's going to fall'," Alvin repeated. "It's going to *fall*," he said. "Ellery, you're smarter than you ever knew."

He ran back inside.

He found his mother crying silently in Hana's arms. They sat on the divan together, Hana with her arms around the woman. They let her cry for a good long moment, and when she realized Alvin was back, she resumed her former poise. "Gracious. I am so sorry. Don't know what got a hold of me…" She wiped her face on her apron. "You're really a dear girl."

"Mum. I've got to go to the tramyards. I'll find Alphonse, and Father and—I can't stay here."

Elise shut her eyes, and nodded tearfully. "I know."

"You—you do? Not going to tell me to—"

"Look at you," she said. "You've grown so much in just a few weeks."

How he'd missed her blessed face, her warm, relieved eyes, red but so joyous now, and Hana there beside her, finally as safe as at least she'd ever been since he'd met her. "Hana, maybe you should—"

Hana bounded to her feet, stretched her arms, and asked pointedly, "So where now?"

And what could he do? More stubborn than his mum, that one.

"Mum, do you still have your things from when you were a nurse? People might still be hurt."

"Then I'll see to them, turn this whole row into a hospital if we have to," she said, rose, brushed off her apron, and regained the regal pose Alvin had long come to expect from his mother. "After all, we're Eskers. Who ever saw an Esker crack under pressure, hmm? Not in *this* household!"

"I'll be back, Mum."

"Alvin, wait! There's—there's one more thing. Your father, he…" The rings under her warm eyes were so dark, and her smile so forced.

"What?" Alvin pressed.

"He … he fears you left because of him."

"Because of … ?"

"The argument you had, that last night here. He blames himself. I couldn't talk any sense into him. Just … thought you ought to know. And Alvin? Please don't rob me of another child."

What could he do? As his mother returned upstairs to fetch her nursing equipment, Alvin and Hana took one last restful breath at the front door of the Esker home. At the end of London Row, they turned west toward Tanno's Landing again, and didn't look back long enough to notice Elise Esker watching them go from the upstairs window with tears on her cheeks.

After a long silence passed, Hana asked, "Do I stink that much?"

"We probably both smell like a bilge dumpster by now, and no mistake. Have you really *never* had a bath?"

"Water shortage? Dry river? Anyway. Who is 'strapping fellow'?"

"That'd be Loftin. I asked him … we had a brief chat."

"About what?"

"Oh, you know: guns, girls, fighting, engineering. Man stuff."

"Uh huh. So what are we doing?"

"Remember that hovering machine thing in the tower?" he reminded.

"You would not stop poking it."

"I—alright, I'll accept that. I think Orphan's flying the same way. Last night, when you were asleep on—well, Ellery told me something was wrong with Orphan. I think he meant it'll fall. He wasn't able to fix it in time."

"And you *can* fix it."

"I *think* so. Look, maybe. He said even Lorecroft don't know about it, but the trams need to slow down, for one thing."

"How do we do that?" Hana panted beside him, arms pumping, breathing through flared nose, mismatched eyes sharp no matter how exhausted she had to be, and it made Alvin laugh inside himself. The withered girl he'd met through the glass in the Agromatic Gardens, after everything, was still running headlong next to him.

"Don't know."

"What do we do then?"

"Free whatever's blocking the toroidal field."

"How?"

"Don't know."

She gave him a slow, sidelong look. "You run fast for somebody who doesn't know what we're doing…"

The old maintenance car shot out of Harchester under Alvin's hand, over the bridgeways and southward toward Ardin Quarter they sailed, Hana staying on her feet holding to the hand grips on the corners of the seatbacks. Then around Bellamy Park, then down around Parliament Hall and the Central Bank and Trust, they soared as fast as the old tram could muster.

Then Orphan Towne dropped without warning.

Hana shrieked when it fell twenty feet or more, and the tram nearly broke the grip it had on the rails. The grind hurt their ears but they kept going, the car rocking on its axles. All the sparking lights of the circling trams dimmed, and gave Alvin paused. The lights across most of Orphan died outright, leaving it cast under the cyan glow of the aurora.

How long did they have before it came crashing down altogether?

And onto what? That great hole in the planet's axis?

"There," said Hana.

For all the absence of Orphan Towne, the tramyard was filled with people—hundreds of people, but even from that distance, Alvin could tell they weren't Orphanites, at least not most.

"They made it," he said. "They actually *made* it."

"For good and bad," Hana added. "What? I do not want them to die. I also do not want them to take this place for their own."

Alvin squeezed the clutch handle and drew back the brake lever as they came to a small branch platform near Steven's Hill Station. Brakes squealed, motors hissed, and they came to a stop. It wasn't long before they heard the voices, shouting back and forth, threats and pleas and things they couldn't make out, and now panic over Orphan's sudden dark.

On the eastern edge of the yard were clustered the great generators of the rail system. The people of Jalóheim surrounded them, and Orphan's constables surrounded *them*, though quite outnumbered. That was all they could see from their distance.

"It's rubbish, being without a proper spyglass, ain't it?" Alvin bemoaned. "Could see what's going on so much easier, if I'd had it still."

"But it's dark, now."

Alvin had no answer. They hurried up the empty lane toward the crowd, but kept to the shadows, which at least now was easier. Though he wouldn't speak it aloud, nor even admit it to himself, Alvin had no idea what to do. He knew what needed to be *done*, but *what* was not the same. As they crept closer, a subtle horror met his worst expectations. In the center of the Galó, among the generators—"Hostages," Alvin realized, among them, his father with a crowbar, along with most of his old mates and most of Orphan's Tramrunners—surrounded by the few scattered Serkers of Jalóheim, and many others among Hana's clan.

"That ain't all of 'em," he whispered to her. "Is it? Not by a long way. Got to be someplace else."

"Or nobody else made it…"

They crept along the walls of the tram sheds, drawing closer to the ruckus ahead. The sudden dark was good for that, at least, but it was also good for hiding people looking for *them*.

Both Alvin and Hana froze when what felt like gun barrels pressed against their spines. "Don't. Not one move. Neither of ya. Got it?"

"Pines! Is that you, then?"

"Bloody right, criminal, and don't you move a finger, or I'll have you off the edge of this hovel!"

"Criminal?!"

"It's *got* to be you! Nearly lost Orphan Towne, didn't we! It's like the *Times* said. And here you are at the scene of the crime."

"What crime?!"

"And with another one 'a them filthy invaders! I'll bet it's you who just blew the light power! Whole band of crooks, you are, and your family…"

"I ain't no crook, Martin Pines, and you watch what you say about my family if you don't want a fat lip!"

There was more than Pines, though, and behind Alvin's back, he and some of the other boys Alvin knew by voice muttered about what to do with them. Albert Glaston, Leland Abernathy, Erik Herschel—all boys his own age from London Row, Tramrunners' sons.

Hana leaned in and whispered, "Can I stab him?"

"What?!" Alvin whispered back through his teeth.

"With my knife? He is a threat. You kill threats. What is the problem?"

"No don't kill *anybody!*"

"Here now," said Pines. "That's enough from you two. Come on, fellas. Over here before they run for it."

The door to one of the sheds opened, and both Alvin and Hana were shoved into the even darker space inside. A single battery torch hung from a hook on one of the old broken tram carriages and lit up the small gathered crowd of more lads from Harchester.

"Here! Caught him trying to join his new mates out there, didn't we?"

"It—it's Alvin!" one of the boys yelled. "Alvin Esker?" said another. "It's him! He's here!" and, "Look! Got one of 'em barbarians with him too!"

And among them, one could not mistake for *anyone.* "Al?"

"Alphonse!"

"Blazes if you didn't come back with your arse intact!"

"Mostly," said Alvin. "I'm a terrible brother."

"Frequently."

The welling up almost overwhelmed Alvin at the sight of his brother, but he kept hold of himself, wishing for his life he had time to do nothing but tell Alphonse all that had happened.

"Alright," snapped Pines. "That's enough of that."

Alphonse growled. "Martin Pines you knock this idiocy off right now! It's Alvin, for land's sake! You've known my family all your life! Put down the stick and shut your gob, while you're at it!"

"Course *you'd* stick up for him!"

"Stick?" said Alvin.

"Don't you turn around, Esker!"

Alvin did anyway, as did Hana, and found Martin Pines shaking, chest heaving and sweat running across his brow. "Is that a billy club? You tried to play off a club like a pistol!"

"It's enough for the like of you, and *her* type!" Pined defended. "Sides, ain't like we've got guns of our own, is it?"

"Will somebody explain what's happening, here?!" Alvin yelled.

From behind the carriage came Sigrie, who lit up at seeing Alvin and Hana, clasping her hands together with a gasp, but not saying anything yet. And with her was Loftin, a head taller than anyone in the shed. Even in the chaos, Alvin noticed how fiercely he stared at Hana with some keen relief washing over him.

Alvin quickly realized they'd stumbled into a sorry excuse for a stand-off, Alphonse on one side, with Sigrie and Loftin, and Martin Pines and the rest of the London Row boys on the other, all posturing and threatening and trying to out-intimidate each other in the honoured tradition of Harchester.

"Should have let me stab him," Hana said to Alvin, looking more than annoyed. She scrambled on top of a maintenance crate and started yelling.

"All of you shut up! Boys acting like—like *boys!* We do not have time for this! Sigrie…"

"Hi, Lofthana." She waved. "Very glad you both did not die!"

"Thanks, Sigrie." She noticed Loftin, then. From under the collar and under his short over shirt sleeve, horrible white veins of scar showed. "You really survived," she commented, but the young man said nothing, and seemed hardly able to look her in the eye. "Hello, Alphonse," she said. "You look good with trousers on."

"What?" everyone asked.

"Now somebody tell us what happened! Where is the *rest* of Jalóheim? Sigrie? Are they…?"

"Most took shelter," Sigrie explained. "In a place by the gate we came through, do not know what it was."

"In the old Warren," Alphonse finished. "The men are trying to take Orphan. Inspector Hartchild and the constables fought them. Martin … Martin's father was killed first."

"Aye, by *their* lot, he was," Pines barked. "So what then, Esker? You fool enough to want us to trust *this* lot? Thieves and killers, that's what they are. They ain't even supposed to *exist.*"

Alphonse sighed, and sat back against the crate Hana was on. "These invaders are threatening to drop Orphan and kill us all if Albany won't give them what they want. Guess the trams keep us in the air, somehow—*Author*, I sound insane—Father and the 'Runners are protecting the generators but Al, they're all but hostages. And if he don't get himself killed he's as like to kill somebody else."

Martin Pines said out low, "All of us was only here checking on our dads. Had enough of being locked up. Now it's like this. We … all we've got is us. None of us knows what to do."

And nobody did. Nobody had anything left to say, ask, or suggest. But neither did Alvin. He was no strategist and certainly no warrior (spyglass combat aside). He had to slow the trams, and then there was the second, much *bigger* problem. One of those *who-in-blazes-am-I* feelings struck him.

This was a tech problem with vikings and sweaty engineers in the way.

"Pines," said Alvin. "I—I'm sorry. About your father. Listen, I know it's all bad enough. But there's more. We have to slow the trams or Orphan's gonna fall. Fall as in drop out of the sky, not—not be conquered or the like. I—I don't know how, though. Or how to stop the invasion. Or how to even get close to—you know, I don't think I know what to do either."

Then from her place on top of the crate, Hana informed them, "I do." All eyes turned to her. Her eyes were fierce as ever, bold colour, and serious.

"Lofthana," said Sigrie. "Please. They are our people."

That is why we stop this," Hana answered her. "You will understand soon. Alvin? Is everything still in your girl bag?"

"Oh come on not here," Alvin sighed, as his mates snickered.

"Good." She hopped down. "We need it."

"Al," his brother interrupted. "There's one more thing. The invaders, they've got a hostage. Real one, I mean. It's Hartchild."

"Bugger. How'd he end up getting himself—"

"No, not the Inspector, Al." Alphonse drew closer. "They've Tabitha."

CHAPTER 28

in which grown people are far too easily impressed

THE CONSTABLES OF ORPHAN TOWNE STOOD OUTNUMBERED three-to-one, only some two dozen men surrounding the situation. In their midst was Inspector General Hartchild, and Albany Finch, facing Chieftain Eaorn and Priestess Tevir, with their own warriors behind them, by the generators for the trams, kept away only by the eight Tramrunners there. Priestess Tevir had an arm around Tabitha Hartchild, a knife to her chest.

"You brought a child to a conquest, not we," said Tevir.

Hartchild had something like an arc pistol in his grip, but larger, like a stubby lectral shotgun aimed at the old woman. "One drop of blood from my daughter, and I'll show you what real barbarism is, woman."

"Enough!" shouted Albany. "You damage those generators and we'll *all* be dead in seconds! Is that what you want?"

Chieftain Eaorn, like his men, trained a powdergun on the Inspector General. The rest of the constables had firearms of one kind or another, and Albany was the only one unarmed. "Surrender your men," Eaorn demanded. "Release control of Iron Hollow to our direction, and *no one* need die. Hostages are not our way—"

"This chariot," said Tevir. "Is the heavenly road for the Last Journey, little Chancellor. "It will carry we faithful into Agarta, and to Imlé itself. If this girl's death is required for your obedience, all the better."

284

"Daddy?" Tabitha pleaded.

She held herself on a crutch, but was continually twisted by Tevir's grip. Then from behind them, through the ranks of Jalóheim, Loftin pushed his way through, and flung a resisting Alphonse Esker to the ground.

"Treachery," Loftin explained.

"You're the traitor, you foul git!" Alphonse protested.

"He was scheming to stop us."

From the generators, the unmistakable voice of Hugo Esker rose over the crowd. "Alphonse? Is that Alphonse?!" It was so dark, now, only lit by the aurora and a dim glow from the generators. Several guns aimed at Alphonse now, dropped by Tabitha's feet. "You blighters hurt my son…"

Hugo Esker didn't finish. He didn't need to. Though armed only with a crowbar, like the tools of the rest of the Tramrunners, the riflemen gave him a wide margin.

And while Tevir pressed her threats, while Eaorn held his resolve and Hartchild ground his teeth and Albany Finch tried his best to negotiate, Alvin Esker watched from the corner of the shed, and whispered to Hana,

"You're sure about this?"

"Nah. But we will do it anyway."

"And you're ready?"

"Are you?" She gave Alvin a knowing wink, and marched out from the corner, straight at the crowd. She muttered something to the constables, and they let her pass, astonished faces watching her, until she came to the center, and every eye turned to her.

"That is not possible," breathed Tevir. "A trick…"

"Is … Hana?" Tabitha gasped.

Hana marched up to Albany Finch, and to Inspector General Hartchild, whose deep, ringed eyes slowly broadened in recognition of her face, then twisted when she informed them, "Chancellor? Inspector? I am Hana Sóholdt, and I am here to surrender myself."

"What is this?" said Albany. "What … Hartchild, who *is* this?"

"Just Alvin's cousin, Sir, on the Cavendish side," she answered, though he had to squint in the dark, a numbing recognition came over him too.

"How can you be here?" said Hartchild. "How—what is going *on?*"

"Now *you* have a hostage," she said out low to Hartchild.

Eaorn bellowed at them all, "This is pointless! That girl was exiled. She is *not* of Jalóheim. Her life means nothing."

"You don't understand, Chieftain," Hana yelled. "*I* am not the hostage. *This* is." From her pocket, she pulled a waterflask. "And my witness."

"What is this?" snarled Eaorn. "The girl is mad, Chancellor."

Albany gripped Hana's arm hard. "What game are you pulling, girl?"

"Please, Sirs. We came to help. Trust us."

"'We'?" said Hartchild.

"Nothing has changed, Chancellor!" yelled Eaorn. "You have one minute. Then Iron Hollow falls. Death, or deliverance…"

He snapped his fingers, and half his men turned their rifles on the generators. Hugo Esker and the Tramrunners growled and postured and spread themselves between the guns and the generators, but everyone knew it would do little good against that much fire.

"Understand we are serious," said Tevir. "Your child's blood first."

"No! Tabby!"

As Tevir raised her knife and the constables raised their arc pistols and the warriors raised their powderguns, one raspy, meager voice shouted over all the rest: "The blood of your own clan not good enough anymore?" Something made the Priestess stall. "Tell your Chieftain, Priestess. Tell them *all* about Faldin. About who its hunters *really* are!" Hana held up the waterflask for every eye to see it glinting in the aurora. "Tell them how I got this from the Faldin Clan, how *you* sent him to kill us."

Tevir's thunderous voice demanded she, "Be silent! No more of this criminal's poison."

"Tell them," Hana continued, "And tell them why it says 'Esig Ganikson cín Jalóheim,' Priestess."

Inspector Hartchild took the flask from her hand and looked it over. "It does," he said. "What does this mean?"

This time Hana looked to the warriors, and to Eaorn. "It means that Faldin has been gone a long, long time, and our old and weak are killed by

Tevir's order." Nobody said anything, but many doubtful eyes among the warriors looked from one to another. "The numbers are always just right to keep us in the village."

Eaorn looked down at the old woman. "She is lying, Tevir."

"Of course she is! May Jalós curse me. A stolen flask in the hands of a thief is no proof of any mad claims. She expects us to believe this because she tries to stall our glorious mission. She brought nothing but deceit."

"And Esig's flask," she reminded them. "Should the Inspector let the *rest* of Jalóheim see it? And if they will not believe a thief, what about a witness?" she added. "With the *blessing* of Jalós?"

From the midst of the constables, a blinding light erupted in the dark of Orphan, forging itself into shape in amber lustre around Alvin Esker.

Tevir stumbled and fell, and Eaorn gasped, "By the mercy of the gods!"

That's when Alphonse grabbed Tabitha, slung her arm over his neck, and got her to Loftin. None of the warriors noticed, nobody did. Every eye was on the luminous boy who may as well have been back from the dead, so far as the Galó knew. He marched with purpose through the constables, who also stood with open mouths, until he came between Eaorn and Albany.

But *his* eyes were on his father's, some ten yards up, who could only mouth *Alvin?* Then rub his eyes, run a hand over his mouth, and watch.

Tevir rose on shaking legs.

"Chieftain," he said. "Hana's telling the truth. Esig and several others from Jalóheim were sent to hunt us down. Dressed like your rival clan, they were. They tried to kill me, and Hana. And he…" Alvin faced the Inspector General. "He killed Ellery, Sir."

"You—you say…" Hartchild couldn't get his breath. No words came, just stuttered noises, and he clutched his chest like his heart might give out.

"Alvin," said Albany Finch. "If this is—"

"I wish it were. I'm sorry."

There behind Hartchild, Alphonse brought Tabitha. She'd no tears on her face, just a stark horror, twisted into rising agony. She fell against Alphonse but he held her up.

A loud *clang* sounded and echoed through Orphan's yards. Eaorn's powdergun dropped to the ground. Gone was the resolve in his face, replaced by a shifting mix of anger and fear. "What has happened?" he said. "Tevir? Is what they say true?"

"It is lies," she insisted, spitting her words by now.

"This boy—this light. How can we…" He looked up at Albany Finch. "There is no honour in this, no victory."

"Chieftain!" Tevir yelled. "You will understand. It was *necessary*. We were growing too large! The water, too scarce! The people would not have waited. It is for Jalóheim that we—"

"You took the lives of your own people." He ordered his warriors, "Put down your guns. It is over." He met Tevir's eyes with fire. "They waited for a *land* to conquer, Priestess, not to be conquered by their own protectors. We are in your hands, Chancellor."

Alvin tapped, and the Halo dissolved into luminous dust at his feet.

Slowly the warriors of Jalóheim lowered their guns, worn, emaciated, their fires all gone out. As it all calmed, one among them escalated, breathed harder and hotter. "Nah," she whispered. "Nah, not after all this. Chieftain, it was my right! Our destiny to see Imlé! Were you not handed this chariot! Was it not because of me that you knew what it was?!"

"Enough, Tevir. It is over—"

"And because you lack the spine to do what must be done, we are robbed of our promised land?!"

Tevir stood as proud as her worn old body would allow, reached to her robes, and in one smooth motion, drew the arc pistol she still had, and among their cries and attempts to dive for it, turned it on the nearest generator.

Hugo Esker dove to stop it. With a ringing *CHANG*, a single thread-thin string of light shot, surrounded by a discharge of lectral current so violent, the generator blew itself apart.

"No!" Alvin screamed, as his father landed hard on the ground.

Then Tevir turned the gun on Alvin, and squeezed again. As the light-thread fired, the burly arm of Alec Hartchild swung around Alvin, and pulled him behind.

"Daddy!" cried Tabitha.

The arcing bolts of current blew against the Inspector General, and he dropped to his knees. Then he lifted his own. Another *CHANG* rang in their ears, and Tevir stumbled, face contorting to shock. Hartchild fired again.

Again.

And again.

Hartchild slumped to the ground, Tabitha throwing herself against him.

But Alvin was too busy rushing through the warriors to the generator, to the Tramrunners gathered around his father on the ground. Alvin seized, his throat tightening as he came near. The main generator sparked and smoked behind them. He prepared himself for whatever bloody sight he might find, or at least told himself he did. He'd lost Agnes. Could he withstand this, too?

"Father?" he breathed. Hana rushed up beside him, and squeezed his hand in her own.

The Tramrunner got Hugo Esker to his feet, and Alvin had never let out a held breath so hard as that one. Hana also fell into heaving relief.

Hugo dusted himself off, looked to the broken generator, and then to his son. Alvin couldn't catch his breath, holding himself on his knees. "Father?" he said. "You're alright."

Hugo looked at his boy, and at the girl beside him. "I thought—I would never see you again," he told him. "I thought…" He squeezed his eyes shut for a single moment, then looked all around at the chaos, at Orphan itself. "Well," he said. "This all quite horrid, is what I think. Mind telling me what that light-show was?"

"Gives me a whanging headache, is what it does," said Alvin, unable to get his mouth to stay serious. "I'm afraid I broke the—earth, I think."

"Huh. Usually you keep your damage to the projects I bring home. How you gonna make this right, boy?"

"Alvin!" It was Albany, calling from where Hartchild had fallen, ushering him over. Hartchild lay on his back, bleeding from the awful wound on his side. "I've sent for a medic. The Inspector, he—"

"Pressure," said Hana. "Hurry! Sigrie! Come help, yah. You, give me your coat."

She nearly pulled Albany's coat clean off him, and held it to the

Inspector's fat body. Sigrie rushed to her side and helped apply pressure. He breathed hard, Tabitha holding his hand in hers. She looked up at Alvin, and at Hana. "You didn't die out there," she said.

"Not for lack of trying," he confessed.

"Ellery…?"

In his delirium, Hartchild only moaned, "Not my boy. Author, please, not my boy."

As Hana held the wound, she told them both, "He died to save us both. He is a hero. You should be proud."

Everyone surrounded them, then. Finch got to his feet, his constables asking what to do with all the surrendered warriors, and even their Chieftain stood over Hartchild as they tended him. Hugo Esker and the Tramrunners came near, and Sigrie, Loftin, Pines, Alphonse, everyone.

Orphan shuddered again, and the axillary generator sparked.

"I don't understand all this," said Albany, running a shaking hand through his hair. "This is all madness. The trams will die and we'll all go with it when the towne falls and—Hartchild and…"

"Albany," said Hugo. "Calm down, boy. It's on you, now."

"I—*I'm* in charge? Author, been Chancellor for all of four days!"

Hugo leaned in. "Inspector General's wounded and in no shape to lead, and the rest of Parliament's hiding in their cellars. As expected. Have the constables escort these folks back with the rest of their relations."

"Right. Yes. Men? Take them to the Warren."

"And start a watch," Hugo added.

"Yes! A—a watch."

"Alvin," said Albany. "What the hell's going on?! What *is* all this?"

Every voice around him echoed the same questions, from Martin Pines to Albany Finch to the Tramrunners, as if he were the one to know everything! But they needed answers, and his were the only ones available.

"Look, everyone," he said. "It's a lot to tell, and we ain't got time for it all now. Orphan's gonna fall if we don't fix it. Don't know when but—"

"Thirty-one minutes," said his father. "If the trams are keeping us alive, they'll shut down in thirty-one minutes. Can't make power with no generator, can you?”

“Well,” said Alvin. “Then it’s between Orphan falling fast-like and Orphan falling slow and easy.”

“How’s that?” asked Alphonse.

“Don’t know. And there’s another problem. Something’s blocking the toroidal field from forming right.”

“The *what?*” everyone echoed.

“It—I don’t really know. But it makes us fly.”

“Then how’d you know something blocking it?” asked Martin Pines.

“Because Ellery Hartchild said so, and he were in charge of the flight system, weren’t he? Sir?” Alvin knelt at Hartchild’s side. The Inspector breathed heavily, but kept himself conscious. “Sir, I need your help. We don’t have long.”

His round head shook side to side slowly. “No,” he muttered. “It’s all lost. My boy … Orphan … is … is too late, now.”

“It ain’t too late, Sir,” Alvin assured him. “Listen. Ellery—you should be proud of Ellery. He was my friend. Hana’s too. He saved our lives, and he’s gonna do it again. We have to unblock the machinery.”

“Al,” said his brother. “What in blazes is blocking it?”

Alvin glanced skyward. “The dome. I think these kind of fields work off an open ring. Orphan’s got a dome blocking it.”

“Blow the windows,” said Alphonse. “There’s a way, ain’t there? Always heard about it. Got to be done from *somewhere*, eh?”

As all their voices argued and questioned and worried, Alvin turned back to Hartchild. “Sir, that’s it, ain’t it? You have to tell me: where is the bridge? Where is Orphan controlled from? We have to release the windows.”

He shook his head. “Can’t do that. Too dangerous. People aren’t … aren’t ready. They’ll see…”

“Of course they’re ready. Sir? Albany?”

“Hartchild’s right, Alvin. You know the *panic* it’ll cause? To see what’s happening out there? The Academy kept them in their homes for a reason!”

“Then get them out! We need them!” He turned to his father. “We’ll need the trams running *faster*, now, if it can be done—keep it aloft long to enough land soft, that sort of thing."

"And how am I supposed to do that, Alvin?" asked Albany.

Hana reminded him, "What about the yelling tubes?"

"The what?"

"Yelling tubes."

"The Broadcast," Alvin corrected. "Albany, go get on the broadcast. Tell the people the truth. Tell them not to be afraid."

"They've reason to be afraid, Alvin! We're all likely to … and what if they can't handle it? What if we lose *more* that way? It's all gone belly-up, is what it's done. What if it all comes … comes down?"

Alvin rose, and grabbed Albany by the arms. "Sure, but they've got reason to hope, too. Albany, don't be so afraid of losing life that you forget to live it."

Albany pressed his eyes shut for a slow moment. "Alright," he said. "We're all likely to die, anyway. Why not?"

"That's the spirit."

Albany and a couple of the remaining constables left the tramyards for the middle of Orphan. Hugo Esker took his men to keep the trams running, and sent Alphonse to round up every engineer he could find, while Martin Pines and the younger ones went to get help for wounded, current and future. Either way, Orphan was coming down.

"Al?" said his brother as he left. "Might need one of these." He threw Alvin his timepiece. "Maybe you'll be on time for something, for once."

Inspector Hartchild still breathed hard, but steadily. Hana assured them he would live, but they still waited for someone to bring one of the medics.

"Sir," asked Alvin. "Where is Lorecroft? Where's the control room? Is it in the Heuridium?"

His round face turned to face Alvin, and blink him into focus. "Were you really his friend?" he asked.

"What—Ellery's? Of course, Sir."

"Never had any friends, did Ellery." Something seemed to comfort him. Tabitha cried silently as her father spoke, but Alec Hartchild turned his eyes up to Hugo in the dim light of the aurora. "You understand?"

"I do, Inspector."

Hartchild nodded to himself. His hound-like deep eyes watched his daughter, Alvin, and even Hana. "Operations." *Breath.* "Bridge." *Breath.* "Old North Op Station." Breath. "In Astorhill. Ellery was supposed to … it was Ellery's job. Wasn't supposed … to go. Without him…"

"Shh, Father," said Tabitha. "Don't strain."

His eyes took in the starry colours through the overhead dome, raining down on them all. "Sort of beautiful. Isn't it?"

Hana got to her feet. "Sigrie. You stay with him?"

"Yah," she answered. "Loftin, too. Yah?"

Tabitha pleaded with them: "Help me get him to a medic?"

Both nodded. Alvin had forgotten Loftin was even there, for a bit. He rose, and found his father there. "I—I'm sorry I missed the memorial," he confessed. Hugo Esker smirked, just a little. "Leastwise," he said. "You had a blonde reason—uh, *good* reason. We'll talk about it later, we will. Go make it right, son."

CHAPTER 29

THE OLD CARRIAGE GROUND ITS BRAKES AT NORTH OP STATION, as Alvin reared back on the lever. His aching hand released the clutch, and the area was anything but quiet, despite being abandoned like the Heuridium. Klaxon alarms were sounding and spinning red across the old building, seated at the top of Orphan's tiers. Masculine statues of men with hammers and chisels greeted them in place of pillars, and the whole place put Alvin in mind of the Central Bank and Trust.

Sixteen minutes left, by Alphonse's watch, and even as their feet touched the platform, Orphan listed all the more, spilling tools from the tram and over the edge of the platform. Hana grabbed for the railing of the tram and held, but when Orphan lurched, the tram snapped its brakes, jolted over the stop, and kept on rolling.

"Hana!" Alvin grabbed her by the waist, and their feet went out from under as the tram hurled over the edge, smashing through the water systems roofs on the lower tiers.

He latched his fingers around the rail, and held them both while Hana scrambled to her feet, and pulled him to his. "Falling?" she panted.

"Feels like it. Starting to, and no mistake."

"Will we die?" asked Hana. "It would be nice to know."

"What sort of question is that?"

"Honest one."

"You didn't have to come with."

"You say stupid things."

The circling trams roared as they want by in their counter-circling course, glowing from beneath and between, generating whatever field was keeping Orphan inconsistent with gravity. It was some of the only light left visible in Orphan, and even Hana's golden mane was silver in the northern lights. All the while, the hollow, crackling voice of Solomon Day droned its way through Orphan Towne.

The final effort of the Great Initiative is well underway.

Hana rubbed her palm. "If I ever see him again, I will crush his hand, stupid old man."

"Hana!"

"What? Stupid old man. Should I stab him, too?"

"Stop trying to stab everybody!"

Worry not over Orphan, good and fellow citizens! These but the growing pains of its new Era. Remain in your homes, and soon all will return as it was, yet with a splendour that will rival the great cities of—what is this? Finch?

Out of the chair, good Marquess. I must insist.

Finch, you have no authority, and this is not the moment for grandstanding when all of Orphan Heights needs its Scholars to—

I am the Chancellor, remember. It's time for a little truth, isn't it? Now kindly rise, or I fear I must remove you.

Choose your words carefully, Chancellor! I am

Sounds of a scuffle ensued. "Are they fighting?" asked Hana. "What is his name?"

"Albany."

"Hey! Hey, smash his hand, Albany!"

"He can't hear you, you know."

Overhead, the aurora slowly shifted to violet. Orphan was drifting, slowly, into the great maw atop the earth, and listing further, side to side, as its power faded and the field destabilized.

"Why are you laughing?" asked Hana.

"It's just Albany," Alvin answered. "Never thought I'd live to see him stand up to someone like Solomon Day. He finally managed to grow some … nevermind."

"What did he grow?"

"Forget it."

"Oh no! Tell me what he grew, Alvin. I am interested."

"Nothing. Radishes. Grew radishes. Has a greenhouse at the family estate in Edgemeadow, he does."

"And he never used to grow radishes before?"

Between the very old and looming doors of North Station hung a very modern bronze dial lock, its letter-code already sitting in display.

L-E-T-S-N-O-T-P-R-E-T-E-N-D

"What does it say?" she asked.

"Says he knows we're coming." Alvin hardly touched the door, and the left door groaned open on balanced hinges. The right wouldn't open, of course, with Orphan's angle.

296

Lights were everywhere, incandescents glowing steady, hung from cables but leaning sideways—or rather Orphan was. The whole sight was disorienting, to have the whole towne listing as it was to Alvin's left.

"Ten-to-one says Lorecroft's already at the top of the stairs."

"Yah, probably. Hey, what does that say?" Hana pointed to the stairs ahead. Along the front of each step was inscribed a line from a poem, or something like it. Alvin read her the stanza:

Nothing unobservable exists

So all that we envision, may it be erected,

And bend all nature's will, though she resists

The place of man arisen and perfected.

Orphan's purpose, however grandiose or surreal, was laid into the brickwork of its founding. From the start, all this was here. Alvin and Hana pulled their way up the ornate stairs by the railings, step by step. The violet and blue aurora shone through the ancient panes of two great windows up there at the top. Through them, clouds billowed, swelled and parted around the immense bow of Orphan Towne as it hovered over newly snow-capped mountains within the deep rim of the great maw of earth. Alvin read her the second stanza.

For that convergence we await

Lighted minds on lighted ray,

Final confluence our self-made fate,

For there at last shall come a day.

—Cornelius Erasmus Hickter

"What does it mean?" Hana asked him as they came to the top.

"Means … I don't know. I think this flight isn't the end of their design for Orphan, is what I think it means."

Scholars, technicians, and a few other Academy types puttered about. At the top of the stairs they stepped onto a wide, arcing floor, cut in half by a drop-off past the railing ahead, but over it, a single bridge led to the outer wall, to whole stations of controls, a central hatch, and those two great windows they saw from down the stairs. As the Scholars saw how close they Orphan was to plunging into the mountains, they left in panic, one by one, until none were left. Albany's voice still sounded across Orphan:

"Now what?"

"There," said Alvin, and he pointed across the bridge. "The master system controls. And that's sure to be the bridge, past that hatchway, there."

They scrambled their way across the slanted floor as Orphan jolted harder and harder, and time ticked down. Two great levers flanked the hatch, among many others, labeled: *Dome Pressure Ejection*.

"There!"

Before they came to the end of the bridge, an unholy *CHANG* sounded in their ears, hot arcs of light tearing by Alvin's head into the far wall. Hana slipped and landed on her back, and Alvin spun against the railing on the bridge. Hana almost fell, but kept her grip.

Far below them circled some kind of enormous lectral coil, too far to jump down even if it weren't dangerous on its own.

"No, no, no. No you will not touch it—any of it." Viscount Pike steadied himself on the back wall, drawing closer as he held to the railings, sparking arc pistol in hand.

"Viscount Pike ... you have to let us go. Orphan's gonna fall if we don't blow the dome."

"And where did you get nonsense like that?"

"From Ellery Hartchild," Alvin explained, cautiously helping Hana to her feet but keeping his eye on Pike.

"Hartchild," Pike scoffed. "Boy wasn't smart enough to stay in Orphan when told. Orphan Heights is only *in* this state because of his failure and your criminal intrusion! Generations of planning, perfection, detail, all blown to the winds because of your childish want to bed a barbarian harlot."

"Hey!"

Viscount or not, Alvin might've decked him in spite of Pike being thrice his size, but the pistol gave him pause. Pike came to the end of the bridge, and Alvin moved Hana behind him.

"Let me stab him," she whispered.

Behind Alvin and Hana, the bridge hatch opened slowly with a hiss.

"You will not touch those levers, boy. I'll not allow your idiocy any more than I'll allow Orphan's common to know beyond their lot. I will never understand how you managed to get through the Heuridium like you did, but you've done enough damage," said Pike.

"For land's sake, Hawthorn, he made it through because I *allowed* him to. How else? Honestly, man…"

Of course it was Lorecroft. Alvin and Hana were stuck on the bridge, back-to-back, Lorecroft at one end and Pike at the other, and Orphan listing more all the while. Even the lights in North Op Station flickered now.

Twelve minutes.

"Allowed?" Pike repeated, his face twisting disgusted.

"You really think these two would've made it as far as they did?"

"Professor?" said Alvin. "Professor, we have to blow the dome! It's what's blocking the toroidal field! Please, we don't have much time!"

"Is it?" Lorecroft mused. "Curious. We have eleven minutes, fourteen, by my count. Give me a moment, if you please."

Lorecroft stepped onto the bridge. He seemed to have no trouble keeping his feet. "I am no fool, Alvin, not even to the ways of youth. I knew when young Miss Sóholdt expressed her intentions back in Bellamy Park that you would do something brash. Once poor Master Hartchild believed he saw you near the Heuridium, all it took was a little lax security, and sending people on errands."

Albany's voice still came through the pipes.

NOT EVERYTHING IS PUT RIGHT. NOT EVERYTHING CAN
BE, AND SOMETIMES THINGS SIMPLY DON'T GO HOW YOU
PLANNED. 'BEST LAID PLANS OF MICE AND MEN,' AND ALL
THAT...

"Why, Hiram?! Have you gone completely mad? All this time, our grandfathers—*great* grandfathers—all our years in the Society, all this preparation, planning, and you let these common wastrels meddle with everything?!"

"That was precisely the problem, Hawthorn..." Lorecroft came closer. Hana grit her teeth and reached to her back for the knife, but Lorecroft put a ginger hand on her shoulder, and ushered himself past them both. "The project had grown rather stagnant, don't you think? Progress comes with planning, of course, but sometimes..."

He stepped off the bridge, as Pike backed away from him a ways, pistol still in his hand.

"Sometimes a system needs a little chaos in order to advance."

"Chaos?! You fool."

"'Shalt thou dispute with him the points of liberty, who made thee what thou art?' Hawthorn?" said Lorecroft.

"They are common *children!*"

"Master Hartchild was one of those 'children,' Hawthorn, yet he was the one best capable of flying Orphan Heights."

Alvin tapped Hana on the wrist, and nodded to the controls while Pike's attention was on Lorecroft. Slowly they made their way closer to the end of the bridge.

"Besides," Lorecroft went on. "For all young Master Esker's flaws, there is something useful there, I think, something Master Hartchild needed as balance."

"So you took it on yourself to gamble three hundred years of progress and labour, gamble all our futures, the Project, everything, on your little *hunch?* Wait until the Grandmaster is told."

"Why? Cannot manage your quarrels yourself, old friend? Besides, I simply permitted nature. A controlled system, suddenly adapting to a new element from beyond itself. It's almost cosmic, isn't it, Hawthorn? An oyster only crafts a pearl when invaded by an irritant, isn't it? Miss Sóholdt was just such an irritant. Besides, I think we both know my hunches are superior to most men's facts, don't we?"

The bridge groaned when Alvin neared the end of it, and Pike spun, kept his pistol aimed at Lorecroft, but slammed his hand down on the lift release, dropping it out from under Alvin and Hana as both dove for the platform.

"Hawthorn!"

Hana's scream resonated, but she latched her fingers onto the lip, and Alvin hooked a leg onto it. A shrill whine sounded from Lorecroft, and Pike's face twisted into shock, shaking. "That's how it is, Hiram?"

I KNOW YOU'VE BEEN ASKED TO STAY IN YOUR HOMES. THAT THINGS WILL GO BACK TO HOW THEY WERE...

With a cry, Pike turned his pistol on Lorecroft, and fired, again and again and again, and as the first shot hit, a golden haze of light erupted around Lorecroft. The strikes were blinding and loud, sparking, reflecting and distorting, but Lorecroft was unhurt.

"Rather rude of you, Hawthorn. Manners of nobility, these days..."

Alvin and Hana scrambled, pulling each other up and onto the far platform by the hatch and control stations. The old banker panted, gripping the railing as Orphan slanted, eyed his colleague sharply.

Then he raised his gun at Hana.

Alvin grabbed her and spun, putting his back to Pike.

The *shriek* of it was deafening, high and deep at the same time, but Alvin felt nothing. The screech blended with Pike's cries, inhuman and twisted, then gone. When Alvin looked, there was only a dissolving trail of sparks and embers in the air where Pike had stood a moment ago, all drifting to the floor, and burning themselves to nothing.

Hana shook in his grasp, and he was sure he did too.

"Well then," said Lorecroft, straightening his waistcoat. The golden shield around him vanished, and he held up a silver rod. "Such unpleasantness."

Alvin and Hana looked on in some muddled mix of horror and relief.

"Did you *kill* him, Professor?"

"Mmm. And don't think it shan't be a headache later on, mark my words," Lorecroft mused. He straightened up his cravat, and adjusted the cuffs of his overcoat. He looked to Alvin, then, and for the first time in the years that Alvin had known the man, he looked … upset, even worried. "Master Esker? Tell me something."

"What?"

"Out there, at the axis. You … you ignited the Oculix."

"And?"

"Why?" he questioned. "By now, you had to have known it would kill you—*should* have killed you. Why would you do it?"

Alvin looked at Hana. "Ain't there anything in your world worth dying for, Professor?"

"Hmm. 'The mind is its own place,' it seems, 'and in itself can make a heaven of hell, a hell of heaven.' Milton. I don't expect you to know what that means." It still seemed to trouble the man, but he pressed it no more. "The secrets we now carry were not meant for common eyes, Master Esker. You should feel honoured. Well, that's all there is, I suppose. I'm off."

"Off?!" Hana yelled.

"You're just going to let us…?"

"Well I'm afraid there's no way over to you, now, or *back*, for that matter, which is unfortunate for you, and I am no pilot. That was young Master Hartchild's job. Nine minutes, twelve, Master Esker."

"I don't understand…"

"Isn't it wonderful when that happens? I wonder what it's like…"

"But…"

"I was pondering your claim about the dome during all that business with the late Viscount, and I do believe you're correct. Perhaps it's time Orphan *did* open its eyes. You'll find the flight controls through the hatch, you know."

Hana yelled over the chasm, "Where are you going?"

"Hmm? What else? Seeing how it all plays out. You'll find, children, that often, affecting the world around you is best achieved with a subtle nudge here and there, rather than an iron fist. Miss Sóholdt? You may need this. Master Esker is frightfully poor at looking after himself, after all."

Lorecroft tossed the silver rod over the chasm, into Hana's grasp.

Alvin and Hana looked at each other, and when they looked back, Lorecroft was gone, because of course he was. It was only them, now. "Come on," Alvin told her.

All the gauges read *Optimal Pressure*, and the ticker readouts printed *Ejection Lines Charged*, or things like that. Alvin took one lever, and Hana the other. They squeezed the clutches, and pulled. Who knows how many years—maybe centuries—they had hung there. They didn't want to move.

IN A FEW MOMENTS, (I HOPE) YOU'LL BE ABLE TO SEE BETTER THAN YOU'VE EVER SEEN BEFORE, BUT NOT FROM UNDER YOUR BEDS...

Hana climbed against the wall and pushed with her feet, and Alvin set all his weight against his. Hana's snapped down with a yelp from her, and Alvin's cranked.

Steam vented from the lines around the two great windows, and each burst from their places, hurling down to the mountains below. One by one, they heard others blow, then more outside North Op Station. Hurricane winds erupted into North Op Station, and both had to cover their eyes.

But it wasn't just the wind.

Light broke through, something like sunlight.

Alvin grabbed Hana's wrist and pulled her in through the hatch, and they found themselves in Orphan's bridge, a cockpit clad in windshields and levers and pipes and lenses bringing every angle of flight to the pilot's eyes, and Alvin knew what to do with none of it.

But he sat down anyway.

"Alvin? Look." Hana stood behind him, and pointed over his shoulder.

Orphan angled inward through the maw of the earth, and ahead of them rose a new light, veiled in smoky haze, but warm and bright, like a golden-white aurora. The northern lights behind them swept like an astral road through the opening, and as they curved, mountains rose along the inside of the crust of the world, an inside-out earth within the earth.

Orphan hit something hard, and nearly sent Hana through the windshield. She landed in a heap by Alvin's chair—grazed a peak, Alvin figured. Through the lenses on either side of the windshield, more and more of Orphan's great panels blew off with pressured release, first from around the perimeter, and then from across the roof, erupting high into the air and catching the wind.

Over half a minute, they gained altitude, and leveled. The horrible trembling subsided.

Orphan became a comet of glass and iron, and when the dome released, Orphan craned hard to one side, then the other, shuddering in the air as it sailed. Alvin instinctively gripped the levers in front of him, and the gauges marked *Toroidal Field Balance* along the panel all shifted their needles just barely into the green.

TOMORROW'S GOING TO LOOK DIFFERENT, BUT MAYBE WE'RE OVERDUE FOR DIFFERENT.

Alvin took in everything he could, the labels of every lever and switch, but knew so little of it. "Hana? What do I do?"

"Fly, silly." She tapped behind his ear three times, and the Halo lit into being around him, its main ring angled. "Like your trams…"

Alvin angled the drive levers, and with a weary groan, dials turned, needles shifted on their gauges, and the whole of Orphan slowly angled flatter. He tried switches, cautiously adjusted levers, and eyed the amber ring around him to keep everything as level as he could.

"Feel like the tram?" she asked.

"Trams ain't two miles wide and hurling through space without rails! Like hobbling to bed after Christmas dinner, is what it's like!"

He'd only a few minutes left, before the trams would give out, and they were still over mountains, breaking through cloud-lines and wind.

EVERYONE, ORPHAN'S COMING DOWN. DON'T PANIC, AND BE READY. WE'LL NEED ALL OF US…

"And the Author's grace, aside," Alvin muttered.

ENGINEERS, MOST OF YOU ARE ALREADY RISKING YOUR
LIVES TO KEEP US MOVING, BY THE AUTHOR'S MERCY, BUT
WE WILL NEED MORE. IF YOU HAVE ANY MECHANICAL
KNOWLEDGE AT ALL, BE READY TO SECURE, AND REPAIR.

They had to slow down. Up ahead, the mountains descended into plateaus near a great river, and valleys beyond that.

But in the midst of it, a deep thrill rose up in Alvin's chest. He let go most of the controls, and drove Orphan from its guidance levers and the Halo's measure alone. She was huge, fat and slow, but she flew. In the far distance, Alvin thought he saw things that he would turn the lens of his mind back to many times, objects in the air he couldn't make out, villages, roadways or the like, even boats on far rivers. He thought he saw a mammoth or two, protruding ruins or settlements, and things he couldn't even put into words.

MEN, GET YOUR FAMILIES TO THE SOUTH EAST END OF
TOWNE. SOUTHERN HARCHESTER, ATTISTOCK, AND
EASTERN WESBELDT. MEDICAL PERSONNEL, BE READY.
THERE MAY BE INJURIES. LADIES, ESPECIALLY YOU
MOTHERS, THEY MAY NEED MORE NURSES THAN USUAL.

"Watch?" he asked. Hana reached into his jacket pocket and drew out Alphonse's timepiece. "Three minutes," he read, and sure enough, the lights were already flickering out. Gauges for the *Toroidal Field Strength* were lowering, and so was Orphan still.

"There." Alvin pointed. "That plateau."

Gingerly he angled Orphan to his left, found the levers controlling the southern propellers and steam vents that propelled Orphan forward, and started shutting them all down. He drew back on the levers, and all the systems started giving out. Three of the gauges burst, and the cockpit went dark of its own lights. Orphan was slowing, leveling, but Alvin lost all control over it. He shut off his own lights, and rose.

"That—that's it."

"Alvin?"

"Hmm?"

"Thank you. For letting me in."

He laughed quietly, and shut his eyes. If he could've chosen, he would've put Hana anywhere else but there, he was secretly so grateful to have her with him.

"Nowhere left to go," he reminded her. "Would've lived a longer life if you hadn't come with—"

"Don't say stupid things," she said. Hana held up the silver rod, and flicked the little switch on the side. Golden light burst forth, and formed a sphere around the two of them and stayed steady. Hana touched it—solid as marble.

As Orphan Towne descended, Alvin Esker and Hana Sóholdt knelt in its leading rim as it sped under a vibrant sky. The broken lens of Alvin's mind angled forward, and while he clutched the wasteland girl to his chest as the land came to meet them, he silently prayed to his Author that she, and his father, mother, Alphonse, and everyone—somehow—live through the day.

Then, Orphan Heights bore its prow into the earth.

Inside the earth.

ENTRY 1: "THE RELOCATION OF ORPHAN HEIGHTS"

For generations, the populous of Orphan Heights awaited what the academic types called "The Great Initiative" with placid readiness and occasional boredom, and when it finally happened, nobody was very much impressed. It upset all the bookends and flatware, said Orphan's many wives, and this wasn't mentioning all the injuries, or even deaths. There were more than a few of those, the day Orphan Heights earned its name, and the towne once known for clockwork order became a bedlam of the sort of chaos that brought on underwashed laundry. For all Orphanites, they were suddenly and undesirably thrust into a world that included *outside*, which nobody asked for. They had to get used to things like wind and insects and direct sunlight. It was unwelcome.

Orphan Heights—or what was left of it—now perched where it crashed: onto the edge of a colossal mountainside, a plateau between two great peaks of the shadow of the new-formed mountains deep within the polar opening. It rested at a reasonable 1.4° slant, which most of the Orphanites agreed was quite livable, even if their hutches did have to be moved to opposite walls to keep the dishware from sliding out. While it was true that nearly all of Orphan's dishes had been destroyed in the collision, the hutches were moved on principle.

And while many of Orphan's husbands complained at being assigned the task of moving all the furniture within their broken and fallen and shattered homes, their wives reminded them that all they were being asked was to move hutches, while they had to manage dinner without any flatware. Interestingly enough, finger-foods came to thereafter dominate Orphan's preference for cuisine.

CHAPTER 30

in which a bedraggled discovery is renewed

THE STAR CAPELLA ASCENDED INTO THE … NO IT DIDN'T. It might've, and probably did, but not within Alvin Esker's view, or anybody else's within Orphan Towne. What *did* ascend was … moons? *Plural?* Through what once was the upper story and rooftop of the Esker brownstone, gazing up bleary-eyed at the greatest discovery in the long and storied history of Orphan Towne, which turned out *not* to be the end of the world, especially since it only came about because Alvin inadvertently obliterated a continent. A song drifted through his senses, a silly little tune in sweet chords.

Die gedanken sind frei…

"Ha—Hana?" he moaned.

"No, sweetheart. So sorry to disappoint. I'm afraid it's me."

"That's Agnes's song."

"Where did you think she learned it, silly?"

Alvin rubbed his eyes, and found his brother over him. "Did you just call me 'sweetheart'?"

"I did not. That was mum. Ain't gonna kiss you, neither."

"Get off me!" Alvin tried to sit up. It was the worst mistake of his life. Only once his eyes were cleared and he had blinked the cobwebs away and Alphonse had been sent off to fetch socks, did he see his mother. She padded his head with a damp cloth.

"How long?"

"Three days."

"Three days? Hana. Did Hana—"

"Rather grown-up of you, isn't it, Alvin? To be so concerned for a young lady? Seems your father and I raised you well—"

"Mum!"

"She lived," his mother assured him. "Wouldn't want you to worry for hours and hours and hours. A little banged up, she was, but less than you were."

"Banged up?"

Elise Esker took her son's face in her hands in her most medical-motherly way, held each eye open and inspected, tilted his head this way and that as she spoke.

"Had her share of bruises but came through alright. Had enough rainwater in the barrels to give the girl a bath, at least. Had to scrub a decade off her." His mother lifted her smirking gaze to his. "Wouldn't leave your bedside for the paying. Had to swear to leave your father *and* brother here with you while we were gone, just so she could have a bath and a meal. It's a miracle at all you survived, and I do mean a *miracle*. Nobody ought've lived through that wreck, not on the north end."

She rose and went back to tending her boy. She washed her hands and inspected his, angling every joint of every finger and elbow.

Alvin took the moment to have Alphonse help sit him up.

He was in his bedroom … or what remained. The wall between it and the rest of the house was gone. Of his beloved brownstone, there was only a couple walls left, and those were shifted and tilted. The table was gone. The artwork was in a pile. The contents of the cupboard still lay strewn across the floor, and the front wall simply wasn't. Divan was fine, though.

"Stick out your tongue."

"Mother I'm fine! Where is she? Hana, I mean."

"Somewhere. Don't rightly know. Left this morning. Past three days, it's rather hectic, isn't it?"

Alphonse added, "Lot of folks are arguing over staying in the perimeter or settling outside. Mrs. Dutch and old George Herschel had an awful row about it just last night, didn't they?" He was busy collecting things. For what, Alvin didn't know, but he collected anything that wasn't too terribly broken, and made piles of them. "Quite a story, that Sóholdt girl told us, Al. I'd say it's rot, the lot of it, but here I am in the remains of my house, dumped onto a new continent, or whatever this is."

Alvin happened to crane his eyes skyward. Sure enough, there was no dome over Orphan anymore. Oh, the old limeiron lattice was still there, bent and twisted and broken in spots, but much of it still overhead. It was the glass that was gone, and from above, a soft autumn-coloured aurora hung like painted light, and for a fleeting moment, Alvin swore he saw *birds* flying in formation up there.

Then came a knock at the door, and the last one tipped the old thing clear off its hinges. It fell like a cut tree, kicking up dust and noise in the living room of the brick skeleton of the Esker brownstone.

"I'm sorry!" said Tabitha Hartchild. She leaned on her crutch still, and coughed through the dust of the entry.

"Miss Hartchild," Alvin's mother greeted her. "Come to see Alvin?"

"Actually, to invite him, if he's quite well enough."

Alvin hobbled into the room, stepping over the wall that used to divide his room from the house. "To what?"

"Alvin! I'm glad. To see you up, I mean. We're having a short memorial. I was hoping you'd come. It's for Ellery. You don't have to!"

"Let me find my coat."

<hr>

There was no body, of course, for Ellery Hartchild's memorial, and the Chapel itself lay in crumbled ruins, like much of Orphan. There was only the cemetery left, and the lone yew tree in its middle, still standing, with a missing bough or three, which was pretty much how everybody in Orphan felt in general.

There was nobody left to say much, at the unremarkable curve on the southwest side of Chapel Hill. Reverend Pattering was badly injured, and of the presiding nobles among the gathered mourners, Inspector General Hartchild was not only bound to a wheelchair with his wounds, but also a fairly non-religious fellow. Tabitha stood beside him on her crutch, but paused by Alvin as she went to leave. Clearly, she wanted to say something, but it never came out. She tried a few times, her eyes still damp from her brother's simple memorial, but no.

It was the first time in her life Alvin hadn't seen her black hair tied neatly in a bright blue bow. But nobody in Orphan was overmuch concerned with appearances, that day.

Her father finally bid her, "Come, Tabitha," as his manservant pushed him along the path, and she followed on her crutch.

They left Alvin alone, under the hickories. It was October, in the now-nonexistent Expanse, and in this place … who knew? Something cracked under his feet, and gave him pause. It was the curved shell of an incandescent. He wasn't far from the pergola he'd never finished wiring, though the pergola itself listed half way over now.

The air was brisk, but the relocation seemed to irritate the trees of Orphan, which no longer knew what season it was at all. A few crumpled "autumn" leaves scraped across the ground at Alvin's feet as he walked, hands in pockets, up the lane, finding himself at a familiar, though often unvisited, marker.

A careless branch had fallen across the inscription *Agnesine Elspeth Esker*, but Alvin took care of that. He dusted off the stone. "Hey, Agnes," he said awkwardly, crouching over the grave. "Listen. I'm sorry I didn't come, before. Your name, written in stone like that, makes it all seem so unchangeable, don't it? I—I should've done better by you. And I'm sorry. For running, when you needed me." Alvin laughed to himself, softly. "Wish you'd have met Hana. Could only imagine what you'd think of her. But she … she would've loved you. Fiercely, too. Does *everything* fiercely, that girl. Hey. I miss you."

There was little more to say, at least on that day. Alvin got up on aching knees, and strolled further up the lane. He was not alone in Chapel Hill.

"Woolgathering, Professor?"

Lorecroft's scarf drifted in the wind. They were new to wind, all of them, but Lorecroft seemed unaffected by it as he stood over his son's grave like an old tree giving it shade.

"Eglantine never comes here, you know. That's my wife. Have you ever known someone who couldn't handle witnessing their own lacerations? Seeing own blood? For her, losing William was too sharp a cut."

"And for you?"

He breathed in sharply. "It is a strange thing, to visit a grave. The dead cannot hear, yet we speak as if they listen. We visit as if dropping by for tea of a summer afternoon, and expect that, at any moment, the graven door of their earthy tenement will open, that they will greet us as before, invite us in, so if we might share a pipe and lark as once we did. And all the while, we pretend it might be so. What self-deluded creatures we are. It is a curious thing, to bury one's child. Death is such an inevitability, yet such a simple break of a universal pattern so upends our feeble minds. Don't you agree?"

"Why do all this, Professor?" asked Alvin. "What was the point? With or without me, your lot would've done all this anyway. Why bring us here? Why not just take us all back to Angland?"

"You think *this* was the goal? How horribly small-minded."

"Then…?"

"This place, Master Esker, is only a step, an open door. Thule, Agarta, call it what you will, is believed by many to be the womb of life itself, the origin of man, and much more. Here there are wonders beyond industry, devils beyond ages, and very strange graves. We are far, *far* off the map, and even under it. As the saying goes, here there be monsters, though there are few outmatching the monsters within us all. The ones enshrined in the boundless skies."

"You can see the Metarcanum too. Can't you, Sir?"

Lorecroft said nothing.

"You used the Oculix. It ain't just me and Agnes at all. 'The secrets *we* now carry,' that's what you said. You can see it."

"I used it long before your sister ever laid mind on it, young man. I would've had nobody else be the subject of such a test."

"Then why did you ever need another? Why make Ellery…?"

Lorecroft shut his eyes. "A 'matchless mind,' that's what they called me, from childhood onward. It was not meant for a child. Master Hartchild was not to be Infused for many years, but mine is a mind *too* logical to see the things you see when you imagine, Master Esker. Halo will only work for such a mind. Maybe it's best that way." Finally he looked up from the marker and turned his face to Alvin. "By the bye, kindly look this way."

"Hmm?" Lorecroft held up a little trident-shaped thing that flashed hot in Alvin's eyes. "Ow! What *now?*"

"A simple activation inhibitor," said the Professor, pocketing the object. "Well we can hardly have an adolescent strutting around Orphan with the power to rewrite physics in his brain, can we? Consider your Halo chained, Master Esker. You realize what you've played with? The kind of power? Would that Miss Sóholdt had perished in that wreck you might understand. The smallest of lives can be among the most valuable to us. Can they not?"

In spite of everything, he had no anger left in his heart for the man. There was only a sort of strange pity left.

"I'm sorry. That you lost your son. Professor."

Lorecroft inhaled, and shut his eyes to think. "'Whatever thing the scythe of time mows down, devour unspar'd; till I in man residing through the race, his thoughts, his looks, words, actions, all infect, and season by him thy last and sweetest prey.'" His eyes opened. "It's late. Go find your woebegone beloved, Master Esker, and kindly leave me with mine."

There was no tram to take Alvin home. There *technically* was, but all of them were ruined, derailed, defunct, and devoid of any lectral power to make them run, like the rest of Orphan. So Alvin walked, light of the red aurora overhead. This strange inner-land didn't have day and night, so much, but the light of the skies did shift, and turned to familiar evening hues.

With nobody around, his curiosity struck him enough to tap behind his ear, and the amber ring wove around his head. But when he tried to activate the Halo program, it appeared well enough, but he couldn't operate it beyond looking. In a way, it made him glad. He shut it off and headed south, as the direct way across towne was now in shambles where the

Merchant Circles used to be, and his path took him by the old Warren, which had largely 'cracked and fallen off' of Orphan. Outside its wreckage, the Galó encamped. He made sure Sigrie and Loftin made it through the wreck, and they did, even Sigrie's father.

Still no Hana, though.

His eyes craned skyward again on his way home, couldn't get used to the sight. The warped arches over Orphan bent and swayed, but stayed mostly up, and the old Heuridium Tower, by some miracle, was still hanging there, though now far worse for wear and listing like a Roman landmark. At some point he turned his attention further up the north end of towne. It was like a great, crumpled can, now. North Op wasn't even visible as something distinct from the rock and ruin, now.

We were in that? he mused to himself, followed by: *what happened to the shield machine?*

The wind was something new, rushing and whistling through Orphan's warping frame and bowing chimneys. But there were people, still, and lots of them. They didn't move in clockwork, anymore, but they still ambled. Alvin started at the flock of pigeons that took off from the grassy clearing and soared in formation into Orphan's sky.

Near Harchester, Alvin found many of the weary men gathered at makeshift tables under the fallen ruins of the *Lager Than Life*, with a new sign crudely painted: *Coming Soon: The Barley Alive.* The men drank, laughed, and wondered at this new land.

Then Alvin Esker came home, to the largely homeless masses he knew from Harchester. Everywhere stood tents, makeshift lean-to structures, and bedsheets covering fallen walls for privacy. Orphan was a shantytowne, for the present, and the old brownstone was no different. The front door fell off its frame again, and Hugo Esker came through the opening.

"Hello, son," he said. "Why don't you come on inside and we can have a little supper?"

"There's supper?" said Alvin, excitedly.

He found his mother labouring over the same pot, trying to come up with something to eat. Alphonse was still collecting things.

"Are we moving?" Alvin asked.

"Afraid so," said his father. "Not much left of the old place, nor of most of Harchester. Chancellery's calling for evacuation of this quarter. First time they've said anything weren't stupid as year-old dairy. Gracious, this towne's had its swings of luck and misfortune. Like a pendulum, it is…"

"But … where'll we go?"

His father and Alphonse overturned the already-overturned counter. Dust and bits of broken ceramics billowed.

"There's my mother's dishes!" Elise cheered. "Oh Author. Look at the state of them…"

"Folks are talking about settling outside the walls," his father continued. "No, really! There's room on the steppes, says the scouting parties, and lots of it. DeWitt's already planning his new pub, isn't he? *And* there'll be space for a piano, he says! Before long, why we'll have a whole *new* Orphan!"

"Right," said Alvin. "Orphan's pianos being sure to've survived the fall."

"No thanks to your rubbish piloting!" Alphonse mocked.

"You … know about that?"

"Hana told us a *lot*," his brother added, handing piles of broken dishware to their mother. "Also, I hear my telescope was quite the saviour of the day, though bollocks if you think I believe all of it."

"Alphonse!" their mother barked. "Where'd you learn that language?"

Neither of them were fool enough to say 'from Father,' so both saying verbatim, "some mates from Wesbeldt" had to do. They were forbidden from seeing such friends, which was fine with them.

The family puttered around the place, packing, repairing, salvaging anything they could for whatever home they would end up in. Alvin found some ruddy old part of some ruddy old engine on the floor where a buffet table had been, and turned it over in his hand. "Father?" he said. "Mum? Listen. I'm—I'm sorry, about all this." The family stilled. "About Agnes. Should've been a better brother to her, shouldn't I?"

"Oh Alvin," his mother sighed. "You mustn't…"

"No, really," he insisted. "If I'd … maybe all this … and we'd not be out a home, and everyone else—"

"Now you listen here, boy," said his father, tossing aside the box of broken glasses, which broke more. "In days coming, there'll be enough people ripe for spilling blame onto you, and anyone who'll let 'em. Don't rightly know what's happened to my boy, nor have the mind to understand it. But you're an Esker, and I understand that. Did the right thing, I trust, best as you knew how. No man's the right to ask more than that. Now. There's work, needs doing. We can't all go lollygagging about for days on end, can we?"

"No, Sir." Alvin smiled.

His family gathered up more, and while they worked, Alvin stepped up to the landing, and his old door, pushing it open on creaking hinges. Most of the outer wall was gone, and the cracking under his feet was all that lay left of his models.

But from his casement window, the only intact window left in the Esker home, light streamed—*real* light, not candle nor incandescent nor even sunlight, but a light he'd never known, warm and young and clear.

"Alvin!"

"Gah!"

He fell on his hind end, and crushed a flying machine. There at the casement window stood the *girl-who-couldn't-exist*, her hand against the cracked glass, bright-eyed, and washed. He hardly recognized her.

"Hana?"

"Yah. You hit your head harder than I thought…"

"You—you're at the window. You know, because the door's off its hinges and the walls are all but—but alright. The window it is. Here."

He cranked on the latches, and opened it. Hana leaned her folded arms on the sill. "You sleep a lot, but your bed is so nice, I understand."

"That's … that's one of Agnes's dresses."

"Yah," said Hana. "Does—does it bother you? I can put on my old—"

"No!" Alvin insisted. "No. She'd want you to have it. Mum give you hat, did she?"

"Yah. Brushed my hair, too. Gave me a bath. Look!" She showed her goggles with a new clasp. "Your brother fixed them. You've a good family."

"I know. Hey. You tell me something? What happened?"

Hana cocked her head. "Huh?"

"When we crashed. Last thing I remember was the power dying."

"Oh." She nodded, her golden hair bobbing aside her face. "Yah. You grabbed tight hold of me when we hit. I remember light. Noise. Then you lying there. It was your father who pulled me out. Lots of others after him. They carried us off, mended us. You were rough."

"Yeah. Feels like it, and no mistake."

"So." She looked around. "All because you flipped a switch, yah?"

"What's this 'you' balderdash?" he protested. "I believe you were there. In fact, I believe it was flipped *because* of you."

"I was looking for a *book*. Nothing more!"

"Bollocks! Regular burglar, you are, and trouble, too. Where have you been, anyway? Mum told me—said you were here, for a couple days."

"She finally made me eat," Hana answered. "And bathe. Then mending things. Not much left of your room, huh?"

"No," he sighed, tossing the remains of a little flight model. "Or of much else, seems. Lots of work ahead."

"Yah." Hana nestled her chin into her folded arms on the sill. "I found grass. Only heard about it from stories, before."

Alvin inspected the remains of his brownstone, and sat himself on the floor against the leaning wall by his door. "We'll have to tear down most of this for building material. The generators are wrecked. Should've seen what's left of North Op Station. You know, I wonder what happened to the stereopticon."

"Yah," she mused. "I think I saw moons. In the sky. (Is it a sky?) Several of them. There's a river, too. Big. And woods."

"The LIT Corps.'s work is all bunk, now, too. Back to oil we go, I suppose. With the continent gone, the pole open like that … I wonder if more will come through. It's just … all so much, you know?"

"Yah," she assured him. Warm 'evening' light settled down from the aurora, and many old lampposts and torches lit up across Orphan where it settled. "Want to go explore?" A brick fell. "Then knock off and find food?"

"Yeah. Let's do that."

Want More?

There's more of the *Axis Gate* world coming, but you don't have to wait for the next book. Explore the world further through the *World Anvil* link below, where you can journey into Orphan Towne, the Expanse (not that it's there anymore), discover secrets, background, lore, and far more stories of these and other characters from the world in this book and in more yet to come.

Check out the author website to support, encourage, yell at, generally complain to, or otherwise contact the author at your own risk (author of *this* book, not *The* Author):

www.danielathasholly.com | captainholly@pm.me

www.ingramcontent.com/pod-product-compliance
Lightning Source LLC
Chambersburg PA
CBHW021403110726

47901CB00008B/2039